"Harrowing. . . . *The Double Bind* has a powerful statement to make about the nature of obsession and mental illness, as well as the lingering effects of psychological trauma. . . . A stunner."
—ST. PETERSBURG TIMES

"Great fiction . . . un-put-down-able."
—PEOPLE

"Ingenious. . . . He's compassionate about mental illness, wise about the healing power of art. He moves easily and convincingly back and forth from different points of view and manages to create authentic voices."
—THE BOSTON GLOBE

"A psychological thriller. . . . A chilling depiction of the ways we choose to remember as well as what we forget."
—NEW YORK DAILY NEWS

"A page-turner with a wicked twist at the end."
—LIFE MAGAZINE

Acclaim for Chris Bohjalian's

The Double Bind

"Imaginatively crafted." —*Newsweek*

"Bohjalian . . . has deliberately wandered into thriller territory. . . . He's playing with our minds in a way that ultimately evokes not Fitzgerald but that master of deviousness, Alfred Hitchcock." —*The Miami Herald*

"A spider's web of a book that combines fantasy and tragedy. . . . A remarkable . . . glimpse of a deeply scarred mind." —*The Washington Times*

"Scintillating ties to *The Great Gatsby* form the skeleton of the new novel . . . part mystery and part psychological exploration." —*The Denver Post*

"Spellbinding. . . . Startling and wrenching. . . . Readers would do well to get bound up in the sheer pleasure of *The Double Bind*." —*The San Antonio Express–News*

"Bohjalian has created another showstopper. . . . He takes a mysterious situation and transforms it into a novel of immense imagination and emotion." —*Rocky Mountain News*

"A chilling depiction of the ways we choose to remember as well as what we forget." —*Daily News*

Chris Bohjalian

The Double Bind

Chris Bohjalian is the critically acclaimed author of ten other novels, including *Midwives* (a *Publishers Weekly* Best Book and an Oprah's Book Club selection), *Before You Know Kindness*, and the forthcoming *Skeletons at the Feast*. His work has been translated into nineteen languages and published in twenty-two countries. He lives with his wife and daughter in Vermont.

www.chrisbohjalian.com

Books by

Chris Bohjalian

NOVELS

The Double Bind (2007)

Before You Know Kindness (2004)

The Buffalo Soldier (2002)

Trans-Sister Radio (2000)

The Law of Similars (1999)

Midwives (1997)

Water Witches (1995)

Past the Bleachers (1992)

Hangman (1991)

A Killing in the Real World (1988)

ESSAY COLLECTIONS

Idyll Banter: Weekly Excursions to a Very Small Town (2003)

The Double Bind

Chris Bohjalian

The Double

Bind

A Novel

VINTAGE CONTEMPORARIES
Vintage Books
A Division of Random House, Inc.
New York

FIRST VINTAGE CONTEMPORARIES EDITION, FEBRUARY 2008

The Library of Congress has cataloged the Shaye Areheart Books edition as follows:
Bohjalian, Christopher A.
The double bind : a novel / Chris Bohjalian.—1st ed.
1. Women college students—Fiction. 2. Photographers—Fiction.
3. Mentally ill—Fiction. 4. Shelters for the homeless—Fiction.
5. Vermont—Fiction. 6. Long Island—Fiction. I. Title
PS3552.O495D68 2007
813'.54—dc22   2006015402

Vintage ISBN: 978-1-4000-3166-5

Book design by Lynne Amft

www.vintagebooks.com

Printed in the United States of America
10 9 8 7 6 5 4 3 2 1

For Rose Mary Muench
and
in memory of Frederick Muench (1929–2004)

AUTHOR'S NOTE

THIS NOVEL HAD ITS ORIGINS IN DECEMBER 2003, when Rita Markley, the executive director of Burlington, Vermont's Committee on Temporary Shelter, shared with me the contents of a box of old photographs. The black-and-white images had been taken by a once-homeless man who had died in the studio apartment her organization had found for him. His name was Bob "Soupy" Campbell.

The photos were remarkable, both because of the man's evident talent and because of the subject matter. I recognized the performers—musicians, comedians, actors—and newsmakers in many of them. Most of the photos were at least forty years old. We were all mystified as to how Campbell had gone from photographing luminaries from the 1950s and 1960s to winding up at a homeless shelter in northern Vermont. He had no surviving family we were aware of that we could ask.

The reality, of course, is that Campbell probably wound up homeless for any one of the myriad reasons that most transients wind up on the streets: Mental illness. Substance abuse. Bad luck.

We tend to stigmatize the homeless and blame them for their plight. We are oblivious to the fact that most had lives as serious as our own before everything fell apart. The photographs in this book are a testimony to that reality: They were taken by Campbell before he wound up a transient in Vermont.

Consequently, I am grateful to Burlington's Committee on Temporary Shelter for allowing me to use these photographs in this story. Obviously, Bobbie Crocker, the homeless photographer in this novel, is fictitious. But the photographs you will see in this book are real.

"Oh, I know who Pauline Kael is," he said. "I wasn't born homeless, you know."

—NICK HORNBY, *A Long Way Down*

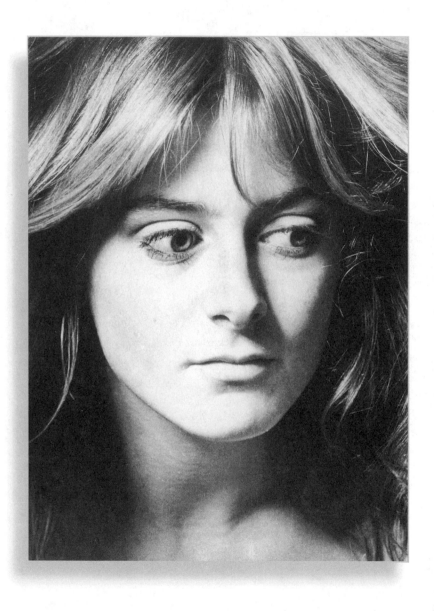

The Double Bind

PROLOGUE

*L*AUREL ESTABROOK was nearly raped the fall of her sophomore year of college. Quite likely she was nearly murdered that autumn. This was no date-rape disaster with a handsome, entitled UVM frat boy after the two of them had spent too much time flirting beside the bulbous steel of a beer keg; this was one of those violent, sinister attacks involving masked men—yes, men, plural, and they actually were wearing wool ski masks that shielded all but their eyes and the snarling rifts of their mouths—that one presumes only happen to other women in distant states. To victims whose faces appear on the morning news programs, and whose devastated, forever-wrecked mothers are interviewed by strikingly beautiful anchorwomen.

She was biking on a wooded dirt road twenty miles northeast of the college in a town with a name that was both ominous and oxymoronic: Underhill. In all fairness, the girl did not find the name *Underhill* menacing before she was assaulted. But she also did not return there for any reason in the years after the attack. It was somewhere around six-thirty on a Sunday evening, and this was the third Sunday in a row that she had packed her well-traveled mountain bike into the back of her roommate Talia's station wagon and driven to Underhill to ride for miles and miles along the logging roads that snaked through the nearby forest. At the time, it struck her as beautiful country: a fairy-tale wood more Lewis than Grimm, the maples not yet the color of claret. It was all new growth, a third-generation tangle of maple and oak and ash, the remnants of stone walls still visible in the understory not far from the paths. It was nothing like the Long Island suburbs where she had grown up, a world of expensive homes with manicured lawns only blocks from a long neon-lit swath of fast-food restaurants, foreign-car dealers, and weight-loss clinics in strip malls.

After the attack, of course, her memories of that patch of Vermont woods were transformed, just as the name of the nearby town gained a different, darker resonance. Later, when she recalled those roads and hills—some seeming too steep to bike, but bike them she did—she would think instead of the washboard ruts that had jangled her body and her overriding sense that the great canopy of leaves from the trees shielded too much of the view and made the woods too thick to be pretty. Sometimes, even many years later, when she would be trying to fight her way to sleep through the flurries of wakefulness, she would see those woods after the leaves had fallen, and visualize only the long finger grips of the skeletal birches.

By six-thirty that evening the sun had just about set and the air was growing moist and chilly. But she wasn't worried about the dark because she had parked her friend's wagon in a gravel pull-off beside a paved road that was no more than three miles distant. There was a house beside the pull-off with a single window above an attached garage, a Cyclops visage in shingle and glass. She would be there in ten or fifteen minutes, and as she rode she was aware of the thick-lipped whistle of the breeze in the trees. She was wearing a pair of black bike shorts and a jersey with an image of a yellow tequila bottle that looked phosphorescent printed on the front. She didn't feel especially vulnerable. She felt, if anything, lithe and athletic and strong. She was nineteen.

Then a brown van passed her. Not a minivan, a real van. The sort of van that, when harmless, is filled with plumbing and electrical supplies, and when not harmless is packed with the deviant accoutrements of serial rapists and violent killers. Its only windows were small portholes high above the rear tires, and she had noticed as it passed that the window on the passenger side had been curtained off with black fabric. When the van stopped with a sudden squeal forty yards ahead of her, she knew enough to be scared. How could she not? She had grown up on Long Island—once a dinosaur swamp-land at the edge of a towering range of mountains, now a giant sandbar in the shape of a salmon—the almost preter-naturally strange petri dish that spawned Joel Rifkin (serial killer of seventeen women), Colin Ferguson (the LIRR slaughter), Cheryl Pierson (arranged to have her high school classmate murder her father), Richard Angelo (Good Samar-itan Hospital's Angel of Death), Robert Golub (mutilated a thirteen-year-old neighbor), George Wilson (shot Jay Gatsby as he floated aimlessly in his swimming pool), John Esposito (imprisoned a ten-year-old girl in his dungeon), and Ronald DeFeo (slaughtered his family in Amityville).

In truth, even if she hadn't grown up in West Egg she would have known enough to be scared when the van stopped on the lonely road directly before her. Any young woman would have felt the hairs rise up on the back of her neck.

Unfortunately, the van had come to a stop so abruptly that she couldn't turn around because the road was narrow and she used a clipless pedal system when she rode: This meant that she was linked by a metal cleat in the sole of each cycling shoe to her pedals. She would have needed to snap her feet free, stop, and put a toe down to pivot as she swiveled her bike 180 degrees. And before she could do any of that two men jumped out, one from the driver's side and one from the passenger's, and they both had those intimidating masks shielding their faces: a very bad sign indeed in late September, even in the faux tundra of northern Vermont.

And so with a desperate burst of adrenaline she tried to pedal past them. She hadn't a prayer. One of them grabbed her around her shoulders as she tried to race by, while the other was hoisting her (and her bicycle) off the ground by her waist. They were, essentially, tackling her as if she were a running back and they were a pair of defensive linemen who had reached her in the backfield. She screamed—shrill, girlish, desperate screams that conveyed both her vulnerability and her youth—at the same time that a part of her mind focused analytically on what might have been the most salient feature of her predicament: She was still locked by her shoes to her bike and she had to remain that way at all costs, while holding on fast to the handlebars. This alone might keep her off the sides of Vermont milk cartons and the front pages of the Vermont newspapers. Why? Because she realized that she couldn't possibly overpower her assailants—even her hair was lanky and thin—but if they couldn't pry her from the bicycle it would be that much more difficult to cart her into the deep woods or throw her into the back of their van.

At one point the more muscular of the two, a thug who smelled like a gym—not malodorous, not sweaty, but metallic like weights—tried to punch her in the face, but she must have ducked because he slammed his fist into the edge of her helmet and swore. His eyes beneath his mask were the icy gray of the sky in November, and around each wrist she saw a coil of barbed wire had been tattooed like a bracelet. He yelled for his partner—who had a tattoo, as well, a skull with improbable ears (sharp ears, a wolf's) and long wisps of smoke snaking up from between the fangs in its mouth—to put the goddamn bike down so he could rip her foot from the cleat. Briefly, she considered releasing her foot herself so she could kick him with the hard point of her bike shoe. But she didn't. Thank God. She kept her foot pointing straight ahead, the metal clip in the sole snapped tightly into the pedal. He tried yanking at her ankle, but he knew nothing about cleats and so he wasn't precisely sure how to twist her foot. Frustrated, he threatened to break her ankle, while his partner began trying to wrench her thumb and fingers from the handlebars. But she held on, all the while continuing to scream with the conviction that she was screaming for her life—which, clearly, she was.

Meanwhile, they called her a cunt. In the space of moments—not minutes, but maybe—they called her a cunt, a twat, a pussy, a gash. A fucking cunt. A stupid cunt. A teasing cunt. Fish cunt. Slut cunt. Dead cunt. *You* dead cunt. No verb. Even the words were violent, though initially three sounded to her less about the hate and the anger and the derision: Those words were spoken (not shouted) with a leer by the thinner of the pair, an inside joke between the two of them, and it was only after he had repeated them did she understand it was not three words she was hearing but two. It was a made-up brand name, a noun, a flavor at her expense. He had reduced her vagina to an aperitif on the mistaken assumption that there could possibly be even a trace of pre-coital wetness lubricating her now. *Liqueur Snatch.* That was the joke. Get it, get it? Not *lick her snatch.* A French cordial instead. But the joke elicited nothing from his partner, no reaction at all, because this was only about his unfathomable hatred for her. What therapists call that moment of arousal? For all Laurel knew, it would come for him the moment she died. The moment they killed her.

Finally, they threw her and her bicycle onto the ground. For a split second she thought they had given up. They hadn't. They started to drag her by her bicycle tires as if she and the bike were a single creature, a dead deer they were hauling by its legs from the woods. They were dragging her to the van, her right elbow and knee scraping along the dirt road, intending to throw her—bicycle and all—into the back.

But they couldn't, and this, too, is probably a reason why she survived. They had so much gym equipment crammed into the rear of the vehicle that they couldn't fit her inside it while she was attached to her bike. She glimpsed discus-shaped weights and benches and metal bars when they lifted her up, and what looked like the vertical components of a Nautilus machine. And so they tossed her back down onto the hard dirt while they made room for her in the van, shattering her collarbone and leaving a bruise on her left breast that wouldn't heal completely for months. She felt daggers of pain so pronounced that she was instantly nauseous, and it was only adrenaline that kept her from vomiting. Still, she continued to grasp the bicycle's handlebars and keep her feet locked to its pedals. One of the men barked at her not to move, which, for a variety of reasons, wasn't an option: She wasn't about to let go of the bike, and with a broken collarbone it was highly unlikely that she could have managed to release her feet, stand up, and ride away in anything less than half an hour.

How long did she lie there like that? Ten seconds? Fifteen? It probably wasn't even half a minute. Her assailants saw the other cyclists before she did. There, approaching them down the road, were three vigorous bikers who, it would turn out, were male lawyers from Underhill on their way home after a daylong seventy-five-mile sojourn into the Mad River Valley and back. They were on road bikes, and when they heard Laurel screaming they stood up on their pedals and started streaking toward the van. It was the sort of into-the-fire valor that is uncommon these days. But what choice had they? Leave her to be abducted or killed? How could any person do that? And so they rode forward, and the two men raced into the front cab and slammed shut the doors. She thought they were going to drive away. They would, but not instantly. First they spun the van into reverse, trying to run her over and kill her. Leave her for dead. But she was, fortunately, not directly behind the vehicle. They had dropped her just far enough to the side that even clipped in she was able to claw the foot or foot and a half away that she needed to save her life. They ran over and mangled both bicycle wheels and bruised her left foot. But her bike shoe and the bicycle's front fork probably spared it from being crushed. Then the men sped off, the vehicle's wheels kicking small stones into her face and her eyes, while the exhaust momentarily left her choking.

When she was able to breathe again, she finally threw up. She was sobbing, she was bleeding, she was filthy. She was an altogether most pathetic little victim: a girl trapped on the ground in her cleats like a turtle who has wound up on its back in its shell. She would realize later that one of her attackers had broken her left index finger at some point as he had tried to force her to loosen her grip.

Gingerly, the lawyers turned her ankles so she could release herself from her pedals and then helped her gently to her feet. The van was long gone, but Laurel had memorized the license plate and within hours the men were apprehended. One of them worked with bodybuilders at some hard-core weight-lifting club in Colchester. He didn't live far from where she had parked, and he had followed her the week before. When he realized that the Jetta wagon with the girl with the yellow hair that fell out the back of her helmet had returned, he saw his chance. Laurel was the first woman he had tried to rape in Vermont, but he had done this before in Washington and Idaho before coming east, and he had slashed the wrists of a schoolteacher on her morning jog in Montana and left her to bleed to death in a field of winter wheat. He had left her tied to a barbed-wire fence, and the tattoos on his wrists—like many a tattoo—were a commemoration. A piece of art that he wore like a cherished memento.

His partner, apparently, hadn't had any idea that his new friend was a murderer: He was a drifter who had come to Vermont and presumed now they were merely going to have a little fun together at the expense of some young female bicyclist.

Afterward, Laurel went home to Long Island to recover, and she didn't return to college in Vermont until January. The spring semester. She took courses the following summer to catch up—she was in Burlington that July anyway for her assailants' trials—and by the autumn she was back on the same schedule with the rest of her classmates and would graduate with them in a couple of Junes. Still, the trials had been difficult for her. They had been brief, but there had been two to endure. It was the first time she had been back in the presence of either of her assailants since the attack, and the first time she had studied their faces in the flesh. The drifter, who would dramatically reduce his sentence by testifying against the bodybuilder, had pale skin the color of cooked fish and a nut-brown goatee that elongated a face already tending toward horsey. His hair was completely gone on top and what remained was gray mixed in with the brown of his small beard. Even though it was the summer, he wore a shirt with a high collar to hide his tattoo. A part of his defense was the contention that he had dropped acid before the attack and wasn't in his right mind.

The bodybuilder was a lumberjack of a man who, while awaiting his trial, had continued to work out in the exterior pen where the weights were stacked at the prison in northwest Vermont—lifting, someone said, even on those frigid days when he would have to brush snow off the Nautilus machines—but it was once more those gray eyes that had struck Laurel. His head was shaved that summer, but she gathered that the autumn before he had merely kept his hair cropped to a tight bristle cut. After his sentencing in Vermont, he was extradited to Montana, where he was tried and convicted of the school-teacher's murder. He was serving a life sentence in a prison forty-five minutes from Butte. The drifter, following his conviction, was incarcerated in the correctional facility just outside of Saint Albans, relegated to the lowest, most demeaning rung of the prison in the eyes of the inmates: the pod with the sex offenders.

Certainly the assault changed Laurel's life in myriad ways, but the most obvious manifestation was that she stopped biking. The cleats had saved her life, but the sensation of being clipped in—of pedaling—brought her back to that dirt road in Underhill, and she never wanted to go back to that place again. She had always been a swimmer growing up, however, and so after a few years away from the water she returned to the pool, taking comfort both in the miles she would mark and the way the smell of chlorine in her hair instantly would remind her of the safe haven of her childhood in West Egg.

The other changes were more subtle: a penchant for older men that her therapist suggested might stem from a need to feel protected—cosseted—by father figures who would shield her from harm. An avoidance of the gym and the weight room. A diary. An even greater immersion in her photography. A distancing from the social world at the college, particularly the fraternities where she had spent most weekend nights her first year. And then, her senior year, the decision to move from the dormitories to an apartment at the edge of the campus. Laurel didn't want to live by herself—though she was no longer an especially social person, she could still have moments of Zoloft-resistant anxiety, especially when she was alone in the dark—and Talia Rice, her roommate since they had both arrived in Vermont at eighteen, volunteered to come with her. They found a couple of bedrooms, a living room, and a kitchen they could share in a rambling Victorian that offered Laurel quiet and detachment, but was still close enough to the campus for her decidedly more extroverted roommate. It was also very sunny, which Talia insisted any place they chose had to be—for her friend's sake.

Still, some people thought Laurel had grown aloof. She could tell. But she shrugged this off and further curtailed her more casual friendships.

Of course, the change that mattered most is this: If Laurel had not been fiercely attacked, she would not have resumed swimming laps. That sounds prosaic, anticlimactic. But life is filled with small moments that seem prosaic until one has the distance to look back and see the chain of large moments they unleashed. Pure and simple, if Laurel had not started venturing most mornings to the school's natatorium, she would never have met the University of Vermont alumna who ran the homeless shelter in Burlington and continued to stay fit years later in the UVM pool. And then she would never have wound up working at the shelter, first as a volunteer while she was still in school and later, after she graduated, as a bona fide employee. And if she hadn't wound up at the homeless shelter, she would never have met a patient from the state mental hospital, a gentleman (and he was indeed gentle) fifty-six years her senior who went by the name of Bobbie Crocker.

LAUREL'S FATHER gave her some advice, too, when she was growing up: Smart is boring. Effort matters. And, yes, she should never forget that while she was being raised in a nice home in an impressive neighborhood with a mother willing to drive her to soccer games and swim team practice, most of the world lived in serious, dispiriting poverty and thus some-day she would be expected to give something back. He did not mean to suggest in ominous tones that a karmic payback loomed before her because she always had enough to eat and never came home from the mall lacking in clothes or CDs or boys with whom she might want to hook up.

Her father knew everything about the consumption, but nothing about the boys. At least nothing of consequence. He died soon after she finished college with nary a notion of either the sexual appetites or the experimentation that occurred in the high school circles in which she had traveled, or the sexual carousel that had marked her first year at the University of Vermont.

He was a Rotarian, which meant that he was a sizable target for comic abuse. But he was firm in his belief that when his two daughters were grown they would have a moral obligation to reach out to others who lacked their advantages. His Rotary Club actually paid for and built an orphanage in Honduras, and he went there himself annually to inspect it and make sure the charges there were content and well cared for. And so Laurel always was careful to defend the Rotary when people around her made jokes about the organization, making it clear to the glib and sarcastic that in her opinion you didn't make fun of people with full-time jobs who put roofs over the heads of children whose parents had died of AIDS or had lost their homes in a hurricane. Her sister, a stockbroker five years her senior, became an active member of that very same Rotary Club.

Laurel was twenty-three when her father died abruptly of a heart attack. She was confident that he knew how much she had loved him, but that didn't necessarily make the hole his death had left in her life any easier to fill. He and her mother had arrived at the hospital in Burlington the night she was attacked in less than three hours. How? A fellow Rotarian was a pilot with a small plane, and he flew them north as soon as she called.

Laurel and her childhood friends were well aware that the country club on Long Island Sound where they all learned to swim and sail and play tennis had once been the home of Jay Gatsby. But, in truth, they didn't much care. Even their parents didn't much care. Their grandparents probably did. But as nine- and ten- and eleven-year-olds, Laurel and her friends didn't care much at all about anything that mattered to their grandparents. The clubhouse and broad, sweeping dining room had been Jay Gatsby's stone mansion, and there were dusty black-and-white photographs of his parties from the early 1920s decorating the foyer. In every image everyone was overdressed. Or pickled. Or both. Laurel sensed that her friends—the boys, anyway—might have been more intrigued by the club's history if the swimming pool in which they spent whole summer days had been the marble one in which George Wilson had shot Gatsby, but it wasn't; that pool was long gone, replaced by an L-shaped monster with eight twenty-five meter lanes along the letter's vertical length, and a twelve-foot deep diving section along the shorter, horizontal span. There was a one-meter board and a three-meter board, and in the grass along the western and northern sides there were long rows of stately crab apple trees. In the high summer, the young mothers would sit among them in the shade with their toddlers. Laurel spent five years at the pool on the swim team and another three as a diver.

In addition, everyone knew that the northernmost of the three houses across the cove in which they capsized their canoes had once belonged to Tom and Daisy Buchanan. Daisy was the Louisville belle Gatsby had longed for and Tom was her husband. The Buchanans' Georgian Colonial was the oldest of the three homes, the other two having been built when Pamela Buchanan Marshfield—Tom and Daisy's daughter—subdivided the estate in the early 1970s. Where there had once been a half-acre of roses there was now a north-south tennis court that belonged to a family named Shephard; where there had once been a barn housing Tom Buchanan's polo ponies there was a sprawling replica Tudor owned by a family named Winston. Pamela sold the remaining property—the house in which she grew up and where she lived as a married adult until she was almost sixty—in 1978, the year before Laurel was born.

Consequently, Laurel never knew Pamela when she was growing up. They wouldn't meet until she was an adult herself.

But her father knew Pamela. He hadn't known her well, but that wasn't because she was an eccentric recluse. Pamela and her husband simply traveled with a much older (and, yes, even wealthier) crowd than Laurel's parents, and for fairly obvious reasons were not members of the relatively casual country club across the cove. Instead, they belonged to a far tonier marina farther east on Long Island.

Nonetheless, when Laurel contemplated her childhood, more times than not the names Gatsby and Buchanan never even entered her mind. If she thought of them at all, she viewed them as insubstantial ghosts, wholly irrelevant to her life in Vermont.

But then she saw the dog-eared photographs that Bobbie Crocker—indigent, good-tempered (most days), and men- tally ill—had left behind after he died at the age of eighty-two. The old man suffered a stroke in the stairwell on his way to his dormitory-like studio in what had once been the city's Hotel New England, but was now twenty-four heavily subsi- dized apartments the formerly homeless could rent for about 30 percent of their disability benefits or Social Security, and as little as five dollars a month if they hadn't any income at all. Bobbie had no family that anyone knew of, and so it was his caseworker who discovered the carton of old photographs in his one closet. They were badly preserved, the images stacked like paper plates or wedged upright into folders like old phone bills, but the faces were clearly recognizable. Chuck Berry. Robert Frost. Eartha Kitt. Beatniks. Jazz musi- cians. Sculptors. People playing chess in Washington Square. Young men tossing a football on a street in Manhattan, a Hebrew National billboard towering overhead. The Brook- lyn Bridge. A few clearly more recent ones from Underhill, Vermont, including some of a dirt road—one with a girl on a bike—that Laurel knew all too well.

And in a separate envelope designed for a greeting card, the snapshots: smaller, though equally as distressed. She rec- ognized instantly the home of Pamela Buchanan Marshfield. Then the country club from her childhood, including the Norman-like tower, when it was owned by a bootlegger named Gatsby. The original swimming pool, with the tower behind it. Parties, such as those that were celebrated on the walls of that country club dining room. Pamela Buchanan Marshfield as a little girl, standing beside a boy a couple years younger, a tan coupé off to their side. Gatsby himself, beside his bright yellow roadster—the car that Tom Buchanan dismissed at least once as a mere circus wagon.

There were just about a dozen of these smaller photos, and hundreds of negatives and larger prints that she presumed Bobbie Crocker had taken himself.

Laurel did not know instantly who the little boy was beside Pamela. But she had a hunch. Why couldn't Pamela have had a brother? Why couldn't he have wound up homeless in Vermont? Stranger things happened every day. But she certainly did not suspect the whole truth when she first tried to make sense of the box of dingy pictures, or imagine that soon she would wind up alone, estranged from her lover and her friends, once more pursued and shaken and scared.

PATIENT 29873

. . . *patient still obsessed with the old photographs. Talks of them constantly, wants to know where we've put them. Plans to have a show someday—a "spectacular show" . . .*

    Plan: Continue risperidone 3 mg PO BID

    Continue valproate 1000 mg PO BID

    Given security issues, no off-ward privileges at this time.

From the notes of Kenneth Pierce,
attending psychiatrist,
Vermont State Hospital,
Waterbury, Vermont

CHAPTER ONE

*P*AMELA BUCHANAN MARSHFIELD saw the ad the homeless shelter in Vermont had placed in the newspaper before her attorney did. She realized right away it was about her brother and her brother's work.

Memory, she knew—especially when you were her age—was nothing if not eccentric. Consequently, when she thought of Robert, she did not recall a grown man. Instead, she thought instantly of the infant she would take from the nurse's arms and show off to her parents' guests as if he were her own. And, in some ways, he was. She was helping to change his diapers, she was helping to feed him. She would carry him out to the garden and hold his face up to the roses so he could breathe in their perfume. She would let him sniff the polo ponies, and the polo ponies sniff him. Her parents' marriage grew considerably less turbulent in the first years after he was born, and it was the only period from Pamela's childhood when she did not recall them fighting. They may even have been drinking less. Her mother was perhaps never happier than when her brother was cuddly and small and smelled of talcum; the myriad disappointments that already had marked Daisy's life—and Daisy herself was still very young

then—must have seemed considerably easier to shoulder
when she cradled her baby.

Unfortunately, it didn't last. It couldn't. The fissures that
were the distinguishing feature of Tom and Daisy Buchanan's
marital landscape were far too wide for a baby to bridge. For
any baby. Nevertheless, Pamela hoped and prayed and craved
nothing less than a lightninglike miracle from that child.
That toddler. That little boy.

Pamela had read somewhere that infants only saw black
and white when they were first born. They didn't yet distinguish colors. She thought this was interesting for a variety of
reasons, but mostly because of one of her earliest memories
of her brother. It was a day the summer after he was born.
Her father wasn't home, but her mother had returned from a
lunch with some lady friends just about the time that she and
her brother were awakened by their nurse from their naps.
They didn't usually nap in the same room, but they did that
humid August afternoon: They had rested together in the
parlor that looked out upon the terrace because the nurse
could open the French doors and a breeze would come in off
the water.

Daisy got out the album with the larger photographs and
portraits, most from her adolescence in Louisville, and
brought her two children with her to the couch. There she sat
Robert upright in her lap as if he were one of his big sister's
teddy bears, while Pamela nuzzled beside her. She smelled of
lemon and mint. Then she proceeded to tell her children—
mostly Pamela, of course, since her brother was barely a season old—the stories of the people in each one. And while
Pamela could no longer recall specifically what her mother
had said that afternoon about her grandparents or cousins or
aunts and uncles and suitors, she did remember this: Her
brother would want to stare at the images long after she and

her mother were ready to flip the page, and often he would reach out with his pudgy fingers and touch the black-and-white faces of the Fays from Louisville who had preceded them.

As a toddler, he gravitated often to that album, and when he was only four and five years old he and Pamela would pore over the entire collection of their mother's photo books. They treated them like fairy tales, and Pamela would use the pictures to craft bedtime stories for him. At some point, he began making up stories for her. They usually weren't violent. And they were considerably less frightening than the traditional stories of giants and witches and fairies that children were spoon-fed back then. But they were strange and largely nonsensical. He was only nine and ten years old, but already Pamela could see that her brother was beginning to live in a boundary-less world wholly lacking in rigid cause and effect.

It was a foreshadowing of what he would become. How he would live the vast majority of his life.

Consequently, as soon as Pamela saw the newspaper ad, she called her attorney and asked him to contact the homeless shelter in Burlington.

CHAPTER TWO

*K*ATHERINE MAGUIRE had luminescent green eyes, and unlike her chlorine-saturated hair they hadn't faded the slightest bit with age. People actually found them a little unsettling. Laurel certainly did. She guessed that Katherine was fifty, not quite twice her age, but she was toned and trim and passed for a woman considerably younger. The two of them had swum together at the UVM pool for six years, ever since Laurel had returned to the water after the attack, meeting at the changing room weekday mornings at 5:45. Two decades ago, when Katherine was only a few years older than Laurel was now, Katherine had founded the homeless shelter—and she had created the institution virtually on her own. Laurel had always viewed this as a daunting accomplishment. She wasn't quite sure she could start a lemonade stand on the sidewalk outside her apartment house on her own. Along with her twin boys in high school, Katherine considered the shelter her life's work.

Katherine strode with her usual confidence into Laurel's office a little before lunch on a Monday in September, cradling in her arms a beaten-up cardboard banker's box. She dropped it with a small thud on Laurel's floor, and then sank into the folding chair opposite her social worker's industrial-strength metal castoff of a desk—a desk identical to the one Katherine used in her own, only slightly larger office.

"There was an envelope, too," Katherine said, "but I forgot it on my side table. And you can't believe the piles of newspapers and junk mail he managed to amass in a single year. The guy was an unbelievable pack rat."

Katherine had a habit that some people (especially men) found annoying, but usually it didn't bother Laurel: She would begin every conversation as if it had been going on for some time.

"Who?"

"Bobbie Crocker. You know he died yesterday, right? At the Hotel New England?"

"No, I didn't know," Laurel said, lowering her voice. When one of their clients died, they all grew a little somber. Sometimes it didn't even matter how well they had known the person: It was the idea that they were the only ones who stood witness to that life at the end. They all keenly felt how small and spare and diminished that individual's existence had become. "Tell me what happened?"

"You hadn't heard?"

"I've been with clients or in meetings all day."

"Oh, Laurel, I'm so sorry. God, I didn't mean to break it to you this way," she said. This might have been true, but Laurel knew it was also possible that this was precisely the way Katherine had meant to share this news with her. Because of her history, people either treated Laurel with excessive delicacy when something tragic or sad had happened, or they steamrolled clumsily ahead. Her sister, Carol, was the one who informed her that their father had died, and they must have been on the phone a solid minute before she realized that Carol was telling her in the most convoluted manner possible what had occurred. Her big sister was so evasive at first that for easily thirty seconds Laurel thought she was phoning with the essentially inconsequential information that their father was on a business trip overseas somewhere and they might not hear from him for a while. She honestly couldn't understand why her sister was bothering to call at all. In the case of Bobbie Crocker's death, Laurel suspected that Katherine may have chosen the opposite tactic, the inadvertent bludgeon, in which her strategy was to act as if Laurel already knew that one of their clients had passed away.

"Go on, talk. Tell me," Laurel insisted, and Katherine did, beginning with the way another tenant had found Bobbie on his way to church, and ending with how easy—how tragically easy—it had been for Emily Young, his caseworker, and her to clean out his apartment on Sunday afternoon.

"Took about two hours," Katherine said. "Can you imagine? Lord, when my parents die it will take about two years to go through all the stuff they've amassed in their lives. But a guy like Bobbie? The clothes went into a couple of plastic bags: the plastic bags for the Dumpster and the ones for the Salvation Army. And trust me: The ones for the Dumpster were a lot heavier. Mostly it was just newspapers and magazines."

"Any letters at all? Any sign of family."

"Nothing really. I mean, there were some snapshots in that envelope, but I only looked at them for a second. I don't think they really had anything to do with Bobbie. You knew he was a veteran, right? World War Two. So he gets a little burial plot up at the cemetery by the fort in Winooski. There's going to be a small ceremony tomorrow. Can you make it?"

"Of course," Laurel said. "I wouldn't miss it."

"He was such a likable guy."

"He was."

"Though also a bit of a lunatic."

"But a sweet one."

"Indeed," Katherine agreed.

"And for an old man, he sure had a lot of spunk," Laurel said, conjuring a picture in her mind of Bobbie Crocker and recalling some of their last conversations. They were, invariably, as interesting as they were demented. They were not unlike the sort of banter she shared with many of the people who passed through the shelter, in that she could safely presume easily half of what he was telling her was a complete fabrication or delusion. The difference—and in Laurel's mind it was a substantial one—was that victimization was rarely a part of Bobbie's anecdotes. This was atypical for a schizophrenic, but she understood it was also likely that she only saw him at his best: By the time she met him, he was once again being properly medicated. Still, he seldom complained to Laurel or lashed out, and only infrequently did he suggest that he was owed anything by the world. Certainly, Bobbie believed there were conspiracies out there: Usually, they had something to do with his father. But as a rule he was confident he had dodged them. "The last time I saw him was two weeks ago at the walkathon," she added.

"Remember what you talked about?"

"I do. He told me he'd been at a civil rights freedom march in Frankfort, Kentucky, in 1963 or 1964. We were all about to begin—well, not Bobbie—and he was hovering at the starting line, savoring the crowds and the sunshine and the breeze off the lake. When I asked him to tell me more, he changed the subject. Told me instead how he started every Tuesday and Thursday with a bowl of bran flakes floating in exactly one-half cup of orange juice instead of milk, because he worried about his cholesterol. He said he cut the sweetness of the juice with a sprinkle of soy sauce. It sounded pretty repulsive."

"You ever hear him bellow hello?"

"Absolutely." It was common knowledge at the shelter that Bobbie's voice, relentlessly booming even though he was now over eighty, was inappropriate anywhere but a ball game or a bar.

"Honey, I'm home . . . less!" Katherine roared suddenly, parroting Bobbie's common cry—a sitcom dad amped on methamphetamines—when he would arrive at the shelter to see if any of the staff he knew were on duty that day. Apparently, he had used that line even when he really was homeless, when he first appeared at the shelter more tired and hungry than he'd ever been in his life. Even then he was no skittish stray cat.

Slightly paranoid and subject to occasional hallucinations? Yes. Skittish? No.

"He used to give me so much grief—"

"Good-natured, I hope," Katherine said.

"Usually. Whenever he was hanging around the shelter and I was here he would tease me for being so green. I remember when we met he thought I was still in college. Couldn't believe I'd been out for a couple of years."

"He share with you any patented Bobbie Crocker wisdom?"

"Let's see. He said I was too young to know the first thing about life on the streets. He told me the only truly safe drinking water left in Vermont was forty miles away in some spring that fed the Catamount River. He told me that Lyndon Baines Johnson—yes, the president—was still alive, and he knew where. He claimed he'd once partied for a weekend with Bob Dylan and Joan Baez. And he said he grew up in a house that looked out across a cove at a castle."

"I loved that man's fantasies. So many of the people we meet think they're Rambo or the pope. Or they have millions of dollars hidden in Swiss bank accounts. Or the CIA—or Rambo, the pope, and the CIA—are after them. Not Bobbie. He dreamed of castles. Gotta love it."

"Well, he did see the devil," Laurel said.

"Excuse me?"

"He only mentioned it to me once. But he told Emily, too. One time he saw the devil."

"Did he say what the devil looked like?"

"He looked like a person, I think."

"Anyone in particular?" asked Katherine.

"Someone he knew, I'm sure. But that would be a question for Emily."

"How serious were the drugs he was taking when he saw him?"

"Maybe the devil was a woman."

"Or her?" Katherine said, correcting herself.

"I'd say very serious. You don't see the devil on Thunderbird."

Katherine smiled ruefully, tilting her head back toward the screen in the one tiny window in Laurel's office, hoping to catch a wisp of the wind. She was, it seemed to Laurel, summoning a memory of the man. Bobbie—and he was always Bobbie to the social workers and the residents of the Hotel New England—was a human skeleton when he arrived at the shelter, but he recovered quickly: One of the side effects of his antipsychotic was weight gain. He never became truly rotund, but within three or four months he had regained the paunch of the poor who live on fast food and the carb-laden breads and pastas that are heaped onto plates at the emergency day station and the Salvation Army. Food heavy enough to help the hungry feel full and keep warm. Lots of peanut butter. He'd shrunk with old age, but he still had presence and bulk. His face was hidden up to his eyes with a white beaver beard that retained a few small patches of black, but those eyes were what everyone noticed because they were deep and dark and smiling, and his eyelashes were almost girlishly long.

"He was quite a character," Katherine purred after a moment. "Did you know he was a photographer?"

"I know he said he was," Laurel answered, "but I don't think there was much to it. I assume it was a hobby or something. Maybe a part-time job he had before his mind went completely. Shooting class pictures at elementary schools. Or babies at Sears."

"There might be more to it than that. Bobbie didn't have any cameras or photo stuff in his room, but he had these. Look in the box," Katherine said, waving languidly down at the carton at her feet.

"These being . . . ?"

"Pictures. Photos. Negatives. There's a ton in there. All very retro."

Laurel peered around the side of the desk. Katherine pushed the box toward her with her foot, so she could reach it and pull apart the top flaps. The first image Laurel spied was an eleven-by-fourteen black and white of easily two hundred teenage girls in identical white button-down shirts and black skirts on a football field playing with Hula-Hoops. It looked like it was some sort of halftime extravaganza: synchronized Hula-Hooping, maybe. The next one, based on the modest two-piece bathing suit the subject was wearing, was from that same era: A surfer girl was posing atop her surfboard on the beach, pretending to ride an actual wave. Laurel picked it up and saw scrawled legibly on the back in pencil, "Real Gidget, not Sandra Dee. Malibu." She thumbed through a few more, all black and white, all from the late 1950s or early 1960s, until she came upon one she thought might have been a very young Paul Newman. She held it up for her boss and raised her eyebrows.

"Yup," Katherine said, "I think it's him, too. Unfortunately, there's nothing on the back. No annotation or clue."

She put Paul Newman back in the box and pawed briefly through the prints. Toward the bottom, she discovered long strips of negatives, none of which had been placed in sleeves. Like the photos, they had been dumped unceremoniously into the carton.

"And you think Bobbie Crocker took these?" she asked Katherine, sitting back in her chair.

"I do."

"Why?"

"They were in his apartment," Katherine said. "And when he was brought in off the street last year, he had this old canvas duffel with photos in it that he insisted were his. I assume most of these were in it. He wouldn't take a bed until he was sure that the lockers were safe—that his locker would be safe. He was literally going to sleep with them, but there were only top bunks left in the shelter, so he couldn't."

The homeless often brought an object or two into the shelter of totemic (and, to them, titanic) importance—that single item that reminded them of either who they were or what their life had been like before it began to unravel. A certificate from a spelling bee they'd won as a child. An engagement ring they'd been unwilling to pawn. A teddy bear—and even the veterans from the Vietnam and Gulf wars sometimes had a stuffed animal with them. Laurel had seen plenty of family snapshots in the mix that was checked into the lockers, too. But she'd never before seen anything that resembled either serious art or professional accomplishment. And she had taken enough photography courses and snapped enough pictures herself to know with confidence that these photographs were interesting from both a journalistic and an artistic perspective. She thought it was even possible that somewhere she had seen the image of the teen girls with their Hula-Hoops—if not this exact photograph, then perhaps one from the same shoot.

"Couldn't someone else have taken the photos and given them to him?" Laurel asked. "A brother or sister, maybe? A friend? Maybe somebody died and left them to him."

"Go talk to Sam," Katherine said, referring to the manager who had been on duty the night Bobbie Crocker had arrived. "He knows more about Bobbie than I do. And talk to Emily. I'm pretty sure he'd told them both he was a photographer. Of course, he wouldn't show them the pictures. Not ever. Apparently, no one could see them—or else."

"Or else what?"

"Oh, who knows? Welcome to Bobbie's World. Emily managed to sneak a peek at the pictures pretty soon after he first arrived, just to make sure that he wasn't some horrid child pornographer. But you know how busy Emily is. The woman's life is chaos. Once she saw they were innocent, she didn't think about them again until she was going through his room with me yesterday."

Laurel considered this for a moment and then glimpsed another photograph. A pair of young men playing chess in Manhattan's Washington Square, surrounded by a half-dozen onlookers all watching the match intently. She guessed this one couldn't have been later than the early 1960s. Something about it definitely felt pre-Johnson to her. Pre—Lee Harvey Oswald.

Beneath it was an image with a completely different sensibility: a dirt road she recognized in Vermont. A girl in the distance on a mountain bike. Black Lycra shorts. A wildly colorful jersey with an image on the front she couldn't quite make out, but that might very well have been a bottle. It was perhaps a half mile from where she had been attacked, and instantly she was back on that road with the two violent men with their masks and their tattoos and their plans to rape her, and her heart was starting to palpitate. She must have stared for a long moment, because Katherine—her voice sounding as if she were speaking underwater—was asking her if she was all right.

"Yes, uh-huh," Laurel heard herself murmuring. "I'm fine. Can I hang on to these?" she asked. She knew she was sweating, but she didn't want to draw attention to it by wiping her brow.

"Do you want some water?"

"No. Really, I'm okay. Honest. I'm just . . . it's just hot out." She smiled for her boss's benefit.

"Well, when you want to go through them—and there's no rush, Laurel—I'd love to know what you think."

"I can tell you what I think right now: They're good. He— or whoever took them—had legitimate talent."

Katherine dipped her chin just the tiniest bit and grinned in a manner Laurel knew well: coquettish and ingratiating at once. Katherine had built the shelter and kept it afloat these many years through a combination of inexorable drive and the ability to charm the world with her smile. Laurel knew she was about to be asked to tackle a project.

"You still have your privileges at the UVM darkroom, right?"

"Well, I pay for them—the way we do to use the UVM pool. But as an alum, it's a pretty nominal fee."

"Okay, then. Would you be willing to—and I'm not sure if I have the right word here—curate a show?"

"Of these pictures?"

"Uh-huh."

"Yes. I think I would." She knew she had said yes in part because of that image of the lean, spare girl up in Underhill. She had to know what else existed in those images. But she also understood that she was acquiescing out of guilt: She hadn't taken Bobbie seriously when he had brought up his photography. If these pictures were his, then she had missed an opportunity to validate his accomplishments at the end of his life, as well as the chance, perhaps, to learn something as an apprentice photographer herself. Nevertheless, she did have reservations, and she shared them with Katherine. "Of course, we don't know for sure if Bobbie took these," she added.

"We'll confirm that. Or you will. And I'm going to talk to our lawyers and our board of directors about spending a little money to make absolutely sure that Bobbie doesn't have some family out there who might want them. Maybe we'll place a small ad in a photo magazine. Or whatever magazine estate lawyers read. Or maybe even the *New York Times.* You'll see a lot of these seem to have been taken in New York. And maybe we'll put what we found on the Web. There are heir search firms with Web sites."

"You know, these are in pretty horrid condition. We can't have a show with them like this. And do you have any idea how much effort it would take to restore them? I don't even know if the negatives are salvageable."

"But you're interested?"

"I am. But make no mistake: It will be a lot of work."

"Well, I think it would be great publicity for the shelter. It would put a face on the homeless. Show people that these are human beings who did real things with their lives before everything went to hell in a handbasket. And . . ."

"And?"

"And these photos—this collection—might actually be

worth serious money if we were to restore it and keep it together. That's why I think it's so important we make certain there isn't family floating around somewhere who's entitled to it."

Laurel carefully reined in the enthusiasm she was starting to feel, because this had the potential to become a task that was daunting. "You said there was an envelope in your office," she reminded her boss.

"Yeah, but it's not as interesting as this stuff—at least in terms of an exhibition. It's a little packet of snapshots."

"I'd still like to see it."

"Absolutely," Katherine said, and she rose from her chair. "You know, I am so sorry I didn't get to know Bobbie better. I knew he was old, but he was so energetic for a guy his age that I figured he was going to be around for a while."

Then she was gone, on to the next project—and there was always a next project because every year there were more homeless and fewer resources to help them.

Laurel kept trying to return to work herself that afternoon: She had a stack of intake forms to review, and she was in the midst of yet another monumental battle with the VA over benefits for a Gulf War veteran who'd been in the shelter three weeks now and was still waiting for a check, but she really didn't get much more done. She kept going back to the box with the photographs.

ORIGINALLY, THE SHELTER had been a firehouse—at least the part of the structure that was original. There had been two sizable additions constructed in the last quarter century. The entrance sat largely shielded behind a cluster of statuesque maples on a quiet street four blocks from Lake Champlain in a neighborhood in the city everyone called the Old North

End. It was one of the small sections in Burlington that looked tired and felt just a little bit dangerous—though, in truth, there were places all across Vermont that seemed dangerous to Laurel that struck most people as harmless. The houses were all in desperate need of a fresh coat of paint, the front porches invariably were collapsing, and almost without exception the eighty- and ninety-year-old structures had been transformed from single-family homes into apartments. But Laurel knew in her heart that it was a safe neighborhood. If it wasn't, she wouldn't have worked there after her experience in Underhill.

The official name of the organization was the Burlington Emergency Dwelling and Shelter—or BEDS. The acronym was designed for publicity (which the group received in abundance) and fund-raising (which, despite all that publicity, was an ongoing struggle). When Laurel first started volunteering there when she was in college, she liked to read picture books and short novels by Barbara Park and Beverly Cleary to the small children (and, unfortunately, there were always small children) who were living in the special section of the shelter for families. At twenty and twenty-one, she didn't believe there was much else she could do to help out other than read aloud. Most days, she found three or four mothers and three times that many children residing there. She never once saw a dad. The single adults were in a separate section of the building with a different entrance and massive doors separating the two worlds. There was a large wing for single men and a smaller one for single women. The shelter had twenty-eight beds in fourteen bunks for the men, and twelve beds in six bunks for the women. This wasn't sexism: There were considerably more homeless single men than there were single women.

The children in the family section where she volunteered

always seemed to have runny noses, and so Laurel always seemed to have a runny nose. Her boyfriend her junior year in college, a professor at the medical school twenty-one years her senior, told her there were about 250 different cold germs, and you could only catch each one a single time in your life. If that were true, she responded, then she would never again have another cold as long as she lived. For a time she tried to keep the sniffles at bay with echinacea and antibacterial hand gel, but ethyl alcohol and perfume were no match for the melting glaciers that ran from the noses of suddenly homeless five-year-old girls—especially when those girls were climbing all over her lap and burrowing into her neck and her chest like small, blind kittens in search of a nipple. She knew even then how deeply glamorous she seemed to them: She wasn't much younger than their mothers, sometimes a mere three or four years. But unlike those other women she was going to college, and she was neither frazzled to the point that she would lash out at them with the back of her hand nor so depressed that she was incapable of rising from one of the shelter's moldy couches to get them a Kleenex.

Occasionally, she would bring one of her cameras and take their pictures. The children all knew just enough about computers and photography to be disappointed when she wouldn't arrive with her digital camera, because they presumed when she started snapping away that they would get to see instantly what the pictures would look like. Consequently, sometimes Laurel would bring her digital for no other purpose than to entertain them. They would have casual modeling sessions, and then she would hook the Sony Cyber-shot up to the computer in the shelter manager's closet of an office and print out the pictures.

The next week the family might be gone, but the images would still be taped to the windows and the walls.

Nevertheless, Laurel always preferred her film cameras, because—unlike most of the aspiring female photographers she had met in high school or in college—she actually enjoyed her work in the darkroom. Printing and toning. Moreover, she preferred black and white because she thought it offered both greater clarity and deeper insight into her subjects. In her opinion, you understood a person better in black and white, whether it was an abruptly homeless little girl in Burlington, Vermont, in the early years of the twenty-first century or a pair of drunken revelers at one of Jay Gatsby's Long Island parties eighty years earlier.

On a certain level she felt voyeuristic, a bit like Diane Arbus, especially when she would photograph the children with their mothers. The mothers all looked dazed and drugged (which, sometimes, they were) and more than a little sociopathic (which, again, sometimes they were). But Laurel also had a thick notebook filled with nothing but contact sheets of her cousin Martin, who had Down syndrome, and she wondered if she would always feel slightly Arbus-like whenever she took anyone's picture because so much of her training since junior high school had involved shooting him. Martin was a year older than she was, and he loved musical theater. His mother, Laurel's aunt, had sewn enough costumes for him over the years to fill a walk-in closet, and Martin would model these for Laurel for hours. The results were pages and pages of contact sheets of a teenage boy with Down syndrome, imitating in his own way everyone from Yul Brynner in *The King and I* to Harvey Fierstein in *Hairspray*. Laurel actually spent much of her recovery after she was attacked with Martin. Her friends from high school were all off at their colleges, and so she was very glad she had her cousin in her life. Her mother still referred to that period as that "awful autumn," but in Laurel's opinion it really hadn't been all that awful once she had returned to Long Island. She slept. She journaled. She healed. She and Martin must have seen a half-dozen Broadway shows together in those months of darkening days, always a matinee, which meant that when they entered the theater it was daytime and when they emerged it was evening and Times Square was an invigorating, phantasmagoric display of light. Then, the next day, careful not to jostle her slowly mending collarbone, they would reenact again and again their favorite scenes. Laurel was content in her own very specialized cocoon. And once she could use both of her arms again, she took even more pictures of a young man decked out in capes and bowlers and *Scarlet Pimpernel* wigs.

Every so often when Laurel was still in college, a single woman would wind up at the family shelter who was only a year or two older than she was. These women were at an age in which they were too old for the emergency shelter for teens run by another group in another section of the city, a small world where they might actually have felt the safest, but they were still too young to be comfortable in the wing of the shelter cordoned off for adults. Consequently, if there was room and they were clean—free of drugs, though not necessarily of grime and lice—they would be allowed to stay in the section for families.

Laurel would photograph them, too, even though more times than not they would try to sexualize the experience. Sex was their only currency and they used it determinedly if inappropriately. They would begin to peel off their tops, unsnap and unzip their jeans, or touch themselves and pout at the lens as if they were modeling for an adult magazine.

They would, as the song said, try to show her their tattoos. It was almost a reflex for them because instinctively they ached even for Laurel's approval, and they knew cold and hunger intimately.

Only when she had been at the shelter close to a year and grown more comfortable with the world of the homeless did she begin to photograph the men, too. Initially, she had avoided that wing because of her experience in Underhill. And, of course, she had seen homeless men on the streets of New York when she'd been a little girl: bedraggled and grimy, malodorous, insane. Screaming or muttering obscenities either at strangers or—and this could be even more unnerving—at no one. But, clearly, she was worrying for naught. The homeless men who wandered through BEDS were frequently among the most gentle people on the planet. Sometimes it was bad luck and (yes) bad choices that had driven them down, not mental illness. And even when they were bipolar or schizophrenic—like Bobbie Crocker—when they were properly medicated often the madness would become manageable. And less frightening. Whenever Laurel looked at the contact sheets that she had made of these men, she was struck either by how broadly they were smiling or by how wistful and unthreatening their eyes really were.

In the fall of her senior year, a twenty-two-year-old woman named Serena came to the family shelter. Serena told Laurel that things in her life had begun to unravel when she was fifteen. The final straw? Her father, who had been raising her alone and smacking her around since her mother had disappeared when she was five, pounded a sixteen-ounce glass jar of mayonnaise into the side of her face, blackening her eye and giving her a deep purple bruise the size of a softball along her cheek. For the first time in her life, she didn't try to hide the marks with makeup, partly because she couldn't—she would have needed an ice hockey goaltender's mask, not a little powder and blush—and partly because she just couldn't stand being beaten up anymore by her dad and wanted to see what would happen if people knew. She figured that things couldn't possibly get any worse.

She was right. But they didn't get better, either, at least not for a very long while. After all, is it worse to have a roof over your head but a father who pummels you weekly, or to move from house to house—a night here, a night there, living often with strangers—before eventually winding up on the street?

Serena hadn't been in homeroom that day sixty seconds when her teacher asked to see her, and within an hour her father was arrested and she was in foster care. Unfortunately, there wasn't an emergency placement available, and so she spent most of the next three weeks bunking with the families of different friends. She'd never been much of a student, and soon she gave up completely. Just stopped going to school. Within months, she wasn't exactly off the foster care radar screen, but she was one of five or six dozen system runaways and no one was even sure if she was still in the state.

A week after Serena had arrived at the shelter and she and Laurel had grown comfortable with each other, Laurel asked to take her portrait, too. The homeless woman agreed. As Serena talked—continually rolling her black T-shirt up over her small stomach, trying to pull her jeans a bit farther down over her hips, pushing her long amber hair away from her eyes—Laurel photographed her. She would use the images for credit in a photography class, as she did many other pictures of the homeless she took. In addition, she planned to give Serena a set of the prints. The young woman wasn't exactly beautiful: She had been on the street far too long for that. Her face was hollow-cheeked, hard, the bones apparent and sharp, and she was thin to the point of emaciation. But she had eyes the blue of delft china, her nose was pert and small, and her smile was fetching. There was something seductive and wanton and undeniably interesting about the whole package.

At the time, Laurel knew enough not to make any of the women or children who passed through the family shelter a personal reclamation project, both because she was still a student herself and because she was a volunteer who really didn't have the slightest idea what she was doing. She had experience, but no formal training as a social worker. Nevertheless, it was almost too tempting not to want to play God with a girl—and that's what she was, it was delusional feminism to call this starving sprite a woman—like Serena. She told herself that she could buy Serena some clothes that didn't make her look like a slut. She could help her find a job. Then an apartment. Isn't that what the BEDS professionals did?

It was, of course, never that easy. Even if Laurel had been able to wave a wand and whisk Serena behind the counter of the McDonald's within walking distance on Cherry Street, the girl wouldn't have been paid nearly enough to afford an apartment in Burlington. At least not without subsidies. Or the help of one of the landlords in the city who worked with BEDS. Or, perhaps, a Rotarian father who was wealthy and generous and all too happy to foot her rent, as well as make sure she had extra money for groceries.

Three days after Laurel took Serena's pictures, she returned to the shelter with a half-dozen prints that she thought the girl would like. It was a gloriously warm Indian summer afternoon, and she had imagined that she would share the photos with Serena and then walk with her west to the lake. There they'd find a bench by the boathouse with a view of the Adirondacks across the water, and they would discuss life's possibilities. Laurel would tell her about her family since Serena had volunteered so much about hers, and she would try to describe for her a world where normal people had normal relationships. She'd learn whether Serena was looking for a job, and she would give her plenty of encouragement. She might even tell Serena of her own brush with death, of the men in the masks who had attacked her, a topic she broached with almost no one.

The conversation never occurred because by the time Laurel returned to the shelter with the photographs, the apparition called Serena was gone. She spent a week and three days there, and then disappeared.

And that, Laurel figured, was that. She didn't expect she would ever see Serena again.

She was wrong. It was BEDS alumna Serena Sargent who brought Bobbie Crocker—literally leading him by the hand—to the shelter. Just about four years later, when Laurel had been working at the shelter as an actual paid employee for close to three years, Serena appeared out of the blue one August evening with a hungry old man who was insisting that he had once been very successful. He was homeless, Serena was not. Laurel wasn't there at the time, but later both Serena and a BEDS night manager named Sam Russo told her the story.

Serena was living in Waterbury, a town twenty-five miles southeast of Burlington known for being the home to both Ben & Jerry's Ice Cream and the Vermont State Hospital for the severely mentally ill. She was living with an aunt who had returned to Vermont two years earlier from Arizona—precisely the sort of good luck that most of the young and homeless needed in order to find their way in off the street—and working at a diner in Burlington.

Apparently, the fellow had spent some time in the state

hospital, though whether this was months or years before he had made his way north to Burlington and Serena's diner was unclear to the waitress. Into whose custody he had been released remained a mystery as well. Bobbie himself no longer seemed to know. He wasn't violent, but he was delusional. He insisted that Dwight Eisenhower owed him money, and he was fairly certain that if his father knew where he was the man would write him a big fat check and all would be well. Serena guessed that his father, whoever that was, had to be at least a hundred by then and was very likely very long gone. Bobbie had been living on the streets of Burlington for weeks—in ATM cubicles, in the kiosks where the attendants would sit in parking garages, in a boiler room at a hotel near the waterfront—and he couldn't seem to care for himself. He wandered into her diner and paid for a cup of coffee and a couple of eggs with money he boasted proudly he'd raised Dumpster-diving for recyclable bottles and cans. He told her that once, a long time ago, he had been from a wealthy family on Long Island and that he had seen more of the world than she'd believe: He had met, he said, people she'd read about in books and magazines and encyclopedias.

Serena presumed that most of his babble had only the most tenuous connection to reality. But she remembered her week and a half at BEDS, and how the people there had been very nice to her. She didn't know whether Laurel might still be there, but she figured that even if that other woman wasn't it would be a reasonable place for her new friend to get help. And so Serena brought him to the shelter, where Sam Russo got him a bed in the men's section. In conjunction with a doctor at the state hospital, a chemical cocktail was found that stabilized his behavior and again synchronized his personal reality with the rest of the world. Bobbie didn't see the planet precisely the way most people did, but he was no longer a danger to himself. Then, once the shelter had established that he was capable of living independently—he was even using a food stamp debit card to buy groceries—BEDS found him a room at the Hotel New England. Two hundred and forty-five square feet, a single bed, a closet. A hot plate and a dorm-room-size refrigerator. He would share a bathroom with the other tenants on the floor and a kitchen with the other residents of the building. It wasn't glamorous. But it was a room with a roof and plenty of heat in the winter and excellent ventilation in the summer. It beat the street, and with federal subsidies it cost him almost nothing.

LAUREL'S BOYFRIEND that autumn was nearing forty-four. This meant that although he was eighteen years older than she was, he was considerably closer to her age than her previous boyfriend, a fellow who had insisted he was a mere fifty-one but Laurel was quite sure was lying. He used a face cream for wrinkles (though he called it a hydrating lotion), and he seemed to be popping Viagra—and then Levitra and Cialis—like M&M's. This made the bedroom a frequent location for petty squabbles, because while he was on Viagra (needlessly, in her opinion, given that his unenhanced libido would have been impressive on a nineteen-year-old fraternity letch) she was still taking an antidepressant. It was a small dose and she had been tapering off it as she gained both distance and perspective on the attack. But while she was chemically slowing her sex drive, her boyfriend was souping up his with every drug he saw advertised on *Monday Night Football*.

Still, that isn't why they broke up. They broke up because he wanted Laurel to move into the meadow mansion he had built on a parcel of what had once been a dairy farm ten miles south of Burlington—he was a senior executive with a group that had pioneered some kind of hospital software—and she didn't want to live in the suburbs. She didn't want to live with him. And so they parted.

Her current boyfriend, David Fuller, was an executive as well, but he was profoundly commitment-phobic—which she considered at the time an endearing and helpful part of his nature, and thus far it had actually given their relationship considerably more longevity than most of her romantic liaisons. Laurel still had moments when she needed to be around people, especially nights, hence the importance of her friendship with Talia. But as her therapist had observed, she was still, apparently, unprepared for an adult commitment herself.

And while David was content to allow their relationship to idle in neutral, he wasn't cold. Part of the reason why he was uncomfortable with their relationship maturing into something more serious was that he was a divorced father of two girls, the older of whom was an eleven-year-old aspiring drama diva who Laurel thought was adorable. She wished she got to see more of the girl. His children were his priority, especially since his ex-wife was getting remarried in November, and Laurel respected that.

David was the editorial page editor for the city newspaper. He had a glisteningly modern, beautiful co-op apartment overlooking Lake Champlain, but because of the time he wanted to devote to his girls and because his first marriage had wound up a train wreck there was no chance he was going to pressure Laurel into moving in with him anytime soon. Consequently, she spent no more than two or three nights a week at his place. The other evenings he either had custody of his daughters, a sixth-grader named Marissa and a first-grader named Cindy, or he was working late so that on those days when he did have them he could lavish his full attention upon them. Thus she only saw the girls a couple of times each month, usually for picnics or movies or (one time) to go skiing. Twice she had convinced David to let her have Marissa alone for a Saturday, and both times they'd had a spectacular day shopping at the vintage clothing stores Laurel frequented and experimenting at the endless cosmetics counters at the one elegant department store in the city's downtown.

He was always careful to drop Laurel off at her apartment first when his children were with them. She never left any sign of her occasional presence—a toothbrush, a robe, a couple of tampons—at his co-op.

David was known professionally for tough, sardonic editorials when he felt there was either a colossal injustice or a monumental stupidity that needed to be addressed. He was firm-jawed and tall, easily six feet and change, and despite his age he still had thick, straw-colored hair: He kept it cut short now, but when he had been younger—before he became the editorial page editor and had a persona to project—he had actually looked a bit like a surfer. Laurel had seen the photographs. He didn't swim, but he ran, and so, like his girlfriend, he was in excellent shape.

Sometimes when they were together at a restaurant, a young waiter would say something that would suggest he presumed that David was Laurel's father, but this happened less often with the two of them than it had with her other boyfriends in the years since the attack. After all, he wasn't quite two decades her senior; most of the others had been at least that. Moreover, she was getting older, too.

She had a date with David the night Katherine shared Bobbie Crocker's photographs with her, and it was the first time they had seen each other in four days. They went to a Mexican restaurant not far from the newspaper's offices. Whenever they tried to talk seriously about what they had done in the days they had been apart, however, Laurel found herself steering the conversation back to the once-homeless man and his pictures. She grew a little light-headed and excited whenever she contemplated the images that existed in the box. Over coffee, she brought up Crocker again, and David said—his tone characteristically dry, every syllable distinct—"I think it's fine that you're interested in this fellow's work as an artist. As a photographer. I applaud that. But I hope you see that Katherine is foisting on you a serious time sucker. From what you tell me, this project has the potential to eat every spare moment you have—and then some."

"She's not *foisting* it on me."

He smiled and sat back in his chair, folding his arms across his chest. "I have known Katherine a long, long time. Years longer than you. I have watched her in board meetings, at fund-raisers, at phonathons. I've stood beside her and read the names of the homeless at the annual BEDS service at the Unitarian church. I've probably interviewed her a dozen times for stories. *Foist* may not be the right word for her methods. She's far too seductive to be a . . . foister. But she's a seducer, and she's very good at getting what she wants. What her people need. And right now her people need a lot. Hell, you know that better than I do. You see the effects of the federal budget cuts daily."

She had actually met David the previous December, when the two of them had wound up walking beside each other in the candlelight parade that followed the BEDS vigil down Church Street. It had been one of those nights when it's so cold the air stings, but the flickering line of candles stretched nearly two blocks, and when they reached City Hall the two of them had melted into a dark little restaurant for hot chocolate. "Well, if she doesn't mind my focusing on Bobbie's work, why should I?" Laurel asked. "Why should you?"

"I don't mind. That would suggest I have more antipathy to the notion than I do. But I don't believe for one moment that Katherine expects you to curate this show—research the pictures, restore the pictures, annotate the pictures—on BEDS time. You'll be spending your nights and weekends in the darkroom, and when you're not in the darkroom you'll be at your computer trying to figure out who these people are."

Laurel didn't honestly believe this was a sudden burst of midlife male selfishness on David's part. She understood that he wasn't concerned the endeavor would take her away from him on those evenings when he wasn't with his children. Nevertheless, there was a hint of condescension in his remarks, and it made her defensive. This wasn't the first time he had tried to lord over her the wisdom that he thought came with age. And so she responded by telling him, "If you're worried about me not being available when you want to play, don't. It's not like there's some kind of deadline. I'd work on the photos when I felt like it, and only when I felt like it. It would give me something more to do when you're with your girls."

"Honest, Laurel, this isn't about me. It's about you. Once your initial enthusiasm for this elephant of a project wears off, I think you'll find it profoundly frustrating to be printing and processing someone else's work."

"Then I'll stop."

He toyed deliberatively with the handle of his coffee cup, and she thought for a moment he was going to say something more about the subject. But David was a man who took great pride in the sheer equanimity of his personality with his family, with his friends, and with his young girlfriend. He saved his volatility and his righteous wrath for the politicians and the policymakers who offended him, and he unleashed it only in print—never in person. In the nine months Laurel had known him and the seven in which they had been lovers, she had never once heard him raise his voice; nor had they ever endured a serious fight. It could be—*he could be*—maddening.

Finally, he reached across the table and gently massaged her fingers. "All right, then," he said. "I don't mean to pressure you one way or the other. I have some incredibly decadent hot fudge sauce left over from my dinner the other night with the girls, and some vanilla ice cream in the freezer. Let's go have dessert in bed. If we leave now, we can be naked in time for the last of the sunset over the lake."

A moment after he released her hands, the young waiter arrived at their table. "So," he said abstractedly, hoping to make a little small talk as he reached into the pocket of his apron to find the folder that contained their bill, "are you two in town looking at colleges?"

CHAPTER THREE

*T*HE APARTMENT THAT Laurel and Talia shared was the same one they had begun renting together as students at the start of their senior year of college. It was two-thirds of the second floor of a beautiful Victorian in the hill section of Burlington, a mannered neighborhood of elegant Georgians and Victorians and even a few arts-and-crafts homes from the 1920s, only a few blocks from the university's row of fraternity houses in one direction and the city of Burlington in the other. The vast majority of the homes were lived in by single families—the town's lawyers and doctors and college professors—but a few, such as the one in which Laurel and Talia resided, had been carved up into apartments. It was a fifteen-minute walk to the BEDS shelter in the city's Old North End, or twelve to the Baptist church where Talia worked as the youth pastor. It was also close to the campus darkroom in which, once a week, Laurel was still printing her own photographs. When the two women first moved there, they were the youngest of the house's tenants. No more. Now it was inhabited mostly by students in their very early twenties, and Laurel and Talia were the only two people who actually had full-time jobs.

Across the hall from them in the smaller apartment that

comprised the final third of their floor lived a first-year student at the medical school, a slim young man from Amherst who seemed to have puppylike energy. He had delicate, almost girlish features, thin bay-colored hair that was already receding, and a glib sense of humor. He was an avid bicyclist—and his friends who came by all seemed to be enthusiastic bicyclists—and since he had moved into the house in July he had twice asked Laurel if she wanted to go for a ride. He actually owned two bicycles: a hybrid and a road bike. His name was Whitaker Nelson, but he said that everyone called him Whit. Clearly, he wanted to get to know Laurel better, but he had sensed instinctively that it would be difficult to simply (and obviously) suggest they go out.

The other tenants included three women and one man scattered above and below them in four single apartments. The most interesting among them, at least in Talia's opinion, was actually the dog owned by an aspiring veterinarian named Gwen. The animal, Merlin, was a sweet-tempered mutt from the Humane Society that was part springer spaniel and part—based on its size—draft horse. It was gigantic and looked a bit like a Shetland pony. Sometimes when Gwen was away for the weekend, Talia would have the pleasure of trying to walk the beast. Usually, it simply walked her.

In Talia's family faith seemed to skip generations. Her grandfather—her father's father—was an Episcopalian minister in Manhattan, and he actually officiated at her parents' wedding. Talia's father, however, always called the sanctuary the First Church of the Holy Brunch, and it angered him the way attendance dropped off in the summer as the congregation migrated east each weekend to the Hamptons. He had drifted away from the church by the time Talia was in kindergarten, and so she only set foot in the place when she was staying with her grandparents. And her mother? She had always been allergic to anything that resembled religion. Talia feared that when her mother died the woman was going to want show tunes sung at her service instead of hymns.

Talia had started to return to the church after Laurel had gone home to recover from the attack early in their sophomore year of college. Suddenly, she was living alone in their small suite at the school, and she was scared. That one small voice? She heard it. This was not a Pentecostal talking-in-tongues sort of voice. It was instead a gentle and reassuring little murmur, and before Talia knew it, she was—much to the astonishment of both herself and her parents—taking comfort from the fellowship of a congregation on Sunday mornings. She shopped around and wound up at the Baptist church, because they seemed to be doing so much with the fringe people—the poor and the homeless and the drug-addicted—who populated the downtown. And there she started to pray for Laurel. And for the men who attacked her. It seemed to her that it was easier to pray for the change of heart of two evil people than it was to pray for the thousands who were their possible victims. It was, in her mind, all about statistics and probability and her sense that God had to be pretty damn busy.

Initially, friends gave her grief and said she was going Baptist because the church was near the very best shopping in Burlington. That was an inducement, she would admit. But she enjoyed her Sunday mornings in the sanctuary. And the minister was a vegetarian, and she liked the way animals figured often in his sermons.

Nevertheless, when she graduated she was as unsure of what to do with her life as Laurel: She was considering divinity school, but she thought it was equally as likely she might wind up at Wharton. She did, however, know that she loved Burlington, and so when the minister asked if she would be interested in remaining in town and starting a program for teenagers in the congregation, she jumped at the chance. Fifteen months later, she was enrolled in the graduate program in theology and pastoral ministry at nearby Saint Michael's College, driving to and from her classes each day while continuing to work with the teens at the church. Other than Laurel, her friends were incredulous. But they were also in attendance—as were most of the teens and even some of their parents from her church youth group—when she was awarded her master's.

She had been at the church over four years now, the program was thriving, and most of the time she was having more fun than she'd ever had in her life—and Talia was a woman who'd had a great deal of fun in her two and a half decades on the planet. She had always been drawn to men with eyes that could scorch off a skirt; in truth, she had eyes a bit like that herself.

She had grown up in Manhattan and her decision to attend the University of Vermont had been a rebellion: It had meant that she was no longer going to be wearing stilettos with three- and four-inch heels that cost as much as a mountain bike, or retain any friends with the audacity (or lack of self-awareness) to actually call themselves *Muffy*. Consequently, she and her parents continued to have what she still considered an uncomfortable relationship at best. They viewed Vermont as an outbacklike mountain range peopled largely by sanctimonious liberals in rusted-out Subarus who dressed exclusively in flannel and fleece. This was a misperception that Talia tried to correct: She reminded them that a lot of her neighbors actually drove Volvos. Still, her parents never came north, and she only returned south on the major holidays: Easter, Christmas, and the Bergdorf's personal shopper sale (some habits died harder than others).

She and Laurel would often have breakfast together when Laurel returned from the pool at the university, and they did the morning of Bobbie Crocker's funeral. She was reading the newspaper on the floor when Laurel arrived, her roommate's hair still damp from her swim. She had already set out a small feast on the mirror-topped coffee table that Laurel had discovered years earlier at a yard sale. There were sliced apples and pears, bagels beside a tub of blueberry cream cheese, orange juice, and hot steeping tea.

"I think you should stay out of the water for a while," Talia remarked, barely glancing up from the paper.

"Why, do I look pruney?" Laurel asked from the bathroom, as she hung her wet suit in the shower.

"Not at all. But water is getting awfully dangerous," she answered. "Have you seen today's newspaper? Just when you thought it was safe to go trudging through the swamps of Alabama, they tell us there's a twelve-foot, thousand-pound gator prowling around. Apparently, he escaped from the zoo during the hurricane last week. Answers to the name *Chucky*. Meanwhile, a seventeen-foot great white shark has made the Woods Hole area of Cape Cod its new home—in water as shallow as three and four feet."

"I don't think there are carnivorous predators in the school pool. I don't think I have to worry about getting eaten."

"Maybe not by gators and sharks. But watch out for those snarky undergrad frat boys in Speedos."

"I wear a Speedo!"

Talia folded the paper and stretched. "Speedos on women are suitably modest. Speedos on men are unsuitably . . . instructive. Too much information. And, somehow, the package always looks a little off. Know what I mean? It all looks so lumpy. What kind of turnout do you expect at the funeral today?"

Laurel had told her about Bobbie Crocker and the photographs he had left behind, and they were both worried about the attendance at the cemetery because the man hadn't any family that they were aware of.

"I think it will be okay. Small but respectable. If nothing else, there will be a group from BEDS big enough to pack the van."

"Good. Intimate, but not lonely."

"No, not lonely," Laurel said, sitting across from her. Talia started to hand her a bagel, but Laurel was too fast and grabbed one herself. Sometimes, Talia knew, she treated her roommate like an invalid. She tried to do too much for her. "Still, I'll be very interested to see who else will be there," Laurel went on. "I might learn something. Maybe there will be someone who can help me make some sense of the photos we found."

Her friend picked up the local section of the newspaper and glanced at the headlines. After a moment, Talia brought up the subject that was most on her mind that morning: "So, are you doing anything a week from Saturday?"

"That's pretty far away," Laurel said. "Probably the usual, I guess. Take some pictures. Maybe swim. See David."

"Want to play paintball with me and the youth group?"

"What?"

"Paintball. You know, get in touch with your inner child?"

"My inner child is not a Green Beret. Why in the name of God—"

"Careful."

"Why in the world would you take your church youth group out to play paintball? What possible theological lessons are there to be learned from running around the woods shooting one another?"

"Absolutely none. But it's early in the school year and I

want the group to start bonding and working like a team. I want them to get to know each other. And—and this is no small *and*—it's always good to show the kids there are adults out there who care enough about them to give up a Saturday to play paintball with them."

"Couldn't we just go for a hike? You know, woods. Squirrels. No guns."

"Oh, come on, they aren't real guns. And this is something that will build a little camaraderie and juice up the boys. The truth is, I need an activity right now that will get the kids' engines running."

"Can I think about it?"

"Nope. I need another chaperone and I know the group adores you."

"Is this your way of trying to get me to go to church more often?"

"If it gets you there the next morning, fabulous. But no, that's not my agenda. I just don't think you get out enough."

"I get out plenty. You're the one who's boyfriend-less at the moment."

Talia ignored this, but only because it was true. "You might get out," she said simply, "but not with a Piranha-brand automatic paintball rifle and a couple hundred marble-size pellets of paint. Now *that's* getting out."

Talia knew that Laurel found it hard to say no to her. The reality was that most people found it hard to say no to her. She took pride in her powers of persuasion. In the past, Laurel had joined her when the youth group had built giant slingshots to hurl water balloons at each other across the UVM rugby pitch, accompanied the group to an alarmingly creepy community theater production of *Jesus Christ Superstar* (Judas was hanged from the ceiling over orchestra row M), and been among the chaperones when they built a raft for a regatta across Lake Champlain to raise money for the local food shelf. The catch was that all the boats had to be home-made and the materials weren't allowed to cost more than $150. Their boat cost nowhere near that much. It was built largely of plywood and old oil drums (though they did paint them an attractive robin's-egg blue), and it moved gracefully through the water for easily a minute and a half before start-ing to list, then sink. Still, the teens' sponsors came through with their pledges.

"I should warn you," Talia continued, "there is a downside to paintball—and it's a big one."

"The fact it's a tad violent? A wee bit antisocial?"

"Oh, don't get all PC on me."

"Then what?"

"We'll have to wear these goggles that are big and gangly. I mean really big. And really gangly. They're a very bad fashion statement."

"We will, huh?"

She nodded. She noticed that Laurel had used the word *we*. Laurel hadn't said yes yet, but it was clear to them both she was going.

CHAPTER FOUR

*A*LTOGETHER, THERE WERE ten mourners at Bobbie's funeral at the soldiers' cemetery in Winooski, and that included a minister Laurel met for the first time; Serena Sargent, whom she had called with the news of Bobbie's death; a woman who served lunch at the Salvation Army; and a representative from the VFW who wanted to present someone—anyone—with a beautifully folded American flag. But there were also three tenants from the Hotel New England who had known Bobbie the last year of his life, all of whom Laurel guessed were in their forties and fifties. And joining her from BEDS were Katherine Maguire and Sam Russo, the night manager who had been on duty when Serena had first brought Bobbie in. It was drizzling, but it was a warm autumn rain and they were not uncomfortable as they stood beneath the black umbrellas the funeral home had provided and listened to the minister read Psalms for this man he'd never met. Then Katherine shoveled some moist dirt onto the modest casket in the hole and they were done.

Laurel was glad she had come for many reasons, the most important of which was her desire to say good-bye to this often confused but occasionally charismatic old man. When she had been having breakfast with Talia, she realized that

Bobbie had become a mascot of sorts for many of the case-workers at BEDS: not a poster child—though that was, clearly, something Katherine thought he might become posthumously—but a laudably indefatigable and eccentric spirit. A survivor. He actually liked hanging around the day station. On his good days, he was capable of coaxing smiles from the shell-shocked who stumbled in, once and for all out of options.

She was touched to witness the friendships Bobbie had made with these other once-homeless men in the short time he had lived at the Hotel New England (but not surprised), and she was glad to see Serena—and to see that Serena was surviving, if not necessarily thriving. Serena remarked that she wanted out from under her aunt's roof and wanted to do more with her life than to be a waitress. But, still, she looked considerably healthier than the last time Laurel had seen her, and so Laurel told her that she wanted to learn all that she could about Bobbie. Serena agreed to meet her the following week.

On their way back to the BEDS van they had used to bring everyone from downtown Burlington out to Winooski—everyone, that is, except for Serena and the dignified Korean War veteran who had appeared out of nowhere with that flag—Laurel tromped through the wet grass beside Sam. Sam was only a few years older than she was, perhaps twenty-eight or twenty-nine. He was a former Phish-head with an unruly mop of red hair that he kept back in a ponytail and an unfashionably rotund spare tire on a man so young. But he viewed himself as ample, not fat, and he was capable of quickly making the homeless who arrived at the shelter feel secure—which, for most of the social workers, was no easy task.

"I'm just curious," she began. "What do you think: Do you believe Bobbie took all those pictures?"

"No question. They were all he had with him when he was

brought into the shelter. The guy didn't even have any underwear except the drawers he was wearing—but he had those photos."

"But how do you know he was the photographer?"

"He just knew so much. He could talk about Muddy Waters—"

"Muddy Waters?"

"Blues singer from the 1940s and '50s—when rock and roll really began. I gather there's a photo of him and his band in that box. Bobbie told me stories about taking his picture at one of the old Chess Records recording sessions. And another time he told me this incredible tale where he was dangled by some crane over a football field to take a shot of, like, two hundred cheerleaders wiggling around inside Hula-Hoops. It was for *Time* magazine, or something. No, that's not right: It was for *Life*. He did a ton of stuff for *Life*."

"Did you ever see the pictures?"

"He wouldn't show them to me. It wasn't safe," he said, looking left and right histrionically, pretending to check to make sure that no one was listening.

"Katherine alluded to the same thing. What was he worried about?"

"Laurel, the man was schizophrenic! For all I know, it was aliens!"

"He never said—"

"One time, he said something that led me to believe his paranoia went back to his dad. He wasn't scared of him—that wasn't it. But it sounded like Bobbie feared that some people who knew his old man were after the pictures."

When they reached the van, Laurel pulled his arm back so she could ask him one more question before they were surrounded by Bobbie's friends inside the vehicle. "Tell me: How does a person who's taking photos for *Life* magazine wind up homeless? I know he was mentally ill. But how did the wheels come off so completely on the poor guy? Didn't he have any family? Any friends? He was so likable, how could he not?"

Sam Russo motioned to the men who were piling into the van in their ratty sneakers and thrift-store Oxford shirts, their pants that smelled always of the street: Howard Mason. Paco Hidalgo. Pete Stambolinos. "How do the wheels come off for any of them? Bobbie may have been a pretty good photographer once—you'd know better than me if he had actual talent—but, as you said, he was mentally ill. And, it was clear, he had serious attention deficit problems. Thirty, forty years ago, there wasn't a whole lot we could do. We had Thorazine. We were just starting to experiment with haloperidol. But that was about it. And let's face it, Laurel, you only saw him after he was back on his meds. You didn't see him—or, forgive me, smell him—after he'd spent a night in a parking garage. Or when he was being kicked out of a diner because he'd been there for hours, ordering and eating like there was no tomorrow, but didn't have a penny in his pocket. Or when he was trying to tell me that he had once hung with Coretta Scott King. I mean, I could see him with some of those musicians. But Coretta Scott King? That's a stretch. And God only knows what chemicals he ingested in his life—you know, recreationally—or what sort of substance-abuse problems he'd had. Or what kind of demons he brought with him into adulthood. I sure don't. Emily might. Emily Young. But trust me: The things I don't know about these people—any one of them—could fill a book."

WHILE LAUREL HAD been at the funeral, Katherine's assistant had dropped off the small envelope with Bobbie's other pictures in her office. There were a dozen snapshots, some browned and yellowed with age. Laurel had just begun to thumb through them when she paused with a flutter in her chest and sat perfectly still. There, in a black and white so old the edges were scalloped, was the house across the cove from the country club where she had spent so much of her childhood. Pamela Buchanan Marshfield's mansion. She recognized instantly the terrace and the adjacent portico with its eight wide columns. The balconies that overlooked the water. The dock. Behind it was a second, different image of the house.

It had never crossed her mind that Bobbie Crocker could somehow be related to the Buchanans of East Egg. Why would it? She hadn't thought much about either Jay Gatsby or that family across the water since she'd left for college and stopped spending her long summer days at the club. She hadn't really thought much about any of them even when she had been living in her Speedo suits there.

She placed the photos upright against her computer monitor and turned to the next one. There it was, the country club itself, complete with its thick, massive stone tower. Behind that print was one of the original swimming pool—Gatsby's swimming pool. And then there were a pair of images from the parties, one of which was dated in pencil: Bastille Day, 1922. There was a man she presumed was Gatsby himself, standing with a look of almost subdued bemusement beside his canary-colored roadster. And, finally, one of the children: a girl Laurel guessed was nine and a boy perhaps five, posed beside the Buchanan portico with a tan convertible parked behind them. It was evident that this image, too, was from the 1920s.

She recalled what Bobbie had once told her, one of the many remarks that Laurel had presumed were phantasms founded on nothing. He said he had grown up in a house that looked out across a cove at a castle. The Gatsby place wasn't a castle, but it was made of stone and it had that tower that looked a bit like a turret.

She picked up the phone that moment and called her mother, hoping she didn't have bridge or tennis that afternoon, or she hadn't taken the train into the city to go shopping with friends or visit a museum. Since her husband—Laurel's father—had died, she had taken an existing tendency toward busyness and allowed it to become all-consuming: She was always out somewhere. Sure enough, Laurel heard her mother's voice on the answering machine and hung up. Next she phoned her aunt Joyce—her cousin Martin's mother—because she, too, had lived in the area since she'd been married and was a member of the club. Aunt Joyce hadn't spent the time there that either Laurel's mother or father or certainly Laurel herself had, but she knew the local history and the social land mines that peppered the terrain as well as anyone.

Martin answered, his voice the tirelessly good-natured mush that Laurel's family alone could translate with anything that resembled accuracy. Because Martin had been born with both Down syndrome and partial deafness, he spoke like his mouth was filled with a giant popover. But Laurel understood him most of the time, even over the phone, and he might have been the only person she knew who would probably live an entire life without ever speaking badly of anyone. His heart was huge, his soul nonjudgmental. He called her Daughter Laurel instead of simply Laurel, since she was named after their grandmother (who had passed away when Laurel was in high school). For Martin, that much older woman had always been Granny Laurel.

After Laurel had reassured him that she would visit him soon and suggested that they see a musical over Thanksgiving, he put her aunt on the line. The two of them probably spoke more often than many grown nieces and their aunts both because Aunt Joyce lived near Laurel's mother and because of Laurel's friendship with her cousin. The woman was, in some ways, a second mom to Laurel, and so she didn't presume when Martin told her who was on the phone that Laurel had especially interesting news.

Oh, but she did, and she got to it right away. She told her aunt about Bobbie Crocker and the photos and snapshots he had left behind, her voice just a little bit giddy, building to what she thought was her big discovery: "And Pamela Buchanan Marshfield had a younger brother, didn't she?"

"As a matter of fact, she did," her aunt replied with supreme calmness. "He died when he was a teenager. I must have been an infant at the time. Obviously, I never knew him. It's just one more way that poor family was cursed. More money—and more bad luck, it seems—than anyone you could ever meet. What made you think of him?"

In the background, Laurel heard the strings that announced the beginning of the overture to *The King and I*. Martin had just slipped the disc into the CD player, and in her mind she saw him climbing into the regal Siamese vest and silk trousers his mother had sewn for him.

"He died as a teenager?" she asked her aunt, a little stunned. She picked up the photo of the two children. The boy was wearing plaid shorts with suspenders. The girl was in a summer party dress with a scooped neck and poufed ballroom sleeves.

"I'm quite sure he did. Why does that surprise you?"

"That homeless man I told you about. That very old homeless man. Bobbie Crocker. I was thinking—I guess I am thinking—that he was really a Buchanan."

"Bobbie might have been the boy's name. But it might also

have been William. Billy, perhaps. Yes, Billy rings a bell. But so does Robert. Of course, none of it matters because that boy was killed in some accident when he was sixteen or seventeen years old."

"The man I'm talking about spent a couple of weeks in the shelter before we found him an apartment," Laurel continued. "But he hung around the offices and the day station a lot. He died the other day with absolutely no family that we know of, but the social worker who went through his possessions came across an envelope with old snapshots. And there are some of the Marshfield mansion—the place where Tom and Daisy Buchanan had lived—and one of a little girl and a little boy with the old house in the background. They're standing beside a car from the 1920s."

"You're sure it's the same house?"

"Yes, absolutely! And there's another one of Jay Gatsby's place—the country club—and the man himself with that sports car of his."

"Well, I still don't see why you would jump to the conclusion that this homeless man was a Buchanan. The son died. It's common knowledge that Tom and Daisy's son died. And you said this fellow's name was Campbell, didn't you?"

"Crocker," Laurel corrected her.

"I think that effectively closes the case. Why would he be calling himself Crocker if his last name was Buchanan?"

She sat back in her chair and took a deep breath to calm herself. She could see her aunt's nose and lips scrunching together the way they did whenever the woman was discussing something she considered unpleasant. Laurel's mother had the same tendency. They both looked like they were eating lemons, and it was an extremely unattractive family tic.

"Maybe it closes the case. But maybe it doesn't," she said.

"Why do you think he had all these pictures?" Laurel knew that she sounded argumentative. But she kept thinking about what Bobbie had said about his childhood. She feared for a moment that she was bunching up her face, too.

"Oh, Laurel, please don't be disappointed with me."

"I'm not."

"You are, I can hear it in your voice. You're angry because I don't share your belief that this homeless man—"

"He wasn't homeless. We found him a home. It's what we do."

"All right, then: formerly homeless. You're angry because I have my doubts. Maybe the children in that picture really are Pamela and Billy—or Bobbie. Whatever. But how do you know that this person didn't come across the pictures in a Dumpster somewhere? Or some antique store? Maybe he found a photo album in the garbage and saved a few of the images. As you've told me yourself, the homeless—excuse me, formerly homeless—sometimes save the damnedest things."

She stared for a moment at the little boy, trying to find a resemblance to Bobbie Crocker. A glimmer in the eyes, maybe. The shape of his face. But she couldn't. It wasn't that there might not have been a resemblance. But it was hard to discern one because so much of Bobbie's face was obscured by that impenetrable beaver beard.

"And, of course, this all presupposes that the little boy in the photo is Pamela's brother and the little girl is Pamela," her aunt continued. "Why would you make such a leap? Why couldn't they be two other children visiting the house? Guests, maybe?"

"I guess they could be."

"Yes! Maybe they were friends of the family. Or cousins," the older woman added, her voice regaining its typically agreeable lilt. In the background, Laurel could hear that Martin had skipped ahead on the CD all the way to the king's first big number, and was belting out "A Puzzlement" with his usual flair. What Martin lacked in pronunciation, he more than made up for in enthusiasm.

"But I really have a hunch I might be on to something here," she said.

"Then maybe you should talk to Pamela Marshfield. Why not? Show her the pictures. See what she says."

Laurel reached for the photo with her phone on her shoulder and gazed at the little girl. The child looked entitled and intense; when she envisioned her as an elderly woman, she saw someone who was more than a trifle intimidating.

"Do you know where she lives now?"

"Haven't a clue. But the Daytons might. Or the Winstons."

"The Daytons are the family that bought her house?"

"That's right. And the Winstons built that elegant Tudor on some of the land she'd once owned. Mrs. Winston is very old now, too. I believe her husband has passed away. I think she lives there alone."

Laurel's office door was wide open, and she saw a slightly wall-eyed young man with spaniel ears and a scrawny turkey neck hovering in the hallway outside it. His hair was dyed the color of orange Kool-Aid, and he had long cuts on both emaciated arms, one stitched till it disappeared beneath the sleeve of his sweat-stained gray T-shirt. He was a mess, and Laurel could tell by his deer-in-the-headlights stare that he couldn't believe he was here at the city's shelter for the homeless.

"I have a client," she told her aunt. "I think I need to go now."

"All right. You let me know if you find out anything interesting about your mystery man," Aunt Joyce said, and they exchanged their good-byes and hung up. Then Laurel rose to greet her new client. She had the sense that he had been hungry for a very long time, and so she suggested that they stroll to the kitchen for peanut butter and jelly sandwiches. The intake forms could wait until after he'd eaten.

CHAPTER FIVE

*H*IS MOTHER NAMED HIM WHITAKER, which was also her father's name. His older brother recast him as Witless when they were arguing siblings in Des Moines. His resident adviser his first year at college christened him Witty, because he tended to hide his nervousness and insecurity behind a thick veil of irony. The RA thought this was clever, and for a while the young man had feared the name was going to stick. It didn't. Thank God. That would have been too much pressure. And so most people simply viewed him as Whit. At least that was how he introduced himself, and that's what the other tenants in the apartment house, including Talia and Laurel, called him that summer and autumn.

He had two buddies helping him move his stuff in, including a bruiser with whom he'd once played rugby, but Talia and Laurel were around that Saturday morning and offered to help, too. He was instantly smitten by both. Talia had exquisite, almond-shaded skin and a raven's black mane that she wore in a single long braid that fell almost to her waist. She managed to make gray sweatpants and a yellow UVM T-shirt look like loungewear from a lingerie catalog. She was disarmingly tall and moved with the grace and poise of a dancer. He assumed that every one of the teenage boys at her church had a crush on her—that is, if she didn't leave them intimidated and mute—and every one of the girls wanted to emulate her. She was, clearly, a rock-and-roll pastor.

Laurel was wearing a ball cap with her homeless shelter's slogan on the front, "Homeland Security Begins with a Home," and her blond ponytail rose over the plastic fit strap in the back like a fountain. It actually bounced against her neck as she raced up and down the stairs with boxes of his CDs and plastic garbage bags full of his clean shirts and socks. She was wearing a pair of pink Keds and denim capris, and he was mightily impressed by those calves. Gastrocnemius. Soleus. Peroneus longus. The muscles that were extending her feet as she moved. The girl had calves that were glorious. A biker's calves. A swimmer's calves. A—okay, he admitted to himself, it wasn't merely a professional's appreciation— lover's calves.

He might have become infatuated with either woman. They were both four years older than he was, and that alone was a powerful aphrodisiac. Why? It meant, pure and simple, that they were no longer in school. Any woman who actually had a job seemed indescribably exotic to him at the time.

But it was Laurel who inadvertently cast the first spell. Perhaps because it was so unintended. So accidental. Early that afternoon, when they were just about done moving him into the house, they were standing together on his little—and *little* was indeed the apt word; it was more like a ledge with a railing—terrace. They'd wandered out there to catch their breath and drink their water. They were hot and sweaty and breathing heavily from their exertions, and Laurel asked him about Iowa and his family and the house in which he had grown up. She asked him why he wanted to be a doctor. She seemed so honestly—and intensely—interested in his responses that briefly he worried that she viewed him as one of the lost causes who appeared at the shelter. But then he let that fear go, because he realized this was just how this new housemate of his was hardwired. She asked about others because she cared about others—and, perhaps, because it meant that she was less likely to have to talk about herself. Regardless of the reason, she made his heart pound as he babbled on about who he was, until she did something so extravagantly intimate and unexpected that his breath caught in his throat: While he was describing for her his grandfather's farm, she took her water bottle and sprinkled a few drops on a delicate handker-chief she had in her pants pocket, and then leaned in close to him and pressed it against his jaw. Apparently, he had cut himself at some point and the small wound had once more started to bleed, and he hadn't noticed it yet. They stood that way, close enough to kiss, for easily half a minute.

There was something about her that was at once nurturing and deeply vulnerable. He could see it in what she had cho-sen to do with her life and in her relationship with Talia: Talia was like a big sister who watched over her.

Whit was not awkward around girls, but he had always been a little shy. He once had a girlfriend who said he was attrac-tive in an unthreatening sort of way. He presumed she had meant this as a compliment, but then she broke up with him a week after making the observation. In college he had been considered discreet. He sometimes wondered if he'd been born a generation earlier whether he would have been every girl's best male friend: the one who is there after they've been hurt by some jerk on the football team or college radio sta-tion and helps to pick up the pieces. But, of course, always goes home alone. Consequently, he was grateful he was born when he was.

Whit didn't pretend to understand women, and he found Laurel particularly enigmatic throughout August and those first weeks of September. They went to a couple of movies together and dancing once—as friends, nothing more, always in a group—and a few times they walked together into the downtown for ice cream. All very wholesome. He knew his Iowa grandparents would have been proud. He found her to be an enthusiastic conversationalist when they spoke about her work with the homeless, about medical school, about the films they had seen. They could talk about politics and religion, and they did—sometimes briefly in the apartment house's hallway and sometimes for longer periods on the house's front stoop. But other subjects seemed to transform Laurel in seconds from pleasant to distant, and he began to grow increasingly careful about what subjects he brought up. One time he offered to take Laurel biking on the spectacularly beautiful roads west of Middlebury, and it was as if he had suggested that they take in a funeral. She grew remote and then excused herself and returned from the stoop to her apartment. Another time he had been prattling on—charmingly, he supposed, in a Comedy Central sort of way—about slasher movies and the idiocy of the women and men who always get themselves killed in the woods, and she withdrew completely. Laurel didn't ever demean or dismiss him; it was clear to Whit that she didn't demean or dismiss anyone. But she would break off their discussions abruptly, and continue on her way to BEDS or the university darkroom or the grocery store. Other than Talia, she didn't seem to have any friends.

Of course, he understood that if she were to examine his world she wouldn't have seen an especially frenetic social life, either. But he had an excuse: He was just starting medical school. For biochemistry alone he could have spent his life memorizing names and structures and pathways. And, yes, he could be blushingly self-conscious around pretty women.

Still, he had a sense there was going to come a time when he would regret a sizable number of the things he had said, no matter how innocuous the remarks had seemed at the moment. One conversation in mid-September was indicative in his mind. It was a weekday morning, and he was standing in his bike shorts and a black T-shirt on the terrace off his apartment that looked out over the street just as Laurel raced through the front door below him and started down the sidewalk toward the city. He was probably staring (though, he would hope later, not too feverishly). Suddenly, she turned back toward the house, swiveling almost balletically on the toe of her sneaker. She looked up, saw him watching, and smiled.

He waved back with a pair of fingers, a small salute, and hoped the intense way he had been scrutinizing her hadn't been obvious. Maybe that two-finger wave would look casual. It hadn't: He could tell by the way she had glanced up at him and then quickly away that his colossal interest was evident.

"Forget something?" he called down.

"I did," she said, and she raced back inside. A moment later, she reemerged. He had barely moved.

For a second, he was unsure whether it would be more polite to show his interest by inquiring what she'd returned for, or whether he might risk embarrassing her if he did. For all he knew, she'd forgotten her diaphragm. After all, she had a boyfriend, an older man who worked at the newspaper. But after a brief pause, as she jiggled the keys on her ring after locking the front door, he went ahead and asked, "So, what was so important?"

"A book on rock and roll. The roots of rock and roll. There's a chapter in it about Muddy Waters."

"I didn't know you were so into music history."

She rolled her eyes and smiled. "Trust me, I'm not. But we had a client who might have had a connection to some early rock musicians." She had a red backpack draped casually over one shoulder, and she slung it in front of her now so she could unzip it and drop the book inside.

"Someone homeless?"

"Uh-huh."

"Was he a musician?"

"Nope."

"A songwriter?"

"No. A photographer."

"Where's he living now?"

"He died."

"Oh, I'm so sorry."

"It's a little sad. But he did live a long time. He was an old man."

"And so you're researching rock music now because . . . because why?"

"It's complicated. I'm actually interested in the photo credits. I could tell you more, but it would take up most of the morning. And I have to be at work. I'll fill you in later. Okay?"

"And, yes, I have to go for a ride," he said, hoping he sounded suitably slackeresque, but was afraid after he'd spoken that he'd sounded only cavalier and irresponsible. "I don't have class today until ten-thirty."

"We do keep different hours."

"You know, it wasn't all that long ago that you were a student, too."

"Sometimes it feels like it was."

He leaned over the balustrade. He wasn't precisely sure how, but he had the disturbing sense that he was about to say exactly the wrong thing. Again. He just knew it. But he felt he had to say something, and so he forged ahead. "This is going to be a pretty short ride. I thought I might go for a much longer one this weekend. Maybe up in Underhill. There are some wonderful logging trails up there, you know. I guess I bike the way you swim. Tell me again: Why did you swap your bike for a swimsuit?"

"I don't think I told you once," she answered, not looking at him at all, but focusing intently on the process of zipping up her knapsack. It was the kind of remark that coming from anyone other than Laurel would have sounded curt and left him feeling profoundly diminished. But from her it seemed merely wistful. As if, suddenly, the topic had made her tired.

"Any interest in coming with me? I have two bikes, you know. I could lower the seat on one and you'd be incredibly comfortable. I was up there a month ago—up in Underhill—and there is one stretch where the woods just open up completely, and the view—"

"Whit, I have to run. Forgive me," she said, not even looking up at him as she cut him off.

"Oh, I understand," he said.

Though, of course, he didn't really. Not yet. And not at all.

CHAPTER SIX

IN THOSE FIRST DAYS after Katherine had given Laurel the photos she had found, the young social worker was fixated most on the one of the girl on the bike. She caught herself staring at the jersey, the hair, the trees behind her for long moments until—almost suddenly—she would be nauseous. She would, as she hadn't in years, see again in her mind the faces of the two men precisely as she recalled them from those long summer days in the courthouse in Burlington. One time she had to put the photo down and duck her head between her legs. She almost blacked out.

Certainly, she was intrigued as well by the odd coincidence that this mysterious Bobbie Crocker had owned pictures of the country club of her youth. She wondered what it meant that he might have grown up in her corner of Long Island— swum, perhaps, as a boy in the very same cove as her—and then, years later, been on the dirt road with her on the Sunday she nearly was killed. That he had photographed her hours (perhaps minutes) before the attack. But that would presume she really was the girl on the bike. And that the picture had been taken that nightmarish Sunday—versus either of the two Sundays that had preceded it. And Laurel just couldn't be sure. On some level, she didn't want to be sure, because that would put Crocker in a closer proximity to the crime than she wanted to contemplate.

It was easier to focus instead on the tragedy of a man of such obvious artistic talent and accomplishment winding up homeless. Still, she tried not to obsess even on this thread too much. Other than skimming a few heavy tomes on old rock and roll and photography in the middle part of the twentieth century, she didn't do much in the way of investigating his identity—especially when she didn't come across Bobbie's name in any of the photo credits in the books. Still, at his funeral she had made a lunch date for the following week with Serena, and the next day she left a voice mail with Bobbie's social worker, Emily Young, asking to see her when she returned from vacation. Emily had cleaned out Bobbie's apartment at the Hotel New England with Katherine, and then left immediately for a lengthy Caribbean cruise. It was why she hadn't been present at the man's burial at the fort in Winooski.

And so for two more days that week she did her job, and she went out again with David, and she swam each day in the morning. She actually went bowling with Talia and a guy her roommate was considering dating, and then, when they returned home, surfed the Web with her friend so they could both learn more about paintball.

She brought the box of photographs back to her apartment, but—with the exception of that image of the girl on the bike—she did nothing more serious with it than flip through the pictures abstractedly while doing other things: Brushing her teeth. Chatting on the telephone. Watching the news. She did not begin to carefully archive the photos to see what was there or take the negatives up to the university darkroom to start printing them. There would be time for that later. And then, on Friday, she went home for a break. Neither

Katherine nor Talia had to ask why. They knew. The anniversary of the attack was approaching, and Laurel made it a rule never to be in Vermont on that day. Her plan was to return to Vermont the following Tuesday, after the anniversary, and then resume work on Wednesday at BEDS.

After breakfast, she threw some clothes and cosmetics into her knapsack, checked the stove one last time, and prepared to start south in her tired but functional Honda. She wasn't sure whether she would try to see Pamela Buchanan Marshfield while she was home, but just in case she got the telephone numbers for both the Daytons and Mrs. Winston off the Internet and made sure that she had Bobbie Crocker's snapshots in a safe envelope in her bag.

IT HAD BEEN ALMOST too easy for her to find Pamela Marshfield. Laurel hadn't even had to bring the woman up: Rebecca Winston did that for her.

She was holding the phone against her ear in her childhood kitchen and watching the fog outside the window slowly engulf first the pines at the edge of the lawn—an edge not on Long Island Sound, but separated from the shore by a mere spit of preserved state forest—and then the wooden swing set and attached playhouse that had sat in the backyard like a great, hulking massif almost her entire life. She saw a blue jay land on the peaked roof of the playhouse and survey the grass. It was nearing lunchtime on Saturday, and she had only just woken up. She'd slept for close to twelve hours.

Rebecca Winston had already described for the social worker the leaf-peeping bus tour she had taken five years ago through the tortuous roads that crept up and over the Green Mountains. It sounded nauseating, but Laurel didn't tell her that. Then Rebecca had volunteered her fear that all too soon she would be unable to live alone in her house, and the conversation had turned naturally, seamlessly, to Tom and Daisy Buchanan's daughter.

"I know there are some very nice retirement communities nearby, but I love my home. Right now I'm looking out at the water—as we speak. It's lovely. Soothing. Especially with the mist. And I have resources. Obviously. But I couldn't possibly bring in all the help that someone like Pamela Marshfield can. Did you know she has nurses who live with her? Two!" the woman was saying.

"Where is she living now, Mrs. Winston?" Laurel asked. "Do you know?"

"You must call me Becky."

"I couldn't possibly," she answered. Mrs. Winston was somewhere between three and four times her age.

"Please?"

"I'll try."

"Let me hear you say it. Indulge an old woman."

"Mrs.—"

"Come on!"

"Okay." She swallowed. "Becky."

"Was that so bad?"

"No, of course not."

"Thank you."

"Do you know where Mrs. Marshfield is living now?"

"Now *her* you'll have to call Mrs. Marshfield."

"I understand."

"She's living in East Hampton. I hear she has a spectacular place."

"More spectacular than her old estate—the one next to you?"

"It's not quite as big. But who needs six or seven thousand square feet when your husband has passed away and you don't have any children? Still, it's not petite. And people tell me that the view of the water is absolutely breathtaking. I've got this little cove filled with boats and houses. I used to watch you kids take out your Sunbirds from the club. Capsize your kayaks. Pamela, on the other hand, has a long stretch of the Atlantic Ocean and her own private beach. Someone told me when it's warm they carry her onto the chaise on the terrace, and she watches the waves."

"She's that infirm?"

"No, she's that wealthy."

"Would she mind if I called her?"

"She'd probably prefer you wrote. She's of that generation that still writes letters. And she is a particularly eccentric letter writer. She's known in some circles for long, formal letters that are chock-full of opinions and stories. We corresponded for a while after she moved."

"Do you still have the letters?"

"Oh, I doubt it. We lost touch a long time ago."

"I'm only here for a couple of days, so I think I'll risk the telephone," Laurel said, and Rebecca gave her Pamela Marsh-field's telephone number—although, because it was unlisted, Laurel had to promise that she would share it with no one. And then, as soon as they had hung up, she dialed the Marsh-field estate in East Hampton.

LAUREL NEVER UNDERSTOOD precisely what Tom Buchanan saw in Myrtle Wilson, the woman with whom Tom had that ridiculous affair in 1922, and who Daisy would accidentally run over while driving her own lover's car. Tom Buchanan might not have been very nice—he might, in fact, have been an abusive bully who once broke Myrtle's nose—but he was handsome and he was rich. Laurel knew the house. She knew where he had kept his polo ponies. But Myrtle Wilson? She had never met anyone who actually knew her. But clearly the woman was neither particularly bright nor especially kind: She was a dowdy screecher with a tendency to put on airs. She wasn't even all that attractive. Obviously, she didn't deserve to die the way that she did. No one did: Laurel, too, had nearly been killed by a car—run over while clipped to her bike. Like Myrtle, she had been left for dead as the vehicle sped away. But Laurel still didn't view Myrtle as a kindred spirit. She just didn't see why a man like Tom might be attracted to a woman like her. She always presumed that his next lover was a more predictable trophy catch.

Laurel found herself thinking about Tom and Daisy most of the next afternoon, Sunday, since on Monday morning she was going to meet their one daughter. A woman, either a nurse or a personal assistant of some sort, took her call on Saturday, put her on hold, and passed along her message to Mrs. Marshfield. Laurel actually apologized for phoning instead of writing. But she explained who she was and told the woman that she had some snapshots of the old Buchanan estate and what she believed was Mrs. Marshfield when she'd been a little girl. Laurel added that she wanted very much to bring them by and introduce herself. She made no mention of the boy in one of the photos or Bobbie Crocker. After a moment of silence, the woman returned and said that Mrs. Marshfield would be delighted to see her on Monday at eleven.

She spent most of Sunday in the playroom in her cousin's home. Martin was in a *42nd Street* phase, and so they devoted a sizable part of the afternoon to tap dancing. His mother had recently found him a black top hat and cane at a vintage clothing store, and the two of them sang "Young and Healthy" a half-dozen times. Martin was almost a head shorter than Laurel, the difference in their heights attributable both to his

Down syndrome and the reality that Laurel was a lanky five-nine. He had deceptively broad shoulders, however, and one of those male frames that seems designed for formal clothes. He looked dashing in blazers, and danced with a charismatic abandon. Laurel had the sense from the embraces Martin received from the young women he knew with developmental disabilities that he had the potential to be a real heartbreaker, but the truth was that those young women—like the young men—hugged absolutely everybody. Whenever she had been a volunteer timekeeper for the Special Olympics, an awful lot of the athletes sacrificed precious seconds so they could wrap their arms around her and tell her how much fun they were having or how much they loved her.

"You dance divine," said Martin gallantly. Then, perhaps because he had just said something of emotional consequence and was embarrassed, he added quickly, "You're so silly," a non sequitur he used to fill any conversational silence that made him uncomfortable. That night the two of them watched *Snow White* for the third time together that Laurel could recall, skipping all the scenes with the witch and the apple and the thunder that Martin found frightening.

Laurel felt it was the perfect way to spend the afternoon and early part of the evening. The year after she had graduated had been a leap year, and so the actual anniversary of the attack would not occur until tomorrow. But the assault had taken place on a Sunday, and so this year she was especially grateful to be away from Vermont. She loved the Green Mountains, but as sunset approached she found herself short-winded and anxious. She was relieved she was six hours to the south—in a world where she could tap-dance with her joyful cousin, while wondering about a series of eighty- and eighty-five-year-old snapshots of a romanticized bootlegger and a mysterious little boy.

. . . speech is rapid and intense, but can be easily interrupted—not at the level of pressured speech. (Note: Patient speaks/socializes very little outside interviews.) Inferred mood is moderately irritable, affect full, thought process coherent.

Thought content: denies ideas of hurting self or others. Still preoccupied with unusual beliefs, not willing to discuss much else. Denies hearing voices—though occasionally observed on ward talking to self (insists just "reviewing" material).

Beliefs still cause functional impairment; little interaction with others, either in hospital or with friends outside, evidently out of concern that discussing beliefs would lead to disagreements and feeling invalidated. Moreover, appears unwilling to focus on practical issues such as future community treatment and discharge planning.

From the notes of Kenneth Pierce,
attending psychiatrist,
Vermont State Hospital,
Waterbury, Vermont

CHAPTER SEVEN

A GIRL, ELEVEN, SQUATTED on the ground in the apple orchard and held in her hand the McIntosh she had just picked from one of the lowest branches of the tree. Then she took a bite, surprised at both how tart and how juicy it was. She was wearing an elegant jumper the color of jade, with a horseshoe-shaped headband that matched it. Her hair still had the sweet, clean aroma of her strawberry shampoo.

Her sister, six, now tried to roll toward her, but the hill in this part of the orchard really wasn't very steep. Moreover, the ground was littered with fallen apples. Consequently, the younger girl had to push her way toward her big sister with her elbows and her feet, and she moved more like a box than a wheel on the small incline.

"That's stealing, Marissa," she said, rising and motioning toward the slightly gnawed apple in her older sister's hand. In the sky behind her were undulating waves of white clouds, a series of wings against an otherwise blue sky. It reminded Marissa of the venetian blinds in the windows of the bathroom in her father's apartment.

"What is?"

"Eating an apple that Daddy didn't pay for."

Marissa sighed and took another bite. This time she

chewed with a great, exaggerated motion, moving her chin like a mechanical stamp press. She noted that the younger girl's mouth was covered with caramel from the candy apple she had eaten when they had first arrived at the orchard—one their father *had* paid for—and the front of her white sweatshirt was dotted with spots from the rotting apples in which she had just rolled. She looked like a kid from a TV commercial for a laundry detergent.

"I should tell," the younger girl added.

"You should do a lot of things," Marissa said after she had swallowed—again with an obvious dramatic flourish. She had been acting with grown-ups, most bankers and teachers and hairdressers by day, in community theaters for three years now. She hoped that someday she would get to do even more: She fantasized about Broadway. "Maybe you should start by not rolling around on the ground like one of those pathetic messy kids from the preschool," she continued. "Or maybe you should think about washing your face every couple of months."

The younger child—a plump girl named Cindy—seemed not especially stung by the rebuke. She shrugged. Then she used her sleeve to try to wipe the caramel off her face, but already it had coagulated like blood. It was going to take a lot more than a dry sweatshirt sleeve to clean up that mess.

When their father had suggested they go to the orchard this afternoon, Marissa had expected that his new—newer, anyway—girlfriend would be coming along, too. The one named Laurel who their mother dismissed for being so young. But Marissa liked Laurel, and so she was disappointed when their father had said it was just going to be the three of them and they would not be picking Laurel up at her apartment on the hill by the college. "You still have caramel on your face," she said after a moment.

Once more Cindy tried wiping it off, this time licking her fingers and rubbing the mess that framed her lips like clown makeup.

"Is it gone?" Cindy asked.

"Much better," Marissa lied. No point in driving home to her sister the reality that she was a complete slob. Still, Marissa wasn't sure why she felt so cranky this afternoon. She and her sister and their dad had had a reasonably nice weekend so far. After going to the lawn sale yesterday at one of their mom's neighbors, they had seen a surprisingly unbabyish movie that they'd all liked a lot and then gone out for pizza for dinner (a slice of which, predictably, Cindy had managed to spread on the cuffs of her sweater, resulting in the sort of stain that would cause Mom to roll her eyes in frustration and say something snarky about Dad when she noticed it). Their father had made waffles for breakfast this morning. She hadn't done her homework yet and that was vexing her slightly from the very back of her mind. But she could always dive into her math when they got back to Dad's, and do her reading in the bath after dinner.

She wondered if her bad attitude at the moment had something to do with Mom's plan to marry Eric Tourneau in November. She had overheard her parents squabbling about the logistics on the phone this morning, arguing over where she and her sister were supposed to be in the days before and after the ceremony. (Unfortunately, she knew precisely where she was expected to be on the big day itself.)

"Are you gonna eat all that?" asked Cindy.

In the distance, easily seventy-five yards away, their father was standing on his toes as he stretched for a cluster of apples on a particularly spindly tree. When he had dropped another pair in the wicker basket at his feet, he glanced over at them again. Marissa really wasn't sure how and when she had wandered off here. She knew she had been working on a different tree from her dad and then had passed over a series of ones that didn't have apples low enough for her to reach. She had no idea how this chasm had appeared between her father and her.

"Okay, you tell me," she asked Cindy. "Which would be worse? Eating all of this apple, which would be stealing a whole piece of fruit? Or not finishing it, which would be wasting food?"

The little girl thought about this, but only for a second. Then she smiled and did a somersault in the sloppy ground, crushing an apple against her back and leaving a long cider stain along her spine. *This kid,* thought Marissa, *is hopeless. Completely hopeless.* Sometimes, she knew, Mom's fiancé seemed to think Cindy was cute. But that was probably because Eric didn't have any kids of his own yet and didn't know any better. He didn't know what to expect from a six-year-old. Besides, he really didn't have a choice: He had to like Cindy because he was marrying Mom.

Marissa had a sinking feeling that he and her mother were someday going to have more children. This, too, made her dislike Eric—and made her angry with her mom. It also caused her to like Laurel even more. Her father had told her that she and Cindy were his priorities, and he had no intention of dating any woman right now who wanted children. This further endeared Laurel to Marissa.

"Think Daddy will buy us another candy apple when we leave?" Cindy asked her the moment she finished her tumble, her eyes wide with pride from her small gymnastic accomplishment.

"I didn't have a first one."

"Yeah," said Cindy. "'Cause you wanted to wait to steal the regular ones from here."

This was it, the last straw: the final petty, stupid, completely illogical, totally childish remark. It was time to silence her sister—or at least send her packing.

"I did," said Marissa, aware on some level that she needed to be careful now in her anger not to narrow her eyes. That would ruin the effect. Instead, she looked back and forth slowly, histrionically. She was slightly amazed that the waves of clouds high above them were cooperating on cue and bunching together to block out the sun. The orchard was growing darker before their eyes.

"What?" her sister asked. "What?"

"Shhhhh. Don't move."

"Tell me!"

"I will. But don't move—just for a second. Okay? I'm listening. This is very important." She added a tiny, warbling quiver to her voice that she hoped sounded at once pleading and . . . scared. Really, really scared.

It worked. The kid stood like a statue. Then, almost desperate, her voice little more than a whisper: "What?"

"I heard something. And then . . . then that apple tree behind you. It just . . . moved."

"'Cause of the wind."

"No. Not because of the wind. It started to reach . . . and stretch."

Cindy paused, trying to decide whether her big sister was teasing. "Did not," she said finally, but she had spoken in a nervous murmur that was only faintly audible. Marissa knew that the child still believed in fairies and trolls and some bizarre prankster dwarf she'd read about in a picture book called a Tomten. It was a wonder the girl didn't believe the Teletubbies were real—though it was possible she believed in them, too. Best of all, Marissa knew that Cindy was terrified of the angry, talking trees in *The Wizard of Oz*—a dread that absolutely dwarfed her fear of the flying monkeys. They had watched their DVD of the movie just the other day, and the moment the trees had started hurling apples at Dorothy and her pals, Cindy had (once again) burrowed underneath the throw pillows on the couch until it was over.

"It did," Marissa said softly, ever so softly. "I would not lie to you about something this important."

"You're making this up. Trees can't move."

"Of course they can. How else could they have filmed that scene in *Oz*? They went to the apple trees and asked them, and the trees said—"

"No. They did not!"

"Laurel has pictures!" Marissa had no idea where this whopper came from, but both sisters knew that Dad's girl-friend was a photographer, and the lie was almost reflexive.

"Of trees talking?"

She nodded slowly, almost imperceptibly. "Of apple trees. And they look . . . furious."

Cindy seemed to digest this, and to build in her mind a portrait of furious apple trees that combined what she recalled from the movie (and, in truth, it couldn't have been much since she had had her head buried for most of the scene) with what she could see in the orchard around her. The talonlike claws made of twigs. The long, grabbing reach of the branches. The angry faces that formed in the bark. When you were six, it didn't take much imagination to become deathly afraid of an apple tree. Marissa sensed that her sister didn't completely believe that the tree behind her had moved, but Cindy probably had just enough doubt that it was worth running to Daddy—if only to tell on her big sister and get her in trouble. Abruptly, almost like a time bomb, the little kid exploded. "Dad-dy!" she wailed, her voice a two-syllable ululation of desperation and panic, and then she turned and sprinted toward her father as fast as her pudgy legs would carry her. She looked like a terrified munchkin.

Marissa guessed that her father would say something to her about frightening Cindy, but she didn't think he would be all that stern. After all, torturing a sibling was practically in a big sister's job description. She wondered if, by any chance, her dad's girlfriend really did have any pictures of apple trees. Not likely, but you never knew. She made a mental note to ask Laurel what kinds of things she photographed the next time they were together. Maybe Laurel could even take her picture. A headshot. A really professional headshot. She didn't have one, and it frustrated her every time she went for an audition. And there were a couple of shows coming up at a theater in Burlington that had parts for a little girl, and so she had to be ready.

Laurel, of course, was a girl with a serious secret. Marissa didn't know quite what it was, but it wasn't a happy one. She guessed that someday she'd know, especially if Laurel and her dad continued to date—which she hoped they would. Laurel was more like a big sister who never bossed you around than her dad's current squeeze. They'd gone shopping for clothes a couple of times, just the two of them, and had a blast. And Laurel had a cousin who was into musical theater, too, and so she actually knew the words to some of the songs from the shows Marissa had been in. But Marissa had also spent just enough time around Laurel to get a glimpse of the darkness behind the curtain.

She took a final bite of her apple and then hurled the core toward one of the posts on a nearby split-rail fence (missing it completely), and started walking up the slope to her father and her sister. She realized she was facing an especially gnarled old apple tree, one with twin knots a foot or two above her that looked more than a bit like eyes that were weeping: The eyebrows were arched, there were tears descending the runnels in the bark. Before she knew it, she was running hard to catch up to Cindy and her dad. She decided when she got to them she would have to tag her sister and act as if this sprint had all been a part of a game.

CHAPTER EIGHT

SUNDAY NIGHT, LAUREL detoured into the room that had been her father's study and sat down at the computer she'd helped her mother pick out when she'd been home for Christmas just about nine months earlier. On the Internet, she had an agreeable time surfing the *Life* magazine Web site— she spent forty-five minutes looking at old covers—but there was no trace of the old photographer who had died in Vermont. Of course, this really meant nothing: The Web site only offered covers and a smattering of classic images. Then she expanded her search by Googling names for over two hours. She found a great many Robert Buchanans, including a nineteenth-century British poet and a twentieth-century American actor. There were Robert Buchanans who were radiologists and real estate agents and professors at colleges great and small. Likewise, there was a Bobbie Buchanan who was a writer as well, still alive it seemed, and residing some-where in Australia. There were also a half-dozen high school students with that name who had their own Web sites—some impressive, some prurient and offensive.

Next she went to the Crockers—the Roberts and the Bob-bies. There were only thirteen Bobbies, and they seemed all to be high school athletes or security guards (two, as a matter of fact, one in New Mexico and one in West Virginia). On the other hand, when she tried Robert, she found almost fifteen thousand possibilities, including field-target shooting champions, wrestlers, and all manner of expert or professional—including a Cambridge-based Platonist and a scientist with an impressive knowledge of an insect called a white grub. Even scrolling quickly, she viewed the Google summaries of only a tiny fraction of the page possibilities.

Consequently, she tried narrowing the field with other words: "photography" or "photographer" or "*Life* magazine." Eventually, she was able to narrow her search to a workable number of entries—in some cases, as few as eleven.

When she was done, however, she had found absolutely no references to the fellow she thought might be the son of Tom and Daisy Buchanan. And it was after midnight. Three hours of work and she had discovered no one who could have been her once homeless man in Vermont, no photographers anywhere near the age of the former BEDS client. Laurel's Bobbie Crocker—or, perhaps, her Robert Buchanan—seemed not to exist in the infinite, virtual world that existed online.

HEAT HAD BEEN added to the pool at the club in West Egg just before Laurel had left for college, and so although the air was brisk Monday morning with the first serious taste of autumn, she went for a swim. She swam a little more than a mile, and even dove a half-dozen times from the one-meter board, savoring the way she would fly abruptly from the crisp air into water that was downright balmy. She was out of practice and not nearly as limber as she'd been when she was fifteen, but it felt good to soar high off the board.

Before leaving, she took her towel from the spot on the grass by the crab apple trees—an image of the young mothers with their toddlers came back to her from her adolescence—wrapped herself in the cloth like a cape, and climbed the ladder to the three-meter board. She had no plans to return to the water one last time: She had never felt any real proficiency from the higher level. But she wanted to see whether the view of the old Buchanan house was different from this height, or whether she might see more. She couldn't, not really. But she gazed for long seconds at the rows of French doors and the bay windows, and the bright vines of ivy that positively smothered the brick. She studied the portico off to the side, and the dock that jutted out even now into the cove. She tried to imagine the patch on the country club lawn where Jay Gatsby had stood hypnotized in the dark by the lights across the water, and what in particular that one light at the end of the dock had meant to him. Only after a long time did she finally drive home to have breakfast with her mother.

While some spouses age considerably when their partner dies, Ellen Estabrook actually seemed invigorated by her husband's passing. Laurel had no doubts that her mother had loved him. She had no doubts that her parents had loved each other. But her father was a very big presence in all ways: He must have weighed over two hundred pounds when he died, and he towered over most men at six feet three inches. He was well muscled and in excellent condition: His death from a heart attack was a shock to them all. Moreover, he hadn't had a sedentary cell in his body: He was always in motion, whether he was at the law firm on the Island in which he was a senior partner or barbecuing chicken at a Rotary fund-raiser in the park or meeting with people as inherently charitable as he to help fund the orphanage in Honduras.

Since his death, Laurel's mother had begun to henna her hair, and her choices in lipsticks were now the vibrant shades of cherry that Laurel was quite sure the cosmetics companies had designed with girls even younger than her in mind. Ellen had also started to wear lots of black, but not because she was in mourning. She was wearing tight black T-shirts, black jeans, black skirts. As far as Laurel knew, she hadn't dated anyone seriously (though she did seem to have plenty of male friends), and Laurel didn't presume she was reinventing herself because she had a particular plan to snare a second husband. But her mother was only fifty-five and she had resolved, consciously or unconsciously, to reinvigorate her life. She was a beautiful middle-aged woman—still imposing and statuesque—and Laurel could see herself contentedly in the lines of her face in twenty-nine or thirty years.

Laurel had been awake for close to three hours by the time the two of them had breakfast a little past eight. She had told her mother about all of the photographs Bobbie had left behind, with the exception of the one of the girl on the bike. She had shared with no one her suspicions of who the cyclist might have been; the very idea that she was revisiting this part of her life would have profoundly alarmed Ellen Estabrook.

Her mother had already informed her that she knew almost nothing about Pamela Marshfield, and so they spoke mostly about the trip on which Ellen was embarking that Saturday for Tuscany. This was something else that had emerged since her husband had died: A passion for travel. Laurel's parents had been to Italy once before, but it had been decades ago and they had spent most of their time in Rome. Now Laurel's mother was going with a girlfriend to a Tuscan cooking school just outside of Siena for two weeks.

When Laurel was putting her coffee mug in the dishwasher before heading upstairs to brush her teeth before leaving, her mother cornered her. "Be careful, sweetheart," she said. "I know some people around here think the Buchanans were this sad, cursed little family. Even your aunt believes that. But I don't. I think they were all pretty creepy."

Laurel studied her mother. The woman was wearing a delicate black cotton T-shirt with scalloped edging around the collar. Clearly, it had cost a bundle at Bergdorf's. She considered briefly making a joke about being attacked by a geriatric who had to be in her mid-eighties, but she restrained herself. Neither of them was capable of verbalizing the word *attack* in any context other than out-and-out warfare. The two of them rarely talked about that period when Laurel was living at home after the assault, even on the anniversary. Her mother worried often about her daughter's safety and the wounds that remained from a very close call, and Laurel knew discussing it with her only made it worse.

"Well, Pamela's father was, I guess," Laurel said instead.

"Her mother was awful, too. Don't forget: It was her mother, Daisy, who actually killed that poor woman. Ran her over and left her to die in the street. Your father always said that if Myrtle Wilson's sister had been better educated—or more litigious—she would have sued Daisy in a wrongful death lawsuit."

"I don't think she's going to run me over. I don't even think she drives anymore."

Instantly, she regretted her glibness. Her mother took a long sip of her coffee, and Laurel could tell she was envisioning, once more, her daughter clipped to her bicycle while two men backed over her before speeding away. "She's richer than God," her mother continued after a moment, recovering. "But she never gave a cent to any of the charitable projects your father worked on. Not even the orphanage. He himself went to her house one afternoon and was part of the ask. That's what they call it in fund-raising, you know. *The ask.*

She agreed to see him and someone else from the Rotary. It might have been Chuck Haller. But she was absolutely unreceptive when they arrived. Uninterested in the whole endeavor. Your father had no idea why she took the time to see them."

"How long ago did Mr. Marshfield pass away?"

"Not long after they sold the house. Twenty-five or twenty-six years ago, I guess."

"Why do you think they never had any children?"

"Oh, I couldn't begin to answer that one. Maybe they couldn't. Maybe they didn't want any," her mother said. She raised her eyebrows and added melodramatically, "Maybe they knew enough not to continue the demon seed."

Laurel smiled and watched her mother as she girlishly checked the post on one of her earrings with her forefinger and thumb. Then she leaned forward, kissing Laurel on the cheek and purring, "Ummm. Chlorine. I love the smell of chlorine in your hair. It makes me think you're still my little girl."

"Is it that apparent?"

"The chlorine? Only if she gets very close. And I don't believe she gets very close to anyone."

Laurel was returning to Vermont the next day and she didn't know if her mother had something special in mind for them for dinner: Her sister, Carol, was joining them that evening. And so she asked if there was anything in particular she should pick up on the way home.

"Nope. You just drive safely. And—and I mean this—stay on your toes around that woman."

"You're really worried about me, aren't you?"

"I guess a little. I don't like that family. And, yes, I don't like you getting so caught up in this fellow's work. There's that, too. It makes me a little anxious. I know . . ."

"You know what?"

"I know how seriously you take your job. I know how much you care about the people who come to the shelter."

"You don't need to worry, Mom. I liked Bobbie, and I've been impressed by the work he left behind. I want to understand how he wound up at BEDS. But at this point it's all just academic curiosity."

Laurel felt her mother's fingers entwining themselves among hers, the older woman's slim and elegant hands squeezing hers softly. Her mother gave her a fretful, tender smile. Laurel honestly couldn't tell whether she was more concerned that her brittle little girl was involving herself in a project that was going to upset her, or whether this instinctive maternal concern was grounded firmly in what she knew about Pamela Buchanan Marshfield.

AMONG LAUREL'S FIRST THOUGHTS? Mrs. Winston was completely mistaken: Pamela Marshfield didn't need or want to be carried anywhere. The woman was elderly, but she was far from frail. Like her brother, she was in astonishing shape for someone so old. Say what you will about the Buchanans, Laurel thought when she first laid eyes on Pamela, it was one hell of a good gene pool. The woman was eighty-six, but she was formidable, entitled, and confident—and just caustic enough to keep Laurel uncomfortable. The social worker kept her guard up, because it was clear that Pamela never let hers down.

"I'm surprised it took me so long to extricate myself from the North Shore," she said soon after Laurel had arrived in East Hampton. She was wearing a sleeveless white blouse that revealed the seashell-sharp points of her collarbone, and a flowered skirt that fell almost to the Italian tile on the terrace where they were sipping their tea. A manicured swath of lawn perhaps two hundred yards wide separated the terrace from the beach. The sea was calm, and the waves at the shore were more ripples than breakers: a bucket of foamy water over-turned on a suburban driveway. "I never get back there."

She was gaunt in the way that many wealthy elderly women are: Her skin was pulled back tight from her eyes, but it hung like drapes from her upper arms and her neck. Her hair was the white and gray of old fireplace ash, and it was cut as short as a man's. Laurel saw white patches on her arms and the backs of her hands where once she presumed there had been moles and age spots and precancerous growths.

"I liked growing up there," said Laurel. "I don't expect to settle in West Egg—"

"No one settles in West Egg," the old woman said with a slight, dismissive sweep of her hand. "The very word, *settlement,* implies a pioneering spirit and a desire to put roots into the ground. There are no roots there. People pass through there as they . . . climb. It has always been that way."

Laurel understood the reference: West Egg had never been as fashionable as East Egg—it had always been a world of newer money—and like Tom and Daisy, Pamela Marshfield seemed to view everyone who lived on the other side of the cove as a Gatsby-like interloper.

"My family has always been happy enough there," Laurel said, hoping she sounded serene and self-possessed.

"I'm glad. I understand you're a swimmer."

"It's how I keep fit, yes."

"I believe you told Julia—my secretary, the girl you spoke with on Saturday—that you used to swim at the club across from our old home."

She had to restrain a small smile at the way her hostess had referred to Julia as a girl: In addition to speaking on the phone two days earlier, they had met while she had been waiting at the estate, and this *girl* was at least five years older than her mother.

"I did. I spent most of my summers in that pool and in the cove behind your old house when I was growing up."

"I was always a bit surprised my parents never moved. I would have thought the . . . the view . . . might have been troublesome."

"Did it bother you?"

"The view?"

Laurel nodded.

"No."

In the distance to the south the horizon was interrupted by a line of cauliflower-shaped cumulus clouds, a row of great Doric columns supporting the sky. Pamela watched them with her for a long moment before adding, "I understand you have some photographs you want to show me."

"Yes, I do." She reached into the leather bag that her mother had given her for her birthday that summer, and took out the envelope with the pictures she had brought with her from Vermont. The first one she placed on the glass table between them was the image of the little boy and girl near the portico at the woman's childhood home. Laurel tried to gauge the dowager's reaction to the shot, but she revealed little. Finally, Laurel asked, "Is that you and your brother?"

"It is indeed. I'd say I'm nine in it, wouldn't you? That would have made my brother"—she paused for just the slightest moment, perhaps trying to pull from the air precisely how much older she was than her sibling—"five."

"Do you remember when the picture was taken—what you were going to do that day?"

"Oh, it could have been taken anytime. Clearly, we were off to someplace rather interesting. But we were always off to someplace rather interesting."

"I imagine you had a lovely childhood," Laurel said, but she didn't mean it. She was merely trying to say something polite to fill the silence that seemed to envelop the terrace whenever one of them finished speaking.

"I think it's fairly common knowledge that my parents had a deeply troubled marriage. And so they did things. *We* did things. We went places, we were a body in constant motion. It was how my parents dealt with the rift. My brother and I understood this early on, and so while I would say that we had a privileged childhood, I would not have called it lovely."

"I see. I'm sorry."

"You have other pictures?"

As if Laurel were telling the woman's fortune with tarot cards, she laid the few others she had of the house down on the table before her. She had brought with her the photos of Gatsby and his parties as well—and of his home and his pool—but she decided at the last moment to keep those tucked snugly in the envelope. They could only antagonize Pamela Marshfield.

"I loved that room, there," the woman said, pointing at a pair of mullioned windows on the second floor in one of the images. "It was a game room. There was a card table where my mother sometimes played bridge—with her friends and with mine—a Victrola in a cherry cabinet, and a billiard table. Robert loved billiards. Bridge, too. He was a very good card-player, even when he was a very little boy."

"Robert? He didn't go by Bobbie?" asked Laurel. She realized that she had sounded a little startled.

"No. He was always Robert, right up until the day he died," Pamela said, but there was something false in her tone—something more practiced than sad. "Where did you get these?" she continued.

"They were in the possession of a man who passed away last

week in Burlington. A very sweet gentleman who was eighty-two years old." Laurel watched for a reaction—the tiniest of nods, a sudden intake of breath, an eyebrow raised in sadness or surprise—but the woman held her gaze and said nothing.

"He had been homeless," she went on. "We—my organization, BEDS—found him a modest apartment. These pictures were among the only possessions he had when he arrived at the shelter."

"Are there more?"

"Yes. There are a few snapshots and there are some of the prints and negatives he took as a photographer. That's what he did for a living. He was a photographer—quite good, as a matter of fact."

"Did you bring any others with you?"

"I didn't," Laurel lied, and she watched as the other woman studied them, focusing mostly on the picture of herself and her brother.

"I presume I may keep these," Pamela said. "I actually have very few photographs of the two of us."

"No, I'm sorry," Laurel told her. "You can't."

"No?" She seemed taken aback. Laurel guessed that people probably didn't say no to her very often. "Young girl—Laurel—why would you want them?"

"First of all, they're not mine. The man died intestate, and as a BEDS ward his photo collection will go to the City of Burlington. The city attorneys will then dispense with the images as they see fit, but I'm sure they'll keep the collection together. Intact. Even the snapshots, I presume. Bobbie didn't have much, and those photos are the only thing he had of real value when he died."

Pamela's eyes widened slightly when Laurel said the word *Bobbie*. "You haven't told me," she said. "What was this fellow's full name?"

"Bobbie Crocker."

"Sounds like a cake mix for men," she mumbled, and Laurel smiled politely at the small joke.

"He was a bit of a character. A real social animal. Even after we'd moved him into his apartment, he still hung around the shelter sometimes. He helped make the newcomers feel a little better. Big, booming voice. Good sense of humor."

"Well, I don't see the value of a homeless man's photographs and why you can't indulge an old woman's request. I'm sure the city wouldn't care if you gave me the snapshots—especially since, clearly, they once belonged to my family."

"I'm sure you're right. I just can't leave them with you now. They're not mine. But I will talk to the city attorney who works with my group. Perhaps you can have them once the whole collection has been archived."

"It sounds big. Just how large is it?" the woman inquired, and Laurel realized that she was starting to fish. "Are there many more of my brother and me? Any of my parents?"

"I don't know. I don't believe so. But I haven't really begun to review all the negatives."

"Ah, you're a photographer," she said, offering the girl a small sarcophagus smile. "A photographer and a swimmer."

"That's right."

"And you're interested in this because you live in West Egg and see in these pictures a . . . a what? Help me, please?"

A flock of seagulls swooped en masse down onto the beach in the distance, and began strutting along the moist sand. "I presumed the man who died was your brother," she answered carefully. "And I was interested in how a person of such—and I will use your word here—privilege had wound up homeless in Vermont."

"Your homeless man was most certainly not my brother. My brother died in a car accident in 1939. He was sixteen years old."

"I'm sorry. My aunt didn't know the details, but she thought he might have died when he was a teenager."

"Thank you. But you needn't feel sorry. That was, quite literally, a lifetime ago."

"Were you there?"

"With my brother? Heavens no. I was at Smith College then. Robert had had a . . . a somewhat contentious relationship with our parents and left home rather abruptly. He was with a friend, another boy seventeen or eighteen. Their car blew a tire and rolled into a ditch in North Dakota. The both of them were probably too drunk to walk, much less drive."

"Did his friend die, too?"

"It was just someone he met in Grand Forks. Maybe *friend* suggests a greater connection than there was. Yes: He died, too."

"What was his friend's name?"

"I couldn't possibly tell you."

"You don't remember?"

"No."

"Do you recall the town?"

"In North Dakota?"

Laurel nodded.

"It was near Grand Forks. It may even have been in Grand Forks. It was on old Highway 2. I do remember that."

"Would any of your cousins know anything about the accident—or about your brother?"

"Oh, we both played often with our cousins from Louisville. The Fays, William and Reginald. But they've passed away. Maybe they told their children something, but contacting them would be a lot of work for little gain."

"So you don't believe this homeless person, Bobbie Crocker, was your brother."

"Why would you believe that he was? My Lord, even if Robert hadn't died, why would he have disappeared? Why would he have changed his name?"

Laurel had to restrain herself from answering simply: mental illness. Suddenly, she was nervous that if she didn't scoop up the pictures that very moment Pamela Marshfield would, and so she slid the images toward her and then dropped them into her envelope. She saw the woman was watching her.

"You have more pictures with you, don't you?"

"No," she said simply. Technically, she knew, she couldn't give the pictures to Pamela anyway because they weren't hers to dispose of. But would anyone really have cared? Unlikely. Nevertheless, Laurel couldn't bring herself to part with them—neither the snapshots she had with her, nor the material back in Vermont—and there was one critical reason why. She had the sense that Pamela was lying. The woman was denying that Bobbie Crocker was her brother and dismissing a BEDS client as a person. Laurel considered this unforgivable. Here she was living in an estate on the ocean while her brother had died in the stairwell to his small single room in what had once been a run-down hotel. Withholding the photos was a way of penalizing her.

Besides, if she was going to unravel the mystery of how the man had gone from the mansion across from her childhood swim club to a dirt road and a homeless shelter in northern Vermont—and Laurel wanted to know now more than ever—she might need those pictures in her research.

Did she think there might be consequences? It crossed her mind. But she understood as well as anyone that often the trajectories in one's life were built entirely upon unintended results. Obviously, none of her clients ever planned to wind up at BEDS.

"What else then is in that envelope?" Pamela was asking her.

"Oh—"

"If they're pictures of my brother, don't you believe I have a right to see them?"

"They're not, they're—"

"Child, please, hand them to me now. I insist," the old woman said, and then she reached across the small table with the speed of a snake and simply pulled the envelope from Laurel's fingers as if the twenty-six-year-old were a toddler who had hold of a piece of precious crystal. Laurel was too surprised to stop her.

"Well," Pamela said, drawing the single syllable out into a short sentence as she began to flip through them, lingering on the one of Jay Gatsby. "I shouldn't have doubted you. They're not of Robert now, are they?"

"No."

"My brother, of course, never knew this awful man. Apparently, I met him once or twice, but I was too young to remember anything."

"Where did you meet him?"

The woman glanced up at her, offered a small practiced frown, and then proceeded to ignore the question completely: "People only know his side of what happened, you know. Gatz's, that is. That, of course, was his real name. James Gatz. He *changed* it to Gatsby. That's the sort of man he was. And yet everyone was always completely under his spell.

See? Just look at the people at this party. Or this one. Gatz hypnotized people with his money."

"And your parents didn't?"

"No."

She seemed to be contemplating the image of the old pool, the one in which Gatsby was murdered, before returning the pictures to the envelope. Then she leaned it up against her cup and saucer. Reflexively, Laurel reached across the table to retrieve it, inadvertently toppling her hostess's teacup as she did. It fell into the woman's lap, but it didn't break and it was, fortunately, empty. Still, it was an awkward moment, and Laurel rose to apologize.

"I am so sorry," she said, fumbling. "Please tell me it didn't spot your skirt."

"You might simply have asked for the pictures, Laurel," she said, her voice a low rumble of condescension. "Trust me: I had no intention of stealing them. Merely touching that one of Mr. Gatz has left me with an almost overwhelming desire to wash my hands."

"Your skirt?"

"My skirt is fine."

"I'm really sorry," Laurel repeated, aware even as she spoke that she had allowed whatever power she had to be eroded completely by one paranoid rush. Nevertheless, she still had the sense that had she not grabbed the prints back, Pamela Marshfield would indeed have held on to them.

Now the woman shook her head and folded her arms across her chest. "So, tell me," she said. "What do you plan to do next?"

Laurel wasn't precisely sure what she meant, and so she told Pamela of her intention to try to restore Crocker's work and see what images existed in the negatives. She admitted that she hoped someday BEDS would give the man the solo show that his photographs deserved. When she was finished, Pamela rose and she knew they were done—or almost done.

"I presume you understand now that this photographer was not my brother?" she asked, and they started through the French doors and into the living room, the heels of their shoes echoing along the strip of gleaming white hardwood floor that separated two great, thick Oriental carpets. The ceiling was vaulted, and from it hung a massive art deco chandelier, the hundreds of bulbs encased in globes the shape of delicate angel wings.

Laurel thought for a moment about the woman's question. She believed just the opposite was true. "Where is he buried?" she asked, instead of answering her directly.

Pamela stopped. "You want proof? You want the body, is that it? Would it put your mind at ease if we exhumed my dead brother's corpse and had strands of his hair DNA-ed?"

"I'd just like to see the plot . . . if I may."

"No," said Pamela. "You may not."

"Because . . ."

"Fine, go see the plot. I can't stop you. It's in the family mausoleum in Rosehill."

"Rosehill?"

"Chicago, young lady. It's a cemetery in Chicago—where my father's people are from. You can go there and see it for yourself. It's not far from the crypts for the Sears family and Montgomery Ward. My advice, however, is that you leave this alone. Just let go of this bone—and, yes, I am aware that was a rather grisly pun—and leave it alone. Surely you have better things to do with your life. And I would hate to see you compromise your years with a dangerous obsession."

"Dangerous?"

She smirked. "Unhealthy, perhaps, might have been a better choice of word. Nevertheless: my brother and your homeless people. It doesn't sound like a promising combination."

Laurel didn't feel threatened—not yet—but she did have the distinct sense that she had been warned. And that only made her want to continue her search with more vigor. When she climbed into her car, she found it interesting that her hostess had never once asked how a homeless man had come into possession of the family pictures.

CHAPTER NINE

AFTER THE SOCIAL WORKER had left, Pamela Buchanan Marshfield sat alone in her study and flipped dolefully through the only photo album that remained that still held pictures of her brother. Her—and now it was official— late brother. He had been gone, literally or metaphorically, for so long that she was surprised at the depth of her grief.

Her father had thrown away or destroyed all of the other books with photos of Robert, or they had been lost over time. This one album she had was ancient, nearly as old as she was. Many of the photographs were no longer even attached to the dusty pages, and there were two- and three-inch-long yellow stripes where once there had been pieces of Scotch tape. Her mother had never thought much about archival preservation. In truth, her mother had rarely thought much about tomorrow. In most of the images, Robert was a very little boy; in a good many, he looked just about the way he had in the snap shot that Laurel had brought by the house.

Clearly, the girl had the negatives. And it sounded as if she had a lot.

When she had met with the social worker, she had chosen to wear a pair of earrings that once had belonged to her mother. She was quite sure they had been a gift from James

Gatz, because the diamonds—and there were many—were set in big, ostentatious daisies, and her mother only seemed to wear them when her father was out of town or with the latest in his unending string of mistresses. Moreover, virtually every other piece of fine jewelry her mother owned seemed to have a story attached to it. *"These rubies were Grandmother Delia's"*— her grandmother, a Louisville Fay—*"and she was given them by her own parents when she debuted in 1885. Your father gave me these pearls on our ten-year wedding anniversary. This diamond? A gift from him after he fucked that awful Lancaster woman."* Her mother's language had actually grown considerably more colorful as she had grown older, and she had started to drink on occasion even when she was alone. Daisy had always been a heavy drinker, but usually she had been able to hold her alcohol well. Tom Buchanan, too. They would be drunk, but you wouldn't necessarily know it until they grew violent.

For a few years, in that period when he had been friends with an advertising executive named Bruce Barton, her father had stopped drinking altogether. Barton was the second B in BBDO, and the author of a slim little book that became a massive bestseller, *The Man Nobody Knows.* In it, Barton portrayed Jesus Christ as the world's first great businessman: the sort of decisive individual who would have been welcomed into the boardrooms of the decade's biggest corporations and who would have felt right at home at the parties that peppered the era—perhaps even those Dionysian debauches that James Gatz threw for strangers across the cove. In Barton's view (and so, for a time, in her father's), Jesus was a man's man, a reveler who would turn water into wine, and a most impressive storyteller—the creator of parables that were models for ad sloganeers everywhere.

In hindsight, Pamela really was not all that surprised that her father had glommed on to *The Man Nobody Knows* and then to its author, and for a few years had tried to live a more exemplary life. Her father was often looking for what he referred to without a trace of irony as "scientific stuff," and Barton was a serious improvement over some of the other titles to which he had attached himself: Goddard's *The Rise of the Colored Empires.* Melckie's *Commandeering the Oriental.* And a particularly angry, brutish little screed called *The Pure American* by someone named C. P. Evans. She could still recall their dust jackets, and the angry fights her parents would have when her mother would say something catty about one of the books and her father would grow defensive.

She honestly hadn't expected the girl to comment on her earrings. But she had still hoped she might. It was why she had worn them in the first place. Big, garish daisies. She had wanted to see how much the social worker knew, and she thought the jewelry might provide an opening. She found it interesting that Laurel hadn't planned on showing her the pictures she had brought with her of Gatz and his parties, and Pamela wondered now if this detail alone didn't tell her all that she needed to know. The child was still worried about her feelings. Hadn't wanted to dredge up her mother's infidelity.

Still, it was very clear to Pamela that she had to get the pictures back. All of them. The negatives, too. She had spent a not insubstantial part of her life salvaging her parents' reputation, and she shuddered when she imagined what sort of truth might be conjured from among those old photos. Perhaps her father did not deserve rehabilitation, but her mother did. Her mother always had done the best she could.

Robert hadn't believed that, of course, which was among the reasons why he had run off. What did he see when he saw Daisy or Tom or her? Clearly, he saw something more. Something different. There was the periodic laughter when there hadn't been a joke. Or before there was a punch line. There were the occasional off-color asides he would offer at inopportune times. At a dinner party. The debut of one of her friends at the Plaza. When the cousins were in town from Louisville. She recalled the occasions when she or one of her parents had found him alone in a room in the house as an adolescent—the kitchen or the living room or his bedroom, the door open—muttering to himself, once rocking in a ball on the dining room floor, half in and half out of the cold fireplace, the fingers on both hands clenched tightly around his windpipe. Another vision she would never forget, and among the worst: the amount of blood—his blood—he had left on his bedspread after he had smashed the kings and queens of his cherished glass chess set and then collapsed atop his mattress. She had just come home from shopping for college with one of her girlfriends when she heard him sobbing, went upstairs to investigate, and wound up pulling the daggerlike shards of black and blue glass from the palms of his hands while the two of them waited for the ambulance. He would never tell her precisely what had occurred, or why, but it appeared that he had been trying to decapitate the pieces.

And yet there were still long periods of perfect lucidity and charm. He was strikingly good-looking, and he always had girls interested in him. He danced as well as any of the boys in East Egg, and he was invited to parties often. He was always very funny. When he was fifteen and sixteen—while she was at Smith—she understood he had actual girlfriends. There was one who, with Daisy or the girl's mother as a chaperone, he would take into Manhattan for movies or stage plays or concerts. He had no interest in learning to play an instrument, but he liked Duke Ellington and Artie Shaw and Horace Heidt and his Musical Knights. Her mother had told her one time that a monitor at a dance had reported that Robert had kissed a neighbor girl named Donelle while the two of them were dancing to a ballad by Billie Holiday. It was clear that Daisy was pleased.

And the occasional violence—such as that chess set? Well, wasn't Tom violent, too? And certainly Daisy herself could be mercurial. She had thrown her share of plates and wineglasses—usually, but not always, at her husband.

Unfortunately, Pamela had only the vaguest outline of what her brother had been up to in all the years he had been gone. She lacked the specifics. For most of their lives, she hadn't even known where he was—what he was doing or where he was living. It was a testimony to the measure of his distaste for her parents and her. He did not merely avoid them, he had not merely shunned them: Over the years, he had resisted completely her sporadic efforts to get him help.

No, that wasn't accurate. Once—one time she had convinced him to check himself into the Oakville Retreat.

Still, each of the photographs in her album was rich with memory. She paused over one that her father had taken of her mother and Robert and her when she was sixteen. That meant her brother would have been twelve. She and her mother were seated on the side of the sailboat her father had bought in one of the brief and (as always) not completely sincere periods when he was trying to find things for the four of them to do together. It was, she believed, the last time he would make such an effort. The boat was anchored in the sand on the beach behind their house that her father had created soon after that pathetic George Wilson had murdered James Gatz. Within days, as if to signal to the world that he didn't give a damn if people wanted to stand around the mansion across the water and gawk at the light at the end of his own family's dock, her father had buried the part of the lawn that sloped into the cove beneath a small mountain of soft white sand. One morning, three dump trucks arrived filled with the makings of his new shoreline, accompanied by a half-dozen men with shovels and rakes, and by the end of the day the dock jutted into the cove from beach instead of lawn.

Most of the time they rarely bothered to tie the boat to the dock, because it was easier to simply drag it up onto the sand. The craft was far too small to take much beyond the secluded walls of the bay. And really only three of them could safely sail it at one time anyway, a further indication in Pamela's mind of the disingenuousness of her father's contention that he had bought it for the Buchanan *family*.

In the image, she and her mother were wearing suitably modest bathing suits. She was struck—as she was often when she saw pictures of her mother—by how much more beautiful Daisy was than she. Daisy Buchanan was only thirty-six then, a mere twenty years older than her daughter.

Pamela saw her brother was barefoot in the photo, but he was wearing long khaki pants and a shirt with horizontal sailor stripes. No doubt their mother had bought the outfit for him as a part of her codependent attempt to support her husband's halfhearted effort to convince the world (to convince themselves) that this boat was just one more indication of the great fun they always had together as a family.

Soon after the picture was taken, her brother and her father fought. Again. By the time Robert was twelve, they were fighting often. This one was particularly nasty because it marked the first time that her brother had physically tried to intervene in one of their parents' venomous little spats. Even now, Pamela could remember vividly what had triggered it. By accident, her father had positioned the three of them for the photograph in such a fashion that he could see in the background the house that once had belonged to James Gatz.

Apparently, her father didn't want that. At least that's what he said. He said he wanted only blue sky and water behind them. And so, when he discovered what he had done, he had them all pose on the other side of the sailboat. But then the sun was going to be a problem. Consequently, he and Robert dragged the boat a few feet farther up in the sand so one would see only the gently rolling waves and the high summer sky, and the picture in the photo album finally was taken.

Oh, but her mother simply had to tease her father over the way he had insisted on rearranging the boat so this image of family harmony would not have behind it the shadow cast by a house that looked like a French estate with a tower that once had belonged to a bootlegger.

"Really, Tom," she'd said, motioning behind her with her thumb and one finger, her hand limp at the wrist, "you act like there are ghosts over there. If you don't want to see that old hulk of a house, we should move. We probably should have moved years ago."

Instantly, the mood was curdled.

"I want you to see that house," he told her. "I don't care."

"I don't see why," she answered. "You ought—"

"No, we shouldn't have moved," he snapped decisively. "I won't be bullied, and I won't have you bullied."

"I have never been bullied by anyone. Present company excepted."

Her mother was sitting and her father was standing, and their eyes met and neither would look away for a long, horrid moment. It was her father who blinked first, but as he turned away, he told her, "It wasn't that house that I didn't want in the picture. It was any house. I didn't want any house in the picture."

"Oh, Tom, please. Now you're a photographer? You actually think about things like composition?"

"You need to see it," he said again.

"I just told you, I don't need—"

"Consider it penance."

"Penance? Do you even know the meaning of that word?" Then she rolled her eyes, craned her neck like a swan, and slowly shook her head. She allowed herself a small chuckle at his expense. This was too much for him.

"Fine, you want that house in the picture? We can do that!" he snarled. Abruptly he grabbed both her wrists, the biceps in his arms tensing against the short sleeves of his shirt, and he dragged her first to her feet and then down the beach a dozen steps so that her ankles were in the water. There he pushed her hard into the small breakers, where she landed with a splash on her bottom. Before she could rise to her feet, he squatted, brought the camera up to his eye, and snapped a picture. Then another. She squinted back at him defiantly but didn't say a word or make a move to stop him.

"You will always see that house," he told her. "Always!"

Both Pamela and Robert had seen their father manhandle their mother before. But never outside. Never when the two of them hadn't been drinking or weren't enduring the pain of a serious, lights-out hangover headache. And so before either Pamela or their mother could stop him, Robert ran at Tom and pummeled him so hard in the stomach and with such unexpected ferocity that he knocked the wind out of him. Had the large camera not had a strap that Tom had looped around his neck, it probably would have splashed into the water when he doubled over and the film inside it ruined.

"Stop it!" Robert screamed at him. "Don't hit her! Stop it!"

Sometimes Pamela had tried to de-escalate her parents' fights before they grew this violent by changing the subject. By bringing up a boy in whom she had some interest—a sure-fire way to get both of her parents' attention. Some evenings she even had the foresight to water down the gin. On this occasion, however, she simply stood by as a few churlish comments had mushroomed into this public midsummer explosion, and now—for the first time but not, alas, the last— her brother had involved himself by attacking the proud and arrogant and physically intimidating Tom Buchanan.

Their mother quickly climbed to her feet, rising so fast that the water poured off her bathing suit in streams and her emergence made a great sucking sound in the small spot in the cove where she had fallen, and she managed to get between her husband and her son just as Tom wheeled on the boy with the back of his hand. Instead, he hit Daisy, and he hit her so hard on the cheek that her head whirled around as if it were on a spindle and Pamela screamed because she thought he had broken her neck. He hadn't, but Daisy corkscrewed into the sand and would have a bruise on her face that would last into the autumn. Both of her children fell upon her and hugged her. They were desperate to know how badly she was hurt.

Still winded, Tom watched them for the briefest of moments, then stomped from the shallow water with his camera bouncing heavily against his chest and started back up the manicured lawn to the house. Pamela remained with her mother and her brother on the beach for at least twenty minutes, until they all heard first the creak of the broad doors on the carriage barn opening and then the roar of the man's new black-and-red Pierce-Arrow. Only when the sound of the engine had completely receded in the distance did they shuffle like wounded soldiers up to the house and start to ice down Daisy's face. The woman didn't even try to lighten the mood with a remark at her husband's expense.

Pamela found it interesting now that her mother hadn't bothered to save the other photos Tom had taken that day—the ones of Daisy staring back at him after he had thrown her into the shallow water. Most likely this was because they were so unflattering. Had they been at all becoming, her mother most certainly would have kept them. Years later, who would know what really had occurred that afternoon? At least that's what her mother would have told herself. It could all have been innocent horseplay. Daisy probably went to her grave believing that she had redeemed the family image.

But, of course, she hadn't. Not completely. Some people viewed their family merely as luckless and ill-fated—which, given her brother's tragic life, might actually have been the case. Who could say? Maybe her own inability to have children was a sign, too. But Pamela knew that others saw her family as decadent, careless, unfeeling. Some considered them cruel.

Nevertheless, Pamela was confident that her mother had lived for her children in the years after her summer with Gatz. She didn't remember what her mother had been like when she had been carrying Robert, but she had heard enough stories growing up to know that Daisy had loved every moment she'd had with that little baby inside her, and her relationship with Tom had never been better. Nor would it ever be that good again. The greatest tragedy in her mother's life? Not the death of James Gatz, though Pamela knew how much her mother had loved him. Nor was it Daisy's own culpability in the death of her husband's lover, Myrtle Wilson. It was the way she would lose her son.

That was the great tragedy of Daisy Buchanan's life.

And now, Pamela thought, *once and for all I have lost him, too.*

She contemplated for a moment the ad she had seen in the newspaper on Friday. She had phoned her attorney that afternoon. And then the next day, Saturday, this social worker from West Egg had called her. She wondered if the girl was aware of the ad—of what her shelter was doing. One would suppose that she was. Still . . .

She recalled Laurel's stricken face that morning after she had toppled the teacup. The child was peculiarly interested in the pictures. She wanted them. But Pamela knew that she wanted them, too—precisely because she didn't know what images might exist in those negatives or what Robert might have photographed later in life. She had only a hunch.

And so she resolved that she would get the pictures back, every last one. It was the least she could do for her mother.

CHAPTER TEN

ALIA RICE SAT in the dimly lit espresso bar Tuesday afternoon sipping a hot chocolate all but smothered by a giant puffball cloud of whipped cream, while chatting with four of her young charges from the church youth group. The café had once been a ritzy craft cooperative with shelves of hand-thrown pots, handblown martini glasses, and hand-made silver jewelry. The shelves were gone now but the dark paneling remained, and the current owners had covered the walls and the ceiling with lush plants and meandering vines. Talia imagined it was a bit like sipping coffee in the Colombian jungle—except for the blue glow of the laptops on which the students tirelessly searched the Web from the small rustic tables and the varied rings and whirrs from their cell phones—and her high school kids liked coming here because it was usually filled largely with college kids. Talia had sat in this very spot often when she'd been in school.

Occasionally, she glanced down at her hot chocolate and her mind roamed to a question that she pondered more often than she figured was healthy: Exactly how much longer would she be able to eat like this? Her Botox-shooting, carrot-crunching, gym-junkie mother on Manhattan's Upper East Side could no longer eat the way she once had—at least, that is, if she wanted to remain the anorexic size four that she claimed to be with her friends (though Talia knew that more and more of her mother's wardrobe was actually a size six). She guessed that she had at least another half a decade, but a lot would depend on when she had children. And she wanted children, she wanted them badly.

Of course, that meant having a husband. And Talia hadn't even had a serious boyfriend since college. She'd had plenty of sex in that time: If you were young and female and breathing in this town, you couldn't help but have a lot of sex. But it had largely been hookups with friends she had met at parties: nice boys. Fun evenings. No future.

And lately even the casual, hormone-satiating sex had dwindled. It was as if her time at the church—proximity alone to something that just might represent a moral compass— was proving sufficient to minimize the usual days of the week when she was quite sure she was in heat. Not that heat, in Talia's opinion, was immoral. But the more time she spent with teens as young as twelve, the more she found herself slinking back to her apartment and wondering what the hell she'd been thinking when she'd been having sex with her friends in Manhattan when she was fifteen and sixteen years old.

"So, like, how many fund-raisers do we need?" Matthew was asking her. He was wearing a Boston Red Sox baseball cap backward, the bill so far back that it was flirting with the collar of his faux army jacket. The four high school students whom she was treating to hot chocolate and snacks that afternoon were the youth group's activities committee. Talia was a little disappointed that Matthew was bringing the subject back to fund-raising, but she wasn't surprised: A few minutes earlier, at the instigation of her disarmingly scholarly high school sophomore, Vanessa, the conversation had turned briefly to free will and what the apostle Paul had meant when he wrote that the path to freedom was to be found in obedience. There was little that unnerved Matthew—that unnerved many of her teens—more than in-depth biblical deconstruction. Usually, Talia had to remind them that two and three thousand years ago people were even more primitive than their grandparents, and it wasn't impossible to find a lesson in all that violence, disrespect, and abuse.

"I think we need one every other month," she answered. "But it all depends on how successful the fund-raisers are and just how ambitious we want to be with our mission work." *Mission work* was the term they used for the money they were planning to raise that year and turn over to BEDS in June—the end of the school year. Laurel had given a presentation to the teenagers about the homeless in Burlington, and the group had agreed instantly to make them their cause.

Of course, Talia knew that they also needed money for what they called their "activities" because trips to rock concerts—even Christian ones—and amusement parks and movies and (yes) paintball didn't come free.

"How much is this paintball thing costing?" Randy, the other young woman on the activities committee, asked her, seeming to read her mind and not even trying to hide her disgust with the activity they had planned for that coming Saturday. Over the summer, Randy had cut most of her hair and dyed what remained a creosote black, moussing it up most days into a series of small, prickly daggers. This week she had added a strip of blue a bit like a Mohawk. The girl probably hoped that she looked a little scary, but her eyes were too wide—even with all that black mascara—and her face too cherubic. She actually had dimples. In the end, Randy looked like nothing more than a little girl playing dress-up.

"Not a whole lot," Talia answered. "Laurel and I are paying

for ourselves, and the folks at the paintball park are letting all of you onto the field at half price because we're a youth group. And a member of the congregation has agreed to pay for all of our ammunition." The irony of this last sentence caused her a moment of introspection, but the moment was brief and—through force of will—shallow. She didn't like the juxtaposition of the words *congregation* and *ammunition.*

"Well, I know I am totally psyched!" This was Matthew. Predictably, the boys in the youth group were considerably more enthusiastic about the paintball outing than the girls. Lightly, but certainly not gently, he thumped Schuyler, the other boy on the committee, on the shoulder and added, "Wear a ton of sweatshirts, bro. Those paintballs hurt!"

Schuyler took a massive slurp of his hot chocolate and nodded, expelling an immense sigh that suggested orgasmic satisfaction. He had already finished a chocolate chip muffin the size of a grapefruit.

"Where have you heard that?" Talia asked Matthew. No one had told her that paintballs might hurt. She thought they were little marbles about the consistency of a gelatinous bath bead—the sort of thing that would more or less melt in your fingers if you held it too long.

"Heard that? I've felt 'em!" said Matthew. "I played once, last year, and I was, like, completely humbled. I walked like an old dude for days."

This was news to Talia—and, clearly, to the two girls at the table. Out of the corner of her eye, she could see they both looked a little sheepish.

"Oh, come on, how painful could it really be?" she said. "Middle-aged executives play it all the time as a team-building exercise. They get a dozen employees—all white-collar geeks, most of whom are in serious need of defibrillation when they're done—"

"Defibri-what?" asked Randy.

"Electric shock. It gets the heart beating . . . after it stops."

"Is it that hard?"

"Paintball? No! All I meant is that it can't be all that difficult or all that painful if a lot of out-of-shape, middle-aged—"

She stopped when she felt a hand on her shoulder and turned around instantly. It was David. Laurel's boyfriend. Laurel's *middle-aged* boyfriend. The latest in her roommate's string of *middle-aged* boyfriends. The three of them had had dinner together a couple of times, but he had never spent the night at Laurel's and her apartment. Why would he when he had a place of his own that looked out on the lake, and he and Laurel could make all the noise they wanted when they were there? Consequently, she didn't know him especially well. She certainly didn't know him well enough that she thought he might see the humor in her dissing out-of-shape, hypochondriac, middle-aged, white-collar . . . geeks.

And, she realized with embarrassment, she had used that very word.

"Do I really seem that old and infirm, Talia?" he asked, his voice playful and bemused. He had at least a decade on everyone else in the café. He was wearing a gray tweed blazer and his eyeglasses had retro tortoiseshell frames. At least Talia hoped they were meant to be retro. It was possible he really had owned them for decades. Middle-aged people weren't nearly as bad as senior citizens when it came to wearing dowdy old frames, but they sure as hell didn't update them often enough.

"I was generalizing," she said and started to rise, but with a gentle downward pressure of his fingers he suggested she needn't stand on his account. Then he pulled back his hand and waved—more of a salute, really—at the students crowded around the table beside her.

"How are you?" Talia asked him, surprised at how small her voice sounded. Was she really that mortified by what she had said?

"Still a few years shy of a respirator, I hope."

"I was just kidding. I—"

"And I'm just kidding, too. I wasn't offended, honest."

"So, what are you doing here?"

He rolled his eyes from side to side conspiratorially, as if he wanted to make sure no one was listening. Then in a stage whisper he said, "They sell coffee here. You can buy it and"—again the eyes darting from one wall to the other—"bring it back to your office."

She nodded. The newspaper building was right around the corner.

"Yo, you ever play paintball—like as a team-building exercise or something?" asked Matthew. Everyone at the table, even the girls, started to laugh.

"Can't say that I have. Are you all about to?"

"Saturday, man!" the burly teen announced. "And I am pumped!"

"Well, then, I am pumped for you," he said patiently to the boy before turning back to Talia. "Have you heard from Laurel since she went to Long Island?"

"An e-mail or two. Nothing major."

"She back yet? I know she was planning to drive home today."

"She might be. I haven't been home since breakfast."

"Well, I'm seeing her tomorrow night. Say hi to her for me," he said, and then he retreated to the rear of the café where three young adults with significant parts of their faces pierced danced like dervishes behind a counter to grind and brew and steam a lengthy menu of coffee and espresso drinks.

"That dude"—the word stretched out into two lengthy syllables—"is dating Laurel?" Vanessa asked, unable to hide the incredulity in her voice. Vanessa was Talia's young biblical scholar, and she looked up at the youth pastor now with wise eyes and straight hennaed hair—hair so straight that it fell like curtains down the sides of her face.

"Indeed he is."

"Isn't he, like, old enough to be her dad?"

"It's close. But I think he may only be old enough to be her uncle."

She made a mental note that when she saw Laurel next she should tell her that she might get some grief from the youth group about the age of her boyfriend. And, she realized, she had better warn her that paintball might be more painful than she had let on—than, in all fairness, she had known. Well, maybe not *warn* her—at least not use that particular word. She knew that occasionally she treated Laurel with more delicacy than was really necessary, but something about the violence of the game had her questioning now whether it might have been her very best idea to insist that Laurel join them in the woods that coming Saturday: Yes, it had been years since her roommate had been attacked, and they hardly ever discussed it. But her friend was far more damaged than she ever let on. The girl still made a point of being out of state on the mere anniversary of the attack.

Sometimes Talia wondered if she really knew all that had occurred that Sunday night up in Underhill. Sometimes she wondered if anyone did.

Quickly, she caught herself. This was paintball. A game. And, the truth was, Laurel didn't get out a whole lot. She saw David a couple of nights a week, swam with her boss, but otherwise spent most of her time with the homeless who just

wanted in from the cold. Talia was practically her only serious friend. Which, of course, led to another inscrutable ele-
ment in Laurel's personal history: Why had her roommate
allowed her to remain a part of her life when she had consciously exiled herself from the rest of the herd? Laurel had
been a part of one once. They both had been in one, travel-
ing through school in a pack: a group of young women who
dressed alike and talked alike and through sheer force of
numbers could help each other endure even the most awkward or intimidating social situations. But Laurel had ban-
ished herself from the rest of her coterie ever since that
nightmare at the start of her sophomore year of college.

"Remind me," Vanessa was asking Talia now, her voice an
up-and-down wave of adolescent uninterest and boredom
that brought the youth minister back into the conversation.
"Just why are we doing this paintball thing?"

She leaned in toward the younger girl, her elbows on the
knees of her second-skin jeans, and smiled as broadly as
she could. "Because—and you will have to trust me on this
one," she answered, "it will be absolutely, positively massive
amounts of fun. Okay?"

She thought to herself that she would have to tell Laurel
this, too—and to say it in precisely this fashion—when she saw
her next.

SOMETIMES LAUREL and her boss swam side by side and sometimes they were separated by any number of lanes. It depended upon how crowded the water was when they arrived at the pool. The two of them didn't race. They didn't speak. They were, in fact, largely oblivious to each other as they counted their laps. Once Laurel asked Katherine what she thought about as she swam, and her boss remarked that she didn't think much at all: She said that she tended to zone out, and when she considered any idea it was usually of the most prosaic nature. How quickly little cuts seemed to heal in the midst of all that chlorine. Whether her bathing cap was pinching her earlobe. Why she still hadn't mastered an underwater kick turn, despite her social worker's patient tutelage.

Laurel didn't craft particularly great thoughts, either— she didn't ponder black holes, she didn't contemplate Wordsworth—but often she solved small problems in her life or found solutions to the dilemmas that confronted her homeless clients. How to get someone back on Temporary Assistance. Whether a woman with a baby might be eligible for a supplemental food program. Who had recently passed successfully through BEDS and might be willing to take on a roommate. On occasion, she might think about her boy-friend, and wonder whether this might actually be one with whom someday she might live.

She had returned to Vermont on Tuesday afternoon, and by Wednesday morning she was back in the pool, a lane away from the woman she viewed as both a mentor and a boss. That morning, she found herself replaying her conversation with Pamela Marshfield in her head, just as she had for hours the day before in the car. Despite the woman's denials—despite the doubts of her mother and her aunt—she was now more confident than ever that Bobbie Crocker was Pamela's younger brother. She had no plans to fly to a cemetery in Chicago to see a tombstone or mausoleum wall with the name Robert Buchanan carved into the marble or granite—at least not yet—but that was only because she wasn't sure what this would prove to her. She tried not to think conspiratorially, but she had spent enough time with paranoid schizophrenics that clearly she was capable of imagining the worst, too. After all, even paranoids had enemies. Moreover, she kept coming back to a likelihood that would cause her to fume in the water: The Buchanans—Daisy and Tom and their daughter, Pamela—had deserted a family member who needed them. A brother. A son. Like so many of the homeless she saw, Bob-bie had been hung out to dry by the very people who were supposed to be there for him no matter what. And, unlike so many of those families, this clan had the resources to have provided for Bobbie when he was in need, instead of viewing him as a madman of the attic to be hidden away or discarded.

Consequently, almost angrily, Laurel began to build a plan in her mind. She already had a lunch scheduled with Serena Sargent for Friday, but there were other people with whom she could meet as well, including some of the tenants at the Hotel New England. She would begin with the three men who had come to the funeral. And she needed to do more with the photos that Bobbie had left behind than merely glance through them while spooning the last of a cup of yogurt into her mouth or watching the news. She should produce an inventory of the images that were already printed, and try to annotate them: Who was in them, where and when they were taken. She should start to make contact sheets from the strips of negatives he had left behind and examine what was there. She should see if there were any more connections to a house in East Egg, or any other markers on the sad picaresque that had brought him from an estate on Long Island Sound to a hotel for the homeless in Burlington and, at least briefly, to the dirt road on which she nearly was murdered.

Moreover, somewhere in his file at BEDS was his VA number—his identification as a veteran—and a Social Security number. Those digits alone might open all sorts of possibilities. She wasn't supposed to abuse her access in this manner, but Crocker was dead, and at the moment he didn't seem to have left anyone behind who might care.

No one at BEDS thought anything of Laurel rummaging through the client files. Tom Buley, a caseworker who'd been working at BEDS probably since she had been in elementary school, was thumbing through the drawers when she wandered casually into the cramped, windowless utility room in which the social workers stored the paperwork on the homeless who arrived at their door. Tom made a catty remark about the group's ancient metal filing cabinets: They belonged in B movies about atomic bombs from the 1950s, he murmured, and must already have been very old when they were donated to BEDS. She smiled, discovered Bobbie's thin folder quickly, and spent a long moment with his intake form.

She saw he had told Emily Young that he had completed eleventh grade, no more, and that he was a military veteran. And he was single: Not only was the box for single checked, but scribbled beside the married box—in what Laurel had to presume was Bobbie's own hand—were the words "Maybe someday!" There was no emergency contact. No sign of employment. For the question "When did you last work?" Bobbie had written in, "When people still listened to disco." He said he had no current health problems except being "too damn old," and no dental problems "cause I got no teeth." She wasn't sure what to make of the fact that Emily had allowed him to write so many comments on the form himself, or that he had ended some of his answers with exclamation points.

Bobbie had acknowledged that he had a documented mental illness, and Emily had written on the line beside it, "Possibly bipolar, possibly paranoid, likely schizophrenic." She had checked off the boxes that said he had received mental-health counseling and mental-health case management, and that he had been treated in a psychiatric hospital. The dates were listed simply as "recent." He admitted (boasted, actually) that he had once had a serious problem with alcohol, but he had "licked it!" years earlier. He had no address and said he was chronically homeless. There was a Medicaid number, a Veterans Affairs number, and a Social Security number—all added by Emily, it appeared, at later dates.

On a yellow Post-it note Laurel scribbled the key numbers and slid the folder back into the drawer.

WEDNESDAY NIGHT, even before they had gone to dinner, she and David went to the editor's apartment on the lake and fell into his bed with its spectacular views of the Adirondacks.

Once he tried gently to climb on top of her, but as always she resisted—pinning him flat against the mattress with her hands on his chest, pushing off him for purchase as she slid up and down on his penis—and he relented. She had not had a man atop her since the summer between her first and second years in college; despite her therapist's observation that this was a phobic—albeit natural—reaction to the attack, she didn't believe she ever would again.

Then, afterward, she told David the details of her visit with Pamela Buchanan Marshfield.

"Want a tip the next time you're interviewing someone?" he asked. She was content in a postcoital stupor. They both were. She was curled with her head in the small valley between his shoulder and his collarbone, gazing abstractedly at the way the gray hair was starting to encroach seriously on the black on his sternum. David, of course, never saw her chest because she wouldn't allow it; even when they made love she would wear a top from her extensive wardrobe of slips and chemises and elegant little tees. That night it was a silk camisole the catalog had said was the color of sunlight. She had the sense that David might be feeling slightly guilty for testing once more her receptivity to making love with him on top, and she considered reassuring him that he had done nothing unreasonable—she felt he was laudably patient with both her secret and her visible scars. But she didn't want to risk ruining the moment.

"Absolutely," she answered simply.

"When the person you're interviewing has finished responding to your question—said all he or she wants to say—you say, 'Uh-huh.' And then go silent. Wait them out. Don't worry, you won't have to wait very long. Nine out of ten times they'll feel compelled to add something. And, invariably, it's a real golden nugget."

"Really?"

"Works almost every time—even with seasoned subjects. The most important things they tell you will be after the 'uh-huh.' "

"I'll keep that in mind."

"Have you Googled Bobbie Crocker?"

"I have. Buchanan, too. And I found nothing. And that was after trying every combination I could think of for Crocker and Bobbie and Buchanan and Robert. I also went to his intake form and got things like his Social Security and VA numbers."

"As a journalist, I'm proud of you. As an ethicist, I'm not so sure."

"Do you think it was wrong of me to get those numbers?"

"A little dubious, maybe. But I think it's fine. Really. It's not like you're going to steal his identity," he said lightly. "Are you?"

"I don't know, Bobbie's a pretty androgynous name . . ."

"True. Especially in parts of the South."

Instead of deodorant, David wore powder that smelled like verbena under his arms. She never noticed it except when they were in bed, but she loved the aroma.

"I should also see if there's anything about a car accident in Grand Forks," she said.

"You should, but it was so long ago that it's highly unlikely there is . . . unless . . ."

He yawned, and so she poked him good-naturedly to continue.

"Unless the kid who died with Buchanan—"

"Assuming Buchanan really died," she interrupted.

"Yes, assuming. But you might be able to figure that out from the Social Security number. In any case, my sense is there won't be much about a car accident unless the other kid was the son of an important family in Grand Forks, and a newspaper did a retrospective on the clan in the last decade. If you'd like, I could do a LexisNexis search at my office."

"You wouldn't mind?"

"No, of course not. I must confess, I don't expect we'll find anything. But it can't hurt to check."

"Thank you."

"And this Long Island woman said her brother was buried in Chicago, right?"

"Yes. Rosehill. In 1939, I think."

"Well, there should be a death certificate we can track down that would verify—or, if we can't find one, perhaps dispel—her story. Let me do a little work online. There are research services we subscribe to at the newspaper that are only available to journalists. Let's see what else we can come up with. And if that doesn't work, there's always shoe leather."

"Shoe leather?" she asked. "Is that another search engine?"

He laughed and she felt his chest rise. "No. If you're really excited by your new hobby, it's you going to Rosehill and examining the records. It's you going to the county courthouse in your corner of Long Island to see what papers exist. The local library, too. Come to think of it, there may be a newspaper article there if her brother really did die in a car accident."

On the bureau opposite his bed was a photo of his two daughters at the top of Snake Mountain, a foothill to the south with a flat summit. Their hair was windblown and wild, their round little faces were smudged with grime from their hike, and they looked more than a bit like beautiful, feral children. David had taken the picture that summer, and Laurel imagined him kneeling five or six feet away from them, not even the slightest bit winded. He was trim and athletic and strong: He would live a long time. She guessed that he would outlast her own father by decades, and suddenly she was very glad for those girls. They had a father who was committed to them and who took good care of himself. The man might not be a part of her life in the distant future, she thought, but he would most certainly be a part of his children's.

It was a long shot and Laurel expected nothing. HIPAA, the Health Insurance Portability and Accountability Act, prohibited health-care providers from revealing information about their patients to outsiders not connected to the individual's ongoing care. Its purpose was to protect people's privacy and ensure that their medical records were never used against them or became public without their consent.

Nevertheless, the next day, Thursday, Laurel did call the state hospital in Waterbury to see if anyone there would tell her anything about a patient named Bobbie Crocker. No one could—or, to be precise, no one would. She spoke with a nice young guy she imagined to be about her age who worked in patient care, and then a polite but guarded assistant in the director's office. She explained to them both that she was from BEDS and told them exactly why she was interested in any information they felt they could offer.

They could offer none.

Neither was even allowed to acknowledge that an old man named Bobbie Crocker had once been a patient at their hospital.

Laurel was going to the darkroom that evening, but she stopped by her apartment on the way there and discovered a note that Talia had left for her on the coffee table in the living room.

What's up, stranger? Is it my breath? I should be back around 6 or 6:30. Let's have dinner and catch up. I want to hear all about your trip home.

xoxoxo, T

She hadn't seen Talia since before she had left for Long Island. Her roommate had been out with friends on Tuesday night, and she'd spent Wednesday night at David's. They might have had breakfast together on Wednesday morning after Laurel had been to the pool, but because she hadn't been to the office in a couple of days she went straight to the shelter. It was almost unheard of for the two of them to go this long without connecting when they both were in town. She considered changing her plans and not going to the darkroom until after dinner, but she decided in the end that she didn't want to wait that long. Besides, she figured she would see Talia on Friday, if only so she could get the details on their excursion the next day to play paintball. And so she scribbled a short note with her apologies, and then packed up Bobbie Crocker's negatives and prints and even the snapshots. She had decided that she would keep everything together in her cabinet beside the UVM darkroom in the event she wanted to cross-reference a pair of images. Then she padded softly down the steps and back into the brisk autumn air. She'd planned to get something to eat while she was home, but in the end she hadn't wanted to risk it. The longer she was there, the greater the chance that Talia might return—and then it might be hours before she would get to work.

SHE COULD SEE how badly the negatives were damaged from the contact sheets, but dutifully she continued to clean and print them, hoping in each case for the best. Some of the photographs, until she found someone willing to restore them digitally, would have great scratches and cracks running through the center, or whole sections smeared and blacked out. At one point, a student five or six years younger than Laurel who was working that night in the university's large darkroom as well peered into one of her trays. He was a chunky little character in a baggy T-shirt, with a line of studs along the cartilage of one of his ears and waves of shaggy hair the color of a rooster's comb. In the red light of the darkroom, he looked almost like he had been pulled from the pages of a comic book.

"That's Eisenhower," he told her triumphantly, pointing at the image in the tray.

"I know," she murmured. She recalled the story she'd once heard about Bobbie claiming that this president owed him money.

"You didn't take those, then. They must be ancient."

"Not ancient. But old."

"Very." He gazed for a moment into the chemical bath and then added, "That's the World's Fair. Nineteen sixty-four. Queens. That globe thing is still standing, you know. It's by Shea Stadium."

"Right." She kept her voice as flat as she could without being obviously rude. She hoped she merely sounded busy. Preoccupied. Focused.

"Who took them?"

"Old fellow. Recently passed away."

"He sure didn't take very good care of his shit."

"No," agreed Laurel, "he didn't."

"Too bad," he said. "He was good."

"Yup."

"I take mostly metal, you know?"

She didn't, but she nodded. She wondered if she remained

silent whether he would continue to chatter. She worried that he was going to insist that she look at his work.

"Yeah, cars and bikes and close-ups of chain link. That sort of thing."

Again she bobbed her head. A small motion, barely perceptible.

"Sometimes when I tell people I take mostly metal, they think I mean rock shit. Bands. You know, as in heavy metal?"

She sighed, but this was a reflex, not commiseration. She was going to have to be rude. Or, at least, cold. She made a big production of staring at a strip of negatives dangling from a wire behind her, as if he were completely invisible, and when she didn't say anything more he muttered importantly, "Man, I got a lot to do. Tons. Aloha."

"Hang in there," she said, a conversational bone that she tossed him impulsively, and much to her relief he returned to his own prints. She worked for another two hours, long after he'd left, staying until the darkroom closed for the night. She watched as not one but two presidents appeared in the shallow tubs (Lyndon Johnson in a big hat and a bolo tie was the other), as well as an actress she couldn't quite place from a musical she didn't know, a flashy jazz drummer smoking a cigarette, a line of hair-salon hair dryers—the helmets resembled chamber pots with wide accordion hoses attached—a very young Jesse Jackson beside a woman she believed was Coretta Scott King, a character she might have guessed was Muddy Waters (but could have been anyone), cars with fins, a lava lamp, Bob Dylan, an elderly woman she presumed was a writer, saxophones (three), a vegetable stand somewhere near Manhattan's Fourteenth Street, the arch at Washington Square, the very tip of the Chrysler Building, a half-dozen more photos from that 1964 World's Fair, and—from a much newer strip of negatives taken with a different camera—the dirt road she detested in Vermont. In one there was that young woman on a mountain bike in the distance. Again, as with the distressed image Bobbie had carried with him that she had first seen in the box Katherine had brought to her office, the girl was too far away for Laurel to distinguish the details of her face. But she was tall and lanky, and certainly the bicycle frame resembled her beaten-up Trek.

And, sure enough, there were also three negatives from a large-format camera of the curve of the horseshoe-shaped driveway that looped from the shore road in East Egg to the Buchanan-Marshfield estate. In them, Laurel could see a car parked beside the front steps, and though she knew little about automobiles, she could tell it was a Ford Mustang. A white body, a black hardtop. It was, she was quite certain, from the 1960s.

CHAPTER TWELVE

*K*ATHERINE MAGUIRE turned her face up toward the mid-morning September sun, eyes closed, as she walked with a city attorney named Chris Fricke down the brick road that had anchored the Burlington pedestrian shopping concourse for decades. She was listening to this lawyer carefully, but she was also savoring the warmth on her eyelids.

"The attorney's firm is in Manhattan, but he actually has a place up in Underhill—a second home, not an office. So he knows a little about BEDS," Chris was telling her, the woman's heels clacking on the bricks underneath every third or fourth syllable. Chris had been one of the city attorneys who assisted BEDS for six years now, almost since the day she had passed the bar and started working for Burlington. She was a little older than the BEDS executive—Chris was in her mid-fifties, Katherine guessed—and genuinely inspiring: She hadn't even started law school until the younger of her two sons had started high school. Like most of the City Hall minions, she was energetic, determined, and absolutely confident, despite all the evidence to the contrary, that what she did made a difference in the world. She actually volunteered time at the shelter, which was more than most of the attorneys who worked with BEDS ever did. She had made an effort to get a sense of just how rotten it was on the streets and what the homeless population really needed, and thus had won Katherine's loyalty as well as her respect.

"He saw the ad we placed in the newspaper?" Katherine asked her.

"Or his client did. Either way, he heard about what we found and he thinks the photos might belong to his client. He said she's an older woman, lives way out on Long Island."

"And he wants us to turn them over to him?"

"You sound disappointed," the lawyer said.

"Well, I am. I wanted to make sure they didn't belong to someone because that's the right thing to do and because I wanted to cover our bases. But of course I want BEDS to have them. I honestly never thought a real owner would ever show up."

"We don't know for sure this is a real owner. I described the stuff that was in the box, and she could be. They could be pictures of her house, and she could be one of the kids in the snapshot."

"You said this is an older woman. How old?"

"Mid-eighties. Old enough to match the girl in that one picture. But she's no crumbly," said Chris. "She may be well into her dotage, but it sounds like she is one very tough old bird. Still healthy, still with it."

"Did the lawyer say why she wants the photos?"

"Because she's in some, I guess. Or her house is. And she's an art collector, and some time ago some of her photos disappeared. Some negatives, too. So she wants us to turn over the whole kit and caboodle. And she certainly doesn't want Laurel to print anything. She wants us to send everything to the lawyer so she can recover the images that she says are hers."

"Is she claiming to be any relation to Bobbie?"

"Just the opposite. Insists she's no relation. Says she did

have a brother, but he died some time ago. She and her lawyer aren't sure where Bobbie got the snapshots of her family or her house or the prints that were part of her collection. But she feels violated, and she wants the images back."

Katherine stopped where she was and turned from the sun to the attorney. "Do we have to do that?" She realized that she sounded petulant, and she didn't like that tone in her voice. But it had been a reflex.

"Not necessarily. We need to examine this a little more closely. Here's the irony: If this woman were related to Bobbie Crocker, then she might have a right to the photos as the sole surviving member of his family. But because she isn't related to him, it's much more difficult for her to claim ownership. Just because she's in them doesn't mean she has a right to them."

Katherine felt a little flushed and decided it wasn't just from the sun. "Look, I want Bobbie to have an art show. He deserved that, you know. But we denied it to him when he was alive because we didn't take him seriously. At least I didn't."

"You really feel bad about that, don't you?"

"A little, yes. But there are other issues, too: First of all, those photos are great PR for the people we serve. They show that a person who did something extraordinary with his life, who had met important people, could also wind up homeless. Second—and maybe this isn't second at all—I'm hoping that the collection might be worth serious money for BEDS, if we can sell the show as a fund-raiser."

"That's not a problem—assuming, of course, we don't have to turn everything over to this woman on Long Island." Chris glanced at her watch and resumed clicking her way down Church Street to her office at City Hall. After a moment, she added, "And don't be surprised if this lawyer calls you—or Laurel."

"Really?"

"He might. He didn't get what he wanted out of me, and so he might try to reach one of you."

"Oh, I hope he doesn't call Laurel."

"Any special reason why?"

"Bobbie—or whoever—took some photos of the swim club where Laurel hung out as a child. And I gather there's at least one of a girl on a bike up in Underhill—on the same dirt road where Laurel was attacked."

"A girl Laurel's age?"

"I think so. I haven't seen it, but Laurel came across it and told me about it. It seems to have shaken her up. And the combination of those photos has led her to become very . . . involved."

The lawyer knew Laurel's history, too, and Katherine saw her glance nervously at her now. "That's a creepy coincidence."

"The swim club or the girl on the bicycle?"

"Both," said Chris.

"But it is just a coincidence," Katherine told her, suddenly feeling a little defensive. "Nothing more. Has to be, right? And I had no idea there were pictures of either when I suggested she look through them."

Chris shook her head. "Still. It had to be a little unnerving for Laurel to know a homeless schizophrenic was taking pictures of that swimming pool. And then of a girl on a bike."

Katherine considered reminding her that Bobbie probably wasn't homeless back then. But she also understood what Chris was getting at, the vulnerability, and so she restrained herself. For the first time, she began to wonder if she'd made a serious mistake when she'd given Laurel that box of old photos.

CHAPTER THIRTEEN

*H*OWARD MASON, Paco Hidalgo, and Pete Stambolinos had all come to Bobbie's funeral service at the soldiers' cemetery in Winooski. On Friday morning, Laurel skipped her swim and went directly from home to the Hotel New England, where she had breakfast with the three of them in the kitchen the residents there shared. She wasn't precisely sure what she would learn, but she was so excited that she was up and out of the house before she had heard even the faintest stirrings from behind Talia's bedroom door. And because she was going to be having lunch later that day with Serena Sargent, she was optimistic that by nightfall she would know considerably more than she did now about Bobbie Crocker's identity.

The kitchen at the old hotel wasn't much bigger than the kitchens in most suburban homes. It was functional, and that was a great gift if you had been living in a homeless shelter— and before that on the street—but it wasn't about to be featured in a home-decorating magazine. The cabinets, donated by a nearby kitchen and bath remodeling store, were made of pressed wood, and the linoleum on the floor had been given to BEDS from a high school that was redoing its cafeteria. Moreover, it was never easy for eighteen separate tenants to

share a stove with four burners, a single oven, and a refrigerator that would have been fine for an individual family but was
far too small for the army of quarts and pints and the occasional half gallon that was wedged upright onto the top
shelves. The room had a single round kitchen table.

When Laurel arrived Friday morning, she was surprised to
find that the three men had whipped up a feast. There was a
Mexican breakfast pie filled with jack cheese and red peppers,
French toast slathered with confectionary sugar and butter,
and jelly doughnuts from the convenience store around the
corner. Laurel thought the meal probably should have come
with an angioplasty, but she was moved by the effort they had
made. She guessed they didn't have a whole lot of company.

Howard waved his hand solemnly over the counter where
the food was displayed like a restaurant buffet and demanded,
"Good, huh?"

"Looks scrumptious," said Laurel. "I don't know where to
begin."

"Always start with the salt. Then end with the sugar," Paco
told her. Paco was roughly her mother's age, but his skin was
so weathered and gray that he looked old enough to be her
mother's father.

"Or, you could live by that slogan you see on bumper
stickers," said Howard. " 'Life is short. Eat dessert first.' I've
always liked that."

She parceled a little of everything onto her plate. She
poured some hot water from the kettle on the stove into a
mug and took the chair that Howard had graciously pulled
out for her. Then she started steeping her tea, watching and
waiting as each of the three men built for himself a small
mountain of food.

"So, you want to know about Bobbie," Pete said gruffly
once he had sat down. He rested his chin in his hand, and

there was a bracelet of untanned white skin where he normally wore an old wristwatch. Like most residents of the Hotel New England, he spent a lot of time outside in the summer and autumn: It was both necessary for him to escape the confines of his Spartan room and a routine that gave him comfort. Laurel knew that he liked to hang out on a bench not far from the Salvation Army that had sun in the morning and shade in the afternoon. Sometimes he would hold court there, and sometimes he would simply sleep. He no longer drank, but she hadn't any idea how he'd stopped: He glared at the world too much to be a member of AA.

"He used to be rich," Howard informed them. "Filthy rich."

"Yeah, so was I," said Pete.

"No, you weren't," Howard said.

"Maybe we're all rich in different ways," Paco offered.

"Nah, Bobbie really was rich," Howard insisted.

"Now how do you know that?" Pete asked him, his voice at once bleak and annoyed. Howard's face fell like flaking spackle. "How could you possibly know that? Bobbie didn't even know where he was from half the time. And the other half he was having long conversations with his father. His dead father, Laurel—just so you know. Let's not lose sight of the fact that the guy had been in the state mental hospital."

"What kinds of things did he and his father discuss?" she asked.

"Hey, he was the one who heard the voices. Not me."

"Oh, I understand. I was just wondering if maybe he told you what they were saying."

"When people are talking to themselves in public—and especially when they're getting frustrated with a person who's been dead for a while—I'm a lot more likely to ask them to pipe down than to let me in on the big secret."

Laurel wasn't surprised that Bobbie was angry at his father, and so she pressed for more: "So you must have overheard what Bobbie was saying."

Pete rolled his eyes. "He said his dad had a lot of connections, a lot of clout with the right people. You know, he'd done them favors. And so he didn't understand why his old man wasn't calling some in to help him out. Or, better yet, to help someone else out. I have to admit, more times than not Bobbie wasn't asking his dad to help him. Sometimes, even some of us figured in the conversations. Once, just to try and shut him up, I told Bobbie that I didn't need any help from his old man. And when this didn't quiet him down, I told him that his dad had really good hearing and he didn't have to talk so loud. And that, thank you very much, at least got Bobbie to whisper for a change."

"He knew everybody," said Paco suddenly.

"Bobbie's father?" Laurel asked.

"No. Bobbie."

"He said he knew people whose pictures he took," Pete explained, shoveling a forkful of French toast into his mouth. "Supposedly, that's how he got to know them."

"He never showed you his pictures, did he?" said Laurel.

Pete chuckled loudly, a great yelp, and sat back in his seat with his arms folded across his chest. "Not a prayer. He insisted someone was after them. Or him, maybe."

"Any idea who?"

"The all-purpose they. Half the nutballs in this hotel think someone's after them."

"Laurel, the French toast is very good with grape jelly, too, you know," said Howard. "If you can't afford real maple syrup, don't compromise with the imitation stuff. Just use grape jelly."

"Did he tell you where he lived when he was a photographer?"

"If," said Pete.

"No, I've seen the photos," Laurel said. "I spent last night in the darkroom up at the university making contact sheets and prints from some of the negatives. He really was a photographer."

"Son of a gun."

"Son of a gun," she repeated.

"What are they of?" Paco asked. "Are they really of famous people?"

She told them of the images Bobbie had left behind, and what she had seen in the negatives she had printed the night before. And then Pete surprised her by inquiring, "You been to the library yet? Looked through the old magazines on the microfilms? Tell you what: You go to those *Life* magazines and those *Looks*. They got 'em all. Then you'll know for sure whether Bobbie really took those pictures or not by the photo credits."

"That's a terrific idea," she agreed.

Howard smiled broadly and looked at his friend with pride. "Pete may be the surliest son of a bitch I know, but he's also one of the smartest."

"I made the French toast. I'm not surly."

"Bobbie told someone I know that he was from Long Island," she said. "Did he ever tell any of you that?"

"Yeah. And he grew up on a cove on the Sound," Paco answered, and instantly she felt a thrilling flutter in her chest.

"What else?"

"He said he lived in a mansion."

"Did he ever mention any siblings?"

Howard licked sugar from the doughnut off his fingers. "I can't think of any."

"He once lived in France," said Pete. "At least he said he did. He said he fought there in World War Two."

"When did he live there?" Laurel asked. "Did he tell you?"

"I guess it was right after the war. He fought there and then went back. Or maybe he just stayed. I don't know. He was in Normandy."

"And then I think he might have lived in Minnesota," Howard said.

"Minnesota?" The surprise in her voice was apparent.

"What, you don't think Minnesota is possible?" Pete asked. "Seems a lot more likely than him shacked up in some French villa with a lot of sunflowers around it."

"I think anything's possible. I just never imagined him living in the Midwest—or, for that matter, in a French villa with sunflowers."

"Hey, I have no idea if the villa really had sunflowers. All he said was that the Nazis took it over for their officers and trashed it pretty badly, and then the U.S. shelled part of it. He said there had been a vineyard and rows of grape arbors, but they were long gone by the time the war was over. One wing of it—not the wing they were living in, of course—was little more than a big ash heap."

"Why did he go back? Was there a woman?"

"So he said."

"Did he tell any of you her name? Or the name of the town?"

The three men looked at one another blankly. Clearly, he hadn't.

"Okay then, what did he tell you about Minnesota?" she asked. "When did he live there?"

"Look, maybe *live there* implies too much. I don't know if he was there a month or a year."

"Either way: Why?"

"He said he had family there. Course, that don't mean a damn thing, because he also claimed he had family in Kentucky," Pete said, lifting his plate to a jaunty angle and then using the side of his fork to scrape the very last of the Mexican pie from the plastic. "Ask him on the right day and he'd have told you he had family on Mars."

"Well, I think he really did have cousins in Kentucky. Who do you think he had in Minnesota?"

"That I don't know," Howard murmured, and his voice almost instantly grew deflated.

"Did he ever mention a town?"

"No. Yes—yes, he did. Saint Paul. Is Saint Paul in Minnesota?"

"Absolutely."

"And . . ."

"Yes?"

"Now that I think about it, maybe he did say something about a grandfather living there," Howard continued, the act of remembering so physically taxing that he was scrunching up his forehead with the effort. "Is it possible that he had a grandfather living in Minnesota?"

"Certainly it is. What else? A neighborhood? A name? A street? Anything?"

"Oh, I wish I knew more. He mighta said more. But my memory? You know? It's not what it once was."

"What about Chicago? Did he ever say anything about Chicago?"

"Maybe," Howard said, but Laurel could tell from both his voice and the way that Pete was glowering at him that he was stretching the truth for her benefit. He was telling her what he thought she wanted to hear.

"Okay, here's one of the main things I can't figure out," she said when the awkward silence had grown too much for her. "Perhaps he left behind a clue with one of you: How did a guy who may have come from a very wealthy family wind up without a cent to his name? I know he had schizophrenia. I know he had emotional problems. I know he drank way too much. But why didn't his family take care of him? Isn't that what families do?"

"Not mine," Pete said.

"Or mine," Paco agreed.

"Besides, you're assuming that ol' Bobbie liked his family," said Pete.

"And they, in turn, liked him," Paco added, as he leaned back in his chair and lit a filterless cigarette off a burner on the gas stove behind him. He inhaled deeply, and then blew a halo of blue smoke into the air.

She thought about the Buchanans for a moment—Daisy and Tom and Pamela—and how dislikable they all really were. Likewise, she considered how much people seemed to enjoy Bobbie. Perhaps he was the black sheep of the family for the simple reason that he was a nice guy. A decent fellow. It was possible that the Buchanans had cut him off, but perhaps it was more likely that he had untethered himself from them— from the rampant thoughtlessness and casual lack of decency that seemed to mark that whole awful tribe.

"Tell me a story about Bobbie," she said.

"A story?" Howard asked.

"Something he once did—or you once did together."

"Anything?" Paco inquired, squinting against the smoke from his cigarette.

"Anything. Something to help me understand who he was as a person."

The men looked at one another, not exactly stumped but unsure what Laurel was searching for.

"He was scared of the devil," Paco said finally, shrugging.

"Aren't we all," said Pete.

"No, really. Bobbie once saw him."

She sat forward in her chair. "You know, he told Emily that, too. Emily Young—his caseworker. What did he say to you, Paco?"

"He took the devil's picture."

"He did?"

"So he said."

"What did it look like?"

"I don't know. Maybe it's why he went crazy. You know how we can't ever see the face of God? Maybe we can't see the face of the devil, either."

"Oh, please," said Pete. "He was crazy long before he took the picture of some carnival freak he thought was the devil."

"A carnival freak?"

"Yeah. A carny. This was some time ago. But from the little he said that made sense—and, trust me, Bobbie did not make a whole lot of sense in this case—our late friend met the devil at the fair they have in Essex at the end of the summer."

"The Champlain Valley Fair."

"Right. Eight, ten miles from here. Whatever. It goes till Labor Day. You got the sheep shearing and the milking and the giant pumpkins. The farming stuff. And then you got the midway with the carnies. The geeks who run the games and the rides. I am sure Bobbie met his so-called devil there. Maybe it was someone who hurt him—you know, physically. Beat him up. Or stole what little money he had. Or maybe it was just some creep who in Bobbie's eyes looked even scarier than he was."

"Maybe you'll find him in those pictures of his you got," Howard said.

She considered this for a moment. So far she hadn't come across anyone demonic. Nor had she found any images from the county's annual end-of-summer exposition and fair. She wondered, based on the photos she'd printed, if Pete was mistaken and it was actually someone from Bobbie's childhood she should be looking for, perhaps an image of someone he'd known growing up. Someone from his own family.

"Are you sure he was talking about the Champlain Valley Fair, Pete?" she asked.

"Not completely. You can't be sure about anything when you're talking about Bobbie. Maybe it was a carny in New York. Or Minnesota. Or Louisville. You said he had family there, right?"

"I did."

"Look, you want a story?" Pete asked.

"I do."

"Then here you go. This is the Bobbie Crocker who was my friend. Our friend. This past summer, we were watching the cranes as they put up that new building by the lake. The one that will have the luxury condos and the shops. It was just me and Bobbie, and we were sweating like pigs. It must have been July. I don't drink anymore, but I was really hungry for a beer. I could just taste it. An ice cold beer—in a bottle. Maybe even one of those Budweiser liters. I haven't had a drink in three years—not quite three years then—but I had a couple bucks in my wallet and there's that convenience store right near where the apartments will be. And I was thinking: a beer. What the fu——heck? Really, what's one lousy beer?

Even a liter? What, is it gonna put my ass back on the streets? Well, of course the answer is yes, it will—because I can't have just one. I have to have, like, a case. But I was gonna do it: I was gonna get me a beer. And Bobbie, thank God, read my mind and got me out of there. Took me to a shady bench and sat me down with a couple of Yoo-hoos. You know, that chocolate milk in a bottle?"

"Yogi Berra used to drink 'em," said Howard.

"Well, he used to say he did in the ads. I think he probably drank beer, too," Paco observed.

"Those Yoo-hoos kept me clean. Sometimes cold sweets help. And it was Bobbie who was looking out for me."

Laurel thought about this for a moment, and she remembered what David had told her to try as a researcher the other night when they were in bed. "Uh-huh," she said simply, nodding. And then she went silent.

Sure enough, Pete—even cool and jaded and skeptical Pete—continued. "We were sitting in the shade under one of them maples they didn't cut down, looking at the water and the Adirondack Mountains, just sipping our Yoo-hoos. And Bobbie says, 'You think this view is grand? You should have seen the view I had from my bedroom when I was a boy. The Long Island Sound out one window and a mansion with a turret out the other.' A turret! Imagine! Course, I was sure he was in Bobbie Crocker la-la land, so I just smiled and changed the subject."

Suddenly, Howard pushed his plate aside and clasped the fingers of his hands together on the table. "You know what was the best thing about Bobbie?" he said meaningfully.

They all waited.

Finally: "He was just a regular guy."

Pete allowed himself another of his hard, short, bitter laughs: "Yeah, that was Bobbie Crocker. While some old codgers are playing golf in Fort Lauderdale, he was summering behind a Dumpster on Cherry Street and spending his winters in the state mental hospital. Just a regular guy, that Bobbie Crocker."

When Laurel looked back at Howard he was nodding in agreement, his eyes wistful and slightly downcast, absolutely oblivious to the anger and the irony that laced so much of what Pete Stambolinos said.

MID-MORNING, KATHERINE put her head into Laurel's office. Laurel was with a new client named Tony, a young man who claimed to have been a high school football star from Revere, Massachusetts, eight or nine years ago, and had spent last night in the men's wing of the shelter. He was estranged from his family—like Pete and Paco and Howard and (yes, she thought) Bobbie. The only difference was that he was a lot younger. He fidgeted in his seat and had a habit of flexing and fanning his fingers, and he had bitten his nails to the point where all of his cuticles seemed to have bled in the night.

"I'm sorry to interrupt, but I have to leave right now for a meeting in Montpelier and I wanted to snag you before I left," Katherine began. She gave Tony a small wave of apology, and held up her hands in a gesture that suggested she was helpless to do anything but interrupt. Laurel joined her in the hallway.

"You may get a call from a New York lawyer asking you to stop printing Bobbie Crocker's photographs," she said. "He might even ask you to turn them over to him—or to someone. And you are not to do that, do you understand? Do not feel intimidated."

"Whoa, lawyers? When did we bring in the lawyers?"

"We didn't," said Katherine, and Laurel understood instantly who had—and why Katherine's demeanor was slightly frenzied. She was feeling coerced, and she wasn't going to stand for it. Nor was she going to allow what she perceived to be the desire of one of her clients to be cavalierly ignored. She told Laurel about her conversation with the city attorney, and then continued, "The woman didn't phone herself, of course. The entitled never do. Her lawyer did. He called Chris Fricke. Anyway, this old crone believes the photos belong to her family because she's in some."

"She's in one."

"And her brother's in some."

"Her brother's in one."

"And there are some of her old house."

"Yes."

"Anyway, she's claiming that Bobbie must have stolen a box full of photos and negatives from her family or found it somewhere, and she wants everything returned intact—exactly as Bobbie left it. She wants to see what else is there that might belong to her."

"Bobbie didn't take anything from her family: He is her family! He's her brother!"

Katherine paused and studied her closely. "Do you honestly believe that?"

"I don't believe it," she said quietly, irritably. "I know it. I am absolutely sure of it."

"Well, don't be. Please give up that notion right now. Do you understand?"

"What? Why?"

"If Bobbie really was her brother—which, I gather, is completely impossible—then we might actually have to turn everything over to her."

"I have news for you, Katherine, I have no doubts whatsoever," Laurel said, trying (and failing) to keep her voice calm.

"Everything fits, it's obvious. Just this morning I had breakfast with some of the guys from the Hotel New England—"

"Let me guess, Pete and his pals? That must have been a trip."

"It was great. They made me a feast. But my point is that even the things they shared with me indicate that Bobbie is this woman's brother."

"Really?"

"Bobbie told them he grew up on Long Island. He told them he had family in Kentucky!"

"I understand the Long Island connection. What's in Kentucky?"

"It's where his mother was from. His mother was born and raised in Louisville."

Katherine sighed and gave her arm a small squeeze. "When you first told me what you recognized in the snapshots, I thought he might have grown up near your swim club, too. Really, I did. And you might still be proven right. Who knows? But—"

"He was taking pictures of the house—his childhood house!—as late as the mid-1960s! I printed a couple just last night!"

"Or someone else was—perhaps at this woman's request."

"Look—"

"Laurel, this woman's lawyer was pretty clear that his client's brother died years ago. Decades ago. No one knows how Bobbie got the pictures and the negatives, but this woman wants you to leave them alone. And she wants us to give them back. Which we do not have to do—at least not yet—precisely because she insists that Bobbie wasn't her brother. No relation. That's the key, and that's my point. As long as this Long Island dowager keeps saying that she and Bobbie aren't related, then she isn't an heir and thus can make no claim on the estate based on family."

Laurel contemplated this for a moment: The irony wasn't lost on her. If she acknowledged who Bobbie was, then Pamela Buchanan Marshfield would have reason to demand—and, perhaps, be given—the photographs. Apparently, there really were people out there who wanted them. Bobbie's fears might have been disproportionate to reality, but they were not wholly delusional.

"If BEDS keeps the prints once I'm done working with them—" she began.

"Not BEDS, the City of Burlington. The legal term is *escheat*. Because Bobbie died without a will, his possessions go to the city to dispose of. And in Burlington that means selling the assets with the money going to the school system— though in this case I'm pretty sure the city will sell them to us for, say, a dollar, so we can use them as a fund-raiser."

"Which is why you want us to hang on to them."

"That's part of the reason. But I also want them because they were the only thing in the world that mattered enough to one of our clients that he brought them with him wherever he went. We need to respect that. And I want us to give Bobbie the show he deserved. I love the idea of an exhibition reminding the city that the homeless are people, too, and have talents and dreams and accomplishments."

"And so I can continue to print them."

Katherine paused, and for a moment Laurel feared that she was going to tell her to stop. Finally: "Yes. Just . . . just remember that these photos belonged to a man who . . . who wasn't who you imagine he was. And"—she looked at Laurel in a way the young social worker recognized because it was precisely the way her mother gazed at her when she was worried—"try not to talk to any lawyers who call you. But, if you must, certainly don't insist that Bobbie was anyone's brother. Okay?"

Laurel nodded, but she was so angry that she felt the corners of her eyes start to quiver. She was furious both because she felt she was being muzzled and because it was clear that not even Katherine believed what she knew was a fact.

Katherine gave her a hug and waved into her office at Tony, but he glared at the director with a look of such condescension and contempt that Katherine rolled inside like a wave and apologized to him formally. Then she turned from the two of them and started down the corridor. Before she was around the corner and gone, however, she stopped and added, "And I'm serious about this identity thing. Okay?"

Laurel nodded, but her mind was already on the photos and the work she would do that weekend in the university darkroom.

PATIENT 29873

. . . no interest in the other patients or socializing in the dayroom. Auditory hallucinations appearing to diminish, but still has denial of key event and significant gaps in memory compatible with dissociation.

From the notes of Kenneth Pierce,
attending psychiatrist,
Vermont State Hospital,
Waterbury, Vermont

CHAPTER FOURTEEN

*D*AVID FULLER was sitting in the pediatrician's waiting room with his older daughter on Friday morning, painfully aware that every plush animal, plastic toy, and glossy magazine was a veritable petri dish of infectious agents. Worse, the small children in the room with them were coughing and wheezing and sneezing. He wanted them quarantined somewhere far, far away from Marissa—who, at the moment, felt just fine. In fact, she was practically the only kid in her class who did not have strep throat. The only reason they were here was because a cut on the pinkie toe on her right foot wasn't healing: too much time, he guessed, with sneakers, tap shoes, and ballet slippers rubbing against it.

Marissa, of course, was absolutely thrilled that the only moment their HMO-sanctioned pediatrician could see her was on a Friday morning—when she was supposed to be in math class. She sat beside her father now on the orange Naugahyde couch, her uninjured foot curled up on the cushions beneath her thigh and her head buried in a *CosmoGIRL!* magazine that he thought was completely inappropriate for this waiting room. (Just where, he wondered, was *Highlights* when you needed it?) He feared her silence had to do with the usually forbidden things she was getting to read about in the magazine. Consequently, to break the periodical's spell, he asked (ponderously, he feared), "Other than your pinkie toe, how are you doing?"

"Okay."

"Is the magazine really that enticing? I certainly hope you're not taking too much pleasure in whatever decadence you've found—if only so your mother doesn't kill me."

"She won't."

"Anything on your mind?"

She looked up from her magazine. "You mean, like, right now?"

"Sure. What are you thinking about . . . like, right now?"

"Well, since you ask, Mom thinks Laurel is way too young for you." His ex-wife, an attorney, was in court that morning.

"Why is your mother even worrying about the age of the women I'm seeing?"

"I don't know."

"Wrong question. Forgive me. Does it bother you that your mother is, suddenly, unnecessarily interested in Laurel's age?"

"Oh, it's not sudden." She dropped the magazine back into the rack beside the couch and yawned, then stretched. She leaned her head against the side of his arm.

"Thank you for letting me know," he said simply.

"No problem."

"So . . . does it bother you?"

"Laurel's age? Nope."

"Does it bother Cindy?"

"She is, like, totally unaware of age. For all she knows, Laurel is Mom's age."

"I think you can give your sister more credit than that."

"Not much."

"For a kid with a sore toe, you are impressively sassy this morning," he said.

"Hey, it was pretty gross last night."

"Uh-huh."

"So?"

He pulled his arm free and wrapped it around her in a hug. "So, nothing. I'm glad we're taking care of this."

After a long moment in which neither of them said anything, she asked, "You seeing Laurel this weekend?"

"I am."

"Tonight?"

"Yes."

"Saturday, too? Or Sunday?"

He thought carefully about her inquiry. Was she asking because she wanted to see Laurel, or because she was worried that his girlfriend was going to impinge upon their time as a family? She and her sister had both been more clingy ever since their mother had announced she was going to marry Eric Tourneau, another lawyer in her firm, in November. Marissa probably didn't view Laurel as an impediment to her parents ever reconciling—a reconciliation that was wholly inconceivable even before his ex-wife and Eric had fallen in love, but an idea that he understood a child might cling to tenaciously nevertheless—but perhaps she felt Laurel was stealing away her father's attention.

"I'm going to be with you and your sister this weekend," he said, hoping he sounded casual. He had the girls, as usual, from the moment he picked them up on Saturday until they left for school on Tuesday morning. He hadn't planned on Laurel and his daughters spending any time together in the next couple of days: He was having dinner with Laurel that evening precisely because he wanted to be able to focus entirely on his girls over the weekend. He had carefully compartmentalized his life, and an advantage, he had discovered, to dating a woman as young as Laurel was that she made no demands that he contemplate marriage. She felt no pressure yet to have children because she still had lots of time. Whenever he dated women even close to his age, he felt on the first date that he was being scrutinized as a marriage prospect; if he passed—which invariably he would because he was breathing and employed—by the second or the third the subject of children would arise. And the reality was that he had no intention of becoming a father again. It was not that he didn't love children; rather, it was that he was devoted to his two girls and would never do anything to make them feel replaced or replaceable. His own father had a daughter and a son from his second marriage when David was still shuttling between his parents' homes as a child, and he always felt like a second-class citizen after they arrived.

Was this fair to Laurel? Probably not. In this regard—and, yes, in other ways, too—he knew that he was not an especially suitable companion for her. For many women. What he viewed as a mere compartmentalization, other people had told him was coldness. He was emotionally indifferent, one girlfriend advised him when they were breaking up. Given Laurel's own wounds, this may have been a particularly damning flaw. But he was confident that she didn't see it this way. He thought that precisely because of her own need to cocoon, she saw his distance as an indication that he was an apt partner. And, of course, his age helped. He knew she desired only older men, and he understood why.

Did he feel bad about the way he remained so detached? Yes, on occasion. But not enough that he had any intention of changing.

As early as that morning in the pediatrician's office, however, he had begun to question Laurel's interest in Bobbie Crocker. And so when Marissa brought her up, it crossed his mind that it might actually be good for his girlfriend to be spending a little more time with his kids. Anything to focus her interest away from that old photographer who had died.

"Why are you wondering about Laurel?" he asked Marissa.

"I need a headshot."

"Excuse me?" He honestly wasn't sure he had heard her correctly.

"You know, a picture that makes me look really professional. I'm going to audition for *The Miracle Worker*, and I'm going to be up against like fifty other girls for Helen Keller. It will be a real cattle call, so I figure I need all the help I can get."

"And you want Laurel to take your picture?"

"I could pay her my allowance for the next couple of months."

"Oh, good Lord, I doubt she'd accept money."

"Do you think she'd mind? I don't. I know it's a huge favor and all . . ."

He exhaled, relieved that the whole reason she was bringing up his girlfriend was because she wanted a headshot. "I wouldn't call it a huge favor," he said.

"Well. It would still be a favor. Especially if I didn't pay her. And Laurel has already done tons for me."

"Tons?"

"She knows every cool clothing store in town, and she must have taken me to them all. You saw the skirts and scarves she got me when we were together."

"I remember."

"I think that's what got Mom really jazzed up. The idea that your college-age girlfriend—"

"Laurel finished college four years ago. Your mother

knows that. She has a master's in social work. Your mother knows that, too."

Marissa thought about this briefly. Then: "I have a question."

"Yes?"

"Laurel sometimes seems a little, I don't know, faraway."

He knew his older child was perceptive and empathetic, and so he wasn't surprised that she had sensed that something was slightly wrong with Laurel. A little off. In his opinion, Laurel was always going to be a beautiful but wounded little bird. Nevertheless, he wasn't about to discuss what had happened in Underhill. Not that moment, anyway. Someday, maybe. Marissa needed to know that the world was a dangerous place. Even Vermont. But he wasn't about to go into any details. "Oh, I guess like the rest of us she can be sad sometimes," he answered simply, hoping he didn't sound evasive.

"Not sad. It's different than sad."

"Then what is it?"

"It's that she's . . . wispy."

"Wispy?"

"Like the curtains in Mom's dining room? The ones you can sort of see through?"

"I know the ones."

"But I really do like her. You know that, right?"

"I do."

A woman with a clipboard—a nurse Laurel's age—gently called, "Marissa?" and scanned the small crowd for a reaction.

"That would be us," he said, raising an arm, and then—because it struck him as funny—his daughter's.

Marissa giggled at the idea she was a puppet, but turned to him as she rose to her feet. "So, Laurel can take my headshot?"

"We'll ask her," he said, but he guessed she would. And he was glad. Suddenly, he was intrigued by the idea of

Marissa sharing her interest in drama with Laurel. And he liked the notion of Laurel doing something—anything—in her free time that did not involve the work of a schizophrenic photographer.

"Really?"

"Sure."

She jumped up and down two or three times in quick succession and pantomimed a short staccato clap with her hands. Then, abruptly, she flinched and closed her eyes because, clearly, she had just landed exactly the wrong way on her toe.

CHAPTER FIFTEEN

*L*AUREL HADN'T FOCUSED on Serena at Bobbie's funeral the week before, and they'd chatted only long enough to reconnect and set up a date for lunch.

When Laurel saw her on Friday, Serena looked older than she would have expected, but the once homeless teenager looked healthier, too. Serena was already at the restaurant when Laurel arrived, a bistro on the waterfront not far from the diner where she worked. She was seated at a table that faced the ferry dock, and one of the large boats had just drifted into the slip from the New York side of the lake. The passengers—mostly tourists—were streaming into the midday autumn sun. The boat was big, but there were so many people disembarking that it nevertheless reminded Laurel of the clown cars at the circus.

Serena's eyes were the vibrant blue that Laurel recalled, but her cheekbones had disappeared into a face that had softened and grown round. Her hair still cascaded over her shoulders, but at some point Serena had made it a shade or two blonder than Laurel remembered. When Serena saw her, she raised her eyebrows in recognition, stood halfway up, and gave her a small salute from her chair. The young woman's pink T-shirt fell to the base of her ribs, and she had a glistening stud in her naval that emerged from a small rope of flesh like a rivet on jeans. She was wearing a pair of thin silver hoops in her ears, each of which was the size of a bracelet.

"We go years without seeing each other, and now twice in two weeks," Serena said.

Laurel had brought along the eight-by-ten photographs of Serena she'd taken years earlier, and she pulled them from her bag soon after they'd taken their seats. "I have a surprise for you," she said, and she watched Serena's eyes grow wide as she began to study the images.

"I was this close to the edge. Man, heroin chic was never a good look on me," Serena murmured, shaking her head in slight disbelief. Then—afraid that she had hurt Laurel's feelings—she added quickly, "I mean, they're great photos. I just look kind of scary. You know?"

"I do know. Heroin chic isn't a good look on anybody," Laurel answered.

"Can I keep these?"

"That's why I brought them."

"Thank you. Someday I'll show these to my kids to scare them straight. Then again, I might not. Who wants to see their mother looking like this?"

"You were in a bad place and it wasn't your fault. You landed on your feet."

She rolled her eyes. "I got lucky. My aunt moved back and took me in. Now I have to find a place of my own. It's time."

It dawned on Laurel that she didn't know if this aunt with whom Serena was living was her mother's or her father's sister, but since her mother had disappeared when Serena was so young Laurel had a feeling the woman had to be related to her dad. And so she asked Serena if she ever saw her father or spoke to him.

"No, he keeps his distance. And my aunt keeps us apart. She knows her brother's a creep. One time he sent me a check. I wasn't going to cash it, but my aunt said I should. And so I tried. It bounced. Another time he showed up uninvited—and drunk—at Easter, but there was a big group of us at my aunt's, and even wasted he could see he wasn't wanted. So he split. But he knows where I work and where I live. He'll appear again."

Serena watched the two waitresses chatting at the bar while they waited and smiled. "Man, if I gave service like this, I'd be fired."

Eventually, one of the waitresses greeted them, and Laurel ordered a garden salad and a diet soda. She was still feeling the weight of the massive breakfast she'd eaten.

"How fresh is your curried egg salad?" asked Serena.

"Very," smiled the waitress, a rail of a girl who seemed too young to work there, and Serena agreed to give it a try.

They were surrounded by businessmen and women whose offices looked out on the lake, and tourists who were visiting Burlington. The two of them talked about their jobs, and Serena told Laurel about her boyfriend. She was dating a guy who worked the night shift at the ice cream factory in Waterbury, but had just applied for a position in the marketing department. Serena thought he had a shot because he was sharp and the company was more interested in good ideas than whether someone had a college degree—and, apparently, he had a lot of experience with ice cream. Laurel described her relationship with David, and wasn't completely surprised when Serena remarked, "It's kind of casual, huh?" Laurel thought she sounded disappointed for her.

"Yes," she said simply. "It's kind of casual."

Finally, Laurel brought up Bobbie Crocker, and told Serena how he had died with snapshots of the country club where she had spent a large part of her youth in his possession, and how she believed he had grown up a child of plenty in a mansion just across the cove. Laurel asked her to recount the story of how she had found him.

"It was real clear he didn't have a place to go," Serena said. "I mean, he was supposed to be *somewhere.* The hospital doesn't just open the door and say, 'Fly, little bird, fly.' I've lived in Waterbury long enough to know there's always a plan for the patients. He was supposed to go someplace. He was supposed to be with someone. But he couldn't tell me where or with who. Or he wouldn't. Who knows? He couldn't even tell me how he'd gotten to Burlington. A bus? Hitchhiked? Beats me. The thing is, with a lot of these people it only takes the slightest wobble and they fall off the horse. They stop taking their meds. But I liked him a lot, and I thought with a little help he could probably get along on his own. I didn't guess he needed the hospital anymore. Not really. He wasn't a danger to anyone. That's why I brought him to BEDS. I talk to enough troopers and sheriffs at the diner to know that's all they would have done." She leaned back in her chair and clasped her hands behind her head.

"What did you like about him?" Laurel asked.

"Oh, he was very kind. I mean, he kept wanting to help me. It was, of course, a little insane."

"How so?"

"Well, he offered to make phone calls to the presidents of record labels. I told him I didn't sing, but that didn't matter. He went on and on about all the record-label presidents he knew who owed him favors, and how he could get me a recording contract with a single phone call. Why was he doing this? Well, because I gave him extra coleslaw. And then seconds for free. That's it. I mean, this old man comes in and he has barely enough money for a grilled cheese! And, you know, he was very funny—despite the fact he had to have been starving. He strolls in that night telling me knock-knock jokes about homeless people, and how many homeless it takes to screw in a lightbulb. And because he had, like, no money, he kept giving me advice as a tip. 'Here's a tip,' he would say. 'One good turn gets most of the blanket.' It was corny, but sweet. Unfortunately, he just wouldn't tell me where he was supposed to be. That's the thing. I have no idea where he'd been sleeping before he wound up on the street."

"You're right," Laurel said. "There had to be someplace between the hospital and BEDS. Obviously, they released him to someone besides us."

Serena shrugged. "I kept asking him where he lived. And he finally rubbed his eyes really hard—like a little kid, you know, using his fists—and said he was pretty sure he was going to sleep that night where he'd slept the night before."

"And that was?"

"The boiler room of that hotel just up the hill. That's a ridiculous place for someone to end up. I didn't know how long he'd been there, but I didn't want him to spend another night in that room."

The waitress returned with their drinks and momentarily they both grew quiet. Laurel watched Serena wrestle her straw free of its paper.

"So, you brought him to us," she said.

"Yup. And he didn't mind at all. You hear all about homeless people being real resistant to coming in off the street—hey, look at what I was like—but he was happy as a clam."

"Did he understand where you were taking him?"

"He did. He just wanted a little assurance that no one would take his bag from him. I asked him what was in it that was so important, and he said his pictures."

"When did you see him next?"

"Oh, I didn't see him a whole lot before he died. Once his caseworker—a woman named Emily, you probably know her—brought him by the diner so he could thank me. She's very nice. And another time I saw him at that candle vigil you do on Church Street just before Christmas. You know, the march where you say the names of the homeless?"

Laurel smiled. "You were there? I'm sorry I didn't see you."

"Yeah, I was in the crowd. I was too shy to say a name in the church, but I had my candle and I marched. Hell, look what you did for me."

"As I recall, you spent about a week and a half at the shelter. We really didn't do all that much."

"But it was a week and a half when I really needed a place," Serena said adamantly, meeting Laurel's eyes with an intensity that surprised her.

"Did Bobbie ever tell you anything about his sister?"

"His sister? I didn't even know he had a sister."

She nodded.

"I didn't see her at the funeral. Is she alive?"

"She is."

"You know her?"

"A bit. I met her last week."

"Is she a little wacky, too?"

Laurel thought about this briefly before responding. "No, she's not. At least not like Bobbie. She's actually pretty nasty."

"I guess she and Bobbie weren't real close."

"No, they weren't. He ever mention any family at all?"

"Not a word," Serena said, and her voice grew solemn, as if she were trying to conjure in her mind a family for Bobbie Crocker. "Not a single word."

"What about that first night he came into the diner? Think back. When you were asking him if he had a place to go, what else did he say?"

Their food arrived, and Laurel could see that Serena was contemplating that August night when Bobbie had appeared at the counter with his duffel and a pocketful of change.

"Let me think," she murmured. Her egg salad was orange with curry and sat like a globe on a palm-shaped leaf of iceberg lettuce. "You know, he did say one thing that might be important."

"Uh-huh."

"He said something about a guy he'd worked with at a magazine somewhere. Name was . . . Reese."

"Was that his first name or his last?"

"I don't know if he told me. But something about it is on the tip of my tongue."

"Tell me."

"This was, like, a year ago."

"I know," Laurel said, hoping she sounded patient.

"I'm going to say Reese was his first name. And . . ."

"And?"

"And you know what? He might have been living at Reese's. After the hospital. That might be it."

"Why would he have left?"

Serena was chewing the egg salad carefully. "They don't put celery in it. We do. You have to have celery in your egg salad."

"I agree," she said politely. "Why do you think Bobbie moved out?"

"Maybe he was kicked out."

"Bobbie kicked out? You don't really believe that, do you?"

"Oh, not kicked out because he was a bad roomie or whatever. Maybe kicked out because he wasn't helping with his share of the rent."

"He would have been eighty years old! How much help could this Reese person have expected—especially if Bobbie came to him straight from the hospital?"

"People are cruel," Serena said offhandedly. "You know that, Laurel."

"But Bobbie was . . . old."

She leaned forward in her chair, her chin over her plate. Her eyes grew wide and her words were soft but angry: "Old doesn't matter. My dad shows up at my house when he's eighty? I got a choice of giving him a room or letting him chill on the street? I can't see me opening my doors. And I don't think I'm a bad person. But cruel is as cruel does. Or whatever."

Laurel thought about this. "I'm sure Bobbie never did anything to hurt Reese—at least not the way your father abused you."

"I agree. I'm just saying, we don't know. I think if you want to get the answer for sure, you got to find this Reese person."

"Bobbie give any hints where he—"

"Or she. I keep saying he, but for all we know Reese could be a she."

"Or she might live?"

"I'd start in Burlington—or the suburbs. Maybe Bobbie got from Waterbury to Burlington before he was homeless. Maybe he was released into the care of someone who lives around here."

"That would be an irony."

"Hey," Serena said, studying a pair of beautiful young women their age in miniskirts—young public relations executives, Laurel guessed. "Life is all about irony. Irony and luck and . . . advantages. Why did I get a mom who lit out at first light and a dad who thought my head was a punching bag? Why did those two over there get parents who made sure they did their homework and then sent them to college? I'm not bitter. Really, I'm not. But I also know life isn't always fair—and I have a feeling, my friend, that you know that just as well as I do."

LAUREL LEFT WORK promptly at five that day, despite the reality that she had gotten so little done. But she wanted to get to the library in Burlington before the reference desk closed at six, because she was keenly interested in making a dent into the microfilms there or the hard copies of the old *Life* magazines.

The library only had bound volumes dating back to 1975, but it had microfilm all the way back to 1936. She was thrilled, and with an eager librarian's help randomly selected a spool from 1960. Then she sat down at a carrel and began to scroll through images that ranged from a Woolworth's lunch counter in Greensboro, North Carolina, to Charles de Gaulle boasting of the detonation of his country's first nuclear bomb. She saw David Ben-Gurion and Nikita Khrushchev and an American U-2 reconnaissance plane. And there was a story about a fellow named Caryl Chessman, a man Laurel had never heard of but whose face gave her the chills because he was going to be executed for kidnapping and sexually assaulting two women a decade earlier. It sounded, based on the article, like he might have been innocent.

She tried to slide past the ads, but they were hypnotic: the mild cigarettes touted by singers and actors, the Air Force bombers used to sell automotive motor oil, the recipes that anchored the ads for canned soups and cake mixes and containers of Borden's cottage cheese.

And, always, she squinted at the small type that occasionally—but only occasionally—ran up the sides or underneath the photos. Much to her disappointment, only a small fraction of the images actually had photo credits. She was probably up to May and almost out of time for the day when she discovered why. There, toward the front of the magazine, was a long, slender masthead rich with names, including the editors and the writers and the photographers.

And there he was: not Bobbie Crocker or Robert Buchanan. That would have sent her spinning like a top in her seat in her carrel. Instead, she saw what seemed to her at the moment to be the next best thing. Above a paragraph-long block of thirty photographers, an alphabetized litany that included Margaret Bourke-White and Cornell Capa and Alfred Eisenstaedt, was an assistant picture editor with the name of Marcus Gregory Reese.

BEFORE LEAVING the library, Laurel printed out the masthead so she would have the full list of names, and then she checked the Burlington phone book to find a phone number for Marcus Reese. He wasn't listed. Nor was he in the Waterbury, Middlebury, or Montpelier areas. Then she went to the newspaper offices, a mere two blocks farther west on College Street. She was supposed to meet David at the movie theater at 6:45, but she was excited by what she had found and wanted to show him the copy of the masthead she had made.

He was on the phone in his office when she arrived, but it was apparent that the call was winding down, and so she slipped the masthead atop an unruly pile of papers on his desk and pointed at the photography staff. He nodded politely, but it was clear that the name Marcus Gregory Reese meant nothing to him. Only then did she realize there was no reason why it would. He didn't know yet what she did; he hadn't been with her when she'd had lunch with Serena. And so the moment he hung up she shared with him all that Serena had told her.

"Son of a gun," he murmured.

"I couldn't find Reese in the phone book, but I figured I'd Google him. And I want to use those research services you subscribe to here at the newspaper. Now that we have Bobbie's Social Security number, let's see what we can find."

"We? Weren't *we* going to a movie?"

Laurel paused. "This won't take long."

"It'll keep," he said, rising from his chair. "We should scoot."

"Let me do this," she said, blurting out the short sentence with a manic intensity that caught them both off guard.

For a moment, David said nothing. Then: "Laurel, let it go for the night. Lighten up."

"It's important," she said, unable to soften her tone.

"To whom?"

"To me. It's important to me. I would think that would be enough."

He looked at her carefully. Their relationship was so completely void of emotional intensity that she didn't believe either of them had ever scolded the other. "Be my guest," he said, though it was clear that he would have preferred that she wait till tomorrow. Nevertheless, he motioned toward his chair and his computer.

"Really, this will just take a second," she continued. "Aren't you curious?"

"I am curious. Not obsessed."

"Well, I'm not obsessed, either. I simply want to find this Reese so I can call him. I want to ask him why he kicked Bobbie out—or why Bobbie chose to leave on his own."

"Maybe he just died," David said, unable—or unwilling—to hide the exasperation in his voice.

"Reese?"

He nodded. "It could be just that simple. The man died, and Bobbie went back to the streets. Tell you what: You Google Reese and see what comes up, and I'll go check the obits. What month last year was Bobbie brought into BEDS?"

"August."

"Fine. I'll look through last summer."

Laurel had the sense that he was making the offer both because he felt bad for being short with her and because he still hadn't done his promised LexisNexis search on a car accident involving Robert Buchanan. Nevertheless, she was grateful for his help.

RIGHT AWAY they learned two things: There was a sizable number of sites on the Web where Reese's name appeared, and—exactly as David had suggested—the old photo editor had passed away fourteen months ago, in July of the previous year. David returned with the obituary that appeared in the newspaper, while she found a series of shorter obits online. She read the clipping about his death at David's desk, while David stood beside her, pleased with what he had discovered.

MARCUS GREGORY REESE

BARTLETT—Marcus Gregory Reese, 83, died unexpectedly on July 18, at his home in Bartlett. Marcus who used his full name professionally but was always called "Reese" by his friends—was born in Riverdale, N.Y., but moved to Bartlett after he retired from a distinguished career as a photographer and editor with a list of esteemed newspapers and magazines.

Reese was born on March 20, the youngest of Andrew and Amy Reese's five children. After graduating from Riverdale High School, he enlisted in the United States Navy, where he served with honor as a seaman in the Pacific theater in the Second World War. When he returned to the United States he took his interest in photography and turned it into a career, shooting pictures first for the *Newark Star-Ledger,* then for the *Philadelphia Inquirer,* and finally for *Life* magazine—where he served also as a photo editor for almost thirty years.

Along the way he married twice. His first marriage, to Joyce McKenna, ended in divorce; his second, to Marjorie Ferris, ended when Marjorie died of cancer in 1999.

Reese is survived by an older sister, Mindy Reese Bucknell, in Clearwater, Fl.

A funeral service will be held on Wednesday, July 21 at 11 a.m. at the Bartlett Congregational Church, with interment to follow in the New Calvary Cemetery.

Arrangements were made by the Bedard McClure Funeral Home.

The fellow in the photo looked closer to sixty than eighty-three, so Laurel presumed it was an old picture. In it, Reese was a heavyset man with wild eyebrows and wavy white hair, and a chin that slid without interruption into a neck the size of a log. He was wearing tinted eyeglasses and a crewneck sweater with an Oxford button-down shirt, and he was grinning at the camera in a manner that could only be called rakish. Perhaps even smug.

David smiled grimly when they had finished reading the obituary. "I've always loved that phrasing: 'Died unexpectedly.' How unexpected can death be at eighty-three?"

"It always sounds like someone was murdered or killed himself, doesn't it? Or some doctor made a howling error."

He sat on the edge of the credenza behind his desk. "Heart attack, probably. Nothing mysterious, I imagine."

She presumed he was right, but said nothing. In large measure because of her meeting with Pamela Marshfield and the lawyer's phone call to BEDS, she was primed to see mystery everywhere.

"And I think we now know where your Mr. Crocker got those photographs," he continued, his chin in his hands.

"What do you mean?"

"He probably took them from this Reese fellow. From what you tell me, Bobbie wasn't exactly a paragon of mental health."

"You think he stole them?" she asked, astonished by the very notion.

"First of all, I didn't say steal. That implies too much mental competence. All I'm saying is that maybe he . . . commandeered them. Maybe after Reese died."

"I think that's still stealing."

"Okay, then: He stole them. Or, perhaps, this Marcus Gregory Reese gave them to him."

"But why would you think that?"

"Because neither of us saw Bobbie's name on the *Life* masthead."

"That doesn't mean he didn't take the pictures!"

"Laurel, the obit said Reese was a photographer," he insisted, cutting her off, and then he motioned at the computer monitor on his desk that showed the Web sites she had found with Reese's name. "And look there: That site is all about Reese's photography. And so's that one. And that one. I wouldn't be surprised if you actually find that Hula-Hoop image or one of Muddy Waters with Reese's name as the credit."

It was possible, she thought, but there was a missing step in his reasoning. She tried to remain calm, to not become defensive. Eventually, it came to her.

"We're presuming that Bobbie did live with Reese," she said slowly.

"Yes."

"And that he was living with him because the state hospital had released him into Reese's care."

"Agreed."

"And that they knew each other because they had worked together at the magazine. That's what Serena told me, remember? It seems to me, Bobbie came to Vermont because he knew that Reese lived here. I only looked at one year of *Life*. Nineteen sixty. Maybe Bobbie worked for *Life* in the mid-fifties or the mid-sixties. Maybe when I have more time at the library, I'll find whole years of *Life* magazines with Bobbie Crocker's name on the masthead."

"And so you're suggesting that Bobbie knew Reese because Reese was his editor."

"Am I vindicated?" she asked.

"No. That's a big leap. They could have known each other at the magazine in a thousand ways that had nothing to do with Reese being his editor. Even if the two men did meet at *Life,* for all we know Bobbie was the custodian. Or the security guard. Or the elevator man. Years ago, they did have elevator men, you know."

"I should check 1964—the issues of *Life* magazine from 1964. The other night I developed some pictures from the 1964 World's Fair. I might find Bobbie's name there."

David nodded carefully, the way a father might at his child when he is on the verge of exasperation. Then he rose from the credenza, reached for the mouse, and started clicking the boxed Xs in the upper-right-hand corner of his monitor to log off. He had already clicked off the browser before Laurel was able to stop him, but he hadn't yet begun to shut down the computer. "What are you doing?" she asked.

"I'm getting us out the door so we don't miss our movie. We need to leave now if we have any chance at all of getting there before it starts. Incidentally, I have something very funny to tell you about Marissa. She wants you to take her headshot. Can you imagine?"

He said more, but she was no longer focusing. With the browser disconnected she couldn't see the summaries of the pages and pages about Marcus Gregory Reese and, almost as if she were an addict, she had to. Physically. She didn't *want* to see them; she *needed* to see them. And so, even though she understood that he was trying to get the two of them out the door and was starting to tell her something about his daughter, she clicked back on the icon for Internet Explorer.

"I'm sorry," she said. "Can't we just go to the next show? There must be a nine o'clock."

"Laurel!"

"If you really want to go, you can go. That's fine. I can meet you for dinner afterward."

"I don't want to go to a movie alone on a Friday night. I want to go out on a date with my girlfriend. This is no small distinction."

She went to the computer's history of the sites it had visited that day, and returned to the Google results for Reese. "I can't stop right now," she said, and her voice was so halting and soft that she didn't recognize it as her own. "I know I'm getting close."

"Let me make absolutely sure I understand this: You want to spend your Friday night at my desk scrolling through sites about a dead photo editor from *Life* magazine. Is that accurate, Laurel?"

"Not all of Friday night. Just give me half an hour. Okay? Then we can go to dinner or we can go back to your apartment. Whatever you want. I just don't want to leave now. I . . . can't. And . . ."

"Yes?"

"And those research services for reporters. Can you show me one? Please? Just so we can see what we can learn from Bobbie's Social Security number?"

He rubbed his eyes and then threw up his hands in a gesture of defeat. Once again he reached over her shoulder, but this time he clicked on the part of his browser marked Favorites and pointed the sites out to her. "Try this one," he said, clicking an icon, "and type in his Social Security number in this field." Then he flopped himself down in one of the chairs across from his desk and started to browse through a pile of newspapers on the floor beside it. "I'm giving you half an hour. And then I'm shutting off the lights and we're leaving."

REESE, SHE LEARNED, was a journeyman photographer: capable, but not, from the images she found online, especially gifted. He was probably a better editor, which explained his long tenure in that role with *Life* magazine. The Web sites she visited suggested that toward the end of his life, he was most likely to be displaying his work in such venues as the meeting room of his church—which he did about a year and a half before he died. She made a mental note to spend a day visiting people from the congregation, beginning with the pastor. She thought she might even attend a worship service that coming Sunday in Bartlett and meet the folks who had known Reese—and, perhaps, his eccentric friend, Bobbie Crocker.

One longer obituary in a photography magazine said that Reese had been a sports photographer back when he'd worked in newspapers, but with the exception of the print of the Hula-Hoopers there hadn't been any sports shots in that box Bobbie Crocker had left behind—and viewing the Hula-Hoopers as a sports image, she decided, was a stretch. Nothing in Reese's history suggested the interest in music or jazz or entertainment that marked Crocker's work, and so—unlike David—she remained confident that Bobbie was responsible for the prints that had been found in his apartment.

The last thing she did before turning to Crocker's Social Security number was to Google the names Crocker and Marcus Gregory Reese together. She came up empty.

Moreover, her research with Crocker's Social Security number only left her more frustrated, more puzzled. The number did not in actuality belong to a Robert Buchanan, as she had thought for sure it would. Instead, it was linked to Robert Crocker. Her Bobbie Crocker: He was born in 1923 and he had died, according to the site, earlier that month. In Burlington, Vermont.

Likewise, there was no Social Security number in existence for Pamela's little brother, which would make complete sense if what she had told Laurel was true: Pamela's brother had been born before Social Security existed, and—if he had died in 1939 as she insisted—he would have died before he would have been assigned one for the purpose of declaring his income.

Of course, for this very reason the site also couldn't confirm for her that Buchanan had passed away six and a half decades earlier.

Consequently, the jubilation she had experienced in the carrel at the library all but evaporated. David was not the sort who was ever going to whisper, "I told you so," but Laurel was feeling silly and small. She still believed that Bobbie Crocker was Pamela's brother, but she understood when she verbalized that notion that she sounded as delusional as a good many of her clients. She knew there was more she could do with Bobbie's Social Security number, and she would, but they had already missed their movie and so she agreed to David's entreaties that they shut down his computer and leave.

CHAPTER SIXTEEN

ITH A COUPLE OF FINGERS, Whit could hoist his Bianchi road bike up and over the wheelbarrow in the old Victorian's crowded carriage barn, as well as the other tenants' detritus: skis and snowboards and skateboards and boots and his own second bicycle, plus the cardboard computer cartons packed with books and clothes and hot plates and mugs. Vaguely aware that Talia was somewhere behind him in the driveway skimming her mail, he lifted his bike in precisely this fashion now as he put it away for the night. It was early Friday evening, and the last of the sun had just disappeared behind the Adirondacks across the lake. It was still light out, but it wouldn't be soon, and the air was moist with the coming dark. He wasn't sure whether he was lifting his bike with two fingers now to demonstrate how light the frame was—which, in his mind, was an indication of his prowess as a rider and the sophistication of his bicycle—or because this little maneuver would strike the girl as a casual indication of his brute strength. As inherently contradictory as these motivations were, he guessed the reason was a combination of both. Though he was not interested in Talia, he was in her roommate: This meant that the laws of hormonal transitivity invariably led him to gravitate toward her now. The truth was, he thought about Laurel often when he wasn't focused on classes and labs, despite his awareness that she was involved with some other guy. She seemed lonely and kind and the possessor of a secret that almost made him ache when he saw her.

Quickly, he locked the bicycle to the jack post. When he emerged from the barn, Talia was seated on the house's front steps. It was clear that she hadn't had the slightest interest in how he had put his bike away or noticed the ease with which he had handled the frame.

He decided that he hadn't ridden far enough or hard enough to smell especially repugnant, and so he joined her on the steps. He was nonplussed to see she was reading a brochure about paintball. He presumed she had received it as part of a bulk mailing.

"Junk mail, I see," he said.

She looked over at him and seemed momentarily perplexed. Then, understanding what he was referring to, she said—her voice dramatically defensive—"I *ordered* this. I *requested* this. Be careful, young man."

"You ordered a brochure about paintball? Whatever for?"

"Oh, you weenie cyclists in your tight little shorts are all the same."

"Has my manhood just been insulted?" He smiled as he asked this, but a part of him wondered always just how seriously Talia meant half the things that she said.

"I just call them as I see them."

"Really. Why do you need a brochure about paintball? Please don't tell me you're actually going to take your church kids there someday this fall."

"Tomorrow."

"You're shitting me."

"Nope."

"Really?"

"Which word didn't you understand? We're meeting at the church and leaving around nine o'clock. Want to come?"

"I don't think so."

"You could ride in the church van. Seats seventeen. And there's no better way to vomit up breakfast than an hour-long drive in a church van."

"And no better way to wind up on the front page of a newspaper. 'Church van' is Latin for 'tragic accident involving children and well-meaning grown-ups.' You could look it up. It's part of the first-year curriculum at the med school: biochemistry. Embryology. Church vans."

"Laurel will be there." She looked down at the glossy piece of paper in her hands. He had a feeling she'd looked away because she wasn't able to keep a straight face when she told him this tidbit. He wondered if his interest in Laurel was that obvious.

"What exactly do you do when you play paintball?" he asked. "I have this vision of a lot of paunchy, poorly social-ized guys in camouflage pants running around the woods shooting blobs of paint at each other."

"That sounds pretty accurate. But there are teams. And a referee."

"A referee?"

"Uh-huh."

He had little desire to spend the day with the high school kids in her church youth group. But there wasn't anything else he had planned for Saturday until early in the evening, when he was meeting his aunt and uncle for dinner. They'd come to Vermont to see the foliage, which—much to their disappointment—was still a few days away from its colorful, almost hallucinatory peak.

"What time will you get back?" he asked.

"No later than four or four-thirty."

He reached over for the brochure and scrutinized the map of the field. He couldn't imagine himself doing this. But, then, he couldn't imagine Laurel doing it, either.

"We're going to spend most of our time there," she said, pointing at a series of waving topographic lines. "That's Calamity Ridge. There's a fuel dump we're going to capture."

Something about the words *fuel dump* made it all seem less abstract to him. "Doesn't any of this make you uncomfortable in light of Iraq?"

Talia turned and stared squarely at him. "I have three friends from school in the Guard, all of whom have been to Iraq or are there right this second. One spent a month in Tikrit. If you come with us tomorrow, you will meet two kids who have older siblings in the Guard, one of whom was in Fallujah. I am neither an oblivious chick who hasn't a clue about what's going down in the Middle East, nor a sociopathic neocon who gets off on playing war. Okay? This is a game. And in my opinion, it's a heck of a lot more wholesome than their PlayStation games—than *your* PlayStation games, for all I know—about snipers and terrorists, if only because they're running around outside in the fresh air instead of sitting around inside their stuffy rooms hunched over their game consoles. The kids *want* to do this. Some do, anyway. They view it like capture the flag or touch football. I view it as a way to build teamwork and show them that there are adults out there—and, I know it pains you to admit this, Whit, but you are an adult in their eyes—who care about them. Who feel like hanging around with them. So, to answer your incredibly agenda-rich little inquiry: No, it does not make me uncomfortable. Okay?"

He nodded, slightly shell-shocked. He had a PlayStation.

He told himself that he still played it on occasion to blow off steam. Reduce stress. He told himself it was . . . medicinal.

"You in?"

He nodded again. He sensed instantly after her little diatribe that he didn't dare say no.

ONE NIGHT in early August, Whit had gone dancing with Laurel and Talia and two of their friends from UVM—a nice-enough guy named Dennis and a girl named Eva. They were a pack, or what Talia liked to refer to as a herd. It was a Thursday night and they met their friends at a club on Main Street a little past ten. Whit was still getting to know Talia and Laurel, and so he was flattered when they knocked on his door and absconded with him. He felt considerably younger than his housemates across the hall then, because he had only finished college three months earlier and was going to be a student for the next couple of years. Consequently, Talia and Laurel were not merely older women: They were older women with jobs. Granted, they both worked in fields that allowed them to dress essentially as they had when they were students, but they still had a weekly paycheck—something he didn't.

The club wasn't especially crowded because the area colleges weren't yet back in session, and so it might have been one of those evenings that grew awkward quickly. But it didn't, largely because they were a gang. He danced with Laurel and he danced with Talia and he even danced for a few minutes with Eva. She worked in the marketing department of a large shopping mall just outside of Burlington, and was the only one in the group who had that urban chic look down.

He was already attracted to Laurel and savoring their

opportunities to talk when the band was between sets. His sense, even at the time, was that he was far more interested in dancing than she was. Still, she was having fun. He could tell.

It was on the way home, however, that he understood precisely why he was falling for her. Talia and Dennis were going to stay at the club for the last set, but Eva and Laurel were ready to go. They had more rigid hours than Talia and actually had to get up in the morning. And so the three of them left about midnight and started walking home, planning to drop off Eva first before he and Laurel continued up into the hill section of the city where they lived.

They had gone three blocks when they saw the transient. He was sitting on a red plastic milk crate, slumped against a brick wall, enveloped by a black raincoat with the sleeves cut away. He was in the shadows, and so they smelled him before they saw him. His face was long, though much of it was hidden behind a thick nest of beard, and his hair hung in twisted, dirty ropes down the sides of his head. He was bald on top, and his skull there was dotted with sores. Whit guessed he was fifty-five or sixty, but Laurel would tell him later that he was probably no more than forty-five. Eva noticed him before Whit and Laurel did, and she took Whit's arm and started to lead them across the street and away from the man. Whit wasn't aware of what she was doing, and so he allowed himself to be led. But then he inhaled the stench and turned and saw the fellow. He was awake and whispering to himself. He wasn't shouting, but his low mumbling, once they were aware of it, might have been even more disconcerting.

Laurel went right to him. She squatted before him and got his attention. Asked him his name and told him hers. She certainly didn't pull him completely from his own planet back to theirs, but while Whit and Eva had stood unmoving and mute, fearful, Laurel was taking his hand in hers—and

Whit understood clearly that taking the soiled hand of a transient was an act both of mercy and of bravery—and leading him to his feet. Laurel told them that they should go on ahead, but they didn't. They went with her as she escorted the man to the shelter. There were beds left because it was summer and the homeless can endure a lot longer outside, and with the night manager's help she got him showered and fed, and then she convinced him to sleep inside that night. It took her about an hour to get him settled. The fellow didn't talk to the rest of them. He really didn't say a whole lot to Laurel. But he stopped his murmuring and his eyes no longer darted like the orbs in a pinball machine. They locked on to Laurel's, and it was clear he felt safe around her. Whatever conspiracies were after him, whatever delusions had led him to the street, momentarily were checked.

When Laurel rejoined Eva and Whit, she apologized for costing them an hour of sleep, and the three of them resumed their walk up the hill. Whit was shaken both by the stink and the utter hopelessness of the fellow Laurel had brought in from the street and by his first view of the inside of the shelter. But after four years there, plus her time as a volunteer, Laurel, he saw, had thought nothing of it.

And he, in turn, was left not merely smitten. He was awed.

CHAPTER SEVENTEEN

*L*AUREL KNEW SHE hadn't been much of a date Friday night—either at the restaurant or back at David's apartment—because she had felt the clock ticking on the time she had with Bobbie Crocker's photographs. The lawyer's call had made her uncomfortable. She wanted to be printing the negatives, especially since she had decided that she would spend at least part of Sunday in Bartlett. Consequently, she and David never quite warmed up to each other, and Saturday morning she went home well before breakfast so she could change her clothes and start work in the UVM dark room. When she had kissed David good-bye in bed, he hadn't even tried to hide his frustration with her.

"Why are you suddenly so consumed by this? At this point, what does it matter who Bobbie Crocker really was? Why do you care?" he asked her, his face still half-buried in his pillow. Sometimes on Saturday mornings they would have breakfast in bed and then go for a walk before he left to pick up his children. Other times he would go get his girls and then meet her at some predetermined activity far from the sheets where, hours earlier, they had made love.

"Why must you use that word?"

"Consumed? Because you are. Two of your three meals yesterday were with people who knew Bobbie Crocker, and last night you broke our date—"

"I did not break our date!"

"You upended our date, so you could spend time researching a man who may or may not have once been his photo editor. Now you're leaving to spend a beautiful autumn Saturday in a darkroom. And why are you doing that? So you can spend tomorrow—no doubt, a beautiful autumn Sunday—with people you've never met, talking about two dead men who may or may not even have known each other."

"I don't know how long I'm going to have these pictures! I told you, Pamela Marshfield has started to bring in the lawyers. For all we know, any day now I'm going to have to turn them over to her!"

He pulled the sheet over his head and wrapped it tightly around his face. She could tell it was meant as a silly, boyish gesture to de-escalate their disagreement before it could become a serious squabble, but they had been so short with each other since the night before that she actually took offense. She had already left the bedroom when he called out, "What did you decide about taking Marissa's picture? What should I tell her?"

She was lifting her small backpack off the floor by the counter that separated the kitchen from the living room. "I said it's fine," she reminded him, aware that she sounded short. But hadn't they been through this on Friday night? She adored Marissa, and she thought it would be fun to take the girl's picture. She'd told David that.

"I mean when? She's going to want to know when."

Laurel knew there was something she was supposed to be doing one day that week. Monday, maybe. Or Tuesday. A part of her even thought she had something scheduled for that day. She was no longer sure, or—at the moment, anyway—she couldn't remember. Finally, she suggested, "Monday afternoon, maybe, around four-thirty? Let me check. Maybe I could leave BEDS a little early. I'll let you know. But if I can't do it on Monday, we can always do it next Saturday. Okay?" After she'd spoken, she realized instantly that she was hoping he would shout back that Saturday would be fine. Although she knew she would enjoy taking Marissa's headshots, she was feeling the overwhelming weight of Bobbie Crocker's photos. And there were just so many other people with whom she needed to speak.

She waited a moment for a response, but didn't get one. Sometimes, she thought, David seemed to believe that his age alone gave him the privilege of judgment. Lately, whenever they weren't in bed, she had felt more like another of his daughters than his girlfriend—and a stepdaughter at that. She got the advice, but not the attention. She wondered if she had sounded testy, but then decided she really didn't have the time that morning to deconstruct everything that she and David had said to each other and left.

When she got home, her apartment smelled musty, and so she opened the window to the small balcony on which she and Talia would sometimes sit and read in the summer. It didn't have much of a view, but it offered morning sun and there was a glorious maple tree just beside it. Talia's bedroom door was still shut tight, which didn't surprise Laurel because it was barely past seven. But she saw her roommate had left a Post-it note for her with the information that there was a message she should listen to on the answering machine. When Laurel pressed the button, she heard an unfamiliar male voice.

"Good afternoon. My name is Terrance J. Leckbruge. I'm

a lawyer with Ruger and Oates. Our firm represents Pamela Marshfield. I love your state. My wife and I have a little cottage not far from you up in Underhill, and I'll actually be there tomorrow and Sunday. It's just before three o'clock on Friday, and I'm leaving for the day—sorry to call you at the start of a weekend. Please ring my cell when you get in or my place in Vermont tomorrow morning," he said with a soft southern accent, and then left what sounded to Laurel like a small phone book's worth of numbers. In addition to his cell phone and his cottage in Vermont, he had provided an office number and another one for his regular home—both of which had a Manhattan area code.

She had felt herself physically tense when he'd said the word *Underhill,* and she considered erasing the message and going about her day as if she'd never heard it. Moreover, it was so early that she really didn't need to return his call for hours. But she couldn't resist knowing precisely how Pamela Marshfield was going to try to bully her for the pictures. And so before she had even changed into clean clothes or sat down with a bowl of yogurt and a banana, she decided she would ring him back. She imagined there was at least a chance she would pull him from bed.

A woman answered, wide awake, and Laurel thought her voice was nothing like the genteel-sounding attorney to whom she was married. Her accent was reminiscent of some of Laurel's neighbors on Long Island. Quickly, the social worker introduced herself and explained that she was looking for a lawyer named Leckbruge. Terrance Leckbruge. The woman asked her politely if she knew what time it was, and Laurel said she would only be home for a moment and that her father had been an attorney.

"When lawyers call me," said Laurel, "I call them back as soon as I can." This was actually a complete fabrication: The only times lawyers—other than her father—had ever called her had been in the year after she nearly was raped, and usually she procrastinated as long as possible before calling them back. She hated rehashing the incident, but she seemed to have done so endlessly in those months. A moment later, she heard a screen door whine open and then clap shut.

"So, Laurel, pleasure to speak with you," said Leckbruge, his voice the reassuring drawl that she had heard a moment before on the answering machine. "You're an early riser, too? How are you doing on this glorious day?"

"I'm doing okay, thanks. What's up?"

"Let's see now, what's up? Well, I had a very nice, very cordial conversation the other day with one of your Burlington attorneys who represents BEDS. Woman named Chris Fricke. I have to tell you, I am mightily impressed with the work you all do at that shelter. You're an inspiration," he said, and then he took a sip of his coffee just loud enough for Laurel to hear it in the pause.

"Thank you," she said.

"I don't know all the details about this gentleman—your Mr. Crocker—but it appears to me as if your group really was his saving grace."

"We found him a home. It's what we do."

"You're modest. Trust me: The work you do is infinitely more important than the work I do."

"That's nice of you to say."

"I mean it," said Leckbruge, and Laurel had the distinct sense that he did. "I was wondering if we might have coffee together while I'm in Vermont. You could come to our place out here in Underhill. It's not flashy, but it's nice. Used to be, of all things, a giant sugarhouse. Woodsy on three sides, but I have a stellar view of Mount Mansfield to the east. The dirt road will beat the dickens out of your car during mud season. But it's fine the rest of the year. I am presuming you have a car. True?"

"I do," she said. "But I'm not coming to Underhill."

She spoke with such unmistakable finality that for a moment he was silent. Eventually, Leckbruge said, "Well, then. Should I read anything particular into your . . . firmness?"

"Nothing I care to discuss." An image: the fingernails on the thinner of her two assailants. He had just wrapped his hands underneath the handlebars of her mountain bike as he lifted it—lifted her—off the dirt road, so the nails were facing the sky. There were black lines of grime beneath the tips. Her stomach already was queasy from the way she had been lurched up and into the air, as she heard once again that appallingly stupid joke. Liqueur Snatch. Meanwhile, the one who would prove to be the real bodybuilder was calling her a cunt, roaring the word at her through the mouth hole of his wool mask.

"Very well, very well," Leckbruge was saying. "Shall we meet in Burlington? Would that be possible?"

"What do you want to talk about?"

"The photographs that were in the possession of your late client. But I'll bet you knew that."

"I have nothing to say. I'm sorry. And even if I did, my sense is I should only be talking to Chris Fricke—as should you."

"Burlington has a lot of eccentric little coffee bars. I love them all, especially one near that theater. The Flynn. Has a hot chocolate that's downright indecent. And I also know of a gloriously idiosyncratic wine bar. How 'bout we meet at five o'clock? Your choice: coffee or wine."

She thought she heard stirring behind Talia's closed door. Suddenly, she had a vague notion that she and her roommate had some outstanding business together—a nagging sense that the two of them were supposed to do something that very day. Perhaps something as simple as shopping. But Laurel didn't believe that was it.

As much as she enjoyed Talia—as much as she loved Talia; the woman had been more of a big sister to her than her real sibling for years now—she realized that she had to be gone by the time her friend emerged from her bedroom. She needed to get to the darkroom. She *had* to get to the darkroom. Which meant that she couldn't possibly linger over this phone call. And so, much to her own surprise, she agreed to meet Leckbruge at a wine bar in Burlington at five, if only so she could get off the phone and out of the house. Then, without showering or changing her clothes or even grabbing a piece of fruit for breakfast, she silently raced down the stairs and out the old Victorian's front door.

WHERE ONCE HAD SAT the ash heaps and the billboard of Dr. T. J. Eckleburg—the optometrist whose looming roadside ad had eyes that were massive, vacant, godlike, and cold—there was now a corporate business park. The buildings were all four and five stories, antiseptic blocks of tinted glass surrounded by parking lots that were dotted with islands of small, stunted trees. There was one fountain, an uninteresting spigot that fanned water into an umbrella near the building that housed a cell phone company. Laurel recognized the complex instantly from the photographs Bobbie had taken, because she had seen it from the highway. That meant that somewhere in the ground beneath one of the buildings was some small remnant of George Wilson's gas station. A tiny shard of glass, maybe. A trace of the cement that once had supported the gas pump. In addition, there was probably a relic or scrap from the coffee shop managed that awful, steaming summer of 1922 by a young Greek named Michaelis—the principal witness at the inquest that followed Myrtle Wilson's death.

Had Laurel not known Bobbie's real identity, she might have puzzled over why the photographer had bothered to snap pictures of an office park on Long Island. It was profoundly far afield from the musicians and actors and news stories that seemed to be his primary subject matter. She might have thought it was possible that toward the end of his career he had been reduced to shooting office parks for real estate ads—and, based on the age of some of the vehicles in the lot, she guessed these were taken in the late 1970s—but she knew just enough area history to understand what he was actually doing. He was chronicling the location where his mother had accidentally run over her husband's lover and then fled the scene.

She paused for a moment, staring at the images of the office park as they bathed in the chemical trays. How hard must it have been for him when he learned the truth about his parents? How old was he? Certainly, everyone discovers things about their mothers and fathers that make them a little uncomfortable, that leave them a little wobbly. Laurel had read enough psychology to know the importance of accepting one's parents' inadequacies, and how we use them unconsciously as a part of our adolescent separation from them. Individuation. Growth. It was, alas, a part of growing up. But it was one thing—in her case, for example—to realize that her otherwise hardworking, disciplined, profoundly giving father gorged on occasion like a Roman emperor. It was quite another to learn that both of your parents were adulterers, and your mother had slammed into a woman while driving her lover's car and left the victim to bleed to death on the side of the road.

She wondered: Was it when Bobbie learned of his parents'

reprehensible cowardice and selfishness—Daisy driving on as Myrtle died, and then Tom telling George Wilson who owned the yellow car so Gatsby would absorb the despairing man's wrath—that he changed his last name?

She didn't know a lot about schizophrenia, but she knew a bit from her master's in social work and from her years at BEDS. You couldn't work with the homeless and not pick up something. She found it revealing that Bobbie was sixteen when he ran away from home, since schizophrenia often begins to manifest itself between adolescence and young adulthood, and on occasion there is one traumatic, precipitating event. A term came to her that they used on occasion at BEDS: the double bind. The expression had a clinical origin, referring to Gregory Bateson's theory that a particular brand of bad parenting could inadvertently spawn schizophrenia. Essentially, it meant consistently offering a child a series of contradictory messages: telling him you loved him while turning away in disgust. Telling him he needed to go to sleep when it was clear you merely wanted him out of your hair. Asking him to kiss you good night and then telling him he has offensively bad breath. Over a long period of time, Bateson hypothesized, a child would realize that he couldn't possibly win in the real world, and as a coping mechanism would develop an unreal world of his own. The double-bind theory had not been completely discredited, but Laurel knew these days that most clinicians viewed nature—brain chemicals—as a much more significant determinant than nurture in whether a person became schizophrenic. Nevertheless, at the shelter they used the expression in much the same way that they would a term like catch-22.

Now, was Bobbie's childhood one long no-win proposition? It certainly seemed possible. Laurel began to imagine a scenario in which the son of Tom and Daisy Buchanan learns in high school what his parents had done the summer before he was born, and then all the bad behavior he has witnessed for a decade and a half—the snobbish arrogance, the marital duplicity, and, yes, the petty carelessness—becomes small change when compared with this nightmare. And so he confronts them. He asks them how much of the story is true and how much is conjecture. His father denies it all, he argues that Jay Gatsby was driving that twilight afternoon in 1922. But Bobbie sees through him, can tell he is lying.

And his mother, that woman whose voice was full of money: What of her? What does she do? Does she confess to her son? Or, like her husband, does she continue to insist that Gatsby was behind the wheel of the car? Or does she simply remain silent?

Either way, Bobbie knows the truth. And that part of his gray matter that had kept his behavior in check—that, to some degree, had kept the schizophrenia at bay—was no longer able to stem the onset of the symptoms.

It was possible, she guessed, that by then even Daisy herself had begun to believe the lie that she and Tom had been telling the world. Who could say? Perhaps Daisy Buchanan had gone to her grave in complete denial, in the end viewing the rumors that swirled about her as a mean-spirited fiction concocted by distant cousins and jealous neighbors.

Memory, after all, can be kind: If you're not schizophrenic, she knew, sometimes a forgiving memory is the only way to get by.

THE REFERENCE DESK at the library was open all day Saturday, and so Laurel worked steadily in the darkroom through the morning and the early afternoon, subsisting on bottled water and a muffin she bought at the UVM snack bar. She was feeling weak, but she couldn't bring herself to stop working. There was always one more picture to print. The images from the World's Fair Bobbie shot that she recognized with certainty were of the New York State Pavilion—the 250-foot tall towers designed by Philip Johnson—and the symbol of the celebration itself, the U.S. Steel Unisphere. She had seen the towers and the Unisphere probably a thousand times from the highway in Queens, and she had had an American history teacher in ninth grade who remembered the fair well from his own childhood and once took the whole class to Corona Park as part of a unit on the 1960s.

She didn't emerge from the darkroom until almost two-thirty, and she left then only because there was work for her to do at the library.

Quickly, the reference librarian found for her the microfilm spool of *Life* magazines from 1964, and she began to move forward from January. She saw a story about Pope Paul VI becoming the first pontiff to ride in an airplane, and a profile of Secretary of Defense Robert McNamara. There was an article about the conviction of Jack Ruby, and another about the way some woman named Kitty Genovese was savagely murdered outside her Queens apartment one night, and how her screams for help were heard by more than thirty neighbors—none of whom came to her aid.

Finally, in an issue in April, she saw the first photos from the World's Fair in Flushing. The fair was formally opened on April 22 by President Johnson, and there were photographs of actual-size models of rockets—surrounded by visitors clad either in jackets and ties or dresses and skirts, many of the women wearing white gloves—as well as the exhibit buildings constructed by General Motors and Chrysler and IBM.

There was a half-page image of the New York State Pavilion (though not the one she had just printed herself in the UVM darkroom), as well as a picture of the monorail with a photo credit—though the photographer was neither Robert Buchanan nor Bobbie Crocker.

She was disappointed but moved on, and within moments she found herself leaning forward in the seat and squinting at a black-and-white image on the microfilm screen. There in the following week's issue was a photograph on the second-to-last page of the magazine, the page opposite the inside back cover, of the Unisphere. The view of the orbital rings from the pedestal and the prominence of Australia reminded her of the one Bobbie had taken. She read the caption, and there he was—waiting patiently for her at the very end.

The U.S. Steel Unisphere surrounded by the Fountain of Conti-nents, the World's Fair, Flushing, New York. The globe stands 12 proud stories high and weighs an Atlas-straining 470 tons. At night the capitals of the world's leading nations are lit, while high above the planet three satellites whiz by. Total cost? $2,000,000, but worth every penny given the glorious way it reminds visitors that for all our political and ethnic differences, we are truly one Earth. The Unisphere is both the symbol of the newly opened World's Fair, and one of its most popular attractions! Photo: Robert Crocker.

Laurel was, perhaps, as satisfied as she had ever been in her life, and she considered calling David on his cell phone that very moment. But she was afraid after the way they had parted that morning that it would sound like she was gloating. Moreover, she was suddenly tired, very tired. Almost light-headed. Probably too tired to talk.

She wasn't due to meet Leckbruge for another forty-five minutes, and so she printed out the page and then returned the spool to the reference librarian and sat down for a long moment on a reading room couch to rest. Finally, she rose, and with the little energy she had left she went to the bakery down the street from the library for a bottle of juice and a scone. She knew that she had to be on top of her game when she met with Pamela Marshfield's attorney.

Chapter Eighteen

PAMELA WALKED SLOWLY along the beach behind her house late Saturday afternoon in her bare feet and a pair of khaki slacks she had rolled up into capris. The autumn light fell upon her like a wave, and for a split second she was indeed unsure of her footing, as if the sand below her were shifting. She paused for a moment to watch seagulls surround a small crab in the sand, circling it. One finally grabbed it and soared into the sky over the surf. The other bird squawked angrily and then noticed her, tilting its head quizzically, robotically in her direction, before lifting off after the seagull with the crab. In the distance, perhaps a half mile down the shore, she could see the colorful dots of the much younger people in their blue jeans and windbreakers who rented shares in the more modest homes on that stretch of beach.

She had not been completely surprised when T.J. had called with the news that the social worker had agreed to meet with him. It wasn't that she thought her attorney was especially charming—though, in her opinion, he was—but because she knew this girl from West Egg was curious. Meddlesome. Nosy. Unwilling to leave her homeless client's legacy alone.

And, thus, unwilling to pass up an opportunity to meet with this lawyer from Manhattan.

In this regard, the girl certainly reminded her of Robert. Asked too many questions. Didn't know when to quit.

That was, after all, precisely why Robert had finally had to leave. Or, at least, why he had decided to leave. Either way, it was hard for Pamela to imagine her father and Robert enduring another night together under the same roof after their final brawl. Of course, Robert had gotten the worst of it: Her father had been a football player. A polo player. An all-purpose brute. Had their mother been home, she would have intervened and wound up in the emergency room at the hospital in Roslyn. Fortunately, Tom and Robert Buchanan had saved their last and worst confrontation for a night when Daisy was off playing bridge. Consciously or unconsciously, Robert had probably chosen that moment because their mother was gone—though his anger at her was as deep and dogged and undiminished as the fury he had felt toward Tom. Even at the end, Daisy loved him—he would always be her mercurial little boy—but he simply could not find it in either his heart or his sadly muddled head to forgive her.

Pamela really didn't know much about either mental illness or teenage boys. How much of Robert's behavior those days was attributable to the insanity that eventually would envelop him completely and how much was the result of being a testosterone-fueled male adolescent was never quite clear to her. She knew he didn't just wake up one day as a madman. It had been a slow and steady deterioration that may have escalated in speed when he was fifteen and sixteen years old. She was no longer sure. Who in their circle even thought about such things in the 1930s? Clearly, Daisy and Tom Buchanan weren't about to. They had plenty of growling demons of their own. But there had been talk of hospital stays (and it was only talk), and at some point they'd made the decision that Robert would be the first Buchanan who could not be trusted at a boarding school. His mood swings were far too intense, and he was completely incapable of focusing on traditional schoolwork. And—far worse, in Tom's opinion— he had no enthusiasm for sports. Only his photography interested him. When he was in one of his periods of absolutely frenetic activity, he would stay up all night in the darkroom their mother had built for him when it was clear he was never going to attend an Exeter or a Hotchkiss or a Wales. Instead, he would go to a private day school in Great Neck.

Then Pamela left for college, which meant that she no longer saw Robert daily. Consequently, she may have noticed the changes even more clearly than her parents. One holiday when she returned from school, he told her he was relieved: He said he had been quite sure she had been kidnapped—and he was serious. Another Christmas, he said he saw things in his pictures that no one else did. Initially, Pamela had hoped that he was merely evidencing a newfound hubris as an artist or critic; when he showed her his photos the next day, how- ever, she realized that he meant it literally. On some level, he was aware of this inconsistency, and her heart sank for him.

When Robert left home, he took few clothes with him, reserving the limited space in his suitcase and their uncle's large Army duffel for his cameras and negatives and stacks and stacks of his photographs. Among them, she knew, was a portrait he had taken of her, because he showed it to her when she tried to calm him down and stop him from pack- ing. But she could only guess what other images—either fam- ily snapshots or his own work—he had with him when he departed. She tended to doubt he had any pictures that included either Daisy or Tom.

Would things have been different if, as their mother had

begged when she'd returned from her card game, Tom had gone after Robert that evening? Pamela honestly didn't think so. The two men, one still a teenager, would simply have found another night to continue their interminable, unresolvable conflict, and Robert would have chosen another night to storm out. Besides, they all expected he would return in the morning. And then, when he didn't slink back in by breakfast, that he would be with them once more by dinner. Even her own effort to convince him to stay had been brief and halfhearted, both because she presumed he would not be gone long and because she would always be loyal to her parents. She knew who they were and what they did. But there was also less for her to forgive.

Still, someone probably should have gone after Robert in those first hours when, in all likelihood, he was still on Long Island. She was home from Smith for the summer, and she knew who Robert's friends were and the places where he was likely to find refuge. She could have retrieved him—or, at least, she could have tried. She did wander down to the dock to see if she could detect a glowing shaft from a flashlight or a campfire near the empty house across the cove. The old Gatz estate had been bought and sold at least a half-dozen times since 1922, but once more it was on the market and empty. Nevertheless, she spent only a moment at the shore: The image in her mind of a solitary figure looking for a light across the water was far too reminiscent of James Gatz's desperate behavior that spring he was stalking her mother. And so she returned to the house and her father's now-silent rage.

A year later, her father announced that he no longer cared if Robert ever returned. The boy was all but dead to him. Soon after that, she heard him remarking gravely to an acquaintance from college whom he hadn't seen in twenty-seven or twenty-eight years that Robert had died. In a car accident. In Grand Forks.

Apparently, their mother had hired a detective to find Robert, and he had been sighted there six months after he had left home. The rest, of course, was a spontaneous, arguably sociopathic fabrication: After Grand Forks, the trail had disappeared.

Eventually, Pamela would hear the story repeated at dinner parties in their elegant dining room in East Egg: The Buchanans' wayward, runaway son had died when his car had overturned in a ditch. By the time she was married in 1946, friends of friends were actually claiming at the wedding reception to have been at her brother's memorial service in Rosehill.

It would be decades before she would see him again, because he did not return for her father's funeral. It was years later, about a month after Daisy was buried, that he reappeared. Pamela came outside one afternoon when she saw him photographing—*documenting* was the word he would use—their house. She hadn't recognized him at first: It had been a long time and he hadn't aged well. He smelled like the homeless she passed on the streets in Manhattan, vinegar-like and sour. He boasted proudly of an idea he was hatching, and she offered to get him help. She couldn't even get him to stay. His disgust with her hadn't diminished in the slightest over time.

Which was why she knew she had to retrieve those photos from the social worker. She could only speculate how far her deranged younger brother had taken his plan.

She watched a wave retreat and dug her toes into the sodden sand. She presumed the girl hated her. *Fine,* she thought. *Let her lionize Robert.* The fact was, it was she—not Robert—who had found it in her heart to pardon her parents.

And now she had to forgive herself. Even if she had gone after her brother that night, she couldn't have saved him. He would still have gone mad, he would still have resisted every attempt the family made to help him. Nevertheless, as she looked back on their lives, she couldn't help but wish that she had been able to reel him in—if only for the sake of their mother.

If only so he hadn't wound up . . . homeless.

The idea stunned her when she contemplated it. Homeless. In the end, her unstable, unhinged, self-destructively self-righteous little brother had actually wound up on the street. It was almost incomprehensibly needless and sad.

Before her, a small flock of seagulls landed en masse on the hard, moist part of the beach where the sea had just been, and began to strut and peck. She sighed and tried to remember specifically what had triggered her father and Robert's finishing quarrel. Then, almost ruefully, she shook her head. She didn't have to think long at all.

CHAPTER NINETEEN

WHILE LAUREL WAS walking to the bar, slightly forti-
fied by the juice and the scone, it dawned on her
that agreeing to meet with this lawyer might prove to be an
egregious mistake. He was, essentially, the opposition coun-
sel. And Katherine had specifically asked her not to speak to
him. Yet here she was, largely—but not entirely—on her way
because early that morning she had wanted to get off the
phone. Of course, she had also agreed to see him because she
was interested in what he had to say, and she thought she
might be able to learn something more about Bobbie
Crocker. Nevertheless, she was anxious, and she found herself brooding upon the consequences and all the things that
could go wrong.

Terrance Leckbruge had told her that she would know him
because he would be reading the *Atlantic*. She decided the
moment she walked into the wine bar that she would have
picked him out anyway. He was sitting atop a tall stool when
she arrived, a glass of something white and a well-thumbed
copy of the magazine on the circular table before him. He
looked about forty, but she wouldn't have been surprised if he
was considerably older than that: His hair, slicked back with a
heavy gel, was so black that she was quite sure he had colored

it. He was wearing the sort of oddly dated eyeglasses that she expected to find on senior citizens: rhomboid-shaped spectacles the color of mustard. The glasses were particularly unnerving because his eyes were a dazzling Day-Glo blue, and his nose was so petite that it was practically nonexistent. She almost wondered whether he epoxied his spectacles to his eyebrows to keep them from sliding off his face, especially since he was, when she saw him for the first time from the wine bar's front entrance, peering down at that magazine, his head slightly bowed, his mouth frozen in a vaguely condescending smirk. He was wearing a gray linen jacket with a beige T-shirt underneath it, and Laurel felt more than underdressed in her jeans: She felt slovenly. She hadn't washed her hair or showered in a day and a half, and she realized that she was wearing the same clothes she had put on Friday morning before leaving for BEDS. She also wasn't wearing any makeup, and she wished at the very least that she had layered on some lipstick and blush.

Leckbruge glanced up as she approached the table, and then slid off the stool to his feet. She thought for a brief moment that he was actually going to try to kiss her cheek, but she was mistaken: He simply leaned in a little closer than most people when he shook her hand.

"You must be Laurel. I'm Terrance Leckbruge, but my friends all call me T.J. They always have, they always will— even if, God willing, I make it to a very old man. Thank you so much for dropping by. Now, you look like you are in serious need of a drink." His accent was lovely in person, even more southern and pronounced than when he'd spoken with her on the phone. She wondered if it was an affectation, but she didn't care. It still sounded nice.

"I am," she agreed, and she reached for the burnished

metal clipboard with the calligraphed list of wines. He must have sensed that she was in way over her head, because he quickly recommended one. Then, when the waitress arrived, he ordered it for her, sparing her from having to wrap her tongue and mouth around the name of an unpronounceable Tuscan vineyard.

For a few minutes, they discussed how much they loved Vermont's quirks and eccentricities, and he told her how he savored the kindness of his neighbors in Underhill. She grew silent when he brought up the town, and it crossed her mind that he might interpret that quiet as coldness—which was fine with her. As soon as her wine arrived, he said, "Really, Laurel, I am so appreciative that you're willing to see me on such short notice. Truly I am. Thank you."

"Well, I have to admit: If I hadn't been trying to get out the door quickly this morning, I probably would have said no. But I didn't want to argue with you."

"And so you said yes."

"That's right."

"I can be very persuasive," he said, resting his chin on his knuckles.

"Not this time."

"And persistent."

"That's more accurate."

"Well, I am grateful that you have been so accommodating." She shrugged noncommittally.

"Where were you today?" he asked. "What was the engagement that was so pressing? May I ask?"

She considered lying, but saw no need. "I wanted to get to the darkroom to work on Bobbie Crocker's negatives. See what's there."

"And?"

"And I saw absolutely no more images of your client, if that's what you're wondering."

"Her house? Her property? Any pictures like that?"

"Look, I shouldn't even be here."

"But you are. Imagine if some individual—a profoundly ill individual—somehow took possession of your family's photographs. Deeply personal images. Wouldn't you want them back?"

"Bobbie Crocker's schizophrenia was under control. You make him sound deranged."

"We don't need to parse mental illness. He was homeless until your group parachuted into his life. I do not believe reasonable senior citizens live on the street in northern Vermont when they have a choice."

"As soon as BEDS gave him the chance to come in off the street, he took it."

Leckbruge swallowed the last of his wine and motioned for their waitress. When she returned to their table, he purred, "This was scrumptious. Every bit as exquisite as you'd said. May I have another, please?"

The waitress had the sort of twin piercings along her left eyebrow that Laurel found painful to look at, especially since otherwise her young skin was as smooth as a model's in a face crème commercial. A lot of Laurel's acquaintances had small piercings and tattoos—even Talia had pierced her navel. Once, soon after graduating, she had toyed with the idea of following Talia's lead and piercing her belly button, too. Piercing one's navel, she knew, was a lot like the decision to pose nude for erotic photographs: It was best done well before you hit middle age. And so it had seemed to Laurel that if she were going to do it, she should do it sooner rather than later. Further goading her toward the body-art parlor was her boyfriend—older, as always, who presumed that a loop in her navel would make it even more apparent to the world both what a trophy catch she was and what a stud he was. In the end, however, Laurel decided that she didn't want to draw attention to her stomach, because then she would risk drawing attention to her breasts. And ever since she had been attacked, that simply had not been an option. Besides, her boyfriend's immoderate enthusiasm alone was enough to nix the idea.

"So," Leckbruge said quietly, almost dreamily, when the waitress had left to get him a second glass of wine, "what will it take for you to relinquish the photos? That is, of course, why we're here. My client feels deeply violated and she would like the pictures back. And, clearly, a part of you understands her deep sense of violation. After all—"

"Why would you think that?" Laurel asked, momentarily afraid that she had read more into his use of the word *violation* than was there. Here she was presuming that somehow he knew what had occurred years earlier on the outskirts of his little village, when most likely he was simply suggesting that she was a particularly empathetic soul. She was about to apologize, or at least try to write off the stridency of her interruption to a lack of sleep or exhaustion—anything—when he reached across the table and rested a warm, gentle hand atop hers.

"Please, I'm so sorry. I shouldn't have said that."

"No, I shouldn't be so touchy. It's just that—"

And this time he cut her off: "You were attacked. I understand. I should have used a different word than *violation*. That was callous of me, and profoundly unthinking."

And so he did know. And she should have guessed that he did. After all, he had a place in Underhill. He was a lawyer. He probably knew all along what had happened. She quickly took back her hand and reached down for her knapsack, planning to leave. But then an image came to her: the girl on the bike on the dirt road. The photo that Bobbie Crocker had taken.

"When was your client's brother in Underhill?" she asked.

"My client says her brother died a very long time ago. He—"

She waved him silent, scything a swath through the air with her fingertips. "When was Bobbie Crocker in Underhill?"

"I didn't know he was. You know considerably more about his life in Vermont than I do."

"He took pictures there. In Underhill. I've seen them. Does your client believe those are hers, too?"

"What are they of?"

"A bicyclist."

"You?"

When she had been nearing the wine bar, she had considered the different mistakes she might make. This thread, however, wasn't one she had contemplated. But then, she wasn't even sure this was a mistake. Hadn't she come here after all to learn what she could? She sighed, and in the abrupt silence at their table she heard for the first time the music and the conversations and the clatter of the glasses all around them. Almost suddenly, the bar seemed to have filled up.

"Me," she answered finally, and then added quickly, "at least it might be."

"You're not positive."

"Not completely. But it's likely."

"My client is a collector. There is no reason not to believe that among the photos that disappeared was an image of a girl on a bike."

"This would have been taken seven years ago. When does your client claim that her collection—"

"A part of her collection."

"When does she believe that a part of her collection disappeared? It would have to have been since then."

"Your point?"

"Did Pamela inform the police of the theft? If the collection was that valuable—"

"Value needn't be judged solely in monetary terms. What she cares about most are the images of her home. Her family. A picture of her and her brother means considerably more to her than it would to, say, the George Eastman House. If you want this picture of you so badly, I am sure my client would be happy to let you have it."

"I don't want the picture," she said, aware that she was starting to grow dizzy, that the table was starting to inch up toward her, "I want . . ."

"Yes?"

"I want to know why he was there."

"Assuming he was."

"I want to know why he was on that road the same day those two men were." The words, she knew, had come out as a mumble, a small sad plea smothered by falling snow. She felt like *she* was being smothered by falling snow—she was starting to feel cold and clammy now, though inside her head she could hear her heart beating like an African drum.

"The men who hurt you?"

"Yes! What other men could I possibly mean?"

"But you don't know for sure it was the same day. Do you?"

"No. Not for sure."

"All right, then. Were your attackers homeless? Forgive me, Laurel, I just can't remember."

"Why would you ask that? Why is that relevant?"

"You sound defensive. You sound like you believe the

homeless never get violent. And yet just last spring two of your clients got into a knife fight in the alley adjacent to that pizza parlor on Main Street, and now one of them is dead and the other is in jail. According to the newspaper, the per-petrator—excuse me, alleged perpetrator—even threatened the victim over peanut-butter-and-jelly sandwiches in your shelter."

She bowed her forehead into the table. Of course she knew the story. But she also knew the two were exceptions: Every-one who had met them at BEDS had feared they were going to come to a bad end the moment they arrived. They spent a mere two nights at the shelter and then were gone. Laurel herself had never met either of the men, and so she had been more frustrated by the utter meaninglessness of their ends—death and prison—than she had been saddened.

"Laurel?"

She flinched when she felt his hand move up her arm to her shoulder, and she forced herself to look up. "One of the men who attacked me was a drifter," she said finally, her voice halting and slow. "But he had never set foot inside BEDS. I checked that years ago."

"May I get you something? Have the waitress bring you water? Are you . . ."

She raised her eyebrows and waited. She recalled the van backing toward her, over her, her mouth and her lungs momentarily filling with exhaust. The weight of the tires on her toes. Her collarbone and a finger already broken. The bruises on her breast.

"Anemic? Diabetic?" asked Leckbruge.

"I just . . . I just felt weak for a second. I'm fine."

"I'm not altogether sure you are. And I would like to help you."

"I don't want your help."

"Look, when you were raped—"

"I wasn't raped," she said, and with the last of her strength she stood, using her arm to lift herself to her feet. His hand fell away and quickly he tried to retake hold of her shoulder, but whether it was to help her or restrain her she couldn't tell. His eyes, once sympathetic, seemed to have grown cold.

"Please, Laurel, you don't want to go home now."

"You're wrong. I do."

"Stay. Sit. Please. I need you to stay for just another moment. I can't . . . I can't let you leave like this."

She breathed deeply and held the air inside her for a long moment, and slowly the world began to return to focus. "This sounds all about you," she murmured. "Why is it that you middle-aged men all think the world revolves around you?"

His lips curled reflexively into a boyish grin. *"Au contraire.* What torments the middle-aged man most is that he has discovered the world does not, in fact, revolve around him. That, alas, is what ails us."

"I'll keep that in mind."

He glanced at his watch. "I would like to continue this discussion."

"And you may: with the Burlington city lawyers. But not with me."

"It need not be antagonistic."

"It is if you bully me."

"I don't mean to bully you. Honestly, Laurel. I don't. There are others who might. But I personally would not bully anyone—let alone someone who has endured all that you have. Trust me."

Laurel thought about this. Was he insinuating that he knew

people who might be willing to intimidate her? "Was I just threatened?" she asked, more nonplussed than fearful.

"I don't think so," said Leckbruge. "But, please, make me one promise. Will you?"

"Unlikely."

"I'll ask it anyway. If you change your mind and realize the reasonableness of my client's request, will you call me?"

She gazed at him, and he raised his eyebrows above those gigantic yellow spectacles in a gesture that may actually have been sadness. Then he looked at his watch once more and sat back down on his stool. She realized as she left the bar that she had never even tasted her wine.

LAUREL FOUND the front door to her apartment was partway open when she returned, and initially she thought nothing of it. She presumed Talia was home. If she imagined anything precise, it may have been her beautiful friend reading on the couch, her iPod in her lap with its cords snaking up to her ears, her head and her shoulders bobbing slightly to the music. Instead, however, she understood as she pushed in the door that Talia wasn't there and they had been robbed. She stood in the frame, momentarily stunned, her eyes taking an inventory of the room. The window to their small balcony was open and the chair beside it overturned. The porcelain table lamp by the couch—a delicately hand-painted Chinese fixture that had sat for years in her parents' living room before her mother had redecorated after her father had died—was smashed on the floor. The coffee table had been upended, the books and newspapers tossed to the ground like so much recyclable detritus. And Talia's small mandarin writing desk had been shoved closer to the door to their kitchen, as if someone had pushed it aside while ransacking its single drawer. The computer was still upon it, apparently untouched, and she was relieved they hadn't stolen that, too—though she still had no idea of what precisely had been taken.

There was no way she was simply going to charge in there alone, and as quietly as she could she brought her backpack up over her shoulders and reached inside for the fist-size canister of pepper spray that she knew was sitting somewhere at the bottom. She had carried one with her wherever she went ever since she had returned to Vermont to finish her sophomore year of college. She had never used it, and she rarely thought about it: She wasn't even sure she remembered how to operate the spray mechanism on this particular model, since she had barely glanced at the directions when she had pulled it from its clear plastic sarcophagus. Still, she was relieved she had it with her now, and when she had the device cradled safely in her hand she stood perfectly still. She feared she had made too much noise already. She didn't even dare cross the hall to knock on Whit's door. And so she remained there, absolutely motionless, and listened. At one point, she felt sufficiently courageous that she considered tiptoeing back down the stairs and leaving the house, but the whole place felt so still. Finally, when there hadn't been a sound from the apartment for almost ten minutes, she cautiously stepped inside. It had become increasingly evident that whoever had been there was gone.

She saw the doors to both Talia's and her bedrooms were open, and she peered into each room. They seemed undisturbed. She pushed her bedroom door flat against the wall, prepared to use the pepper spray and run if she felt the slightest resistance behind it. She saw her CD player on the bureau and her small television set on a shelf in the armoire. She didn't have a lot of jewelry, but the teak box with her earrings and bracelets and a couple of necklaces was still atop her dresser. So was her own iPod. She checked the bottom drawer of the bureau, and sure enough her checkbook and passport were still underneath her sweaters—which were, as she kept them, all perfectly folded. Everything was exactly the way she had left it Friday morning.

She sat down on her mattress, wondering what it meant that nothing seemed to have been stolen. And then it hit her: Nothing had been taken because the only thing the intruder had wanted was in her cabinet at the UVM darkroom. The snapshots, too, because she had wanted to keep everything together. Suddenly, even the way Terrance Leckbruge had tried to detain her at the wine bar seemed ominous—because, of course, it was. While they had been together downtown, Leckbruge had known someone was at her apartment, and he had wanted to keep her with him as long as possible while his associate, whoever it was, tried to find Bobbie Crocker's negatives and prints. She recalled the way he had checked his watch and tried to prevent her from leaving.

"Laurel?"

She looked up, and there was Talia in the doorway to her bedroom.

"Someone was here," Laurel told her, her voice a stunned monotone. "Someone trashed our apartment. They were after Bobbie Crocker's negatives."

"What are you talking about?"

"Something's in them. The negatives. Something's in one of the negatives I haven't printed yet. Or something important is in one of the ones I have, and I didn't recognize its meaning."

"Laurel," said Talia again, though this time it wasn't a

question. She was wearing a gray sweatshirt with the words "Make my day" printed on it, and there was a deep bruise forming along the back of her left hand and a string of badly applied Band-Aids on her right. Her hair was a rat's nest, and she looked exhausted. Instantly, Laurel remembered: paintball. She was supposed to have helped Talia chaperone the youth group's paintball outing that day.

"Oh, Talia, I forgot. I am so sorry. I really blew it, didn't I? I don't know what to say. It's just been a completely weird, completely awful day. I blew off my best friend, and now I've come home to find our apartment was trashed by—"

"Gwen's dog."

"What?"

"Gwen is away this weekend, and she asked me to walk Merlin," Talia grunted as she limped over to the edge of the bed and sat down beside Laurel, trying to massage one of her sore shoulders with her hand. Gwen was the aspiring veterinarian who lived in their apartment house, and Merlin was the good-natured but gigantic foo dog—part canine, part lion—that Gwen continued to insist was a mere mutt from the animal shelter. "You know, I hurt everywhere," Talia continued. Then: "Don't feel guilty. No, strike that. Do feel guilty. Feel guilty as hell: I could really have used you today."

Laurel felt like they were having two conversations at once: paintball and what had happened to their apartment. "Gwen's dog made this mess?" she asked.

Talia nodded. "About, like, fifteen minutes ago. It's my fault. I'd just finished walking him. Actually, he walked me. I hobbled. Anyway, I thought I heard a noise in our apartment, so I went upstairs to give you hell for leaving me alone in the woods with a dozen teenagers with semiautomatic Piranha-brand paintball rifles. You didn't answer, but there was definitely something scratching around inside—"

"There was someone here? Did you see him?"

"Not someone. Some animal. It was a squirrel."

"A squirrel," said Laurel.

"Yeah, our window was wide open, and a squirrel was running along the couch when I opened the door. And Merlin saw it and went nuclear. Chased it everywhere. Toppled that nice lamp of yours, banged off the coffee table. Twice. Practically dove off the balcony when the son of a bitch scooted down the maple tree there. And I was, I am sorry to say, far too banged up to move with the kind of haste I would have needed to grab Merlin before he and the squirrel did in our living room."

"So we weren't robbed."

"Not likely," said Talia. "Not by the squirrel, anyway. I saw him leave, and he left empty-handed. Or empty-clawed."

"There wasn't anyone here."

"Nope. Just the squirrel. Man, I wish I'd had my Piranha. That squirrel would have gone through the winter with neon-colored fur."

"You know, I think I did leave the window open this morning."

"So you were home then. I thought I heard you return from David's. And still you forgot we were supposed to play paintball?"

"Really, Talia, I wish I could make it up to you. I just . . . I just forgot."

"Where were you? You didn't answer your cell. You weren't at David's—"

"You spoke to David?"

"No, he wasn't home, either. Were you with him?"

Laurel shook her head.

"Then where were you?"

"The darkroom."

"You were in the darkroom on a day like today!"

"Well, I also met a man—"

"An older man, no doubt," Talia said.

"Yes, but it wasn't like that. It was a lawyer who wants Bobbie's pictures. That's where I was just now. I was meeting with him because he has a client who believes all those photos belong to her. And I am simply not going to give them up. They're too important! And . . ."

"Go on."

Laurel suddenly had the sense that she was talking too much and she heard a frenetic urgency in her tone that she could tell from Talia's gaze was alarming her friend. And so she stopped speaking. It was all too complicated to explain, anyway.

After a moment, Talia looked away from her and then lay back on the bed. "I think I'm just going to stay here and die," she said, clearly hoping to direct the subject away from Bobbie Crocker's photographs. "Would you mind? There is no part of my body that isn't sore."

"Was it that awful?"

"Awful? It was spectacular! The only thing in the world that's more fun than paintball is really good sex. And trust me: The sex has to be really, really good."

"Are you kidding?"

"I'm not. It was awesome. You have no idea what you missed. I may never be able to sit up again. I may stay like this forever. But it was worth every gash and cut and bruise. We started out really badly. Whit came along—"

"Whit?"

"Uh-huh. Thank God. I needed another chaperone, you know—and a captain for a second team. And Whit took it incredibly seriously—more seriously than I did. It is so clearly a guy thing. Women can do it. But it's not instinctive with us the way it is with guys. He took a team and I took a team. And for the first two hours he just spanked us. I mean spanked us hard. It was pretty harsh, trust me. But then I figured it out. I just, like, totally got it: You actually need to view it like chess at first and plan your moves. And then, all at once, as soon as you're in position, you stop thinking and you pretend you're at the wildest party you've ever been at in your whole life, you're on the dance floor, and you are totally out of control. You just give it up completely. And once I understood that? Well, Whit was a dead man for the rest of the day. We were unstoppable, and I didn't have the kids on my team who live for their PlayStations. I did it with soldiers like Michelle. You know Michelle, right? Shy little Michelle? Well, we took no prisoners. None. Zip, zero, nada."

"It all sounds sort of violent," said Laurel.

"Sort of? Hello? I found myself snaking through a quarter mile of mud and pricker bushes on my stomach so I could sneak up behind a half-dozen teenagers I'm supposed to be mentoring in the ways of the Lord. When I rose up to nail them, I heard myself screaming they better drop their rifles or their brains would be roadkill."

"Did you really say that?"

Talia paused. "Actually, I think I said something much worse. But we won't go there."

"And they dropped their rifles?"

"Well, if you want to know the truth, I didn't really give them the option. I think Matthew tried to get off a round before I gunned him down. But he didn't have a prayer. None of them did. I torched them all. Next time, you have to join us. You simply must."

Laurel smiled politely and hoped she looked sincere. But she wasn't sure that she did. "Okay," she murmured. "I'll really try."

"I'm serious," Talia said, exhaling loudly, contentedly, despite her aches and pains. "And I know I owe you a lamp. Is there any other wreckage? I dragged Merlin back downstairs before I could really survey the damage."

"Just the lamp. And you don't owe me anything. Don't even think about it."

Talia pushed her ragged body back up into a sitting position, resting her weight on her elbows. It was apparent to Laurel that this small feat had taken serious effort. "Well, I'll buy us a new one. And I should clean up this mess myself. Unfortunately, I don't think I can bend over."

"You stay here," Laurel insisted. "I can pick up the pieces. Do you want something to drink?"

"Morphine."

"Will wine be okay? Or juice?"

"Wine's fine. But crush an analgesic in it . . . or morphine."

"Okay," she said, hoping they really did have a bottle of wine in the kitchen. She honestly wasn't sure.

"Tell me something," Talia said suddenly.

"Sure."

"Why haven't I seen you since you got back from your mom's?"

"Is that true?" she asked, though she knew that it was.

"I can't believe you're pissed at me," Talia continued, "because I am far too adorable for anyone ever to be pissed at me. At least for more than, like, a minute. But someone with a less-healthy ego might wonder what's going on here. I mean, I haven't seen you since before you left for Long Island, and then today you left me to the lions."

Laurel felt an eddy of autumn wind in the room, and so she closed the window and locked it. She thought for a moment before answering, because she was of two minds. On the one hand, she had always taken a small amount of pride, perhaps unjustified, in the reality that she was attentive and responsible in the eyes of her family and friends. She didn't let people down. On the other hand, she wondered if the reason she forgot about paintball wasn't that she was so focused on Bobbie Crocker's work; perhaps it was because a part of her understood that the last thing in the world anyone should expect of her was a desire to run through the woods with a toy gun. Perhaps she forgot because Talia should never have asked her to join the group in the first place.

"I didn't mean to leave you to the lions. And I'm certainly not mad at you. Why would I be?" she asked. She recognized a small iciness in her voice and did nothing to rein it in.

"So you've simply been busy."

"Yes."

"With David?"

"No."

"Not with your dead homeless man, I hope."

"Why do people refer to him that way? He wasn't homeless! We found him a home—"

"Hey, Laurel, chill. I didn't mean—"

"And why must being homeless be anyone's sole distinguishing feature? I notice you didn't describe him as a photographer. Or a veteran. Or a comic. He was very funny, you know. Frankly . . ."

"Frankly what?"

"Nothing."

"Tell me."

"There's nothing to say. Just . . . nothing."

Talia lurched slowly to her feet and narrowed her eyes as if to say, *I've had enough of this, thank you very much.* Laurel hadn't noticed it before, but the girl had a gibbous-shaped bruise the color of eggplant on the side of her neck. "I think I'm going to go take a hot bath," Talia said quietly. "I can get my own wine." Then her roommate limped past her into the kitchen, where Laurel heard her reaching into the cabinet for a glass and into the refrigerator for the wine. Laurel waited, unmoving, until she heard their bathroom door close. Talia did not exactly slam it, but she gave the door a demonstrable thwack.

Laurel had a nagging sense that she didn't feel quite bad enough that Talia and she had snapped at each other—that she just might have overreacted when her friend had referred to Bobbie Crocker as homeless. But this had been a stressful week, hadn't it? And it had been a very long day, right? And, besides, what did any of it matter when Crocker's work—when *her* work—might be in jeopardy? When there remained negatives left to print? The most important thing to do now, Laurel decided, was to return to the UVM darkroom and find a secure place for Bobbie Crocker's negatives and photographs. Just because someone hadn't tried to take them that afternoon didn't mean someone wouldn't try to steal them tomorrow.

The rest—Talia and David and Mr. Terrance J. Leckbruge—would just have to wait. The mess on the living room floor would just have to wait. And so she shouted through the bathroom door that she was leaving again, and then she started down the old Victorian's creaky wooden stairs.

BEFORE PACKING AWAY Crocker's photos at the UVM darkroom—the finished ones that he had kept with him all those years, as well as the negatives Laurel had printed herself—she ripped a piece of paper from a yellow legal pad and scribbled a time line indicating roughly when they had been taken. Most of the dates were guesswork based on Internet research: The Hula-Hoop had been invented in 1958 and the craze had run its course by the early 1960s. Assuming that the photograph of the two hundred girls with their Hula-Hoops on the football field had been taken at the pinnacle of the toy's popularity, it had probably been snapped between 1959 and 1961. Laurel's aunt Joyce had looked at the liner notes of her cousin Martin's *Camelot* CD and given Laurel the rough years when Julie Andrews had played Guinevere. Other dates were even more imprecise: Eartha Kitt was ageless, but Laurel guessed she was about forty in the portrait of her Crocker had taken outside Carnegie Hall—a guess based entirely on Laurel's sense that Kitt looked about the age she had been when she had played Catwoman on the old *Batman* TV show, and the performer was thirty-nine that year. Sometimes Laurel gave a picture a date based on nothing more than her profoundly limited knowledge of vintage clothing and cars.

And yet as approximate as the time line was, it was helpful nonetheless.

Crocker Photos: Rough Dates

Mid-1950s:
Chuck Berry
Robert Frost
Jazz musicians (many photos)
The Brooklyn Bridge
Muddy Waters
Plaza Hotel

Late-1950s:
Beatniks (three)
Eisenhower (at United Nations?)

Real Gidget (Kathy Kohner Zuckerman)
Hair dryers
Autos (many)
Washington Square
Train station, West Egg
Cigarettes (in ashtrays, on tables, close-ups in
people's mouths)
Street football underneath Hebrew National
billboard

1960/61:

Julie Andrews (Camelot)
Girls with Hula-Hoops

Early 1960's:

Sculptor (unknown)
Paul Newman
Zero Mostel
More autos (a half-dozen)
Manhattan cityscapes (including Chrysler
building)
New York Philharmonic
IBM typewriter (three)
Greenwich Village street scenes (four)
Chess players in Washington Square

1964:

World's Fair (a half-dozen shots, including the
Unisphere)
Freedom march, Frankfort, Kentucky
Martin Luther King (at Frankfort march?)
Lyndon Johnson (in big hat in a ballroom)
Dick Van Dyke

Mid-1960's:
    Eartha Kitt
    Bob Dylan
    Myrlie Evers-Williams
    Brownstones (in Brooklyn?)
    Mustang in front of Marshfield estate (car
    introduced in 1964)
    Midwestern arts-and-crafts house (looks like
    Wright)
    Nancy Olson
    Fifth Avenue bus
    Modern dancers (a series)

Late-1960's:
    Jesse Jackson
    Coretta Scott King
    Lava lamps (many—a series? for an ad?)
    Jazz club (a series)
    Joey Heatherton (I think)
    Sunbathers at Jones Beach
    Central Park series (picnics, baseball, the zoo,
    hippies)
    Paul Sorvino (and Mira?)
    Love beads and peace medallions

Early-1970's:
    Flip Wilson
    Unknown rock band
    Actors: Jack Klugman and Tony Randall
    World Trade Towers
    Wall Street (many)
    Main Street, West Egg
    Ray Stevens (maybe)

Liza Minnelli
Jazz trumpeter

Late-1970s (or later!):
  Valley of Ashes office park (not real name)
  Plaza Hotel (again)
  Jewelry box (may be art deco, but on negative strip with Valley of Ashes office park)
  East Egg train platform
  East Egg shoreline
  West Egg shoreline
  My old swim club (Gatsby's old house)
  Crab apple tree (a few prints, one with a little pyramid of apples beside it)

Late 1990s/Early 2000s:
  Underhill dirt road scenes (two with a girl on a bike)
  Stowe church
  Waterfall
  Dog by bakery
  Mount Mansfield ski trails (in summer)

She noticed that either Bobbie stopped working through much of the 1980s and 1990s, or those images had been lost. She also found it interesting that he seemed to have returned with increasing frequency as he grew older to East and West Egg and the Valley of Ashes. It was possible that he had been returning there all along, annually perhaps—she had that photograph of the West Egg train platform with cars nearby from the late 1950s—and those negatives and prints had simply disappeared over time. But she had a feeling this wasn't the case. She imagined him in his mid- to late fifties, retracing his steps and the swath left behind by his parents. She noted how he had photographed the Plaza at least twice, and she was sure that he couldn't help but see through the walls of the hotel to the steamy afternoon when his mother's lone (at least Laurel believed it was lone) infidelity had become clear to his father.

She gazed at each of the images before she packed them safely away in the portfolio case. What could have taken ten minutes took close to ninety. Initially, she presumed she was searching each photograph for whatever it was that Pamela Marshfield or Terrance Leckbruge so desperately wanted— the clue to their impenetrable interest. She was looking as well for the devil: a person, an image, a carnival freak. Wasn't that what Pete Stambolinos had said? There might be a photo of a carny. But there wasn't, at least not yet. There certainly weren't any images from the county fair held annually near Burlington. There weren't even any images that might be considered in the slightest way threatening.

And so, increasingly, she found herself studying the compositions themselves, Bobbie Crocker's use of light and dark, and the way he was capable of making even the most journeyman subjects fascinating: A typewriter. A cigarette. Men playing chess. She feared that her printing wasn't doing them justice. He deserved better.

After she had boxed the prints up, she decided she couldn't take them back home. Yes, it had only been a squirrel in the apartment today. But tomorrow? Other people wanted these images; Bobbie had understood that. It was why he had shared them with no one. And so she viewed the squirrel as a sign sent by a guardian angel. The message? Put those pictures someplace safe.

And that place certainly wasn't going to be her office at BEDS. She trusted Katherine, but not the lawyers. David's co-op was a possibility, but that might endanger his little girls if someone broke in. And while his office would be secure—it was impossible to venture inside the newspaper without either an ID card with a strip that could be read by the scanner or being buzzed inside by the receptionist—that security might also preclude her from accessing the materials when David wasn't there. She knew some of the receptionists, but not all.

Briefly, she even considered Pete Stambolinos, appreciating the irony of hiding the photos in the very same building in which they had moldered the last year of Bobbie Crocker's life. But it didn't seem especially prudent to turn them over to a man who had never numbered levelheadedness among his personal strengths.

She needed an acquaintance, someone who Marshfield or Leckbruge would not associate with her, and decided she should try Serena Sargent. She was going to Bartlett tomorrow to visit the Congregational church that Crocker's old editor may have attended, but she figured she could leave the prints she had already made with the waitress when she was done. She could visit the woman at her home in Waterbury or, if Serena was working, she could stop by her diner in Burlington in the afternoon. Meanwhile, she would keep the unexamined negatives—and, in truth, there were no more than three dozen strips left to print—with her wherever she went.

Patient 29873

It would be helpful to know the most recent or pertinent stressor.

In the meantime, it remains difficult to keep a conversation on track. Patient has moments of marked conversational clarity followed consistently by a delusional digression that derails our progress. Still unwilling to discuss treatment and aftercare plans.

From the notes of Kenneth Pierce,
attending psychiatrist,
Vermont State Hospital,
Waterbury, Vermont

CHAPTER TWENTY

*M*ARISSA TOOK HER little sister's hand in hers as they fell into the swarm of people—grown-ups and teenagers and children as young as Cindy—and emerged from the darkened theater into the movie's lobby Saturday night. She blinked once, then squinted against the brighter lights and the crowds by the concession stands. It was a little past nine o'clock, an hour past Cindy's bedtime, but the kid was holding up pretty well. And why shouldn't she? Her big sister and her dad had just endured this completely lamo movie about a circus clown who hated children but had nevertheless wound up having to run his mom's day-care center. The movie had been Cindy's choice, and so the kid didn't dare melt down now just because what their mom's fiancé liked to call the witching hour was drawing near.

She glanced from her dad, who was on one side of her, to Cindy, who was on the other, struck by the difference between an adult who has his act together and a kid who does not. She saw that her sister had popcorn butter all over her mouth and her bulbous, squirrel-like cheeks—it looked as if she had washed her face in the stuff—and a few small remnants of kernels epoxied like craft pebbles to the corners of her lips. Her hair, never her best feature, was frizzed up on one side like a frightened cat, and—was it possible?—she had a Junior Mint in her ear. Why was the kid putting Junior Mints in her ears in the movie? And how could she not know the candy was still there? Marissa remembered well the time Dad had had to take Cindy to the pediatrician two years ago because the kid had stuck a hard little pea up her nose. They'd been making food jewelry at the preschool—uncooked macaroni and peas and colored sugar—and for reasons no one could fathom, Cindy had wedged a pea high and deep inside her left nostril. According to the doctor, kids did this a lot. Still, as Marissa had watched the pediatrician, a nice woman who was her doctor, too, put a pair of tweezers the length of a pencil up Cindy's nose, it gave Marissa one more reason to wish that she and her sister weren't really related.

Recalling that visit to the doctor made her remember her toe. Her doctor had looked at it for about seven seconds, prescribed some antibiotic that tasted like bubble gum, and told her to soak it with her massive amounts of spare time (yeah, right). Still, the appointment had allowed her an escape from math hell. And, of course, it had given her the chance to bring up the idea of getting a professional headshot taken sooner rather than later.

Abruptly she bumped squarely into her dad's side, which meant that Cindy slammed into her. She looked up and saw that her dad had stopped because he had run into someone he knew—though not in the literal way she had just bumped into him. It seemed her dad was always running into someone he knew. This time it was a woman who he was calling Katherine and kissing once on the cheek, the way grown-ups seemed to do whenever they didn't shake hands. Marissa knew that she herself preferred the shaking hands route. Just imagine if right this second you had to kiss a cheek like her sister's? Gross. Way beyond gross.

Katherine had a man beside her whose name Marissa didn't catch, but it was evident they were a pair, and it was clear they had had the good fortune of seeing a different movie from the loser that her family had just had to stomach. Marissa smiled politely when she was introduced and was asked the obligatory questions—she basked for a moment in the woman's approval—but then allowed herself to fixate on the colorful movie posters for the films that would be arriving next. She was just beginning to fantasize that her name was on one—maybe the one with the hunky young film star who was on the cover of *People* and who had told the magazine the parts of his very hot movie-star girlfriend he liked best (the insides of her thighs, she'd read yesterday in the doctor's waiting room)—when she heard a name that caused her suddenly to pay attention. Laurel. They were talking about . . . Laurel.

"I don't know if it has something to do with her trip to Long Island, or it's all about the pictures," this woman named Katherine was saying. "But she didn't come swimming with me on Thursday or Friday, and she was hardly in the office at all the last couple of days—which doesn't bother me the tiniest bit as her boss. Really, it doesn't. I'm just wondering what's going on as her friend—and whether I made a mistake getting her involved with those photographs in the first place. Do you think I did?"

Her father seemed to consider this, nodding the way he did whenever he was thinking deeply about something someone had said. Marissa knew the look well. Finally, he told Katherine, "She was definitely fixated on Bobbie Crocker last night. Wednesday night, too. But last night was . . . worse."

"Worse?"

"More intense. She spent a lot of time researching Bobbie Crocker on the Internet when we were supposed to be going to a movie. And she really didn't stop talking about him all night long. Then this morning she went to the darkroom, and tomorrow I believe she's going to Bartlett. To a church that somebody named Reese, a fellow who might have known Bobbie, went to before he died a little over a year ago."

Katherine stretched out her hands and spread wide her fingers, her elbows pressed against her ribs, in a gesture of confusion. "I don't get it. She's going to a strange church miles from here because a dead person who knew Bobbie—"

"*Might* have known Bobbie."

"Because a dead person who *might* have known Bobbie went there?"

"That sums it up."

The woman reached over and squeezed her father's arm. "All I suggested she do was print the guy's old negatives. I never asked her to become a private eye."

"I understand."

"You didn't answer my question," she said. "Did I make a mistake getting her involved with the pictures?"

He breathed in and out of his nose so deeply that it sounded to Marissa like a small gust of wind. She knew that he was going to say that Katherine had. It all came down to Laurel's secret. The mystery that Marissa thought Laurel took with her wherever she went. Whatever Katherine had asked her to do with some pictures, it wasn't helping. It was making that secret even noisier in Laurel's head.

Marissa found it interesting that secrets made noise. She'd always viewed them as physically heavy—hadn't she seen people on the street who seemed stooped by the weight of what they couldn't tell anyone?—but only recently had she concluded that it was actually their persistent thrum that caused people to slouch. Eventually, her father muttered, "Look, I hate to sound patronizing—"

"Oh, stop it. You love to sound patronizing."

"Because Laurel is an adult. She's a grown woman. But, yes, Katherine, maybe. Maybe you did."

"You're being polite. You think definitely."

Before her father could answer, the man beside Katherine knelt down and said to Cindy, "I hate to be the one to break the news to you . . . but I think there just might be a piece of candy in your ear." The fellow was balding and tall—so tall that even kneeling he had to bend over slightly to speak eye to eye with the girl—and he was wedged a little too tightly into a turtleneck. The result was a very bad fashion statement, Marissa decided: He looked a bit like a turtle himself. Her sister slowly reached up to her ear and ran a pudgy finger and her cork of a thumb over the Junior Mint. It was apparent that she wanted to remove it . . . but couldn't.

"It's an earring," said Cindy. She spoke with great seriousness to the fellow because it was clear to her now that the Junior Mint wasn't going anywhere for a while. "It just looks like a piece of candy."

Marissa smiled, hoping she could salvage a small portion of dignity for both her and her sister, and added, "Cindy has always been her own girl when it comes to fashion and food."

The man nodded equally as earnestly, and then looked up at her father because of something her dad was saying. Instantly, Marissa looked up, too.

"She's fragile, Katherine," her father was telling the woman. "You know that. You've known her a lot longer than I have."

"Which makes it even worse, in your opinion, that I asked her to do this."

"Yeah, I think so," her father said, and Katherine seemed genuinely troubled by this idea. It looked to Marissa as if her

father were about to say something more. He even went so far
as to open his mouth, but at the last moment he must have
thought better of it because he remained silent.

"There's nothing that should have been disturbing in
those pictures. Right?" Katherine said. "Some old movie
stars. Some snapshots of her old swim club and some nearby
house. I guess there were a few Bobbie took up in Underhill,
but still . . . I don't know, I just saw a project that I thought
might be fun for her. And, yes, good for BEDS. That's all. I
would never have suggested this to her if I'd thought the
images might upset her. Never!"

Katherine's discomfort was so tangible that the man she
was with stood up, forgetting completely about Cindy and her
mint—which, Marissa feared, might result in some serious
acting out on the part of her sister—and started rubbing the
woman's back and shoulders in great, slow, circular motions.

"Look, I don't know what it is about the pictures that got
under her skin," her father said. "I have no idea what she sees
in them. But the sooner we can get her off this task and onto
something else, the better."

"I just saw the pictures as publicity, David, that's all. Maybe
a little cash for the organization—assuming the collection is
actually worth something. But it's all proving too much trouble, isn't it?"

"Could be. It certainly doesn't seem worth the anguish it's
causing Laurel."

"As you said: She's fragile."

Her father looked down at her and Cindy and smiled, as if
he had suddenly remembered they were there. Right away he
noticed the Junior Mint.

"Cindy, sweetheart, do you know there's a Junior Mint in
your ear?"

"It's an earring," said Cindy, and she offered him what she

must have presumed was the cutest, most pixielike smile in the world.

"Yeah," Marissa said, unable to contain herself a moment longer, "and the popcorn beside your mouth is a lip ring."

Her sister stuck her tongue out at her. She rolled her eyes, but decided everyone would be better off, including her, if she took the high road and put her arm around the kid. Her sister was as shaken as she was by the reality that soon Mom and Eric were getting hitched. "When we get home, Dad and I will help you take your earrings off—if you want us to. Sometimes it's hard, you know."

Katherine smiled, but it was clear that she wasn't really focused on them. She was still thinking about Laurel. "Of course," she continued, "it might be even worse at this point to take the pictures away from her."

"I think it would be best if we could get Laurel involved in another project," their dad said. "Another photography project, maybe. No, not maybe. Definitely. And I know one. It's not very big. But it is important to someone." His voice had brightened considerably and he sounded almost playful.

"And that would be what?" the woman asked.

"A headshot for my young diva here," he said, squeezing Marissa. "Laurel offered to take a headshot of my rising young star this Monday. Late afternoon, maybe. Or early evening."

Marissa felt a surge of electricity, downright elation, and stood up a little taller against her father's side. She hadn't realized that her father had taken her idea so seriously. "Really? This Monday?" she asked him.

He nodded. "She offered. I said I'd get back to her. You're done with singing lessons by four, but since you'd be the subject of the pictures, I figured I should double-check. Will Monday work?"

"Yes, Monday's perfect! Thank you, thank you, thank you!" She pulled him down by his arm and kissed his cheek. She was already thinking about the headshots she had seen in playbills and beside the résumés of the older girls she knew, and what she would wear. What she would do with her hair.

"David," Katherine began, her voice absolutely flat. "You're treating Laurel like a child. I think we need to confront this head-on—not try to distract her like she's a toddler."

"I'm simply trying to be efficient. Accomplish two tasks at once."

"Look, I think it's very sweet that she offered to photograph Marissa. But you can't possibly believe for even a nanosecond that taking your daughter's portrait could begin to replace her interest in Bobbie Crocker."

"No, of course not. But maybe if we view this obsession a day at a time and keep her busy with other things, we can wean her from the project."

"Wean? That's exactly what I'm saying!"

"It's an expression."

Almost on cue, as if she knew on an instinctive level precisely how to drive her older sister crazy, Cindy interrupted the grown-ups. "She can take my headshot, too! I want a headshot, too!"

"See," their father said, much to Marissa's horror. "The project has already doubled in scope."

A FEW MINUTES LATER, as the two girls were walking with their father down the Burlington street toward their apartment near the lake, Marissa asked, "Dad, is Laurel sick?"

"Laurel is a swimmer, remember? Very healthy. I don't think you have anything to worry about. Why do you ask?"

"You said she was fragile. That was the word you used when you and Katherine were talking."

"I didn't realize how carefully you were listening," he said.

"I didn't mean to eavesdrop."

"Oh, you weren't eavesdropping. Katherine and I were just, I guess, a bit indiscreet."

"So why is Laurel fragile?"

He seemed to think about this, his long strides slowing. "Well, I don't want to scare you. But I also want to be truthful with you. Always. You know that, right?"

"Right."

"Okay. Seven years ago, she had something bad happen to her. She's fine now. Mostly, anyway. She's just been a little delicate ever since."

"What happened?"

He glanced down at Cindy, who wasn't listening to a word they were saying. She was far too busy licking the tip of her finger. For a moment Marissa wasn't sure why, but then her sister brought the finger back to her ear . . . and then back to her tongue. And then she got it: The Junior Mint was starting to melt, and Cindy was scraping her fingernail against the chocolate and cream and tasting it. She shook her head. On the one hand, she was appalled. There was nothing—*just nothing!*—this kid wouldn't eat. On the other hand, at least this meant that she and her dad wouldn't have to get out the tweezers to extract the piece of candy. Body heat was actually doing the heavy lifting on this one. Thank God it wasn't a SweeTart or something hard. Then they might have had to go back to the doctor tomorrow.

Her father was saying—quietly, so Cindy would have to start listening actively if she wanted to hear—"I know at school you've learned about strangers and how you shouldn't get into cars or vans with them. Right? In health class, you watch all those movies about how to stay safe. How there are really bad people out there."

"Uh-huh."

"Well, seven years ago, when she was in college, Laurel went biking in Underhill. She was on a dirt road and it was pretty deserted." He paused, but only briefly, to make sure that her sister was still safely ensconced on Planet Cindy. Then, after a long sigh, he resumed his story. Marissa could tell that he was condensing it to all but its basics, abridging it considerably: He was trying so hard to convey the tale in a way that would not make the world unbearably frightening to her that she really wasn't completely sure what had occurred. Still, it sounded scary, and when he was finished she found herself folding her arms against her chest as they walked. She understood that he had told her even the barest bones of the tale because he was trying to answer her original question, explain to her why—in his opinion, in Katherine's opinion— Dad's athletic young girlfriend was fragile. Nevertheless, it was still a profoundly ominous story to hear as they strolled down the sidewalk in the night, and somewhere in the back of her mind she was dimly aware of the crackle of newspapers as they blew in the wind and the scuffle of footsteps before anyone would pass them on the street.

RA·9444
OHIO · 1956

*W*HAT DID THE neighbors think? Sometimes Laurel tried to imagine. Did the Buchanans care? First, in 1922, there was that nastiness near the ash heaps, the hit-and-run car accident, followed by the investigation and the inquest. There had to have been newspaper articles noting that Daisy was in the passenger seat of that bootlegger's car when he slammed into Myrtle Wilson and left her to die in the street, her left breast literally ripped off by the front of the vehicle. Surely, the neighbors must have pondered, why was she with him? Most, Laurel presumed, came to the most likely of conclusions. Then, a few years later, there were the allegations that it was actually Daisy who had been behind the wheel that steamy dusk. Not Jay. The neighbors must have discussed those stories, too.

Likewise, Laurel was sure that they whispered about Tom Buchanan's extramarital dalliances. The girl in Santa Barbara (a chambermaid), the woman in Chicago. And those were merely the affairs that occurred in the first three years of Tom and Daisy's marriage. Even Pamela Marshfield had wondered that morning over tea why her parents had never moved.

And yet, somehow, the marriage had endured.

Saturday night, Laurel stared at the snapshot of Pamela and Bobbie as children beside the tan coupé, the portico towering high above their small, entitled shoulders. For the first time, it dawned on her that Bobbie might have been a reconciliation baby. A child conceived and birthed to show the world that the Buchanans' marriage was fine. Rock solid. And the neighbors needn't waste any energy at all wondering whether it could or it should be saved.

THE CHURCH SAT ATOP a small ridge perhaps a mile and a quarter beyond the village of Bartlett. Laurel stopped at a gas station on the main street to ask for directions, and found it easily within minutes. It was a classic New England church with a pair of tall, stately sugar maples out front, their colors just starting their transformation into what soon would become a phantasmagoric rainbow of reds. It had a modest, unadorned steeple, and clapboard the color of bone. The stained glass was more ornate, with most of the windows depicting crowns and scepters and crucifixes. The deacons, an elderly man and woman, welcomed her warmly when she arrived: They smelled fresh young blood.

She sat in the back, both because she knew no one and because her family had never been big churchgoers. She was, she realized, slightly overdressed in her lone white blouse and the black broomstick skirt she had found in the back of her closet, since everyone else who was there who was even close to her age was wearing blue jeans or khakis or (in the case of a couple of girls who looked to be seniors in high school) the sort of retro-looking miniskirts that Laurel herself often picked up at the vintage clothing stores near the Burlington waterfront. She felt bad that she was here under what had to be considered a false pretense, guilt that was only exacerbated when the family in the pew before her—a salt-of-the-earth farmer and his wife, a schoolteacher, and their four unkempt but well-behaved children between the ages of, she guessed, five and fifteen—greeted her with unnecessary but completely sincere handshakes and embraces. Even the littlest girl, a shy thing with a sticky palm, insisted on pumping her arm wildly during the moment in the service when the pastor asked everyone to say hello to the parishioners around them.

She restrained herself from asking them how well they had known Marcus Gregory Reese or a man named Bobbie Crocker. She knew she should wait until the coffee hour that, according to the program, would immediately follow the benediction.

When the service was over, the schoolteacher, a woman named Nancy, asked her how long she had lived in Vermont. The woman was simultaneously handing quarters to two of her children to bring to their Sunday school classes, while gathering up their crayons and coloring books and sweaters. The older kids had shot from the sanctuary to their classrooms the moment the service had ended.

"Eight years," Laurel answered. "And you?"

Nancy kissed her remaining children on the tops of their heads and then watched as her husband brought them across the large, suddenly noisy room to their teachers.

"My whole life. I was born here. What did you say your name was?"

"Laurel."

"Well, it's nice to meet you. Did I hear you right earlier: You live up in Burlington?"

"I do."

The teacher stiffened just the tiniest bit, as if she sensed that Laurel wasn't here entirely because she was shopping for a church to call home.

"What brings you to Bartlett? It was probably a pleasant drive this morning. But it won't be come winter."

Laurel smiled in a way that she hoped was at once ingratiating and honest. "I want to learn about a member of this congregation who recently died—and a friend of his."

The woman nodded, and then rested a finger—the nail a near-perfect oval, the white at the tip a crisp sickle moon—on her chin. "And that would be?"

"Marcus Gregory Reese. He—"

"Oh, I knew Reese. That's what he went by. Reese."

"Can I talk to you about him?"

"Sure, but I didn't know him well. I mean, I rarely saw him other than Sundays. A couple of Thursday mornings in the summer, maybe, when the seniors would get together here at the church to play games. Sometimes I'd join them—you know, add a little youth to the mix? Pour the juice, brew the coffee? And I might have run into him once or twice at the grocery store. But that was really about it. Which of his friends do you want to meet? Perhaps I can introduce you."

"That's the problem. He died, too."

"I see."

"Bobbie Crocker. Ring a bell?"

"Huh, Bobbie died? I'm really sorry. I'd wondered what happened to him. He just disappeared off the face of the planet, didn't he? When did he die? And how?"

"A couple weeks ago. A stroke."

"They sat over there," the schoolteacher said, extending one of her long fingers with the lovely nails in the direction of the pews on the other side of the sanctuary. "Bobbie and Reese. I think they might have lived together, but I'm not sure. Why are you interested in them? Are you related to one of them?"

"No."

"Then why? May I ask? I don't want to pry."

Laurel thought for a moment before answering because there were just so many reasons. There was her curiosity about how Bobbie had gone from the Buchanan estate in East Egg to a single room at the Hotel New England. There was her sense that the two of them were connected since he had grown up in a house across the cove from the very club where she had spent a sizable chunk of her childhood, and then, perhaps, been photographing up in Underhill on that grim, tree-canopied dirt road on the day she had nearly been killed. There was her respect for his talents as a photographer and her desire to annotate his work properly, both for a show and for posterity. And, pure and simple, there were the mysteries: Why had his family cut him off years ago, and why was his sister insisting upon the fiction that they were unrelated today? Why was she claiming that her brother had been dead for so many decades? It was all too much to explain to this sweet woman in the back of a church on a Sunday morning, however, and so she simply told Nancy what she did for a living and that she was researching some photographs that were found in Bobbie's apartment after he died. She left it at that.

"Well, if you want to talk to someone who knew them better than I did, try that lady over there. Her name is Jordie."

"Jordie . . ."

"It's short for Jordan. She's another senior in the church, and she moved here from New York, too. She was also part of that Thursday morning seniors' game day I told you about. When Bobbie was living here, he and Reese and Jordie were real staples," Nancy said, and abruptly called over to a slightly stooped old woman in an elegant cardigan with pearl buttons and a short crop of platinum hair impeccably coiffed and slightly feathered. Her face was deeply furrowed, but Laurel couldn't tell for a moment if the wrinkles were all due entirely to age or the way she was laughing in response to something a nearby parishioner had said. She looked more like a peer of Pamela Marshfield than a dowager in a small town in Vermont. Laurel could imagine the woman in a spa or a country club or jauntily waving to a doorman as she passed beneath an immaculate awning on Manhattan's Upper East Side. Nancy called again, this time starting down the aisle toward the woman and dragging Laurel with her. Jordie finally noticed them and smiled at Nancy as they arrived at her side.

"Jordie, I have someone here who wants to meet you," the schoolteacher said. "This is Laurel. She's interested in Reese and Bobbie, and I thought you might be able to help her. Do you have a moment?"

The woman eyed her, bobbing her head and scrutinizing the girl. Appraising her. The seemingly good-natured laugh Laurel had witnessed a moment ago had evaporated completely, and the social worker assumed it was because of the subject of her inquiry.

"I have a moment," said Jordie carefully. "What do you do, young lady? Are you a *writer*?" She said the last word almost scornfully. Are you a *pornographer*? "I've had some bad experiences with reporters in my day, and I'd rather not have another."

"I'm a social worker," Laurel answered. "I work for BEDS. Up in Burlington?" She had surprised herself by turning a simple declarative into a question. Was she that intimidated? She reminded herself that in the last week she had confronted Pamela Buchanan Marshfield and T. J. Leckbruge, and hadn't backed down from either.

"Yes, I'm familiar with BEDS."

"Well, that's how I got interested in them. Bobbie Crocker was one of our clients."

At first she thought Jordie was nodding her head in recognition, but then she understood it was the bounce of a person with Parkinson's. "One of your clients?" she asked, and that glacial veil, part suspicion and part condescension, thawed in an instant.

"Yes."

"He was . . . homeless?"

"He was. He passed away two weeks ago."

"Oh, I feel horrible," she said, her voice growing soft. "Just horrible. I didn't know he had wound up on the streets. I didn't know he had died."

"Jordie," Nancy said, wrapping one arm around the old woman's shoulder consolingly, "don't feel bad. None of us knew."

"He'd been living with Reese, you see," Jordie said, so shaken by the news that she lowered herself carefully down onto the back wall of the pew.

"Yes, that's what I thought."

"It was Reese's house. And when Reese died, his sister said he could stay there till she sold it."

"When was this?" Laurel asked.

"At his funeral."

"And his sister's name is Mindy, right? And she lives in Florida?"

"Yes, I think so."

"So Bobbie was at Reese's funeral?"

"Oh, absolutely."

"Did he say whether he was going to take Mindy up on her offer?"

"This was all such a long time ago. Two years ago, at least. Maybe three."

Briefly, Laurel considered correcting Jordie, reminding her that it was only a little over fourteen months ago that Reese had passed away. But there was no reason. "What do you remember?" she asked, though her faith in the woman's memory had been shaken a tiny bit by this lapse.

"Well, we discovered that Bobbie's mother and my aunt were friends. Isn't that a small world?"

"Jordie, you never told us!" Nancy said lightly, as her youngest daughter abruptly reappeared in the sanctuary. Apparently, the drawing the girl had made for her Sunday school teacher was still in their car and she needed her mother to help her retrieve it. Nancy shrugged apologetically and said she'd be right back.

"Bobbie didn't like to talk about his family," Jordie continued. "I guess they had some sort of falling out."

"Did he tell you his mother's name?" Laurel asked, waiting for the confirmation she could share with David and Katherine and Talia—with everyone who seemed to be doubting her.

"Crocker, I assume," Jordie replied, and Laurel felt a sharp spike of disappointment. "Ladies of that generation—heavens, ladies of my generation!—always took their husbands' last names. That's just the way it was done."

"What about a first name?"

"Oh, I can't remember anymore. If only you'd asked me six or seven months ago. But I'm honestly not sure if I ever knew. I told him my aunt's name, but I'm not positive he ever told me his mother's. Lord, growing old really isn't for the faint of heart, is it? You forget so much."

"Well, then, tell me, please, anything you can remember," said Laurel. "Anything at all." Perhaps, she thought, there would still be a surprising, corroborative detail.

"Okay. He lived on Long Island. He grew up there, you know."

"I did know that, yes."

"And he had a sister."

"Did he tell you her name?"

"No, I don't think so. I'm sorry. But she was older, I am quite sure of that, and . . ."

"And?"

"And my aunt gave that girl a putter once, Bobbie's sister, that is, when the girl was little more than a toddler. A tiny golf putter. It was a present. Bobbie said that his mother had always liked my aunt very much. Yes, very, very much. They didn't always travel in the same social circles because his mother was married and my aunt wasn't, but they went to an awful lot of parties together—including some at that famous bootlegger's estate. You know the one."

"Gatsby's?"

"Well, that wasn't his real name, of course. But, yes, that's who I mean. When Bobbie found out who my aunt was, he said that his mother and my aunt spent a lot of time there together. Really, a very good amount, especially when they were in their early twenties. I don't remember exactly what he said—I don't remember anything exactly these days—but one time he implied that his mother had liked that awful man more than my aunt had. Gatsby. Gatz. Whatever. Can you imagine? I'm sure that wasn't true. People just went to his parties because they were great big festivals. Circuses. No one actually went because they liked him. Good heavens, how could they?"

"What about your aunt? What was her name?"

"Oh, I'm sure you've heard of her, young lady. Her name was Jordan Baker, and I'm named after her. She was a famous golfer on the women's pro tour. A real pioneer. But there are still some people out there who think she was some sort of cheat on the golf course. A sneak! Well, that wasn't my aunt, I promise you. And that's why I wanted to know if you were a reporter. I can't tell you how many people I have had to talk to over the years about my aunt as a result of some malicious and completely untrue story about a tournament she was in as a very young woman."

"Oh, no one thinks badly of your aunt," Laurel reassured her, though she certainly had: She had indeed viewed the golfer as a cheat and a sneak. And, she realized, she was incapable of mustering much respect for anyone who had sided with Tom and Daisy Buchanan that summer of 1922.

Jordie looked up at her now, her venerable head still quivering slightly, and repeated, "Really, Bobbie could have stayed with me. You believe that, don't you? I have so much empty, dusty space. He could have had his own little wing with a room and a bathroom! All he had to do was ask!"

"I'm sure he could have stayed with half the people in this church, if you'd known," Laurel said. "He was . . ."

"Yes?"

She had started to tell her that he was schizophrenic, but at the last moment had reined herself in. Jordie didn't need to know. "He was private," she said simply.

Jordie seemed to think about this. Then: "Did he come straight to you?"

"You mean after he left Reese's house?"

"Yes."

Again Laurel decided there was no point in telling the truth. The woman felt terrible enough as it was. And so she lied. "I think so," she said. "He was very happy. I want you to know that. And we found him a nice apartment in Burlington and he made friends there very quickly. He was okay. Really, he was."

"We used to play bridge on Thursday mornings right here at the church," Jordie continued. "That's when the seniors get together to play games. There was Reese and Bobbie and Lida and me. It was always great fun."

"Yes, Nancy told me."

"No, it wasn't bridge," Jordie corrected herself. "I used to play bridge with Reese and Lida and Tammy Purinton. Bobbie hated bridge. Really, my memory has just gotten so bad!"

"I think that's true for all of us," Laurel said, partly to be polite and partly because there were events in her own life that she imagined she remembered incorrectly. Even at her age the brain was an imperfect mass of gray and white tissue; even at her age there were moments in her past that her own mental health demanded she forget. Or, at the very least, revise. Everyone did that, didn't they?

"I just don't know why he didn't go home," Jordie went on. "He must have had family left somewhere. I think his sister was still alive. At least she was a couple of years ago."

Laurel smiled supportively. "His sister's fine. I've met her. She lives in East Hampton."

"Of course, he did like Vermont. That's why he came back. That, I guess, and Reese."

"Came back?"

"He had come here once before to see his son. One autumn."

"His son?" The surprise and the incredulity had caused her to raise her voice, and the old woman recoiled slightly. "Bobbie had a son?" she continued, trying to soften the sudden reediness in her tone.

"I think he did. Maybe I'm mistaken."

"What did he say?"

"He just . . ."

"Yes?"

"He just mentioned him the one time. Maybe twice. But it was clear Bobbie didn't want to talk about him because he had been in some kind of trouble."

"How old was he? His sixties? Fifties?"

"Younger than that. And the first time that Bobbie had come to Vermont must have been six or seven years ago—when Bobbie had been younger, too."

"Six? Or seven?"

"Please, you're asking too much."

"It matters."

"But I don't know, Laurel."

She thought the lights in the church, already sallow, were growing dimmer still. But she understood this wasn't really the case. It was because the light-headedness was returning. She felt herself swaying in place and looked down at the burnished pine floor to try to regain her equilibrium.

"Do you know what kind of trouble?" she asked finally, carefully articulating each word. "Was he in trouble with the law? Had he committed a crime?"

"Yes, I think that's it," said Jordie carefully.

"What kind of crime?"

"I don't know. That I never knew. But Bobbie came to Vermont to visit him. Wait . . ."

"Go on."

"I think Bobbie came to Vermont to see him, and then something happened—"

"To Bobbie or to his son?"

"To his son. And Bobbie left. Bobbie didn't come here *because* his son had done something. But then he left after the boy got in trouble. He returned to . . . to wherever it was that he came from."

"And this was seven years ago?"

"Or six. Or eight. I just don't know. I can't trust my memory—and neither should you. But it was the autumn. I can tell you that. When Bobbie mentioned his child, he said he had come here that first time because he had wanted to see the leaves change colors before he died."

"Did he say where he was in Vermont?"

"Underhill," she said, and a moment later Nancy returned from the wing of the church with the Sunday school classrooms. The teacher raised her eyebrows quizzically at the two of them, now ruminating silently together, the girl stooped over as if she, too, were desperately old. Laurel reached for Jordie's tired, gnarled hand, the flesh a little cold, and thanked her. Said good-bye. She tried to stand up a little straighter, to regain her composure. Then she found it within herself to smile for Nancy, tell her about Bobbie's son, and allow the schoolteacher to lead her downstairs to the coffee hour that followed the service.

"I DIDN'T REALIZE Bobbie had any children," Nancy was saying as they wandered downstairs from the sanctuary into a large room filled with folding metal chairs and folding metal tables and posters on the walls for the church's different mission offerings. There was a big crowd of adults here, milling about and sipping coffee, senior citizens and the parents whose children were in Sunday school.

"Me, neither. He certainly hadn't told his friends in Burlington. He hadn't told any of us at BEDS."

"You sound angry—like he should have."

"If I had known who Bobbie's son was, we would have had a very different relationship."

"You knew his son? From the little Jordie just told you? How?"

Laurel quickly backpedaled: "I did not definitely know him. But I might have." She was unprepared to explain who Bobbie's son was both because she was still reeling from the discovery and because she didn't want to discuss what had happened to her up in Underhill. Not with this new acquaintance. She never even discussed it with her mother or her closest friends.

"But how?" Nancy asked again.

"His son might have been a drifter. Or a bodybuilder."

"There's more. I can tell."

"I guess I just want to know why this child wasn't taking better care of his father. Or, at least, trying."

"That's all?"

"That's all," Laurel lied. Then: "I'm sorry I made Jordie sad when I told her that Bobbie had been homeless."

"See, isn't Jordie sweet? Some people find her a little unapproachable, a little off-putting, because there is just so much blue blood in her veins. But she's actually very kind—though she used to be a killer when she played bridge. It's too bad her mind isn't as sharp as it was even a year ago. Trust me: You wanted to be her partner if you played."

"She told me Bobbie hated bridge. But I could have sworn his sister said he loved it when I talked to her last week in East Hampton."

"You drove all the way out to East Hampton?"

"It wasn't a big deal. I was already on Long Island anyway. I was visiting my mom. She left for Italy yesterday, and I thought I would drop in before she left."

Nancy eyed her carefully. "Is this really just about those photos that were in Bobbie's apartment?"

"That's how it began," she answered. "There is more to it now."

The schoolteacher reached for a pair of mugs beside a metal coffee urn and handed one to Laurel. Then she motioned for the social worker to help herself to the containers of cream and milk and the dish overflowing with packets of sugar and Splenda. "Well, here's what Bobbie told me about bridge. He said his parents used to fight when he was a boy, and one of the ways his mother dealt with a pretty poor marriage was to play bridge—but not with her husband. It sounded like it was a ladies' league. She started playing the summer before Bobbie was born. She'd disappear most afternoons, leaving his older sister alone with the nurse. Apparently, the game became an addiction for her. Years later, she wasn't even home the day—or the night, for all I know—when Bobbie had some huge blowout with his father and left for good. He said he never saw the man again."

In some ways, Laurel thought, the pieces were fitting together as precisely as a jigsaw puzzle. She wondered what this perfectly nice woman would say if she were to inform her, *Bobbie's mother was Daisy Fay Buchanan. And she wasn't playing bridge that first summer. She was disappearing those afternoons to be with Jay Gatsby. Bridge was just her ruse. Her cover.*

No doubt the schoolteacher would, like everyone else, smile on the outside while believing on the inside that she was either mistaken or nuts. Nancy would probably conclude that she was more paranoid than some of her clients if she knew that the man's photographs and contact sheets and negatives were locked in a case right now in the back of her car—if the woman knew that she was going to hand them off to a waitress at a Burlington diner because there were people who wanted those pictures as much as she did and so she had to hide them someplace safe.

"You said you wanted to meet the minister," Nancy was saying, gently leading Laurel over to him. "I don't know what he can tell you about Bobbie, because Bobbie wasn't with us very long. But he can probably tell you something about Reese."

Laurel thought the minister looked to be about David's age. He had a high forehead beneath a brush cut of reddish-brown hair. His eyes were a little sunken, but he had a strong chin and a wide, infectious smile. His name, she knew from the program, was Randall Stone, but everyone seemed to be calling him Randy. After Nancy had introduced them, she explained to him why the young social worker had driven to Bartlett that morning. His face grew solemn when she told him that Bobbie had passed away.

"And you met him through your work with BEDS," he said to Laurel, not a question but a statement. He was, clearly, enduring precisely the sort of guilt that Jordie had experienced just now when she had learned what had happened to Reese's friend after the old editor had died.

"Yes. But he didn't stay long in the shelter before we found him an apartment. His place wasn't palatial, but it was a bed and it was warm and it was his own."

The minister ballooned his cheeks in exasperation, then exhaled. "He told me he was going to move in with his sister."

"Did he say where she lived?"

"Long Island. East Hampton, maybe. The last time I saw him was at Reese's funeral. I really should have gotten a better handle on his plans. We all knew he was more than a little off."

"Off?"

"I'm not sure where he'd been living for most of the years before he showed up at Reese's doorstep like a stray cat, but his address immediately before moving in with Reese was the Vermont State Hospital."

Laurel had chosen not to tell Jordie the specifics of Bobbie's mental illness, but she saw no reason not to share these details with the pastor. "Bobbie was a schizophrenic," she said. "When he was medicated, he could more or less function. Not completely, of course. And like most schizophrenics, he didn't believe he was ill—and so sometimes he would stop taking his medicine when he wasn't supervised."

"Do you know if he ever married?" he asked. "I couldn't get a simple yes or no answer when I asked him that one day when he was here playing Scrabble."

"I don't know," she said.

"I don't think he did," Nancy answered. "He and Reese had some inside joke about a ballerina he was seeing in the 1960s, but I guess Bobbie wasn't exactly the commitment type."

"But he might have had a son," said Laurel. "Jordie Baker believes that he did."

"That's a news flash for me. I had no idea."

"So he just appeared in Bartlett one day? Reese had no idea he was coming?"

"As I understand it, Bobbie came to Vermont looking for Reese a little over two years ago, but something happened and he wound up at the state hospital. Reese wasn't expecting him. While he was there, someone on the hospital staff located Reese, and Reese was extraordinarily magnanimous. He invited Bobbie to move in with him when the hospital team said he was ready. I gather Bobbie had lived with him once before—years ago, when Reese was married. Reese grilled him a couple of times about where he'd been since then, but the answers were inconsistent. Sometimes Bobbie said he had been in Louisville, sometimes he said he had been in the Midwest. At least once he said he had been near his sister on Long Island. I'm sure he had other answers, too. But in all of his stories, he never once mentioned a son."

"Did he say why he was always on the move?"

"I asked him that when we met. He made a joke about having to stay one step ahead of the hounds."

"It probably wasn't a joke. He might really have thought he was being pursued," Laurel said. And, she thought, it was possible that someone really was trailing him for those photos.

"Is that a symptom of schizophrenia?" Nancy asked.

"Paranoia? Often."

Randy jumped in. "Whoa, I don't know if Bobbie actually meant anything by that remark. It might have been just a joke. I mean, another time when we were chatting he said something like 'Guests are like fish. You keep them around too long and they start to smell.' "

"As far as I know, Reese was a photo editor and Bobbie was a photographer," Laurel said. "Bobbie used to work for Reese. Is that how you believe they knew each other? Or is there more to it than that?"

"Reese was a successful photojournalist, too," the pastor said. "He worked for newspapers, magazines, even *Life* in its heyday. This was the *Life* that my parents—and your grandparents—pored over weekly."

"And what about Bobbie?" she asked.

"Well, like you said: He took some pictures for Reese. For *Life*. The problem was that he wasn't very dependable. Both Reese and Bobbie made jokes about that, too. The man was his own worst enemy in terms of a career."

"Because of the schizophrenia," she said.

"And the drinking. He was an alcoholic, and he was irresponsible. He'd get into trouble."

Nancy glanced quickly at Laurel. When their eyes met, the schoolteacher looked down at the tile floor.

Laurel turned back to the pastor and asked, "Did you ever see any of Bobbie's photographs?"

"I saw the ones he took when he was living here. When he was staying with Reese, Reese would loan him his camera and chauffeur him around. And I saw a bunch Bobbie said he took in Vermont years before that. Fall foliage stuff. A batch of a dirt road up in Underhill—one that might have had a bicyclist in it, I think."

"Was he living with Reese when he took those?"

"Oh, no. He only reappeared in Reese's life the year before last," the minister said, as two other parishioners, an elderly couple, descended on him. Laurel had the distinct sense that she had monopolized the pastor long enough and so she allowed him to be pulled into their conversation.

"I hope you'll come back," Randy said to her.

"I will," she said, though she honestly wasn't sure whether she meant Bartlett or the church.

"I just thought of one more thing." This was Nancy, speaking softly although the nearby parishioners were so engrossed in their conversation that they couldn't possibly have heard what she'd said. Laurel understood this was an invitation of some sort. It was why Nancy had looked at her so seriously a moment earlier.

"Yes?"

"Maybe it was the word *trouble* that made me think of it. That same day we were playing Scrabble—right over there, as a matter of fact—Bobbie said something about jail. It came up right after he'd turned the word *fine* into *confine*. You know, by adding c-o-n? Something about the connection and the moment, I don't know, it made me sure that he was talking about a prison."

"And you thought Bobbie was talking about himself . . ."

She nodded. "I did at the time. But now I learn that his son may have been a criminal. Maybe that's what Bobbie was thinking about. It wasn't Bobbie who had ever been behind bars. Maybe it was his son who had once gone to jail."

"Or, maybe," Laurel said, thinking aloud, "his son is there now."

THAT AFTERNOON, SERENA told Laurel that she, too, had never heard Bobbie Crocker mention a son. She said she could barely imagine such a thing. Now she was gazing at the photographs Laurel had made from the negatives Bobbie Crocker had left behind at the Hotel New England, as well as at the handful of fading, dog-eared prints he had carried with him for years. The waitress was working in Burlington that day, and so she and Laurel were meeting in a booth in the back of the diner, a slightly incongruous world of train-car-slick chromes and panels of dark heavy wood, Bobbie's pictures carefully stacked in a black portfolio case that—when open—took up virtually the entire top of the table. The restaurant was half filled, but the real rush was over, and so the waitress who was working with Serena that day, a matronly middle-aged woman named Beverly, had insisted that her younger associate join Laurel in the booth.

"And you want me to hang on to these," Serena said, her voice hovering on an edge between incredulity and mere bewilderment. She looked older to Laurel in her beige uniform. The dress was too tight across her breasts, and she had pulled her rich mane of hair back in a styleless bun.

"I do. There are still negatives I haven't finished working with, and so I'm hanging on to those. For the moment, anyway. But as I print those pictures I'll bring them to you, too."

"I like this one," she said, stalling for time as she processed Laurel's request. She was staring at the image of the Mustang in front of Bobbie's childhood home. "I know a person up in Stowe who collects vintage cars. He has a Mustang just like that one: white with the black hardtop. Very classic."

"Bobbie was a talented guy."

She nodded and then looked up at Laurel gravely, her face a vessel bracing for bad weather. "Okay, why?"

"Why what?"

"Why do you want me to keep these for you?"

Laurel took a sip of her soda. She had expected this question, but in a diner in the light of day—away from the darkroom and people like T. J. Leckbruge—she feared that whatever she said might sound a trifle insane. Maybe more than a trifle. But she knew this wasn't the case. It wasn't as if she had made up Leckbruge or Pamela Buchanan Marshfield. It wasn't as if she had manufactured the connections between Bobbie Crocker and a house in East Egg, Long Island. She had the pictures to prove the connection was real, and they were right there between them on the Formicatopped table.

"Well, his sister wants them," she answered. "That woman I told you about on Friday. I met with her lawyer yesterday, and I came away with a very bad feeling."

"Meaning?"

"I don't think they're safe with me."

Serena leaned forward across the tabletop. "What are you really saying, Laurel? Do you honestly believe Bobbie's sister or this lawyer is going to send some goon to break your legs for a couple of ancient black and whites of dudes playing chess? Do you really believe someone wants a picture of a Mustang that badly?"

Laurel considered tapping the side of the portfolio case and correcting her: This was far more than a couple of images. But that wasn't Serena's point. "I don't think anyone would hurt me," she said evenly. "I wouldn't ask you to hang on to them for me if I thought someone would hurt you or your aunt. But, yes, I do think it's possible they might have someone try to steal them—or resort to more aggressive legal tactics."

"Which would be?"

"I'm not sure."

"So my having the pictures would be a secret? No one would know?"

"No one but us."

Serena sat back in the booth and rested her hands in her lap. "You know, if I didn't know you and what you did for a living, I might have thought you were the one who had just stumbled in off the streets—or come here from the state hospital."

"Look, I know I seem a little irrational. But I'm not. And until I know why Bobbie Crocker changed his name or why his sister wants these pictures so badly, I need your help. Okay?"

"Of course it's okay. Of course I'll help you. But, Laurel, doesn't this all seem a little, I don't know, beyond irrational? A little . . ."

"A little what?"

She smiled sheepishly. "I'm just worried about you. That's all."

"Why does it seem that strange and absurd? Good Lord,

Serena, you were homeless. I would have thought you would have understood as well as anyone just how strange and absurd life can get!" She was aware that her tone sounded defensive and sharp and just a little bit whiny.

"I was only saying—"

"I know what you were saying. You and David and my boss and my roommate are all treating me like I'm insane. Like this is all something I've completely made up!" She hadn't planned on raising her voice, but she had, and she could see that the other customers were now watching them.

"I didn't say you'd made anything up," Serena murmured.

The waitress was trying to pacify her, and this only made Laurel's frustration more pronounced. But she didn't want to get Serena in trouble by making a scene in the woman's restaurant, and so she tried to make light of her outburst. "I didn't sleep well last night," she said, making a conscious effort to keep her voice friendly and calm while acknowledging that in Serena's eyes (though most certainly not in her own) she had overreacted.

"I understand," Serena said, and then she looked past Laurel, over her shoulder. Laurel turned and saw arriving at her side a short, older man with milky blue eyes. He was wearing a red V-neck sweater with a white polo shirt with an unfashionably large pointed collar beneath it. The collar looked like the wings on a paper airplane. Although he had little hair left on his scalp, he had dwarf topiaries emerging from his nostrils and his ears. Laurel knew she had seen him somewhere before, but she wasn't sure where. Almost instantly he ended the mystery.

"So, I saw you at church just now, talking to my friend Jordie," he said. "Ain't she a peach?"

"She is a peach," Laurel said, glancing quickly at Serena and then starting to rise to be polite.

"Don't get up. Not for an old wolf like me. Are these Reese's or Bobbie's?" he asked, sweeping his hand over the portfolio case as if he had a magic wand in his fingers.

"They're Bobbie's," she answered. "I'm sorry. I must have missed your name."

"Hey, I'm the one who should be sorry. It's Shem. Short for Sherman. My name is Shem Wolfe. I go to the church you were just at. It's a nice church. I used to like a place closer to Burlington. But now I go to Bartlett Congregational. I don't mind the drive. What are your names?"

The two young women introduced themselves. Then, one at a time, he surrounded their fingers and palms with his own oddly meaty, age-spot-ridden hands. "So tell me, how is Bobbie doing? Where is he these days?"

Laurel wondered if the news that Bobbie had died would be a blow, because it was possible that he and Bobbie had been friends. But Shem was old and Bobbie had been even older, and so she simply forged ahead and told him. "He died. But he died quickly—a stroke—and so he didn't suffer. He was living in Burlington. Only five or six blocks from here, actually."

He nodded, absorbing the news. "Oh, that's too bad. I'm sorry. When did he pass?"

"Two weeks ago."

"I wish I'd known. You know? I woulda gone to the service. There was a service, right?"

"A small one."

"I bet Jordie woulda gone, too. Really, I'm sorry. Still, I always say you should be a man's friend when he's living. Not after he's passed." He made a clicking sound with his tongue against his dentures, then sighed. "I'd join you two beautiful girls—well, I'd ask to join you, I wouldn't be so presumptuous as to suppose you wanted more company—but I was just leaving. I teach a journalism class at the community college. I know, I know, I'm too old. I shoulda retired. But I wrote for newspapers when I was younger and I love a good story. Finding one, telling one. Teaching others how to tell 'em. Anyway, I still have lots to do before class tomorrow."

"And I should go help Beverly," Serena said, rising. "That's a pretty big family that just pulled into the parking lot. I'll be back in a couple of minutes, Laurel, okay?"

"I'm not driving you away, am I?" Shem asked.

"No, not at all. I'll be back."

Shem bent over the table to stare at the top picture in the portfolio case, the one of the Mustang beneath the Buchanan portico. He studied the photograph and then exhaled loudly.

"That Bobbie sure grew up with one big silver spoon in his mouth," he said.

Laurel was taken aback. Had this Shem Wolfe really just implied that he knew this was the home in which Bobbie Crocker had grown up?

"You know this was Bobbie's parents' house?" she asked him, wishing she could rein in her enthusiasm and make her voice sound more casual.

"Well, it was his mom's house. The old Buchanan place, right? But Bobbie's old man—his real dad, anyway—lived over the water in West Egg."

"Excuse me?"

"Oh, I guess I'm slicing hairs, you know? Very fine hairs. But maybe not. Tom Buchanan raised Bobbie for a while and put a roof over his head. Bobbie lived with the man for what, sixteen, seventeen years? Something like that. But his real allegiance, once he figured it out, was always to his real dad. Or, I guess, to the ghost of his real dad. Because, of course, they never met. But Bobbie told me twice—really, two times—that he'd never stopped wishing he'd got to meet that Jay Gatsby."

SHEM WOLFE WAS indeed a remarkable storyteller, and that afternoon he told Laurel what he knew of Bobbie Crocker's youth. Apparently, Reese had been aware all along of who the periodically homeless man's father had been, and in the year that Bobbie had lived with Reese in Vermont, Bobbie had grown sufficiently comfortable with Reese's friend, Shem, to share with him his life story, too. The three of them—the two old photographers and the one old reporter—reminisced often.

"Reese always cut Bobbie a little extra slack," Shem said. After Serena had left, he had taken her seat across from Laurel, deciding that his class preparation could wait another half hour.

"He was an addled man, and I guess he had been an addled boy," he told her. "Sometimes even voices-in-his-head addled. And always a little unfocused, a little edgy." Shem had learned that Bobbie hadn't been much of a student and he'd never been much of an athlete. As a result, he had never had much of a relationship with Tom Buchanan, the man he assumed was his father. The family rarely mentioned the baronial estate across the cove, and no one ever dared bring up the car accident. Adult neighbors and schoolteachers never discussed it around Bobbie when he was a child. The other boys, however, occasionally would flaunt the rumors they'd heard, for no other reason than the reality that boys can be cruel. Usually, the tales bordered on the fantastic and had only the most tenuous connection to the all-too-prosaic truth. At least one first-grader liked to insist that Bobbie had Martian blood coursing inside him. A third-grade boy announced to the class that the man Bobbie still believed was his father—Tom Buchanan, of all people—had made his fortune with a string of speakeasies. In the fourth grade, there were stories swirling about him that his mother had killed a man—a tale that Bobbie would later realize had at least a semblance of truth, since his own father might not have died if his mother had told Tom Buchanan who had been driving that tragic afternoon. And, though it was an accident, his mother really had killed Myrtle Wilson.

It first dawned on Bobbie in the sixth grade that he had been conceived in the summer of 1922: the summer of his mother's alleged dalliance with that dead criminal who had once lived across the cove. He wrote this off as coincidence on a conscious level, and for a time even viewed it as corroboration that his mother could not possibly have been involved with Jay Gatsby. Back then, he presumed, his parents had still loved each other.

It was, perhaps not surprisingly, a photograph that had set in motion the final fight with Tom that would cause him to leave home. When he was sixteen he found a greeting-card-size image of a young soldier in one of his mother's ragged old books. The lieutenant was a little older than Bobbie at the time, but the teen couldn't help but notice an uncanny resemblance between himself and the officer. He could see it in the hard, solemn cast of the man's face, the high cheekbones, the firm jaw: the restlessness and ambition in the fellow's dark eyes. There was a note on the back of the photograph in a handwriting Bobbie didn't recognize:

For my golden girl,
Love, Jay
Camp Taylor, 1917

For years now, Bobbie had known the specific allegations about his mother and Jay Gatsby. Sometimes he had given the tawdry claims more credence than at others. But he had still been too young to accept with certainty the notion that his mother could be so deceitful and, ironically, that his father could be so magnanimous—at least when it came to raising Jay Gatsby's bastard son. He just couldn't quite believe the lurid stories could be true, though he had felt his relationship with his mother begin to change. He had found himself looking upon her differently. Less the victim in a turbulent marriage. Less the frivolous Louisville belle, still years short of serious middle-age. Less unreservedly innocent. But he had nonetheless remained confident that his father—or, to be precise, the man who was raising him—was far too arrogant and cruel to raise his wife's lover's baby. It wasn't possible.

But this picture he had discovered in the old book suggested that it was. No, this picture proved to him that it was. He was an aspiring photographer, he knew that pictures didn't lie. At least in those days they didn't. And Tom Buchanan had to know. If he hadn't known for sure in 1923, he had to have figured it out by now. The resemblance was unambiguous. Why then did this conceited, brutish man abide having him under his roof, within a stone's throw of his precious polo ponies and his half acre of roses? And the answer, Bobbie realized, was clear. Pride. Precisely because Tom Buchanan was so arrogant, he was never going to acknowledge aloud that his wife had slept with Jay Gatsby— and thus the rest of the story, including the awful ways George and Myrtle Wilson had died, might be true, too. Tom might allude to the affair, he might allow the subterranean truth a glimmer of sun in a catty remark when he and Daisy were fighting—odd comments Bobbie had witnessed or overheard suddenly made sense—but he would never give public credence to the notion that he had been cuckolded by the low-rent criminal across the way.

In hindsight, Bobbie told Shem, he wished that he had waited until his mother had returned from her card game before demanding to hear what had really occurred in 1922. It wasn't as if he didn't already know. But he was filled with such adolescent rage that when he saw Tom in the kitchen— the very room in which this man and his mother had reconciled mere hours after Myrtle Wilson had died on the street near the ash heaps—he exploded. Here was the man who, in essence, had had his father killed. He took a swing at Tom, but the punch was well telegraphed and Tom decked the boy. Asked him if he wanted to climb up off the tile and take another. His sister made an attempt to calm both men down, but her efforts were doomed to fail because Bobbie knew where her loyalties lay. He understood now why his father always treated her so differently from him. Besides, she had always tried to defend her parents, and their behavior was indefensible. He wanted as little to do with her as he did with Daisy and Tom.

"And after he left?" Laurel asked Shem. "What then?"

"Then the story grows sketchy."

"How so?"

"Sometimes I couldn't tell what were the things Bobbie had actually done and what were the memories he was making up. But Reese knew some details, and between what Bobbie had told Reese years ago and what Reese recalled from the days they worked together at the magazine, you could get glimmers."

"Such as?"

Shem rested his head in his hands, his mind a wardrobe of Bobbie's reminiscences—some real, some imagined. He told

Laurel how Bobbie had claimed to have traveled, but the picaresque paralleled his father's in so many ways that at least some of it, Shem believed, had been fabricated. Ostensibly, Bobbie was looking for Jay's family. He insisted he had been to wintry upper-plains cities in Minnesota in search of his grandfather, and eventually to Saint Olaf, a Lutheran college in the southern part of the state where Bobbie had heard Jay had spent two weeks as a student and janitor. Like his father roughly three decades earlier, Bobbie said he had worked as a clam digger and salmon fisherman on Lake Superior. He'd tracked down the remnants of Camp Taylor, scrupulously avoiding his cousins and his grandparents who still lived in that corner of Kentucky. (He said that years later he had returned to Louisville to see what remained of the Fays, and there he had participated in—and chronicled—a freedom march an hour to the east in Frankfort.) As a young man, Bobbie had briefly considered taking his real father's name, but he wanted anonymity as he visited the states and towns that had even the smallest cameos in the story.

When the United States entered the Second World War, he enlisted. This was, after all, what his father had done. His real father, the one who was a captain, fought in the Argonne, and eventually would be given command of the divisional machine guns. The man who had raised him, on the other hand, had spent most of 1917 playing polo and most of 1918 romancing Daisy.

This entered Bobbie's mind when he signed up to join the Army. He felt he couldn't be a Gatsby given the preconceived notions people had of his father, but he no longer wanted to be a Buchanan. He no longer wanted to be the son of a patrician and bully. He no longer wanted to be Robert. On his way to the recruiting station on a main street in Fairmont, Minnesota, he passed a grocery store that had a window display with a poster of a fictional housewife named Betty Crocker and decided, almost on a lark, to commandeer the name. Why couldn't he be Bobbie Crocker instead of Robert Buchanan? Hadn't his own father changed his name, too?

Moreover, he realized that if he changed his name, it would be that much more difficult for them to follow him—though who, precisely, *they* were Shem couldn't say. Still, it wasn't merely nascent schizophrenia and paranoia that caused him to shed the skin of a Buchanan: It was also a desire to distance himself from the whole hollow, sullen, and morally insolvent little clan.

If the Army had any doubts about the mental health of a recruit whose moniker must have reminded them of a cake mix, they weren't sufficient to prevent them from allowing him to wade ashore at Omaha Beach in one of the very first waves behind the demolition teams. Bobbie would fight that year and into the next in France and Belgium and Germany, somehow escaping the war unscathed. Physically, anyway. He had an affair with a French woman who was in many ways even more scarred than he was, given how much of her family had died in the first German offensive in May 1940 and then fighting in North Africa in 1943. She lost two brothers, a cousin, and her father. He wanted to bring her back with him to the United States, but she wouldn't leave her family—the living and the dead.

And so he returned alone to America with his unit, and after his discharge got work in a photography store in lower Manhattan. He sold cameras and film, and in the evenings he took pictures himself. Sometimes he'd visit nightclubs, largely because he was living alone in a squalid apartment in Brooklyn and wanted to spend as little time there as possible. He didn't have a lot of money, but he spent what he had to keep his seat warm at places like the Blue Light, the Art Barn, and the Hatch. He drank heavily—which only intensified his isolation and exacerbated his mental illness—and found that he could drink on the house if he took the performers' pictures. He didn't have a studio, and so these were all shots of the musicians and singers while they were onstage or relaxing in their dressing rooms. They loved the photographs and (more important) their managers loved them, especially the candids, and in 1953 he took his first assigned photograph of Muddy Waters, a profile of the musician for Chess Records that showed the master with the head and tuning pegs of his bottleneck slide guitar resting against the tip of his elegant, aquiline nose.

Eventually, Bobbie's work came to the attention of editors at *Backbeat* and *Life,* and soon he had become friends with a young photo editor who called himself Reese.

From there, Laurel realized, she could almost tell the story herself. She didn't need Shem's help. He was merely corroborating her suspicions and the details she'd already gleaned: Bobbie's mental equilibrium had never been one of his cardinal strengths, and his instability and schizophrenia were amplified by the alcohol. He grew less dependable. Over the next decade, he would make some deadlines and miss others. He was immensely talented, which only made working with him that much more frustrating. There were seasons in the 1960s when Bobbie would vanish off the radar screen so completely and for so long that Reese would finally conclude that this time Bobbie had died. Usually when he reappeared, Reese would insist that Bobbie find a place where he could dry out once and for all. Shem guessed that Bobbie probably had been hospitalized during some of those disappearances. During others, he was in all likelihood trying to find his family. That meant scavenger hunts in odd little towns throughout the Midwest and Chicago, and brief conversations with the sons and daughters of people who may (or may not) have met the strange men his father knew and who passed, specterlike, through Jay Gatsby's life: Meyer Wolfsheim. Dan Cody. A boarder named Klipspringer.

Occasionally, Shem said, Bobbie had girlfriends. The photographer was, when he was sober, eccentric and talented and interesting-looking—though not traditionally handsome because the alcoholism had reddened his skin and his mental illness caused him to care less and less about hygiene. Still, there was a backup singer who never quite made it and a dancer who never quite made it and a secretary at *Life* magazine who actually would make it, joining Helen Gurley Brown to help edit *Cosmopolitan,* and each time Reese had high hopes that this was the woman who would provide Bobbie with the grounding he needed to settle down. It never happened.

"And his son?" Laurel asked. "Which of these women was the mother of his son? Do you know?"

"I don't know. I don't know much. I know she wasn't one of those more serious relationships he had. She did something in theater, I think—but not on the stage. A costumer, maybe. A seamstress. She died a long time ago."

"Do you know anything about the boy?"

"Bobbie didn't like to talk about him. It was one of those subjects—and Bobbie had a lot, of course—that were off-limits."

"But he said something."

"His son was homeless. I know that."

"Like Bobbie?"

"Worse. Did drugs. Didn't work much."

"Might he have been a carny?"

"Like in a circus?"

"Like at a county fair. At a midway."

"It's possible."

"And eventually he wound up in Vermont?"

"So it seems. Seven or eight years ago. But by the time Bobbie returned two years ago, he must have been long gone. Bobbie never mentioned going to see him."

"There were two men who . . ."

"Go on."

She shook her head; she couldn't. She was surprised that she had even begun to reveal what had happened to her seven years earlier, and guessed that she had spoken only because Shem was such a wondrous and unexpected resource, and because his face was so unthreatening and kind. Even the deep lines around his lips were patterned like the ridges on a scallop seashell. Still, she had to know if Bobbie's son was indeed one of the two men who had attacked her, and—if so—which one.

"Do you believe his son might be in jail?" she asked instead. "Jordie thought he might have been a criminal."

"If he was, he was no petty thief. Bobbie spent serious time on the street, too, remember. He wouldn't have cut his kid off for stealing a sandwich or because he had a substance-abuse problem. It woulda had to have been something much worse."

She gathered herself. Then: "Rape? Murder?"

"Oh, yeah."

"Is rape really a possibility? Or attempted rape?"

She felt him studying her intently, sympathetically, a grandfather's anxious gaze. "I guess anything's possible," he said after a moment.

"Did Reese know?"

"About the son? Or the possibility that the boy may have grown into a very bad person?"

"Either."

"He knew Bobbie had a son. But not much else. Don't forget, it's not as if Bobbie was a great father himself. He had his own devils, his own mental illness. He told Reese and me that the boy's mom had kept him away from the child when he was growing up. Didn't want Bobbie to have anything to do with him. Maybe this saddened Bobbie. Maybe he just wrote it off to one of the many conspiracies that surrounded him. Maybe he understood he couldn't help the boy. Who can say? Reese probably thought this was a wise course of action on the part of the mother. He knew Bobbie's limitations."

"But he liked Bobbie . . ."

"Very much. Oh, very much. Years ago—before you were born—he made it clear to Bobbie that if he ever needed anything, he shouldn't hesitate to ask. And so one day, decades later, Bobbie did. That would have been a little more than two years ago now," Shem said, his voice growing rueful. He explained that Bobbie had come to the Green Mountains in search of Reese. He was old and out of options. But he didn't find Reese right away. First, there was an incident of some sort in Burlington, and Bobbie was brought to the Vermont State Hospital. It was from there that he asked a member of the staff to track down his old editor; two months later, he was released into Reese's care. Bobbie's attention span had diminished to the point that he could barely sit through a half-hour sitcom on the TV Land channel, and Reese had the impression that Bobbie had been in and out of state hospitals in New York and Florida and North Dakota. But he no longer drank. And, properly medicated, he was the same good-natured, well-intentioned, not wholly presentable misfit he'd been thirty-five and forty years earlier.

"What are you gonna do with those pictures?" Shem asked when he had finished this part of the story. He was staring at the print of Julie Andrews as Guinevere and seemed startled by the image, even touched. "I saw this show. It was 1960. The Majestic Theater. I was a newlywed. Has Julie Andrews ever looked prettier?"

Laurel assured him that she hadn't. And she added that unlike most women her age, she actually knew the words to "The Simple Joys of Maidenhood." Then she told Shem of her boss's plan for a retrospective, the idea of giving Bobbie Crocker the show that he had never had in his life.

"Oh, I'll bet his sister will just love that," Shem said, a small, wary chuckle punctuating his remark. "She still living? Or did she pass, too?"

"She's still alive. But she tells people her brother died when he was a teenager—at least that's what she told me. She even dared me to fly to Chicago to see where he was buried. Do you think she knows about Bobbie's son?"

"I doubt it," he said. "You know, she won't be happy about your show. I got the impression from Bobbie that she was very loyal to her mother and father. Very loyal. Not just a daddy's girl and not just a mommy's girl. Both. Bobbie and Reese thought it was a stitch the way she worked so hard for so much of her life to rehabilitate her parents' reputation. She'll go to her grave telling anyone who will listen that all those stories about her mom and Jay Gatsby were a lot of malarkey—and all completely unprovable."

She laced her fingers together on the table before her and thought about this. "What are you suggesting? Do you think there's a picture in this pile that somehow proves Jay Gatsby was Bobbie's father?"

"Maybe not in this pile, but in some pile! Absolutely! That's what our paranoid schizophrenic was doing, don't you see? View those pictures like a crazy man's Post-it notes. Post-it notes in a code. Those pictures Bobbie kept with him? They're like a treasure map."

"Or an autobiography."

"Exactly! You remember that old program, *This Is Your Life*? Actually, you probably don't. It was way before your time. It was an old TV show. From the 1950s. Ralph Edwards was the host. Guests would be paraded out—Nat King Cole, maybe, or Gloria Swanson—and friends and family would come out one by one to surprise them. Well, Bobbie was sort of doing his own *This Is Your Life* with his pictures. He was taking photos of the Gatsby side. Reese told me it was like an obsession with Bobbie."

"Did Bobbie himself ever tell you he was doing this?"

"No. But I do know this: You know that day back in 1939 when Bobbie found the picture Jay gave his mom? The one where Jay's decked out as a soldier boy? Bobbie took it with him. Reese saw it many, many years ago, when he and Bobbie were still working at *Life*. Said Bobbie was still young enough that you could see the resemblance. It was unbelievable. After that, the photos Bobbie took are like the clues in a scavenger hunt. At least some are. You know, maybe you find the house. Then maybe you find the bureau. Then you open the drawer. And there it is—the picture."

"There what is? The photo of Jay from Camp Taylor?"

He put out his hands, palms up. "Oh, I don't know for sure what's in the drawer. I don't even know if it is a drawer. Or a bureau. Or a box. I was just using that as an example. But Bobbie told Reese and Reese told me that it's all in the pictures. That's why he took them with him, no matter where he went or how bad things got for him. They were the proof of who he was, the proof that his old man was that good old sport we've heard all about—better than the whole damn bunch on the other side of the cove."

"I have some snapshots Bobbie had with him at the end. There's one of Bobbie and his sister, and there's one of Jay beside a flashy car. But that photo you told me about—the one of Jay in his uniform. I don't have that one."

"Maybe the boy knows where it is," Shem said. "Or maybe the boy knows how to find it. Maybe that's the real reason why Bobbie came here seven years ago. To plant that final clue."

Laurel knew where the two men were serving their time. The more violent of the pair, the one who had murdered a schoolteacher in Montana, was in the maximum security compound of the state prison forty miles northwest of Butte. The other, a fellow with no previous criminal record, was still in Vermont, at the correctional facility just outside of Saint Albans. She hadn't anticipated ever seeing either of them again once they had been escorted from the courtroom after their sentencing, one to a prison in Vermont and one to be tried next for a murder in Montana.

"It's possible that his son has the picture, isn't it?" she said. "Or some proof of some kind?"

"Sure. But how do you even begin to find the boy? All you know is that he might have done something awful. You don't even know for certain he's in a jail somewhere."

Oh, but I do, she thought. *I just don't know whether the jail is in Montana or Vermont.*

PATIENT 29873

I brought up the book this morning. I expected enthusiasm, but patient was defensive and derisive instead. Eventually settled down. When I asked for elaboration, was told I didn't know what I was talking about.

At this point, the benefits of discussing the book outweigh the risks.

From the notes of Kenneth Pierce,
attending psychiatrist,
Vermont State Hospital,
Waterbury, Vermont

CHAPTER TWENTY-TWO

*W*HIT HAD BEEN EXHAUSTED when he'd had dinner with his aunt and uncle on Saturday night, but the serious paintball-induced pain was still a half day away. By Sunday morning, it had come in with the sweep of high tide. It wasn't, in all fairness, a searing, debilitating, white-lights-dancing-against-his-eyelids sort of pain. But his day in the paintball woods had left him limping gingerly around his apartment. There was a steady throb in his lower back, his calves were almost too sore to stretch, and he felt a sharp dagger slicing into his side whenever he tried to breathe deeply. He wondered if he had cracked a rib. Still, it was a beautiful morning today and he had an evening in the library before him, and so about twelve-thirty he decided he would hoist his bike onto the top of his slightly battered Subaru (battered because his mother was a careless driver, oblivious to curbs and parking meters and great cement columns in parking garages, and the vehicle had been hers before she had passed it along to her son) and drive out to Underhill. He hadn't gotten there the previous weekend as he'd hoped, and so he figured he might as well head out there today. He guessed the most difficult part would be lifting his bike onto and off of the car's roof rack. But the frame was so light he figured even that should be manageable.

He hadn't been out to Underhill since early August, perhaps a month after he'd moved into this house. That day he'd spent time in the state park and then ridden for a while on the logging trails in the nearby woods. He liked the way a ride there was peppered with long stretches beneath a vaguely claustrophobic canopy of leaves, followed by picture-postcard-like vistas of Mount Mansfield and Camels' Hump.

Tentatively, he tugged his bike shorts over the grapefruit-size black-and-purple bruise on his hip, and then held his breath and closed his eyes as he pulled a tight long-sleeved jersey over his chest. Reflexively, he moaned aloud. He wondered briefly if this ride really was such a good idea, but he couldn't imagine spending a day like this inside. Not with seriously cold weather barely a month or two in the distance.

As he was passing Laurel and Talia's front door, he paused. He heard music inside and decided to knock. He wanted to ask Laurel about yesterday, inquire why she hadn't joined them for paintball. Talia answered, and it didn't appear she had been up very long. He guessed she had walked the pony that their neighbor Gwen claimed was a dog and then gone back to bed for a couple of hours, because her hair was wild with sleep and she was wearing a pair of pink-and-black polka-dot pajama bottoms with the drawstring so loose that they hung far—erotically far, hip bone low far, a wisp of mons pubis far—below her waist and a silk camisole that neither matched her pajama bottoms nor hid the vast majority of her breasts. He felt far more guilty than aroused, however, because in the long strip of flesh between the bottom of her top and the top of her bottom he saw a machine-gun line of welts across her abdomen. Even her navel looked bruised.

"Well," she said, her voice thick and tired and in desperate need of a drink of water, "if it isn't Sergeant York."

He motioned toward her stomach. "I think I know when that happened. I have a bad feeling I even know who did it. It was when you came over the top of that rusty jeep and didn't know I was there, right?"

She looked down. "Usually, I have a silver flower in my belly button. A little Celtic charm. It dangles. It's very lovely. If I hadn't had the foresight to take it out before we played, you probably would have shot it through my intestines."

"I'm really sorry. I guess I got a little out of control."

"Are you serious? You can't be serious. Yesterday was the most fun I have had in a very long time. It was fabulous. You were fabulous. *I* was fabulous."

"You make it sound like sex."

She shook her head. "Oh, as I told Laurel, paintball is better than sex. At least most sex. I am so glad you were there. Really, Whit, thank you."

"I had fun, too. Is Laurel home?"

"Nope. Left this morning at the crack of dawn. Enter the crib and I'll tell you the little I know."

He hadn't thought about the possibility that only Talia might be here, and he realized he was looking at a lengthy detour. But he did want to know what had happened to Laurel, and suddenly he liked the idea of commiserating with another grown-up who had spent the previous day mercilessly abusing her body.

"You can't possibly feel up to a bike ride," she said, motioning him inside, waving her arm ironically as if she were fanning it over a wall of game-show prizes. "If you do . . .

then you're a bloody superman. I can barely walk. Really, come in."

The place was a mess: There were blue jeans and tops and bras and thongs (or at least very small bikini panties) wadded up on the couch and the coffee table, and the floor was awash in CD cases and fashion magazines and books, some of which had titles like *The Powerfully Contagious Christian* and *Teen Saviors.*

"So, I guess you just got up?" he asked, wondering for a moment where he should sit. He wasn't sure if he was supposed to move her clothing and her lingerie or sit on top of it. Quickly, however, she scooted in front of him and gathered her underwear and her jeans into a ball and heaved them through the door to her bedroom so he had a place to sit down.

"Just got up? Are you crazy? I just got back from church! I was about to go back to bed, if you want to know the truth. But, no, I suck it up, thank you very much, and get my butt to church every Sunday morning. I am—and this does horrify some people, I guess—a role model. At the moment, of course, I might be a role model who looks like she just spent the night at some nightmarish frat party. But I was in bed last night with the lights out by ten. And this morning I was cleaning and organizing before church. Gwen's dog sort of trashed our place yesterday, and when I was tidying up I decided to do some serious organizing. Even clean out my drawers. Hence, the . . . the chaos. You want some coffee?"

"No, I'm good."

She nodded. "Right answer. It would mean getting dressed and going to Starbucks." She plopped herself down on the couch beside him.

"So, did you see Laurel before you crashed?" he asked.

"I did. And it wasn't pretty."

"Excuse me?"

"Your crush is losing her shit."

"Laurel is not my crush!"

She ducked her chin and looked at him over the tops of her eyes, a glimpse that conveyed in an instant her incredulity. "You have serious longing issues for that girl—and, I might add, ones with little chance of fruition given that she seems to have an older-man jones."

"What do you mean she's losing her shit?" he asked, picking up one of her books about Christians and teens off the floor. "Did you find out why she didn't play paintball with us?"

"Yup. It was those pictures. The ones some old BEDS client left behind at the Hotel New England. She spent yesterday—most of it, anyway—in the darkroom. Can you believe it? She is so obsessed with those loopy old photos that she completely forgot she was supposed to be running around the woods with my youth group. With me! She's actually forgotten about me totally lately. I must confess, I didn't think such a thing was possible, and I am more than a little bent out of shape. But more than that, I am worried about her."

She recounted for him the way Laurel had presumed their apartment had been ransacked yesterday, and her fear that someone was after the old homeless man's pictures. She told him how her friend had been avoiding her since she had returned from Long Island, and how Laurel's life seemed, suddenly, to be revolving around this strange dead man's work. When she was finished, she leaned her head against the back of the couch, closed her eyes, and said almost plaintively, "Really. I don't know what to make of this or who I should call. Her boss, maybe? The minister at my church? What would you do?"

He wondered if she was, perhaps, overreacting. "Isn't this just a new hobby? Something she's jazzed about because it's

all fresh? Obviously, I don't know a whole lot about her life
or how she spends her time. She's from Long Island, she
works at BEDS, she's dating an older guy from the newspaper. She likes to swim in the morning. She used to bike.
That's about it. But she doesn't seem to have a whole lot
going on in her life, does she? So why shouldn't she work on
those photos? It sounds like all they're really keeping her
from is . . . well, you."

He hoped this last remark had sounded like a good-
natured joke, but given the speed with which that sleepy hand
of hers had backhanded him on the chest—a spring-loaded
paddle, it felt like—he wasn't so sure.

"Not everything is about me," she said.

"No?"

"No. There is actually quite a lot going on in our Laurel's
life—or, at least, in her head. You don't know what the girl
has been through. Almost no one does."

Her tone was uncharacteristically wistful, and it made him
wonder: "Does this have anything to do with the fact she was
nearly raped once?"

"Nearly?"

"Yeah, I guess. The other day Gwen said something to me
that implied Laurel had almost been raped. I don't know
anything more than that. I don't know where or when or the
circumstances. I figured it was none of my business and I
didn't want to pry."

She raised her head from the couch and turned toward
him. "It wasn't almost."

"Oh, shit."

"And it wasn't just rape. They—"

"They?"

"There were two of them. You want to know about Laurel?

You want to know why she doesn't bike anymore and why I worry? Okay, Captain Lycra, here's the four-one-one on Miss Laurel Estabrook," she said. Then, her eyes never wavering from his, Talia told him precisely what had happened to her friend up in Underhill, and why she was worried now.

CHAPTER TWENTY-THREE

FTER SHEM HAD LEFT, Laurel went through the photos one last time in the diner, trying to piece them together in a linear fashion. Not chronologically. She'd already done that. This time she was seeing if she could, as Shem had suggested, form a treasure map. She winnowed out the celebrities—pushing aside the likes of Chuck Berry and Robert Frost and Julie Andrews—and then she made two piles, one of places and one of things, and she wrote down on a yellow legal pad what was in each.

Places

The Brooklyn Bridge
Plaza Hotel
Washington Square
Train station, West Egg
Manhattan cityscapes
Chrysler building
New York Philharmonic
Greenwich Village
Street football underneath Hebrew National billboard

World's Fair (including the Unisphere)
Brownstones (in Brooklyn?)
Mustang in front of Marshfield estate
Midwestern arts-and-crafts house (Wright?)
Unknown jazz club (a series)
Central Park
World Trade Towers
Wall Street
Main Street, West Egg
Valley of Ashes office park (not real name)
East Egg train platform
East Egg shoreline
West Egg shoreline
My old swim club (Gatsby's old house)
Underhill dirt road scenes (two with a girl on a bike)
Stowe church
Waterfall
Mount Mansfield ski trails (in summer)

Things

Hair dryers
Autos (many)
Cigarettes (in ashtrays, on tables, close-ups in people's mouths)
More autos (a half dozen)
IBM typewriter (three)
Mustang in front of Marshfield estate
Fifth Avenue bus
Lava lamps

Love beads and peace medallions
Art deco jewelry box
Crab apple tree (a few prints, one with a little
pyramid of apples beside it)
Dog by bakery

There were certain images that Laurel assumed were value-less in this quest: the cigarettes, the lava lamps, the cars. The hair dryers. Likewise, she knew that other photographs had been commissioned assignments, such as the Unisphere. The ones that were most puzzling to her were the pictures of Vermont and the pictures of her that were taken just before her life would be altered forever: photographs Bobbie had snapped on that very Sunday in Underhill, perhaps, or on one of the Sundays that had preceded that awful day. Were those images relevant to her search? Was she actually a clue herself in Bobbie's treasure map? Or was it just an odd coin-cidence that her path and Bobbie's had crossed years before they would formally meet, and that they would cross in that particular month—perhaps on that very Sunday afternoon? Were the photographs of a bicyclist on a dirt road or of a church up in Stowe a part of the pictorial labyrinth he was constructing, or were they irrelevant? After all, there were no indications that either Gatsby or the Buchanans had ever set foot in Vermont.

And what of that house Laurel had presumed was some-where in the Midwest? Was it in Chicago, where she knew Tom Buchanan's family was from? Or was it in Saint Paul, where Howard Mason had said that Bobbie might have tracked down a grandfather? For all Laurel knew, the house with its gently pitched roofs and wide boxlike floors—a second floor that jutted out like a jaw above the first—might very well exist in East or West Egg, Long Island. Or it might have belonged to one of those Louisville cousins.

The prints that Laurel thought had the greatest potential were the ones that most obviously hinted at a part of Bobbie's life. Carefully, she drew a line through the images that she was confident were not clues to his parentage, and decided that what remained was manageable. Doable. She could see the elements of a map, just as Shem had suggested. She would simply tell Katherine that she needed some time off from work—a week, maybe two. Tonight she would make prints from the last of the negatives, and perhaps as soon as tomorrow or Tuesday she would start to use up her vacation days and go . . .

Well, she might have to begin with a prison in northern Vermont. And, if that inmate wasn't Bobbie's son, then one in Montana. Because although the project might be doable, it wasn't going to be easy. There were the trace elements of a map, perhaps, but which were the clues and which were merely the aimless photos (or, perhaps, even the red herrings) taken by a schizophrenic who drank too much she couldn't decide. She had landmarks in East and West Egg: the houses and train platforms and the manicured lengths of beach. Her country club—Gatsby's estate. She had an office park that had risen from the Valley of Ashes. She had the Plaza, the hotel where Bobbie's own mother had been asked to choose between her husband and her lover, and been unable. She had an art deco jewelry box with scalloped mirrors along the lid. Surely there was a chance that the box held Jay's wartime portrait—and perhaps something more. A letter. A locket. A ring with an engraving. But how did one begin to find a box in any of these structures? Suppose she found the arts-and-crafts house? What then? Ask the owner if she could dig up the basement? Ransack the floorboards in the attic? Likewise, what could she do at her old country club? Ask to rummage around the library—the one that had once dazzled guests simply because it happened to have books that were real?

Nevertheless, she felt confident now that no one could possibly question what she knew was true: not David, not Katherine, not Talia. No one ever again would question her sanity.

When Serena rejoined her in the booth, Laurel pushed the portfolio case toward her, reminding her to tell no one she had it. As soon as Laurel had finished speaking, however, she could see by the look on Serena's face that she had been wrong, completely wrong, a moment earlier: People were still going to doubt her. It was clear what the woman was thinking, and Laurel knew more or less what her friend was going to say before Serena had even opened her mouth.

"Laurel, you know there is nothing I wouldn't do for you . . . and I will hang on to these for you. I will. It's fine. But honestly, girl, do you really believe for a second that someone is going to try to steal these pictures from you?"

"Yes. And I don't believe it. I know it."

"But—"

"You think I'm crazy."

"No, of course I don't. But I do think you may be, I don't know, overreacting."

Laurel repeated the word. It was long. A euphemism for misbehavior. For inappropriate behavior. "Well, then," she asked. "What would you do? What would you have me do?"

"Come on, Laurel, don't take that tone with me. I'm just . . ."

"Just what? Worried?"

"No. Okay, yes. Worried. I'm worried."

"Then tell me. What would you do?"

"Well, for starters I wouldn't get so freaked out," Serena said, but after that opening Laurel really didn't pay much attention to the rest of her speech. Serena was sweet and she was well intentioned, and Laurel knew now that she couldn't trust her. Her friend didn't realize the importance of the images she had with her. As soon as Leckbruge or some minion appeared, Serena would turn them over to him. The whole portfolio case. Of course it would be an act of naïveté on her part, not betrayal. But it would have precisely the same effect. The pictures—and all of her work and Bobbie's—would be gone.

And so Laurel thanked her for her time and her conversation, and when she left she took the portfolio case with her. She was polite. So polite that Serena walked her to the diner's front door and assumed, when they parted, that Laurel was going to heed her advice and relax.

SHE WOULDN'T HAVE been able to tell what it was from the negative. At least not for sure. It only started to become clear on the contact sheet.

It was when she first printed the photograph Sunday night, yet another resin-coated print, that the image became unmistakable in the orange light of the darkroom. She studied it for a long moment in the chemical bath, not hypnotized but absorbed. Incapable of looking away.

She thought of something Shem Wolfe had said to her that afternoon about Bobbie, and she felt her face flush:

He had his own devils.

Shem had been referring to Bobbie's mental illness, but the word *devil* came back to her now—along with the other words that had dogged her for years. Cunt. Twat. Pussy. Gash. Fish cunt. Slut cunt. Dead cunt. She saw in the calm waters of the darkroom tray the tattoo. Here was the picture Bobbie had told Paco Hidalgo he'd taken. What she had presumed all these years had been a mere human skull—albeit one with fangs—she saw now was in actuality a tattoo of the devil: skull-like, yes, but it had ears. And it was breathing. Hence the smoke.

And Bobbie Crocker had known this man and photo-graphed this image: a devil amid stubble, an earlobe hover-ing above it like a planet. He was either Bobbie's son or a friend of Bobbie's son.

Because, apparently, even rapists had friends. Murderers, too.

This was the devil who had frightened Bobbie Crocker: One of the very men who had tried to rape her. And then driven a van in reverse to try to kill her.

SHE WAS WEAK when she finished up in the darkroom, but unless she went downtown into Burlington the only places that were going to be open this late on a Sunday night were the fast-food restaurants and the doughnut shops on the neon-lit strip just east of the campus. It was after eleven.

She hadn't been home since early that morning. It hadn't even crossed her mind to stop by her apartment after she had left Serena, because she'd wanted to go straight to the darkroom.

Now she drove to the old Victorian and found a parking spot she could have taken right in front of the building, but—almost reflexively—she continued past it. She had noticed there were lights on both in her apartment and in Whit's, and it was evident that her housemates were awake. This was unfortunate: She didn't want Talia or Whit to hear her arrive because she didn't want to have to speak to either of them. And so she parked instead at the far end of the block, near the corner. Her plan was to wait an hour or two, until they had both gone to sleep. Then she would find the keys to the house's entrance and her own apartment, and have them ready in her fingers well before she reached the front walkway. She would take off her clogs and hold them in her hands, too, so she wouldn't make any noise as she approached the door or tiptoed up the stairway to Talia's and her corner of the house.

And, just in case, she told herself that she would undress and climb into bed in the dark. Wouldn't even turn on the living room light. And did she really need to eat a couple of crackers? Probably not.

None of this meticulous planning would end up mattering, however, because she fell asleep in the front seat of her car. She awoke once, a little before 3 a.m., her back and neck throbbing—was this what some of her clients experienced, she wondered, or did they have the common sense, at least, to crawl into the backseat to doze?—and considered going inside. She had just seen in a dream an Underhill forest alive with flying things: birds and insects and swirling leaves. The birds had the heads of small devils—devil skulls, really, the devil from the tattoo—and she was their prey. She believed that she was trying to walk her bicycle through the tumult, though she didn't recall if there had been a path on which she might ever have been riding. Eventually, she thought, she had been swamped by the swirling creatures. They had attacked her in all the places where she had been hurt by Bobbie Crocker's son and his partner seven years earlier, and when she awoke there was an ache—and this, she concluded, was a phantom pain, because why would she experience any discomfort there from a nap in the night in her car?—on the left side of her chest.

Still, she could not bring herself to open the car door and return to her apartment. The dream had frightened her almost to the point of immobility, brought her to the verge of paralysis. And there was so much she wanted to do—*so much she had to do*—that she was too agitated to move. Emily Young was finally back from the Caribbean and she needed to meet with her, and then she needed to visit the prison in Saint Albans. And that would demand complex arrangements with the superintendent at the correctional facility, the inmate's therapist, and the state's Department of Crime Victim Services. But at the same time she was tired, more tired than she could ever recall being in her life. Suddenly, much to her own surprise, her eyes were watering. She was crying. She heard small sobs and hiccups and a choking little whistle inside her head that reminded her of the shrill sound the brakes had made on her bike years ago, and she didn't stop crying until she had fallen back to sleep behind the wheel.

When she opened her eyes next, the sun was starting to rise, and she felt a twinge and roll in her stomach. For a moment, she couldn't recall when she had last eaten. She turned around to make sure the portfolio case was still in the backseat of the car, where she had placed it the night before when she had finished up in the darkroom. It was. On the sidewalk she heard the brooding scuff of heavy work boots. She looked to her left as a man passed within two or three feet of the glass, a great bearded hulk in a parka. It was a heavier jacket than was really necessary this time of the year, unless it was the only jacket you owned. She noticed the man's pants were tattered at the cuffs and sliced open at the knees. She decided the fellow wasn't homeless, not yet, but there was something about him—his clothes, his posture, his pace—that made her fear that if he didn't get help he might be soon.

She wondered what it would really be like when she ventured north to the prison and saw one of her assailants. She thought she could find the will at the very least to visit Saint Albans, because there she would be meeting with an inmate who had merely—and as the word formed in her mind she winced and felt another sharp pain ripple across her breast—attempted to rape her. He was a horrible man, but at least he had never murdered anyone himself. But what if Bobbie's son had been the one who had slashed open the veins of that woman out West, using a length of barbed wire to leave her tied to a fence as her blood drained into the earth from her wrists? Would she be able to see him again in the flesh? Sit across a table from him? What would she say? Would it even be worth the long trip to Butte?

And then, as she began to envision the confrontation—she knew the technical term for what she was proposing was a clarification hearing—she started to doubt the accuracy of her own memories: What really had occurred on that dirt road in Underhill? She told herself to take this a step at a time—as she had for a week now. To move quickly but carefully. And her next step at this point was Emily Young. And then the prisoner in Vermont. That was all. A tattoo of barbed wire or a tattoo of a devil: Did it really matter? With any luck, she would never have to travel to Montana, anyway.

She decided that if she had any chance of changing her clothes before work, this was it. A shower would be out of the question because that would surely wake Talia. Breakfast, too. She'd have to stop by the bakery on the way into BEDS. But she could, if nothing else, wipe a cotton ball with Clinique over her face and run a brush through her hair. Rudimentary hygiene was one of the first things to go when you lived on the street, and she had to remind herself that—even if the people around her thought otherwise—it wasn't she who was the delusional paranoid in this case.

CHAPTER TWENTY-FOUR

SHE MET WITH Emily Young before eight o'clock Monday morning, as the woman who had been Bobbie Crocker's caseworker was beginning to dig through the small avalanche of paperwork that had smothered a sizable part of her desk while she had been on vacation. Laurel thought she had never seen the woman look so good. So healthy. Emily had once been a vigorous spinner and Nautilus junkie, but a bad back had dramatically curtailed her time at the gym. The result was a woman nearing forty with a round, pert face and wide eyes atop a body that in the last half decade had gone a little soft. The Caribbean cruise, however, had worked wonders. Emily looked like she'd lost weight, she was tan, and she was wearing a cheerful print dress covered with neon-blue irises, the likes of which seldom was seen around BEDS.

"Most of the people on the boat were eating like there was no tomorrow," she said to Laurel as she thumbed through a manila folder with paperwork on Bobbie Crocker. For a moment, Laurel feared it was the folder from the filing cabinet she'd perused the other day and that there wouldn't be any information in it that she hadn't already seen, but then she saw papers she didn't recognize. "But my whole outlook changed on our first day out. I got a massage. And the masseur was this young guy from Argentina who was extremely hot. Before I knew it, I wasn't eating—for him!—and he was working on me each afternoon. And so that was my vacation. I lived on fresh fruit and vegetables, swam and lay in the sun, and I had a handsome—no, he was way beyond handsome, he was beautiful—masseur working on my back and my legs for two hours a day. You do the math."

"How do you feel now that you're back on dry land?"

Emily shrugged. "I have to get back on that boat." Then: "Let's see, when our Mr. Crocker was in the hospital he was on risperidone. And Celexa. It looks like there was also some discussion of clozapine, but then they decided he was too old. They were probably worried about the side effects: screwing up his white blood cell count."

Laurel nodded. She knew that Celexa was an antidepressant and risperidone was an antipsychotic.

"Clearly, Bobbie wound up in the hospital in the first place because he had some sort of event," Emily continued. "He had to have done something that suggested he was either dangerous to himself or to others."

"You knew Bobbie," Laurel said, surprised by the defensive, protective tone in her voice. "I've talked to a lot of his friends. One person said there may have been an incident of some kind in Burlington. But, other than that, I haven't heard anything that would make me think he was violent."

"Not violent. But delusional. Off his meds, he had episodes. We both know that. Now, my sense with Bobbie is that he was much more likely to be a danger to himself than to someone around him. Thank God he was homeless in August. Can you imagine if he'd had to fend for himself on the streets in December or January? Guy that old? He would have frozen to death. And we both know that happens." She flipped a piece of paper and then surprised Laurel by leaning forward and exclaiming, "Ah-ha! He was arrested for theft of services. A restaurant where he ate—and ate—and then didn't pay. It wasn't a big deal. We're talking fifteen dollars and change. But there were also complaints against him for panhandling and unlawful trespass. The trespasses may have gotten a little nasty: Bobbie was pretty agitated at some camera store, where he thought they had stolen some pictures of his he couldn't find. Sounds like he and the owner got into a screaming match. And, let's see, here's another complaint. This one's from a grocery store: He was hanging out in the produce section, eating, and wouldn't leave. Now, this is all petty stuff. The actual point was to get him a psychiatric evaluation."

"But he was never violent, right—other than yelling at the owner of a camera store?"

"Yup. And the owner seems to have yelled back," said Emily. "So, have you spoken to the crowd at the Hotel New England?"

"Pete and his pals? Yes. But I also spent part of yesterday in Bartlett. There I met Jordie Baker. I met a schoolteacher and a minister who knew Bobbie. And right here in Burlington, I met Shem Wolfe. And, of course, I've spoken to Serena Sargent. You might remember Serena. She brought Bobbie to us. Five years ago she was a client herself."

"You're good. Even I don't know who some of those people are. Who's Jordie? Who's Shem?"

Laurel told her how Jordie's aunt had known Bobbie's mother, and how Shem had been friends with Bobbie and his editor. She explained how Bobbie's devil might actually have been a tattoo—though she did not reveal on whose neck the devil resided. Nonetheless, she had the sense that Emily was impressed with her detective work.

"Well, then, what do you need to know from me?" Emily asked when she had finished. Then, almost abruptly, she added, "God, and you think I've lost weight? What the heck is going on with you? Have you been sick?"

Laurel was taken aback: She thought she looked fine after brushing her hair and applying a coat of lipstick. "No," she said simply. "I've just been busy."

"Don't be offended. We're friends, and I was just . . . just wondering. Katherine told me last night on the phone that you had jumped into Bobbie's pictures with real gusto, and—"

"You and Katherine were talking about me?"

"Whoa, it wasn't like that. I knew she had her monthly breakfast with the development committee this morning and so she wouldn't be here when I got in. And so I called her to find out what was going on back at the ranch. I figured I should get a sense of what chaos awaited me on my triumphant return. That's all. Anyway, she happened to mention—and, truly, it was an aside to everything else we were talking about—that you were a little preoccupied—"

"Preoccupied?"

"My word, I'm sure—not hers. She said you were working really hard on Bobbie's photos, that's all. She said you were trying to put together a few bits and pieces about his life."

Laurel could tell that Katherine had told her more. Implied more. Katherine had probably said that her brittle young protégée was obsessed—yes, *obsessed*—with the old photographer and his real identity.

"You don't need to worry about me," she told Emily. "I'm fine."

"Okay, then. No offense intended. Ask away: What don't you know about Bobbie Crocker that I could possibly tell you? I have a feeling you know considerably more about the

Hotel New England's favorite eccentric than I do, but fire away."

"What do you know about his son?"

"His son? I didn't even know he had a son!"

"How about his parents?"

"Next to nothing," said Emily.

"Next to nothing? Or nothing?"

"Nothing."

"His sister?"

"He never said a word to me about her."

"Did he ever say anything about his childhood?"

"I'm sure he did. And I'm sure I can't remember."

"I understand you took a peek at the photos before you passed them on to Katherine. Did you notice anything interesting?"

"The ones Bobbie took? I looked at them briefly. I flipped through them. I thought they were pretty good. But, honestly, you'd know better than I. Were they?"

"Yes. Bobbie was talented."

"And so you'll put together a show?"

"Eventually," Laurel answered. "Did he mention any friends? Any extended family? Any surprising people in his life?"

"Other than the people whose pictures he took?"

"That's right."

Emily sat back in her chair and wrapped her fingers together across her tummy. Irises peeked out from behind her thumbs. "Okay, I'm thinking." After a long moment, she said, "Once, when we were downstairs at the day station together, just hanging around for a few minutes, a man came in. Bobbie didn't need the day station by then, he was all set at the New England. But, you know, we quickly became like his alma mater. Anyway, a guy comes into the day station, and while Bobbie is getting out the Wonder Bread and making him a peanut-butter-and-jelly sandwich, it comes out that the guy had done jail time."

"Where?"

"Vermont."

"Which facility?"

"Saint Albans, I think. But it might have been Chittenden County."

"How long had he been out?"

"Six months. Maybe eight. He didn't want to make a mistake and go back. And Bobbie asked him if he knew someone there. In prison."

"What was the inmate's name?"

"I don't remember. But that doesn't matter; that's not the interesting part. What is, is this: Whatever the guy's name was, this new client at the shelter had known him. He had real contempt for him because this other prisoner had been a sex offender. But he was also scared of him. Really scared. And so was Bobbie. And so I asked Bobbie how he'd met this character, the one who was still in jail. After all, Bobbie had never done any time, at least none that I knew of. And so it had to have been on the outside. But Bobbie wouldn't tell me. Once he had been assured that the man was still behind bars, he wouldn't hear another word about him."

Laurel knew the names of the men who had tried to rape her. How could she forget? The bodybuilder from Montana was Russell Richard Hagen. The drifter was Dan Corbett. No middle initial. Wouldn't abide the name Daniel.

"Was the inmate named Russell?" she asked Emily.

"No."

"Richard?"

"Nope."

"Dan?"

"You know, that rings a bell," Emily answered. "What, did Bobbie ever tell you something about this person?"

"He did," Laurel lied. "It's just one of those sad coincidences. I think this Dan fellow may have tried to bully him once. On Church Street." She didn't want her associate to know that her search was leading her back to the assault up in Underhill. Emily would worry. They all would. And so Laurel thanked her, told her she understood how much paperwork she had to pile through after her lengthy vacation, and returned to her office. She was supposed to meet with a fellow from the Veterans Affairs group who worked with homeless veterans about new VA services, and she wanted to have a list of clients handy who might benefit. And then she needed to craft a memo for Katherine telling her that—and this lie came to her instantly, too—her mother was hospitalized and she'd have to go home to Long Island for a couple of days. She would tell Katherine that she'd call her from the road with the details and her boss needn't worry. Her mother would be fine. And she would be fine.

And if Katherine should try to reach her at her mother's? She'd get only an answering machine, because her mother was now at a cooking school near Siena. She was, literally, on the other side of the world.

But she wanted the memo to be on Katherine's desk when the woman returned from her meeting. She didn't want to have to explain her sudden departure in person.

SHE WAS NOT GOING to Long Island, of course. At least not yet. First, she was going to see the Crime Victim Services department in another part of the state and then meet with the superintendent of the prison in Saint Albans. She was going to set up her clarification hearing with inmate Dan Corbett. And she wanted to meet with him as soon as possible.

She left BEDS through the back entrance, rather than through the front door. Her meeting with the VA staffer had lasted till nine-thirty, and by the time she had written a memo to Katherine that struck the right chord—one that would not panic the director, yet would suggest there had been a need for a certain urgency—it was nearly ten. Katherine would be back any moment, and Laurel didn't want to run into her in the lobby or on the main stairway.

The sun was high in the sky now, unlike when she had left her apartment hours earlier. She'd been careful to escape before Talia had awakened, and she was especially glad now: It would make it easier for her to disappear. To remain patient and focused, unencumbered by her roommate's doubts, while she did the hard work looming before her. She would tell Talia—she would *write* Talia—precisely what she had told Katherine. What she would tell David. She was back home in West Egg.

Shame on them. Shame on them all.

Doubting her. Doubting Bobbie.

All along, she had presumed that poor Bobbie Crocker was scared of his sister, when—the truth was—he was scared of his son.

CHAPTER TWENTY-FIVE

*P*AMELA MARSHFIELD spent most of Monday morning on her living room sofa, feeling older than she ever had in her life. There was an ache in the upper part of her spine, and she wouldn't have been surprised if her physician told her at some point in the coming winter—after, no doubt, an almost killing battery of modern tests—that it was cancer. She was finding herself uncharacteristically short of breath. And her hip—replaced fifteen years ago—was throbbing. In addition, nothing had tasted very good at breakfast. The truth was, nothing had had any taste at all.

Across from her in one of the metallic gold easy chairs that her mother had picked out seventy-five years ago—the chrome siding meticulously restored not once but twice since then—sat Darling Fay, eldest daughter of Reginald Fay of Louisville. Reginald was her cousin, long deceased. His father had been Daisy's older brother. Darling, like most of the Buchanans and the Fays, was remarkably well preserved for a sixty-two-year-old, in part because of those fabulous genes, in part because she'd never married or had children, and in part because twice a year she flew to Manhattan so a cosmetic surgeon could shoot her face full of Restylane. This was why she was in New York now. This morning she was

making what Pamela understood was an onerous and obligatory journey to the tip of Long Island to see her father's dod-
dering cousin, but if Darling wanted to come all the way out
here Pamela wasn't about to stop her. The two women were
sipping tea, though only Darling was enjoying it.

"I'm surprised your lawyer didn't suggest you handle it in a
less antagonistic fashion," she said to Pamela, a hint of a
frown clouding her face. She was wearing a floral skirt with
rickrack trim that Pamela presumed was by Kay Unger, and a
casual, pistachio-colored jacket that offered (in Pamela's
opinion) far more cleavage than was appropriate.

For a moment, Pamela wished that she hadn't opened up to
Darling, hadn't told this young—well, younger, anyway—
woman that her brother had died. She regretted telling her
about the reemergence of Robert's work and his deluded,
malicious attempts to expose their family secrets. She wasn't
sure why she had, except, perhaps, because she was old and
tired and she was fishing for comfort. Trawling for reassur-
ance. And, in this case, wasting her time. She was going to
receive no sympathy from Darling. This cousin once removed
had been born after Robert had run off, and viewed him as
only a deranged family shadow.

"What would you consider a less antagonistic fashion?"
Pamela asked her finally.

Darling gently placed her teacup on the coffee table
between them. "Your father could be a rather blunt instrument."

"Oh, I know."

"But he also knew precisely when to open his wallet. When
a donation to the right charity at the right time might make
all the difference."

"Such as after the accident."

"Precisely." No one among the Fays and the Buchanans

knew the details, but it was understood that in 1922 and again in 1925 Tom Buchanan had made generous philanthropic gifts to a variety of police departments on Long Island as well as serious campaign contributions to the neighboring district attorneys. It had been his way of ensuring that no one carefully investigated who had really been driving when Myrtle Wilson was killed, or seriously investigated the allegations that surfaced three years later.

"And you're suggesting that I should be opening my purse now?" Pamela asked.

"I wouldn't be so presumptuous as to tell you what you should do. You know that. I was simply wondering aloud why your lawyer didn't encourage you to make a donation to that woman's little homeless group. COTS."

"BEDS."

Darling waved her hand in the air as if brushing a fly away from her face. "Whatever! It's just a thought. It is, I'd guess, what your father would have done."

"As blunt as he was."

"Yes. As blunt as he was."

"And you believe this group will give me back Robert's work if I give them some money."

"They might. At this point, what else can you do? What other choices do you have? You want to get the photographs back, don't you?"

"I *have* to get the photographs back. I will not allow their exposure to demonize my mother again. There are two sides to every story, and I will not have Gatz deified and my mother vilified. That's all there is to it."

"Then buy them. Just open your wallet and buy them."

Initially, the idea seemed tawdry to her, and not a little pathetic. Still, she guessed Darling was correct: She hadn't a choice. She wasn't going to live forever. For all she knew, she wouldn't live till the end of the day. And if she wanted to get her brother's malignant, lunatic work quashed once and for all—she could already see in her mind the carcinogenic bonfire she would have on her beach once the photographs were all in her possession—she was going to have to pay someone. The reality was that the malodorous homeless who bunked at the shelter could actually use her money. They needed it. The lawyers in T. J. Leckbruge's firm did not. They would always do quite well, thank you very much, without it. They might miss the legal fees they would have generated obtaining her brother's photographs, but soon enough she was going to die, and the firm would make a tidy sum then when it settled her estate.

She sighed and smiled at Darling. She resolved that as soon as this woman left, she would make the appropriate phone calls. She would instruct her attorney to make a suitable overture to the homeless shelter in Vermont. Offer, in essence, whatever it took to have every snapshot, every negative, every print returned to her.

CHAPTER TWENTY-SIX

*D*AVID'S THROAT went a little dry when he read the note Laurel had left for him at the newspaper's front desk.

My sister called: Our mother went to the hospital last night. She had an appendectomy, but they're doing more tests to see if something else might be wrong. My aunt is with her now, but I can tell she's a little worried, and so I've gone to Long Island for a couple of days to check in. I'll call tonight.

Please tell Marissa I'm sorry I won't be taking her headshot this afternoon. But she's a beautiful girl with a voice like a lark, and it doesn't take a talent like mine (sound of throat clearing) to make her look great. She's the best.

I'll call when I can.

L.

He held it in his hand and studied the handwriting. She'd written with a blue felt-tip pen in her small, nearly calligraphically beautiful script. He appreciated that she was anxious about her mother, but he wondered if she wasn't overreacting. If there wasn't something else going on here.

After all, she had left this note for him downstairs. Hadn't even asked the receptionist if he was upstairs in his office.

He knew that he should have called her on Sunday. At her home. On her cell. Katherine had told him enough at the movies on Saturday night that a more attentive person—a more *involved* person—would have been sufficiently alarmed to do something.

But he hadn't, and so he phoned her now. As he expected, he missed her at BEDS, and so he left a message on her voice mail. He left a second one on the answering machine that she and Talia shared at home. And then he left a third on her cell. Finally, he replaced his phone in its cradle and sat on the edge of his desk, considering what he should do. If, in fact, he should do anything.

He knew Marissa was going to be disappointed. And she was going to be alarmed. Sure, she had spent twenty minutes that morning going through the clothes she had at his apartment because of that afternoon's much-anticipated photo shoot. But after their conversation Saturday night, the real issue in her mind was going to be Laurel's well-being.

And then there was Cindy. He had planned on spending the morning interviewing hospital executives about the skyrocketing costs of their building project, but he'd had to cancel when she had fallen off the swing set at the school playground and taken sizable chunks of skin off her calf and both elbows. Seven stitches in the leg and butterfly bandages on her arms. She had been made nearly hysterical by all the blood. He had met his daughter and a teacher's aid at the emergency room (at, ironically, the very same hospital where he was supposed to be researching an editorial). Then he had brought Cindy back to his apartment, calmed her, and convinced his sister to race up from Middlebury to watch her so he could return to work.

But missed headshots and stitches might turn out to be nothing compared to the big problem: Laurel. And he really wasn't sure what he should do about her. He knew he was a careful, cerebral man. It was a strength of his—and, on occasion, a weakness.

He understood that conceivably he could do nothing. After all, Laurel was a grown-up. She had gone home to care for her mother. Besides, it was an appendectomy—not open-heart surgery. And she wasn't going to be there alone: She had her sister, Carol, and her aunt in the area. She didn't need him, too. Moreover, he had always made a point of not babysitting her—of not, in fact, babysitting any woman. Not girlfriends, not wife. He hadn't the time to babysit Laurel anyway, even if he were the babysitting type. He had a time-consuming job and two little girls, and the last thing he wanted to do was encourage a high-maintenance relationship with—and this was a term he realized he had used Saturday night while talking to Katherine—*a fragile young woman*.

He wondered if this was precisely why he hadn't called her on Sunday. Because it would mean getting in deep, and he was not merely cerebral and careful: He was aloof and detached, and since the divorce he had wanted nothing that resembled commitment.

And going to join Laurel at her mother's bedside certainly suggested a serious commitment. It might unleash a more profound obligation than he was willing to make to any woman right now. It might mean marriage and it might mean more children, and more children remained absolutely out of the question. Not with Cindy six and Marissa eleven. He wouldn't do that to them. It was bad enough that their parents' marriage had fallen apart and now they needed extra TLC because their mother was getting remarried.

On the other hand, Laurel's very fragility suggested that he needed to jump in. He knew Laurel's history as well as anyone; he had a responsibility. Consequently, he reached once more for the phone and rang the Baptist church, where he was connected quickly to the youth pastor.

"Let me guess, you want to know what's going on with Laurel, right?" Talia asked almost as soon as he said hello.

"I do. I want to know how ill her mom really is. I can't tell from the note."

He heard her make a clicking sound with her tongue against the roof of her mouth. Finally: "Her mother's ill?"

"She didn't tell you?"

"No."

"She left a note for me here at the newspaper," he said, and then he read it to her.

"The timing isn't real good," Talia said. "I think her mom was supposed to go to Italy this month."

"That's what I thought, too."

"I wonder if there's a note for me at the apartment," she murmured, her voice a mixture of hurt and concern. "I honestly didn't think Laurel was capable of going anywhere these days except that smelly darkroom or her office at BEDS."

"You really had no idea she was leaving? She didn't call you, either?"

"Nope. But—without wanting to put too fine a point on this—she hardly talks to me these days."

"She didn't tell me you'd fought. May I ask what it was about?"

"We didn't fight. Not exactly. We had a few words on Saturday afternoon, but by then she was already avoiding me. At least that's what it seemed like. She was supposed to play paintball with my youth group, you know. But she didn't make it."

"Huh . . ."

"She went home to Long Island around the anniversary, and when she came back she was like a ghost. She'd sneak into the apartment late at night to change her underwear, but that was about it. Otherwise, she was never home. She was practically living at the darkroom. I left her notes and stuff, but I might as well have been writing in invisible ink."

He rubbed the back of his neck with his free hand. He felt a headache coming on and reached into his desk drawer for his thousand-count bottle of ibuprofen. He was reminded once more that he was closer to Laurel's mother's age than he was to Laurel's, and the reality made him a little disgusted with himself. "I can't believe she's mad at you," he muttered, and then swallowed two of the pills without water.

"Maybe, maybe not. Either way, something's going on, and if she's gone home I think we should be worried."

"I am."

"Are you going to follow her?"

"I just left a message on her cell. I thought I'd wait to hear back from her before I did anything."

"Think I should follow her?"

"Maybe. But let's sit tight for the moment."

"That's it?" asked Talia.

"Is there something else you would recommend?"

"I'm worried!"

He paused. Then: "Do you realize, Talia, how many years I have on Laurel?"

"Is your point you're a middle-aged letch? If so, please get over it. Laurel needs you."

"She needs more than me," he said, not exactly raising his voice, but speaking with a serious snap in his tone. "That's the problem. Why do we only see each other a couple of times a week? Because my children are my priority at the moment, and I won't give her more time than that. I was telling my daughter the other night what happened to Laurel—"

"Are you serious? She's a child!"

"I gave her just the barest bones. But even that, just verbalizing a small portion, made me realize that I represent the two things Laurel needs least in her life."

"And those are?"

"Yet another middle-aged man. And a person who won't commit himself to her completely. To really be there for her."

She was silent, and he sensed a storm surge of anger welling inside her. He braced himself. Instead, however, she said simply, "Call me, please, when you know what you're doing." Clearly, she was sandbagging her fury.

"I will," he said. He almost wished she had vented at him. He felt he deserved a good dressing-down.

After hanging up, he contemplated her observation that Laurel had grown obsessed with the photographs after she had returned from Long Island, and he wondered if something had happened there she hadn't told him about. Or, perhaps, whether this all had something to do with Underhill; in the end, he guessed, everything did. He decided he should call Katherine: see what else might have been in those photographs, and whether Laurel had said anything more to her.

This wasn't doing much. But it was doing something.

SAY WHAT YOU will about nurture and upbringing and really bad parenting, Whit Nelson believed, a good many of the human shells who filled Laurel Estabrook's caseload were going to wind up at BEDS no matter what because of hard-wiring and chemicals. And he didn't mean substance abuse, though there was an obvious connection between substance abuse and mental illness. They fed on each other. He meant brain chemicals. Obviously, not all of the homeless were victims of nature. There were the veterans, for instance, and most of them had been fine until they had seen things or done things—or been ordered to do things—that had sent them over the edge. And there were the people whose parents' addictions—alcohol, cocaine, gambling, sex—had left them scarred, too.

But for most of the mentally ill at the shelter? Whit had concluded that their fate was as inevitable as someone's with cerebral palsy. Their future was already buried molecular deep in the furrows inside their heads the moment they were born. Their demons already were present. Their fears or their paranoia or their reckless hunger for chemical amelioration. Their inability to work. The world needed places like BEDS and people like Laurel, it needed them desperately. But so much of what they did was palliative and quixotic.

Which, he guessed, helped to explain his attraction to Laurel.

That, of course, and her vulnerability. Her history. She was a victim, too.

TALIA WENT HOME that Monday morning immediately after hanging up with David, wanting to see what sort of note Laurel might have left for her. She told Whit, a little breathless from her near-jog up the hill, what David had told her when they ran into each other on the stairway.

"You finished organizing," he said when she unlocked her

front door. The clothes were gone from the living room, the books were piled neatly on the shelves, and the magazines had been slipped vertically into a brass rack beside the couch.

"Yeah, my drawers are a thing of beauty," she said.

They found the note right away on the coffee table. It was brief and distant and vague—and a little defensive. Laurel had offered Talia no more information than she had given David. Immediately after reading it, without telling Whit who she was calling, Talia picked up her phone and dialed. He waited and watched, and saw her shake her head when she got an answering machine. Then she hung up.

"Who were you calling?" he asked.

"Laurel's home on Long Island. I got her mom's machine."

"You thought Laurel might already be there?"

"No. I thought she might be lying about her mother. I almost expected her mom to pick up."

"But she didn't."

"That's right."

"So she might really be in the hospital."

"Maybe," Talia said, and then she beelined for Laurel's bedroom. He followed her.

"What are you looking for?" he asked. "Anything specific?"

"Not really."

He wanted to do something, but he felt it would be a violation to open Laurel's drawers. And so he was standing uselessly in the doorway with his hands on his hips when she waved her index finger in the air and opened Laurel's closet. She rolled onto the floor a piece of black American Tourister luggage, the biggest size an airline might allow in the overhead bin. "This is interesting: She didn't take her suitcase. She doesn't expect to be gone very long."

Then she opened the bottom drawer of the dresser in the

bedroom and started pulling aside Laurel's sweaters. She held up her roommate's checkbook and flipped to the last page of the register. "She didn't take this, either," she said.

"Then do we know for certain she's really left?" he asked.

"No," she said slowly, seeming to consider this possibility. "Maybe we don't." Then they stood there, more like helpless children than young adults, completely unsure what they should or could do next.

KATHERINE MAGUIRE'S meeting with the BEDS development committee had been long and hard and had left her on the verge of despair. The number of people—men and women and families—approaching the shelter was climbing, just as the federal government had slashed programs so severely that they were going to lose $145,000 in the coming year. They were likely to lose as well at least 740 housing subsidies, the result of the government evisceration of the HUD program that provided them. And the cost of oil in the coming winter was expected to skyrocket.

She sat back in her chair after hanging up the phone with the shelter's city attorney and decided that she probably wouldn't like this woman from Long Island if they ever met face-to-face. Pamela Buchanan Marshfield certainly wasn't a guardian angel, descending upon the shelter when it was most in need. She was only making this offer now because her attempts to bully the group had failed. But the timing? Remarkable. It was as if she had known. Katherine had returned from the development committee meeting wondering how they could possibly raise enough money in the short term from the private sector to replace what they were losing in government support. And then, out of the blue, there came this offer from her lawyer.

The BEDS attorney, Chris Fricke, had assured Katherine that the municipality would sell the Crocker collection to the shelter for a dollar, which would then allow them to give it to the Long Island woman. After, of course, she had made her donation. One hundred thousand dollars.

Katherine understood that initially Laurel would be furious. She would feel personally betrayed, and she would insist that the organization was doing exactly the opposite of what one of their clients would have wanted. But Katherine thought that eventually she would come around. After all, half the time Bobbie himself hadn't known what he wanted. And she had to believe that Bobbie would have been happy to see BEDS making so much money off his work. He would have been thrilled!

Moreover, it was certainly in Laurel's best interest to get her away from those photographs. Even if this wealthy dowager hadn't offered to make this contribution to the shelter, Katherine was planning to insist that Laurel turn over the materials and give up on the project. She'd done enough. She'd done *more* than enough. It was time to let it go.

Of course, Katherine wasn't sure how to tell her this. Or how even to get the photos back. It was while she had been on the phone with Chris Fricke, simultaneously going through the papers that had appeared on her desk like mushrooms in a wet summer, that she had found the note Laurel had left: Apparently, her young caseworker had gone home to care for her mother.

At least that was what she had written.

PATIENT 29873

Clearly sees far more in the photos than is there. The snapshots, too.

Tomorrow I need to examine the collection—all the images—and explore

this avenue further.

Patient still writing six and seven hours a day in those notebooks.

From the notes of Kenneth Pierce,
attending psychiatrist,
Vermont State Hospital,
Waterbury, Vermont

CHAPTER TWENTY-SEVEN

*L*AUREL KNEW they were looking for her. She knew they were all looking for her. She finally had to shut off her cell phone when she wasn't calling the prison or the Department of Crime Victim Services, because it never ceased ringing. Eventually, they would stop trying her and they would phone her mother. That was clear. And that would be fine, because her mother was in Italy. But would they finally try to reach her sister? Talia certainly might. And if her roommate reached Carol, they would all realize that she had lied to them, and they would grow convinced beyond doubt—her family, too—that she was losing her grip. Without even meaning to assist Pamela Marshfield, they would help the old crone. They would find her and they would confiscate the photographs. Bobbie's photographs. Her photographs. They would give them to the woman.

And so she understood how little time she had. Consequently, she checked into a motel outside of Burlington, where she showered and washed her hair for the first time in days. She bought a new blouse and new slacks. She wore perfume. She donned sunglasses so no one could see she'd been crying. Again.

Then she was back in her car, shuttling between the different bureaucracies in Burlington and Waterbury to expedite her hearing with Dan Corbett. She had been told at first that it would take days to set it up—perhaps even weeks—but she was persistent, and then she got lucky. She got a surprise. It seemed that Corbett had written her a letter of apology. He had begun the mandatory sex offender counseling program the year before, and as a part of his victim empathy group he was required to pen a note to the person he had injured that expressed his remorse. Usually, the victims never saw these letters, because they wanted nothing to do with their assailants. But here was Laurel, so desperate to see him that she wanted to come to the prison in person. And she would read whatever it was he had written.

Why not? she thought. She already knew better than anyone what had occurred up in Underhill. Perhaps his note would reveal something about his childhood. Whether he had ever had a father in his life. How he had wound up on that dirt road seven years ago. How Bobbie Crocker had.

Perhaps, she told Dan Corbett's prison therapist on the phone, her willingness to receive this letter would help the man with his own healing. His own recovery. His own eventual return to the world.

She didn't quite believe that, of course.

Moreover, she never wanted Dan Corbett returned to the world: She wanted him kept right where he was.

But she was going to say what she needed to expedite that hearing. Nothing else mattered with the clock ticking ever more quickly, and ever more people behind her.

MONDAY AFTERNOON, Whit heard the sounds of a small crowd gathering in the apartment across the hall. It was a little before three. He opened the door, and there was Talia talking to a pair of women older than either of them in the hallway.

"Hello, Whit," Talia said sarcastically. "Care to help me dissuade these two lovely ladies from ransacking my apartment?"

One of the women shot Whit a dart with her eyes, and quickly he extended his hand to her. Talia introduced her as a city attorney named Chris. The second woman, Katherine, was Laurel's boss at the shelter. Talia said the two of them were hoping that Laurel had left the prints she had made from Bobbie Crocker's negatives behind in the apartment.

"I told them," Talia was saying, "there's no way they're here. We went through this place just a few hours ago. And after Laurel's little episode on Saturday, I'm quite sure she's hidden them somewhere. I said we might find some lingerie that will leave us all a little embarrassed. But we won't find the photos."

"Talia, we don't want to ransack your apartment," said Katherine. "You know that. But how do you know for sure the photos aren't here? I've seen them, I know what we're looking for."

"So do I. And it seems to me you're more worried about those photos than you are about Laurel."

"You know that's not true. Of course I'm worried about Laurel. We all are."

The attorney nodded earnestly and then said, "But those photos are worth an enormous sum of money to BEDS right now. We can't let anything happen to them. That's the reason we're here. What if Laurel . . ."

This was too much for Whit: "What if Laurel what?"

The woman rolled her head on her shoulders and made a wide-eyed, eyebrows arched, you-never-know sort of face.

"You really don't get it," he said. "Laurel would never do anything to those photos. They're her life right now."

Katherine placed her fingers gently on his elbow to pacify him. He restrained himself from shaking them off. "I love Laurel. She's like a daughter to me. Someday I hope she's running the shelter. That's how much I care for her and respect her and trust her. But she's in trouble right now. Something about this mad dash home doesn't quite ring true. At the same time, I have a woman willing to make a humongous donation to the shelter if we give her the photos—almost enough to cover what we're going to lose in government support this year. That is one hell of a nice Band-Aid."

"You mean all you have to do is turn over a person's life's work," Talia said mordantly.

"First of all, it isn't his life's work. It's a few hundred images, tops. Bobbie would probably want us to hand it over given the money we've been offered. Bobbie loved what the shelter stood for and what we did. He would want to make sure it remained solvent."

"And what of Laurel?" asked Whit. "What of the work she's put in?"

"They're not her photographs. She has no right to them. Besides," she said, and here she paused for a moment, as if trying to find the correct words. Finally: "Besides, if I'd known she would take this all so . . . so seriously, I would never have let her near them."

"Still, don't you think this is an awfully scary quid pro quo? A very bad precedent?" he continued.

"Here's what I see. I have a friend who is losing her grip over some photos she probably shouldn't have, and I have a benefactor who wants them badly. A hundred thousand dollars badly. I'm sorry, Whit. I'm sorry, Talia. But this is a no-brainer."

Talia shrugged and motioned the two women inside the apartment. "Go ahead," she said. "But you won't find them."

And she was right.

CHAPTER TWENTY-EIGHT

*L*AUREL HAD NEVER been to the prison before. Never driven the long, two-lane road surrounded on both sides by nothing but farmland that led from Saint Albans to the correctional facility. Never noticed that coils of concertina wire have anvil-shaped razors—because, of course, she had never seen the wire up close. She saw that the prison's squat cinder-block buildings stretched out like the spikes on an asterisk. The asphalt basketball court had a wire fence and a wire roof. She saw the remains of two massive gardens on the other side of the walls, one for that summer's vegetables and one for flowers. The vegetable garden was easily a couple of acres: The long rows of tomato cages alone must have stretched the length of a tractor trailer truck. The woman with her, the woman who was driving, told her as they parked that the inmates grew enough vegetables here to feed the prison through the summer and fall. She admitted to Laurel that she honestly didn't know what they did with all those flowers. She was from the Department of Crime Victim Services, and she was with Laurel because the social worker from BEDS was going to see her own perp.

That was the term this woman named Margot Ann kept using. Perp.

And she was not about to let Laurel go alone. Margot Ann was even taller than Laurel, her black hair was just starting to gray and she wore it boyishly short. Originally, she was from Jackson, Mississippi: Hence, she said, the use of two first names instead of one. She had met her husband, a native Vermonter, overseas when they had both been in the National Guard. She helped coach the girls' basketball team at the high school in her community, although her own children were all boys and spent most of the time in the winter on their snowboards. She had shared much of her life with Laurel on the drive to Saint Albans. Laurel guessed this was supposed to make her feel more comfortable, more at ease. They had done all their prep work the day before. In theory—and Margot Ann said theories meant little in a clarification hearing like this—she and Margot Ann would meet with Dan Corbett for perhaps half an hour. She would ask the questions about his father and his grandfather that interested her, and he would share with her the letter he had written. But it wouldn't be simple. Not logistically, not emotionally. Laurel understood. Now, lulled by Margot Ann's conversational drone, she felt oddly airy in the passenger seat of the woman's Corolla, as if she were suspended on a Styrofoam noodle in the swimming pool back in West Egg, a little girl half in and half out of the water.

At the prison's main entrance, she and Margot Ann gave up their keys and their pens and their cell phones. They gave up their vials of pepper spray. (Margot Ann, Laurel saw, carried one, too.) They were met by the facility's superintendent and a correctional officer who would escort them to the room where the small hearing would be held, but who wouldn't actually join them for it. The officer would wait just outside the room's glass door, but there would only be

four of them present at the hearing: Margot Ann, Dan Corbett's therapist, the victim, and the . . . perp.

There is that four-letter word again, Laurel thought, as she sur-
veyed the metal detector in the small, spare lobby. *Perp.* It
almost sounded like one of the names Corbett and Russell
Richard Hagen had called her that day on the dirt road in the
woods.

Inside the prison, she learned that the facility's myriad
metal doors were opened and closed electronically by a correctional officer with a gun in a booth: He was surrounded
by cinder-block walls and bulletproof glass, and he could see
the doors throughout the building on closed-circuit television monitors inside his cubicle. From there, he pushed the
buttons that slid steel bolts back and forth across the entire
prison. Guards would radio to him which door they wanted
opened: "One door." "Two door." "Three door." "J"—
meaning the door to the J-wing, the pod with the sex offenders. That's where they were going. The sex offenders had
their own wing because the rest of the prisoners detested
them. The correctional officer who was accompanying Laurel and Margot Ann said that only last week he had broken up
a fight between two inmates because one had wrongly accused
the other of being a sex offender.

Apparently, the therapist she was about to meet had spent
much of yesterday preparing Dan Corbett for Laurel. His
rights mattered, too.

THEY SAT IN A square room with orange walls and a single
window that looked out upon a small, dark courtyard. There
were drawings that inmates had made taped to the walls—kites
and children and spaceships—and Laurel wondered if they

were a part of the therapy. Four chairs had been placed in a spacious circle, and she was seated in the one closest to the door. Dan Corbett would be seated across from her, a good six or seven feet away. His therapist would sit beside him; Margot Ann would sit next to her. A correctional officer would be watching them through the glass door.

Laurel had brought select photos with her, and she busied herself while she waited for the inmate to be escorted into the room by arranging and rearranging the key ones in her lap. There was the old snapshot of Bobbie and Pamela. The photographs Bobbie had taken years later of the house in East Egg. One of Gatsby's estate. The pair of her on the dirt road in Underhill.

She wasn't sure in what order she would reveal them. It might depend upon whether this prisoner was Bobbie's son, or whether that distinction belonged to the convicted murderer in Montana. Margot Ann kept reminding her that Dan Corbett was not going to be a physical threat to her, but she wouldn't be surprised if he was still a psychological viper. He had been in counseling now for a year and a half, said Margot Ann, but she understood he was still the sort who could turn on her in a moment. And while they could prevent him from touching her, Corbett might say wounding, hurtful things before they could silence him. She hoped he wouldn't: After all, he had written that letter expressing his remorse. But Laurel should never lose sight of what he had done seven years ago.

"You okay?" asked Margot Ann finally.

"Uh-huh," she mumbled.

"Good." She gazed for a moment at the images in Laurel's lap. Then she continued, "So, you think Corbett's father may have taken those?"

"I think so. I hope so."

"Why?"

"Because I would rather believe the man who had taken them was related to Corbett than Hagen."

"And, I presume, because you don't want to go to Butte."

"For many reasons. Yes."

"But you would?"

"I believe so," Laurel said.

"Is that you?" asked Margot Ann. She gestured with her finger at one of the pictures of the girl on the mountain bike.

"Yes," she said. It still surprised her that it had taken her so long to admit this to herself. To admit it out loud. Of course that girl was her. Who else could it be?

THE FIRST THING Laurel noticed when Dan Corbett was ushered into the room—and she noticed it instantly—was the tattoo. There it was, the devil's skull on his neck. The fangs. Her eyes slid down the arms of his navy blue jumpsuit to his wrists, just to be sure there was no barbed-wire bracelet in purple ink, too. There wasn't. She took some comfort in this, but she knew she should be careful: Dan Corbett had tried to rape her. And while he may not have murdered that woman in Montana, something about him had nonetheless scared the hell out of Bobbie Crocker.

His eyes were bloodshot and his skin was so pale it was almost translucent: She could see small road maps of veins on his cheeks and along the sides of his nose. He looked a little cooked. But he also appeared more oily than menacing: He certainly seemed less threatening than he had six-plus years ago in the courtroom. She guessed he was fifty now. He still had an immaculately trimmed goatee, though it had grown as gray as the hair that fell in greasy curtains over his ears. She remembered something a professor had once told her class back in college: In the flesh, malice is not especially impressive. More times than not, it's our size, it fits inside the frames of our mirrors.

"I believe you two know each other," said Corbett's therapist, a tall, slim fellow with a small gold hoop in his ear who didn't look much older than Laurel. He was wearing a blue denim shirt and a casual necktie patterned with the phases of the moon. His name, she knew from their phone calls yesterday, was Brian.

Corbett's eyes were darting around the room, taking in Laurel and Margot Ann. He wove black Converse sneakers that squeaked on the linoleum floor. He wasn't shackled.

"Yes," Laurel said. "Hello."

"Hello." It took only those two syllables, but instantly she heard in her head his cloying, sinewy, disgusting little joke from the dirt road. Liqueur Snatch. The two men sat and Brian outlined the ground rules for their clarification hearing. What he hoped they would accomplish. Something about the whole situation reminded Laurel of a meeting between lawyers trying to hammer out a divorce settlement.

And then they all turned to her, presuming she was ready to start. Caught off guard, she asked the very first question that popped into her mind: "Did you ever work in a carnival?"

Corbett gave her a self-deprecating smile and looked down at the piece of lined yellow paper he had in his lap. His letter, she guessed. "Yup." That was all.

"What did you do there?"

He shrugged. "I ran rides."

"Is there anything you want to add to that, Dan?" asked his therapist. "Is there anything more you wish to tell Ms. Estabrook?"

"It was just a job," he said to Brian. "Paid me a little money."

"Tell Ms. Estabrook."

He turned to face her across the broad circle. "It was nothing special. No big deal. Just work."

"Thank you," she said.

"No prob."

"And your father. What was his name?"

"I see you got his pictures."

"I . . . do." She spoke slowly, haltingly. She felt immediate relief that Bobbie's son was this man, not Russell Richard Hagen. She also experienced a deep and satisfying rush of optimism: In the coming moments—in this very room—she was about to learn all that she needed to convince the doubters around her that she was right and they were wrong. That her mind was sound.

Of course, this also meant that she was going to have to inform him that his father had died, and she wasn't sure how he would respond.

"I didn't really know him," Corbett continued. "He showed up three, maybe four times in my life. He went by Bobbie."

"I have something to tell you about him."

"And that is?"

"He passed away. A stroke. I'm sorry, Mr. Corbett."

"That why you came here?" he asked. There wasn't even a trace of grief in his tone.

"Partly."

"He mighta been my dad, but he was no father. I had no bones to pick with him at the end. But, oh, no, he was never my father."

"How did he find you in Vermont?"

"We'd just run into each other at a shelter in Boston. He recognized me. I said I was goin' to Burlington. You know, 'cause of the fair. I was meeting up with Russ Hagen, and I told him so. Russ had been a carny, too. But then he got a real job at that fitness place."

All morning Laurel had endured an ever-thickening cloud bank of dread; she had felt her nerves thrumming inside her. Now the mere mention of Hagen's name—there it was, out there in the room like a thunderhead—was causing her to tremble. Little electric spasms moved through her like hummingbird wings. She felt Margot Ann's hand on her forearm.

"You want some water, Laurel?" Margot Ann asked.

She shook her head no and continued. "Did he give you anything when he came here? A picture? A box?"

"Bobbie? No way. That man didn't have a pot to piss in."

"He had his photographs."

"And he never let those out of his sight."

"Did you ever frighten him?"

"Bobbie? When I was on drugs, I probably scared everyone." He seemed to take pride in this, and Brian whispered something to Corbett she couldn't quite hear. Then, after they had pulled apart, Corbett added, "Yes. I scared him the day we hurt you."

"How?"

"I was outta control."

"Did he see what happened?"

"What happened?" Corbett asked, and once more Brian looked over at the inmate. This time he didn't have to prod him verbally. Corbett went on, "I don't think so. He heard. We were all pretty noisy. But he didn't see. I think he got there before those other bicyclists did. The lawyers."

"Before?"

"Yeah."

"Was he in the van with you when you drove out there?"

"No, a course not. Remember, he was this crazy old man! He—"

"He was your father!" She snapped at him, and instantly the room went quiet. Margot Ann's hand was still on her forearm, stroking her skin through the sleeve of her shirt.

"I don't have to be here," Dan Corbett said to no one in particular. "I do not have to be here."

"No, you don't," said Brian. "But we're all glad you are. I think Ms. Estabrook was more surprised than angry. Is that correct?"

"Yes. That's correct."

The prisoner filled his cheeks with air as if he were a chipmunk and then exhaled audibly. A balloon that's been untied. "He was stayin' with us, he knew 'bout that road. Liked to take his pictures on it. But he didn't know you were goin' to be there that day. He didn't know me and Hagen were, either. But Hagen knew you would be around. He knew where you parked. He'd followed you, like, two times. Maybe three. I don't know. Anyway, Bobbie just walked out there from Hagen's place. It wasn't that far. Well, maybe to a guy in his seventies it was. But not really. We didn't even know he had been out there till just before the cops came to the trailer. And then he split just before they arrived."

"You never told the police."

"They didn't ask," he said, and for the first time she heard a low rumble of evil in his voice. "And I wasn't about to give them another witness. That wouldn't a made much sense. And neither was Hagen."

She looked down at the pictures before her, and held up for him the large print of the Buchanan estate in East Egg. "Do you recognize this house?"

"Nope."

"But you knew your father took the picture, right?"

"I guess. But I don't assume nothin' with Bobbie."

"Did you ever meet your grandfather?"

"Sure. I knew 'em both."

She sat back in her chair. "Tell me about them. Please."

"What do you wanna know?"

"Whatever you can remember."

"Well, let's see. My momma's daddy was a jazz musician. Played trumpet. He lived in the Bronx."

"And your father's?"

"You mean the man who raised me? The fellow my momma married? Or Bobbie's?"

"Bobbie's."

"I figured."

"Please," said Laurel.

"Bobbie's daddy lived out on Long Island."

"Uh-huh."

"He was a conductor on the Long Island Rail Road. He—"

"A conductor?"

"A conductor. That's right. You know, on a train? His momma was a schoolteacher. First grade, second grade. Something like that. Bobbie used to take pictures of the train platforms out there sometimes. Out on Long Island. I guess 'cause of his old man. And the nice houses out there: He took pictures of them, too. Truth is, I saw Bobbie's parents more than I saw my momma's. And I saw them all more than the parents of the man momma finally married."

Laurel had thought it possible that Corbett wouldn't have any idea who Bobbie's parents were. Likewise, she had imagined he might have known his grandmother was Daisy Fay Buchanan and thought mistakenly that his grandfather was Tom. But she had never for a moment entertained the notion that he could be so profoundly misinformed—that he would have it all so wrong.

"A train conductor?" she asked. "And a schoolteacher? Why would you think that?"

"Because that's who they were, lady. I spent serious time with them as a boy. For a while, my momma thought she could handle Bobbie's craziness better than his own parents, specially after she let him knock her up good—"

"This is your mother you're talking about," said Brian.

"My momma weren't no different from—"

"Tread lightly," Brian cautioned the inmate. "Remember—"

Corbett put up both hands in a gesture of resignation. "Fine. 'Nuff said."

"Is your mother still living?" Laurel asked.

"No. She died a long time ago."

"Do you have any siblings?"

"That word sounds like a venereal disease," said Corbett, lecring. "Siblings. Siblings. Let me ask you: Do you have siblings, Ms. Estabrook?"

Margot Ann turned to Laurel and looked her squarely in the eye. "Would you like to leave?"

"No." Then, to Corbett, she rephrased her question: "Do you have any brothers or sisters?"

"I do not."

"What about the name Buchanan? Does that ring a bell?"

"Nope."

"Daisy?"

"Like a flower?"

"Like your grandmother."

"My grandmother was not named after no flower. I had one named Alice and I had one named Cecilia. Bobbie's momma, the teacher? She was Alice."

"No," Laurel said. "She was Daisy. She was married to

Tom Buchanan. That was their house in the photo I showed you. And in 1922, in the summer, she had an affair with a bootlegger named Jay Gatsby. Gatsby—"

"As in the novel?" This was Brian. Laurel saw that everyone in the room was staring at her.

"He was Dan Corbett's grandfather: Bobbie Crocker's father. That's who Jay Gatsby was!" Had she raised her voice? She hoped that she hadn't. But the exchange had happened so quickly and she had been unprepared for this prisoner's recalcitrance and denial. For his bizarre fabrication. A train conductor? A schoolteacher? She could only presume he had made up such a story to torment her. Torture her further.

There again was that voice. His voice. A recollection: Liqueur Snatch.

"Laurel?" She turned. It was Margot Ann. Otherwise, the room was silent. The drumbeat in her head was the only other noise she could hear. "Laurel?" Margot Ann said again.

"Yes?"

"Would you like a break? Mr. Corbett isn't going anywhere. But we can leave."

She heard someone in the room sniff. Realized it was herself.

"May I still hear the letter?" she asked.

"Still? Of course you may," said Margot Ann. "If you want to."

Corbett looked away, glared at the clock on the wall. Brian tapped the tips of his fingers gently together, and the inmate looked at his therapist—a trained dog, she thought—and then at her.

"Do I just read this out loud?" he asked.

"Just like we did in the group. Just like you did with me," said Brian. Then, to Laurel, he added, "He's becoming accountable for his actions." Laurel thought it was as if he were speaking about an ill-behaved child.

Margot Ann asked her once more if she really wanted to hear this, and she heard herself saying she did. She did. She . . . did. She didn't believe she had repeated herself, but she feared that she might have.

And then, just after that, Corbett started to read. His voice was at once sycophantic and condescending. He wanted, she decided, to demean her while somehow garnering the approval of his therapist. She knew this was an impossible task, and it dawned on her that if he couldn't have both he would choose to make her suffer. That, perhaps, was for him his moment of arousal.

"Dear Ms. Estabrook," he began, holding the paper before him with both hands, as if it were a hardcover novel. "I am writing you this letter to say I am sorry for what me and Russ Hagen did to you seven years ago. I was on drugs, but that's no excuse. I left home early, but that's no excuse neither. Neither is the time I spent just drifting around. I take full responsibility for what I did. And that means I take full responsibility for hurting you. These are hard words for me to write because they are so evil. Sodomy. Rape. Mutilation. But they say the truth will set you free and I will not mince words. And so while I don't remember everything, I remember enough. And I know what came out in the investigation. It's all true, I know. That means that first of all I am sorry for the ways we broke your collarbone and your fingers and your foot. And I am sorry for holding you down while Russ raped you in those two places. I am sorry I raped you there, too. And I am sorry that we forced you to have oral sex on us. And most of all I am sorry that I held you by your arms while Russ Hagen cut you so badly. I do not believe that he really planned to cut out your heart, and I did not really believe it then. But I know I was scared you would be able to figure out who we were, and so I think a part of me was hoping Russ really would kill you when he cut off your breast. And so much of you was bleeding so badly when we left, I thought you really might die back there in the woods. But I was glad then and I am glad now that those men on the bicycles found you and you are alive. I am sorry about your breast and the other scars. I wish I could make it up to you. I wish I could go back in time and not do those awful things to you. But I can't. And so all I can do, Ms. Estabrook, is say that I am sorry. Sincerely, Dan Corbett. P. S. I will never do this sort of thing to another person. I promise." When he finished, he glanced over at Brian. "Do I give this to her?"

"You stay seated. We'll give it to her," the therapist said.

Beside her, Margot Ann's eyes were closed. She was, Laurel realized, fighting back tears. Brian was staring down at the floor. There was again the pulse of her heart in her head and she felt herself sweating. She felt oddly, unaccountably naked. And she wondered why this inmate had been allowed to fabricate so much in what was supposed to be a letter of clarification.

PATIENT 29873

. . . patient showed me a copy of The Great Gatsby, the paperback with the deep blue cover and the flapper with the nymphs in her eyes, and yet continued to dispute that it was a work of fiction. Referred to it as a memoir, a true story. Little reaction when shown the publisher's page with author, publishing date, fiction disclaimer, etc.

The diagnostic problem has been referred to before. Regarding stressors preceding this episode (whatever it's an episode of), there are photographs of a young woman on a dirt road on a bicycle in the collection that appear to have been taken near the spot seven years ago where the rape and mutilation occurred. It is beyond current knowledge to determine whether it would cause the delusions by being found among images of the childhood swim club, i.e., suggesting to the patient a biographic or even karmic connection . . .

From the notes of Kenneth Pierce,
attending psychiatrist,
Vermont State Hospital,
Waterbury, Vermont

CHAPTER TWENTY-NINE

*P*AMELA HAD NEVER told anyone what she had seen, not even her confidant and attorney, T. J. Leckbruge. Partly, this was because she sometimes wondered if she really had seen anything at all. It might have been a memory that in point of fact she had conjured completely. Still, it was vivid, crisp, altogether cinematic in her mind.

One excruciatingly hot summer afternoon, James Gatz was at her parents' home, and her nanny, the young Irish girl with the hair as red as a crayon, was going to walk her down to the cove so she could dip her young charge's pudgy legs into the water. Tom Buchanan was gone somewhere for the day. Gatz was wearing a suit as sparkling white as Pamela's little smock dress, and sitting in a chair opposite her mother, his legs crossed. Daisy Buchanan was draped languidly across the couch as if she were a model who was about to be painted. They both had drinks in tall glasses resting on the coffee table, but the ice had long melted and there was condensation running along the sides and actually puddling atop the coasters. Daisy looked especially enervated, her body seeming to melt into the cushions of the couch.

The nanny had waded into the water with Pamela, holding

her fingers as she lifted the child in and out of the surf, dip-
ping her up to her waist, then her shoulders. The day was so
steamy that even the cove had reminded Pamela of a tepid
bath, and neither she nor her nanny had been especially
refreshed by the dunking. Moreover, they had neglected to
bring either her small floating boat or her toy seal because
the plan had never been to submerge themselves completely—
to go for a real swim—and so she had quickly grown bored.

Fortunately, her nanny had brought a stale baguette, and
she broke off little pieces for Pamela to feed to the seagulls
they'd seen from the house. There may have been a dozen of
them, maybe more. The birds swooped down around the
child's ankles and at first Pamela had been afraid, but once
she understood that all they wanted was the bread she had a
delightful time and felt like a circus performer with a flock of
trained animals around her.

And then, all too soon, the bread was gone and once more
she was aware only of the oppressive heat of the afternoon.
She would guess later that the bread had lasted barely five
minutes when they returned to the house.

They entered through the living room, one of the many
rooms that overlooked the bay, slipping through the French
doors that were slightly ajar. They were both still so hot and
tired—they were, perhaps, even more uncomfortable than
when they had left because the long walk up the hill to the
house had been completely in the sun—that they hadn't spoken since they had emerged from the water, and they moved
almost noiselessly across the terrace.

In the living room, Pamela noticed instantly that Gatz was
no longer on the chair. He, too, was on the couch. And he
was hovering over her mother, lifting his head from hers as if
they had been . . . telling secrets. That was how close his face

had been to Daisy's. Abruptly her mother bolted upright so she was sitting beside Gatz, rather than lying beneath him, the pencil-thin straps of her crepe dress dangling close to her elbows instead of slung tight over her shoulders. She looked more flushed than before they had left as she sheepishly tried to adjust the straps, while—and here was a part that led Pamela to wonder if she were embellishing the details much later in her mind—covering her bare breasts with her forearms as she worked to compose herself.

Sometimes the image was fuzzy, as if it were only a dream Pamela had concocted as an adolescent; other times, however, it was as clear in her mind as if it were happening at that very moment. Eventually, she would begin to recall (or, perhaps, to imagine) that she had actually seen James Gatz's hand emerge from underneath her mother's dress. In college, when she would think back upon that afternoon, she would even begin to conjecture that her half brother had been conceived that very day. It was possible. She was immediately taken upstairs for her nap. Her father didn't return home until after dinner.

And the nurse? Soon, very soon, after that she was replaced. This, Pamela knew, was not a detail that was subject to the frailties and vagaries of memory. That nurse had disappeared completely from her life.

MARISSA WAS TRYING to do her homework in the bedroom, but Cindy was watching television in the living room with their aunt and her dad's condo just wasn't that big. This was the third day their aunt had been with them, and it had grown painfully clear to Marissa that the woman had spent way too much time at rock concerts when she was young, because her hearing seemed worse than their grandfather's. Almost as if it were a ballet, her sister—still beaten up from her fall off the swing—would climb off the couch to turn the volume down on the movie they were watching, and then their aunt would go and get something from the kitchen and turn it back up so the TV was loud enough to drown out a jet engine.

Moreover, Marissa was still disappointed that Laurel hadn't taken her photograph on Monday, and worried that something strange was going on between her dad and his girlfriend. She wasn't sure what, but it was more than just the idea that Dad was troubled by the way Laurel had gone home to Long Island, where she used to live. She had the sense there was more to the story than he was letting on, and it all went back to whatever it was that he and that woman named Katherine had been talking about on Saturday night. She thought it was distinctly possible that her dad was about to break up with Laurel. She didn't think this was fair, but when he had picked her up at school the other day he had seemed more angry than anxious. It was like he didn't believe Laurel's mother really was sick. It was as if he thought she was this crazy girl, and he didn't want her around his kids anymore.

Well, she could appreciate that if Laurel really were insane. That would make sense. But Laurel wasn't. She'd just been through a lot. It was too bad no one, not even her dad, seemed to understand.

MARGOT ANN HAD asked Laurel whether she felt up to returning to work after the draining ordeal of the clarification hearing. They were standing in the parking lot outside the correctional facility, the fence with its coils of concertina wire looming high above Margot Ann's shoulders.

"No," Laurel had answered. "I think I'm going to go home."

"Take the rest of the day off—I agree."

Laurel smiled wanly, hoping to convey emotional fatigue. But the truth was, she wasn't exhausted. She was confused—but she was also energized. She didn't like misleading Margot Ann, but she also didn't believe she had a choice. Her plan was to have Margot Ann drop her off at the parking garage in Burlington where they had met that morning, but she certainly wasn't about to drive to her apartment in the hill section after that. Home, in this case, meant West Egg. If Bobbie hadn't given his son the next clue, then she would follow up on a hunch that had been growing stronger ever since she and Shem Wolfe had parted company in Serena's diner on Sunday: Perhaps she herself was the link to the final evidence. The final proof. Perhaps it wasn't a coincidence at all that she had been given responsibility for Bobbie's images once he had passed away. Hadn't he photographed her himself that day seven years ago on the dirt road in Underhill? Hadn't Katherine asked her to research the images he had left behind?

And if she were a critical link for Bobbie Crocker, then it was surely because he had understood that she had spent her summer afternoons as a girl lingering in the shade of the trees behind Jay Gatsby's house. His father's house. Swimming not exactly in Gatsby's pool, but in the one that had been hollowed out in the very ground where Gatsby's had been.

Perhaps Bobbie had singled her out because he realized that she alone was capable of understanding both his life and his work.

Consequently, she would return once more to his home.

Because if she were Bobbie Crocker and wanted to leave

behind the proof of who her father really was, she would place it there. Where Gatsby had lived and, yes, where he had died.

SHE SPENT THE NIGHT in her house in West Egg. She listened to the messages that Talia and Katherine and David had left on her mother's answering machine. They were checking up on her. Checking up on the notes she had left them.

But she slept little that night, because she had detoured to the country club in West Egg on her way home, arriving just after the dining room had closed for the evening. There she studied the pictures on the walls, including the old black and whites of the small circuses that Gatsby called parties. As the busboys cleared the final tables and the dishwashers in the kitchen inadvertently clanged the heavy pots against the sides of the sinks—as the steam from the hot water slid like mist underneath the swinging doors—she wandered around the dining room and the hallways that linked it with the main entrance and the library. She studied carefully the images of the original swimming pool, trying to envision precisely where Gatsby had been when he had been shot, and where that smaller pool rested in the midst of the Olympic-sized one that existed there now. She noticed there were no crab apple trees in the old prints and remembered a story she'd been told as a girl: A mysterious donor had given the club the crab apples. Then the trees had appeared in Bobbie's photographs—including one picture of a tree with a small mound of crab apples beside it.

That was, she realized with an emotion as close to elation as she was capable of experiencing in her current state, the marker. The symbol. The totem.

By the time she climbed into bed it was midnight and her

plans for the next morning were rumbling inside her head like the din inside a theater moments before the curtain is finally raised into the fly space. She had studied the print with the tree and the pyramid of fallen fruit, and knew precisely where her search was going to end.

She awoke well before dawn, went to the garage for the long shovel her father had used around the house and her mother's small garden trowel, and returned to the country club. She parked in the space nearest the stone Norman tower. For a moment, she sat in her car because she was crying once again, and didn't know whether it was because she was exhausted beyond words or because no one believed her, or whether she was sobbing for a homeless man who had learned as a boy how callous and cruel grown-ups could be. How capable of delusion. Distortion. Disdain.

She listened to the birdsong and gathered herself. She watched the sky lighten to the east and the textured stones on the structure of the clubhouse grow more distinct. A little before six, she climbed from the Honda and started toward the crab apple trees, leaning the shovel against the one where she planned to dig. All of the trees were dramatically wider and taller now, the branches full and broad. At least one tree had been cut down since Bobbie had photographed them, maybe two. But it wasn't hard to see where the small pyramid of crab apples had sat, and why Bobbie had built the small mound where he had. This tree was the middle of a small group of three that had been planted near the northern edge of where the original pool had been. This newer pool, easily three times the size of Gatsby's, had been built where the first one had been constructed, but took up considerably more real estate. Gatsby's pool had existed roughly where the twelve-foot-deep diving section was now, and this tree was about as close as Bobbie could get to the spot where his father had died.

The sun still wasn't up when she first thrust the shovel into the ground, but it felt more like day than like dawn, and after sitting for so very long in the car she was relieved to stand up and take the shovel in her hands, place her foot on the rolled shoulder—the wooden handle cold against her fingers and the edge of the blade sharp against the arch of her foot—and press it into the earth. Through the grass and the roots. Into the loamy soil. She pitched the divots into a pile to her right, and then the dirt upon them. Occasionally, she would fall to her knees and root around in the hole with her arms: She wanted to make sure that she wasn't missing something small but important. A locket, perhaps. A monogrammed wristwatch. But she was confident she was merely being thorough when she did this. Bobbie had given her no reason to believe she was looking for a specific piece of jewelry.

She had been digging for close to half an hour and had just begun to worry that at any moment a stray golfer with an early tee time would wander by or one of the maintenance men would arrive to skim the fallen leaves off the surface of the pool and check the chlorine levels in the water when she heard the blade hit something solid—but not nearly as solid as a rock. There might even have been a faint echo. Now the hole was so deep that to reach the bottom she had to lie flat on the edge and pull herself partly inside it, and even then she had to stretch out her fingers and hands. She pawed away the dirt that surrounded the object and used her nails to scrape more dirt off the top: She could feel one straight edge, then another. She reached for the garden trowel and gently but urgently quarried along the sides. Finally, she felt a clasp. A hinge. And then with both hands she was able to pull from the ground the wooden jewelry box, the one with the scalloped mirrors along the lid.

She knew next to nothing about wood, but when she brushed off the dirt she thought it was cherry. Her parents—now her mother—slept in a bed with a cherry headboard, and it was the same color as this jewelry box. Carefully she used her thumbnail to press open the hook, her heart galloping, oblivious to the sweat that was turning the dirt on her cheeks and her forehead to mud. It was jammed with soil and rust, but finally she was able to pop it open and lift the lid. For a moment, she was disappointed. She had expected to find the inscribed photograph, the one Jay had given Daisy in Louisville, when the two had been young and in love and their lives had not yet begun to unravel. But it wasn't there. Instead, she found an envelope—once beige, now brown. When she flipped the envelope over she saw the single word *Daisy* written in a man's hand on the front, and when she opened the flap she noticed the letter *G* had been embossed on the back. Inside was a photograph of Gatsby and Daisy, taken that summer of 1922. They were sitting together on the stone steps that led from his house to the pool, perhaps a mere thirty yards from the very spot where she was kneeling that moment. Daisy was wearing a black Empire dress, sleeveless, and strings of pearls. Her earrings were daisies. He was wearing a tuxedo, his bow tie slightly askew. Daisy's arm was hooked through his, her head was leaning toward him but not quite touching his shoulder. In the image, they looked slightly flushed, as if they had just been dancing. They were smiling. No, Laurel decided, they were more than smiling. They were beaming. It was night, but their smiles alone might have been enough to illuminate the grounds.

Folded behind the photograph was a letter, written in the same hand that had addressed the envelope.

My Dearest Daisy,

I can only begin to imagine what you are feeling, but you have to understand that her death wasn't your fault. She ran in front of the car! No one could have stopped in time. No one.

Remember: Should anyone ever ask, you must tell them that I was driving. I can take care of myself. And I can take care of us. This horrible unpleasantness will pass and we will be fine. We will be together.

I watched your house last night and I waited. I waited all night. I stayed awake by imagining our future together. It is a future where you won't be bullied, where you won't have to wonder where your husband has gone. We don't have to stay here, you know. We can settle in Louisville, if you'd like. Or Boston. Or Paris. Or London. It makes no difference to me. So long as we're together, we can be happy anywhere.

Can't you see it? I can. I see us: You and me and Pammy and a son. Yes, a little brother for your sweet girl. And we will name him Robert, after your father. That will be our family. A boy and a girl and the most loving and loved mother in the world. That will be us. I will be the husband you deserve and the father our children deserve.

That's precisely what I saw last night as I stood sentinel outside your house.

We will be okay, you know. We will.

I will be home all day today. Just let me know when I should come get you.

Love,
Jay

She knew she should fill the hole back in, but she was hot and tired and she felt dizzy when she stood up. Besides, it was nearing seven-thirty: In the distance, she had been hearing the sound of irons and woods striking golf balls from the first hole for close to half an hour, and at least five or six vehicles had arrived in the parking lot since she had started to dig. And so, with the box with the small envelope under one arm and the shovel and the trowel under the other, she started back toward her car with its apple cores and empty cans of Red Bull littering the passenger seat.

As Gatsby's old house and its once-sprawling sage lawns, now an antiseptic prairie of fairways and putting greens, receded in the Honda's rearview mirror, Laurel began her long journey back to Vermont. Seven more hours. She drove briefly along the Sound, the last of the blue fog having lifted off the water, before veering toward the long strips of expendable plastic and neon that linked West Egg with the expressway. Then she was on the highway itself, rolling past the ambitionless office parks built upon the ash heaps and the remnants of a world's fair. Past the Unisphere and the skeletal remains of the once great pavilions: the visible detritus of that era's unachieved aspirations. Didn't she see daily the castoffs and casualties sprung loose by an ever-spinning globe? Her eyes were small slits, her head heavy with visions and dreams. There was the vindication she anticipated when she shared what she had found to keep her awake—Bobbie's vindication, not merely hers—but there was also her dawning awareness that her past was a part of her future. Always. It was, for better or worse, inescapable.

She arrived at her apartment mid-afternoon, and when she staggered through the front door encumbered by the cherry box and the portfolio case with Bobbie's photographs, for a moment she thought she was feverish.

There before her was a small crowd composed of some of the most important people in her life. Sitting on the couch was her roommate, gazing at her with a look of sodden despair, and her mother—summoned, apparently, back from Italy—in a tight black sweater today instead of a tight black T. And Whit, in the chair by the computer, looking uncharacteristically haggard and gaunt. She saw Katherine in the seat by the balcony, a cell phone pressed up against her ear. She didn't see David, and for an instant she wondered where he was, but the moment was brief because her attention was diverted by another man—not David—who was pacing between the living room and the kitchen. Initially, it was hard for her to place him. She knew him from somewhere—at least she thought she did.

Then, abruptly, it came to her. She hadn't recognized him right away, despite the hours and hours they had spent together since she was nearly killed on a dirt road in Vermont, because she always saw him in the context of his office, where they met.

It was her psychiatrist. Dr. Pierce.

Assessment: Bipolar 1 disorder, current episode manic, severe, with psychotic features; PTSD.

This deserves some comment. The unusual presentation was discussed with Dr. R——. That discussion is reviewed here.

PTSD seems fairly clear, in spite of the psychotic symptoms, given severe trauma, intense distress when viewing the bicycle photographs, and numbing symptoms, i.e., avoiding the site in Underhill, memory gaps, feelings of estrangement. This diagnosis is important in terms of functional impairment and prognosis, whatever else is going on.

The psychosis part is more difficult. There is no language/behavior disorganization, in spite of the patient's wordplay. Mood symptoms, including moderate ongoing irritability, sleep loss prior to admission, and unusual persistent activity, i.e., disappearing from her family and friends, the frenzied travel and searching before admission, her current writing, seem most compatible with a bipolar 1 disorder, which could certainly be associated with psychoses. (Valproate appearing to lower the activity level and mood to a fairly moderate state, in any case.) Main difficulty is that it is unusual to have delusions persist when the mood symptoms are more or less resolved.

One example in the DSM for psychosis not otherwise specified is "persistent non-bizarre delusions with periods of overlapping mood episodes that have been present for a substantial part of the delusional disturbance," and this fits. Since there is only one manic episode—not "periods" plural—it makes sense to go with a mood diagnosis for now.

The construction of the delusions is intriguing. She has written an entire book chronicling those weeks in September, which she considers a true story, but including characters she has made up completely or derived from an 80-year-old novel: Pamela Buchanan; T. J. Leckbruge, an anagram created from the name of an optometrist on the fictional billboard. Shem Wolfe—apparently Meyer Wolfsheim. Then there is Jay Gatsby.

She also has fabricated or revised conversations with her aunt, her mother, and a neighbor from Long Island.

And perhaps to justify her boyfriend distancing himself from her, she seems to have made up two little girls and given them to him. She insists these two fictitious children are the reason her boyfriend has, apparently, broken up with her. (Am exploring how much of the girls are drawn from her own childhood memories and her relationship with her older sister.)

Re—how encapsulated the delusions are. Although persisting in spite of minimal mood symptoms now, they do not appear to extend much beyond the Gatsby idea. They extend to the homeless man for whom she provided services, who is, of course, deceased. But the case is not closed from her point of view, because the homeless man was indeed the father of one of her assailants. Consequently, I would not yet stop the antipsychotic risperidone.

Am adding to the list of visitors her housemate Whit Nelson. Like her friend Talia, he seems to have a moderating effect on her behavior—and clearly he cares for her.

What is really unusual is the patient's capacity to have false beliefs, yet to maintain a remarkable empathy for the people in her "memoir" who do not share them—all the while walling off from herself her painful memories of how brutal the attack was. Her characters' observations toward the end of her story, what she herself has written, imply a dawning realization of how violent the attack was. Nevertheless, at this time she still insists that she escaped years ago with a broken collarbone and a broken finger. She claims to have no conscious recollection at all that she was mutilated and left for dead in the woods . . .

From the notes of Kenneth Pierce,
attending psychiatrist,
Vermont State Hospital,
Waterbury, Vermont

SELF-PORTRAIT: BOB "SOUPY" CAMPBELL

ACKNOWLEDGMENTS

I WANT TO THANK RITA MARKLEY, executive director of Burlington, Vermont's Committee on Temporary Shelter, both for sharing these images with me and then for inviting me into her life to see the shelter she manages.

In addition, I could not have written this novel without the wisdom, guidance, and unfailing patience of two advance readers: Johanna Boyce, a psychotherapist with her master's in social work; and Dr. Richard Munson, a psychiatrist at the Vermont State Hospital in Waterbury.

I am grateful as well to the following people for answering my specific questions about mental illness, the homeless, and the law: Sally Ballin, Milia Bell, Tim Coleman, and Lucia Volino, of Burlington's Committee on Temporary Shelter; Shawn Thompson-Snow, of the Howard Center for Human Services in Chittenden County, Vermont; Brian M. Bilodeau, Susan K. Blair, Thomas McMorrow Martin, and Kory Stone, of the Northwest State Correctional Facility in Swanton, Vermont; Doug Wilson, a psychotherapist with the Vermont Treatment Program for Sexual Abusers at the Northwest State Correctional Facility; Rebecca Holt, of the *Burlington Free Press;* Jill Kirsch Jemison; Dr. Michael Kiernan; Stephen Kiernan; Steve Bennett; attorneys Albert Cicchetti,

William Drislane, Joe McNeil, and Tom Wells; and, finally, the Probate Court of Chittenden County, Vermont.

As always, I am indebted to my literary agent, Jane Gelfman; to my editors at Random House—Shaye Areheart, Marty Asher, and Jennifer Jackson; and to my wife, Victoria Blewer, a wonderful reader who manages to balance candor with kindness.

I thank you all.

Finally, I want to acknowledge my appreciation for three books. Two are nonfiction stories about mental illness that were both informative and inspirational: Greg Bottoms's *Angelhead: My Brother's Descent into Madness* and Nathaniel Lachenmeyer's *The Outsider: A Journey into My Father's Struggle with Madness*.

The third, of course, is F. Scott Fitzgerald's *The Great Gatsby*. There are myriad reasons why—along with millions of readers spanning four generations—I have read and reread this novel. Why, as a novelist, I have revered it. There is the poignancy of Gatsby's great dream, Fitzgerald's luminescent prose, and the writer's profound insight into the American character. There is that wrenchingly beautiful ending.

For the purposes of *The Double Bind*, however, there was something more. Few novels have had the intellectual influence on our literary culture of *The Great Gatsby*, and fewer still have been as widely read. Second, *The Great Gatsby* is a book, in part, about broken people, their lies and distortions: the lies we live consciously, and those we convince ourselves are mere embellishments upon a basic reality. That is, perhaps, among the principal issues the characters confront in *The Double Bind*, too, and why *The Great Gatsby* presents itself as such a unique and pervasive influence on the fictional Laurel Estabrook.

Consequently, I want to express both my admiration for *The Great Gatsby* and my gratitude that it is a part of the canon.

Chris Bohjalian

The Double Bind

A Reader's Guide

A Note to the Reader

In order to provide reading groups with the most informed and thought-provoking questions possible, it is necessary to reveal important aspects of the plot of this book—as well as the ending.

If you have not finished reading *The Double Bind*, we respectfully suggest that you may want to wait before reviewing this guide.

QUESTIONS FOR DISCUSSION

1. Chris Bohjalian begins the novel with a very matter-of-fact description of a brutal attack. Later in the novel, he writes about Laurel, "She preferred black and white [photography] because she thought it offered both greater clarity and deeper insight into her subjects. In her opinion, you understood a person better in black and white" (page 37). Compare Laurel's analysis of photography to the writing style of the author, particularly in the prologue.

2. Bohjalian introduces the world of *The Great Gatsby* seamlessly into his characters' lives, and Fitzgerald's themes resonate deeply within *The Double Bind*: the death of the American Dream, repeating the past, and self-reinvention, to name a few. Discuss how each author (Fitzgerald and Bohjalian) explores these themes, and examine any others that stood out for you.

3. In a feat of narrative turnaround, *The Double Bind* ends with a shocking revelation. Did you find yourself reviewing the novel or rereading it to experience it anew? Did you find the treatment of F. Scott Fitzgerald's characters to be more or less significant in light of the revelation?

4. Discuss Bohjalian's treatment of homelessness, both as a reality and as an abstraction or social issue. Did *The Double Bind* change your thoughts and views on the plight of the homeless in America? If so, how?

5. Why did Laurel, as the author writes, allow Talia to "remain a part of her life when she had consciously exiled herself from the rest of the herd" (page 134)?

6. We learn from Bohjalian that the phrase "double bind" is a psychiatric term for a "particular brand of bad parenting [that] could inadvertently spawn schizophrenia" (page 215). What else, in light of Laurel's history, might the title of the book refer to?

7. Is Laurel's imagined life for Bobbie—and all his psychiatric problems—a way for her to express her own psychotic break? Is the Bobbie Crocker that the reader gets to know really a facet of Laurel's personality?

8. Through most of the book the reader believes, along with Laurel, that she escaped certain rape—and that her ability to hold on to her bike saved her. But after the attack, she gives up biking. Discuss the play between the conscious and subconscious mind—a delicate balance that must have underlined all of Laurel's actions—in this abandonment of the very thing she'd convinced herself was her savior.

9. In what ways is Dan Corbett's tattoo of the devil as a skull with horns reminiscent of the billboard of the pair of eyes that overlooks the Valley of Ashes in *The Great Gatsby*? Is there other imagery in the novel that echoes Fitzgerald's tropes?

10. "For the first time, [Katherine] began to wonder if she'd made a serious mistake when she'd given Laurel that box of old photos" (page 150). Were the photos the catalyst for Laurel's downfall? Would Laurel have eventually suffered a similar psychological breakdown without the introduction of the photos?

11. How was Laurel able to block out what really happened to her when she carried real physical scars of the mutilation to remind her of it? Were there clues in the narrative that part of her did know what happened all along?

12. Laurel suffered a horrendous attack and managed to go on to do great work for the most neglected members of society. Does her breakdown have a negating effect on the seemingly heroic work that came before it? Why or why not?

ALSO BY CHRIS BOHJALIAN

THE BUFFALO SOLDIER

Two years after their twin daughters die in a flash flood, Terry and Laura Sheldon, a Vermont state trooper and his wife, take in a foster child. His name is Alfred; he is ten years old and African American. And he has passed through so many indifferent families that he can't believe his new one will last. In the ensuing months, Terry and Laura will struggle to emerge from their shell of grief only to face an unexpected threat to their marriage: Terry's involvement with another woman. Meanwhile, Alfred cautiously enters the family circle, and befriends an elderly neighbor who inspires him with the story of the buffalo soldiers, the black cavalrymen of the old West. Out of the entwining and enfolding of their lives, *The Buffalo Soldier* creates a suspenseful, moving portrait of a family, infused by Bohjalian's moral complexity and narrative assurance.

Fiction/Literature/978-0-375-72546-3

THE LAW OF SIMILARS

When one of Carissa Lake's patients falls into an allergy-induced coma, possibly due to her remedy, Leland Fowler's office starts investigating the case. But Leland is also one of Carissa's patients, and he is beginning to realize that he has fallen in love with her. As love and legal obligations collide, Leland comes face-to-face with an ethical dilemma of enormous proportions. Graceful, intelligent, and suspenseful, *The Law of Similars* is a powerful examination of the links between hubris and hope, deception and love.

Fiction/Literature/978-0-679-77147-0

ALSO AVAILABLE
Before You Know Kindness, 978-1-4000-3165-8
Trans-Sister Radio, 978-0-375-70517-5
Midwives, 978-0-375-70677-6

VINTAGE CONTEMPORARIES
Available at your local bookstore, or visit
www.randomhouse.com

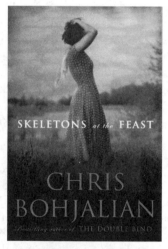